HEART
—of—
GLASS

...L SERIES

HEART
—*of*—
GLASS

A Novel

Book Three

JILL MARIE LANDIS

New York Times **Bestselling Author**

ZONDERVAN®

ZONDERVAN.com/
AUTHORTRACKER
follow your favorite authors

ZONDERVAN

Heart of Glass
Copyright © 2011 by Jill Marie Landis

This title is also available as a Zondervan ebook.
Visit www.zondervan.com/ebooks.

This title is also available in a Zondervan audio edition.
Visit www.zondervan.fm.

Requests for information should be addressed to:

Zondervan, *Grand Rapids, Michigan 49530*

Library of Congress Cataloging-in-Publication Data

Landis, Jill Marie.
     Heart of glass : a novel / Jill Marie Landis.
        p.   cm. — (Irish angel series; bk. 3)
     ISBN 978-0-310-29372-9 (softcover)
     1. Irish — United States — Fiction. 2. Plantations — Louisiana — History — 19th
century — Fiction. I. Title.
PS3562.A4769H423 2012
813'.54 — dc22   2011049848

Cover design: Curt Diepenhorst
Cover illustration: Aleta Rafton
Interior design: Michelle Espinoza

Printed in the United States of America

12 13 14 15 16 17 /DCI/ 22 21 20 19 18 17 16 15 14 13 12 11 10 9 8 7 6 5 4 3 2 1

*For thou art my lamp, O L*ORD*:*
*and the L*ORD *will lighten my darkness.*
2 Samuel 22:29 KJV

PROLOGUE

LOUISIANA, 1861

Four measly years older.

As Katie Keene followed her best friend, Amelie Delany, through a well-tended boxwood hedge on that balmy April night in 1861, all she wanted was to be seventeen.

Thirteen seemed like an endless purgatory on the road to adulthood. Her parents were forever telling her she was too old to run through the house, yet she was too young for Amelie's handsome older brother, Colin, to notice her.

Light spilled from the tall narrow windows of the *garçonnière*, a hexagonal outbuilding where Colin and his friends holed up after dinner to play faro and discuss romantic conquests. All of them were between sixteen and twenty years old and were sons of wealthy planters. The young men spent their days hunting and carousing, traveling up and down the river to visit each other's plantations and flirt with the belles who lived along River Road.

But tonight was different. Tonight talk of war peppered their conversation, and their laughter and ribald shouts sounded forced.

"Do you think they're afraid?" The toes of Katie's black slippers sank into the soft, well-tilled soil of Amelie's mother's flower bed as she gripped the windowsill and rose up to peek inside.

Amelie turned to her in the semidarkness, her wide black eyes huge against the perfectly shaped oval of her face. She blinked twice and shrugged with a toss of her head.

"Papa says the shots fired on Fort Sumter have got the men all primed and ready to fight. That's why he and Colin enlisted. He said it's not going to take more than a week or two to best the Yankees. Why should they be afraid?"

"People get killed in wars. Aren't you scared for them?"

Gilbert Keene, Katie's father, was too old to go to war. He claimed someone had to stay home and make money to bankroll the army while young men like Colin defended their rights and property. Unable to imagine a world without Colin, Katie prayed he'd stay safe.

"Stop being such a worrywart." Amelie shook her head and her dark corkscrew curls danced against her collarbone. Though Katie's looped braids were the height of fashion too, she still envied her friend's bobbing black ringlets.

"They could be hurt, Amelie. Maybe you're not worried, but I'm scared for your papa and Colin."

"They'll never lose to the Yankees." Amelie's mouth set in a firm, determined line for a moment. She didn't sound quite as certain when she added, "Not ever."

Unable to keep her eyes off Colin, Katie turned to the window again. At seventeen he was tall, broad shouldered, and strikingly handsome. His jawline was finely honed, and his hair was black as midnight with a tempting curl to it. His smile was so infectious no one was ever morose when Colin was around.

She watched him shrug off his long, burgundy, fitted jacket before his fingers worked out the knot in his silk tie. He tossed them both over a nearby chair and proceeded to roll up the sleeves of his white linen shirt.

Her heart fluttered at the sight of his suntanned forearms. If only he would turn his dark Creole eyes her way. What did it matter if he caught them spying? His eyes seemed to reach into her very soul.

Truth be told, he took very little notice of her. Her dresses were just as expensive and as pretty as Amelie's and she spent most of her time at the Delanys' house, but, with her plain brown hair, thick spectacles, and still-flat chest, there wasn't all that much for Colin to admire.

Besides, he could have the attention of as many plantation owners' daughters as he desired: girls his own age; poised, blushing beauties who knew how to flirt and pose and hold a man's attention. Girls who weren't a bit shy. Amelie would be just like them in another year or two, but next to her best friend, Katie felt like a wilted wallflower.

"Look at him," Amelie said. "He's trying to act like Papa."

Colin crossed to a low serving table where a tall vase filled with Marie Delany's yellow tea roses stood beside a cut-crystal decanter of brandy. He picked up the decanter and sauntered around the room splashing liberal amounts of the amber liquid into snifters cradled in his friends' hands.

"I'll bet he sneaked that liquor out here." Amelie sniffed.

"You going to tattle?" Katie asked.

"'Course not." Amelie pretended not to care but she worshipped her big brother.

A sigh escaped Katie as she watched Colin pause to light a cigarillo he'd drawn out of his waistcoat pocket. He leaned back, let go a cloud of blue smoke, and then stared at the glowing end of the thin cigar.

With their brandy and cigars, finely tailored cutaway coats, and crisp white shirts, he and his friends played the part of the men they hoped to be as they headed off to join their Louisiana regiments and fight the Yankee War of Aggression.

"This is boring." Amelie sighed and tugged on Katie's sleeve. "Let's go back to the house."

There was nothing boring about Colin, but if Amelie wanted to leave, Katie would oblige her best and only friend. For three years now they'd been as close as sisters. If it hadn't been for Amelie and the Delanys, her life would be a very lonely affair indeed.

And Colin? Though he held a very special place in her heart, she was definitely glad he wasn't her brother.

"I want to go *now*." Amelie stretched and accidentally bumped against the windowpane.

Inside, Colin whipped around. Katie ducked below the sill and crouched in the dirt.

"It's all right." Amelie grabbed Katie's hand. "Come on."

Just as they slipped back through the low hedge and stepped onto the oyster-shell path to the house, the door to the *garçonnière* suddenly flew open. Colin's tall frame was silhouetted in the light streaming through the open door. His hands were behind his back.

"I see you tadpoles. Come over here," Colin said. Behind him the card players let out a shout that was followed by a round of laughter.

Tadpoles.

Humiliated, Katie stared at the dirty toes of her slippers, ashamed to be caught spying like a child.

"We don't have to do *anything* you say." Amelie stuck out her tongue.

"Does Mama know you're creeping around out here in the dark?"

"Does Papa know you're drinking his brandy?" Amelie shot back.

"Here you go, little sister." He held out a yellow rose.

Amelie sniffed it and then dropped her hand to her side. The rose, already forgotten, hung against the folds of her full skirt.

"And one for you . . ."

Before she realized he'd moved, Colin's hand was beneath Katie's chin. He forced her to look up. The very sight of him looming over her took her breath away. Beneath her chin, his hand was warm and strong. Her mind went blank.

"Well," he said, as he shrugged, holding out another rose. "Don't you want this, Katie Keene?"

Katie stared up at him with a lump in her throat and pushed her spectacles up her nose. Praying she looked older and perhaps even a bit pretty in the ring of lamplight, she smiled up at him and nodded. His fingers touched hers as he handed her the flower.

"Th ... thank you." The words came out as a raspy croak.

Raising the rose to her nose, Katie inhaled the heady scent. Without warning she sneezed. Not once, but three times. Colin laughed. Her cheeks caught fire and, humiliated, she ducked her head. When she looked up again, Colin was walking through the door, and an instant later he was once again closeted inside with his friends.

Amelie grabbed her free hand and they started running along the path, the oyster shells crunching beneath their thin-soled slippers. As they reached the wide gallery surrounding the ground floor of the mansion, *Belle Fleuve*, Amelie tossed aside her rose, and it went sailing out into the dark.

Katie clung tightly to her rose, intent upon pressing it between the pages of her book of Irish folktales and keeping it forever.

The girls followed the sound of Marie Delany's tinkling laughter and found Amelie's parents seated at a small damask-covered table just outside the French doors to the formal dining room. Tall tapers burned in an ornate candelabra gracing the center of the table. Melted ivory-colored beeswax slid down the silver, hardening into pools on the tablecloth.

It was customary for the Delanys to share romantic dinners alone beneath the stars on warm, clear nights like this. Katie hung back in the shadows, content to watch in silence. The dancing candle flames flickered off the crystal glasses, casting an almost magical glow over the loving couple.

Amelie broke the spell as she sidled up to the table. She reached for a biscuit on her father's plate, broke off a piece, and popped it into her mouth.

"Papa, may we go riding in the morning?"

"I don't see why not. I'll tell the stable hands to have your mares ready."

Patrick Delany turned the same bright smile on Katie. He wore wire-rimmed spectacles like hers, a feature that endeared him to her even more.

"How are you tonight, Katie? Are your mama and papa in the city?"

She curtsied. "I'm fine, sir. They're staying at the townhouse this week." Forever tied up with various philanthropic causes and hectic business and social lives, Nola and Gil were always in New Orleans these days. "When are you and Colin leaving for New Orleans?" Katie asked.

Marie Delany, with her smooth, plump cheeks, soft hands, and diminutive height, looked more like a young girl than the mother of a strapping seventeen-year-old son. At the mention of Patrick's leaving, Marie turned to gaze into the dark garden, but not before Katie caught the shimmer of tears in her eyes.

"I'm sorry if I've misspoken," she said.

"Not at all." Patrick smiled his reassurance. "We'll be leaving with our regiment at the end of next week." He reached across the table for Marie's hand and covered it with his. She turned to him again. "It will be over before it starts, darling," he promised.

"What about your work, sir?" Intrigued by his intricate rolls of drawings, Katie was in the habit of asking all manner of questions about his architectural projects.

"The work will keep. In the meantime, you continue to take note of all the elements of style we've talked about. When I get back I'll show you how to start drawing plans of your own. There'll be a need for architects to rebuild the North after the war ends. It won't be easy, but if you dream big you just might become one of the first female architects in the country."

"Rebuild the North?" Marie's lip quivered. "I thought you said it would be over soon."

Her lilting voice was barely audible now. She took great care setting her fork upon her gilt-edged Limoges plate. As always, Marie was a vision — the genteel, refined Creole lady of the manor. Her silk gown was from France, and the table was set with the finest china and sterling silver. A house slave hovered a few feet from Marie's chair, silent and watchful, ready to do her bidding at the slightest lift of her hand.

"Surrender *will* come soon." Patrick raised his stemmed wineglass, twirling it as he gazed at the thick, red Bordeaux in the candlelight. "Mark my words."

Amelie was tugging at Katie's wide sleeve. "Come on. I want to show you my new gown," she urged.

Still clutching her rose, Katie bid the Delanys good-night and thanked them for their hospitality, then followed Amelie to the stairs at the end of the gallery. Would she ever have a husband as kind and gentle as Patrick Delany or as handsome as Colin? One who enjoyed candlelight dinners beneath the Louisiana night sky?

Upstairs, Amelie pulled her newest gown out of the massive armoire and held it in front of her while she twirled around the room.

"I just love this shade of yellow silk, don't you?" She stopped for a second to study herself in the mirrors on the armoire doors. "I begged for it to be completely off the shoulder but Mama said it wasn't fitting for a girl my age. The skirt is so full it's going to take a bigger hoop to hold it out. What do you think, Katie? Isn't it just a confection?"

"It's perfect. I love the embroidered trim and the ribbons along the waistline." Katie reached out and rubbed the silk between her thumb and forefinger. The bright fabric reminded her of Marie's roses. No telling how many times Amelie would actually wear the gown after all the young men marched off to war.

"A photographer is going up and down River Road taking pictures of all the men in their uniforms. Papa has him scheduled to come over in the morning, and we're going to have a picture made of all of us, and I'm wearing this." She tossed the dress over the end of her bed. "Will you help me with my hair? That new girl, Bertrice, doesn't know one end of a hairbrush from the other yet."

"Of course."

"Get rid of that silly rose and let's dance." Amelie tried to take it, but Katie scooted away and placed the rose on a table near the door where she wouldn't forget it.

Amelie grabbed her hand and then bowed and laughed. They waltzed around the room and then began jumping through a lively polka. Marie Delany had hired a visiting Frenchman to instruct them both in the fine art of ballroom dancing, but they'd been hopeless as serious students of the art. They'd learned far too quickly and then spent the rest of the allotted time teasing the poor man and falling into helpless giggles.

The girls careened around until they were both out of breath and then collapsed on the bed.

"I think it's high time I kissed someone," Amelie announced.

"You don't mean it!" Katie tried to hide her blushing cheeks behind her hands. She adjusted her glasses, which were slightly askew from their tumble onto the bed.

"Haven't you ever wondered what it will feel like?" Amelie turned her head and Katie found her staring. She was glad Amelie couldn't read her thoughts. She had been curious about the taste of Colin's lips, but certainly no one else's.

"Sometimes," Katie admitted.

"Well, I've been practicing." Amelie grabbed her pillow. "First I'll slip my arms around him like this." She hugged the pillow close. "Then I'll close my eyes and pucker up like this." Amelie pursed her lips and pressed her face into the pillow. She twisted her face all around and then fell back with a sigh.

"There are bound to be victory balls galore when the war is over and you'd better be ready." Amelie snatched up another pillow and shoved it at Katie. "Go on. Try it."

"Should I take off my glasses?"

"Of course."

"I won't be able to see anything."

"So what? Follow your instincts."

Not sure she had any of those particular instincts, Katie slipped off her glasses and squinted as she hugged the pillow close. Before she pressed her face against the fine cotton, she puckered up. When she closed her eyes and her lips sank into the down, the not-quite-imaginary beau she pretended to kiss was Colin.

ONE

LOUISIANA, 1876

Almost home.

Katherine Lane Keene drank in the sight of the familiar landscape as the carriage rolled along the twists and turns of snakelike River Road.

Despite the War of Northern Aggression, despite everything that had happened to the land, the familiar scent of the rich, fertile earth was a constant. Miles of long, rectangular fields of green stretched far and away between levees and the highway that paralleled the Mississippi between New Orleans and Baton Rouge.

Acres once abundant with sugarcane were now overgrown and neglected, as were many of the once-grand plantation houses that dotted the land. As the carriage passed Destrehan, one of the earliest Creole estates in the area, Kate's heartbeat sped up. She had nearly reached her destination. The dream she'd nurtured for so very long was about to come true.

She reached for the long, thick rolls of architectural plans tied with black ribbon on the seat beside her, set them on her lap, and ran her gloved hand down the newsprint. She'd poured years of painstaking work into the plans for the reconstruction and refurbishing of the once-grand house at *Belle Fleuve*. Her mother called it an obsession; for Kate it was a labor of love.

She'd spent almost half of her life preparing for this day. People told her she was crazy, that architecture was a man's field. They said she would be better off getting married and raising a houseful of children. Kate wanted no other home.

For now, all that mattered was the house at *Belle Fleuve* and its owner. She had awaited his return for so very, very long.

"I hear he's insane." Myra O'Hara startled Kate out of her reverie, forcing her to turn her gaze back to the interior of the carriage. Myra straightened her cocoa-brown traveling skirt, folded her plump hands across her ample waist, and lowered her voice as if *he* could hear. "Crazy as a loon. Won't come out of the *garçonnière*. Holed up in there like a madman."

"I've heard the rumors." Kate feigned nonchalance. "They're nothing but gossip, and I'll take no stock in them until I've seen Colin Delany for myself." Who knew what state Colin might be in? She hadn't laid eyes on him since before he went off to war.

If rumors were to be believed, Colin was no longer the dashing, confident young man who had enlisted with his father and gone off to fight for the Confederacy.

"You're obsessed with the place," Myra grumbled. "Much as you are with him."

That much was true. Kate's heart had broken the first time she'd witnessed the neglect and decay that threatened to ruin the place beyond salvation. From that day until now she had labored over the reconstruction plans.

"This isn't just about *Belle Fleuve* or Colin." Kate never tired of defending her vision. She blinked away tears. "It's about how good the Delanys were to me, about how they opened their home and their hearts to me. My childhood would have been terribly empty without them. Besides, if Colin is as bad off as they say, then it's my Christian duty to help him."

Surely Colin would appreciate all the work she'd done, the

details and effort she had put into the drawings. After all, it was his father, Patrick, who'd inspired her love of architecture.

But according to the rumors, Colin had sequestered himself from the world. What if he refused to give her permission to begin?

Kate took a deep breath and reached up to be sure her hat was secure.

Let him try to stop me.

"Did you just say something?" Myra raised her voice over the crunch and clatter of carriage wheels against the oyster-shell drive.

"I don't think so." At least Kate hoped not.

"Wouldn't y' know it? It looks about to rain." Myra stared at the sky.

The carriage turned onto an *allee*, an arcade of ancient live oaks flanking a narrow lane that led to the wide front gallery of the mansion at *Belle Fleuve*. Kate had instructed the driver to pull up near the *garçonnière* next door.

As the carriage rolled past the main house, Kate slid a finger beneath her spectacles and wiped a tear from the corner of her eye. It never failed to upset her—the terrible condition of this once impeccable, glorious house.

The first time she'd witnessed the toll the war had taken on *Belle Fleuve* had been four years earlier. She had just returned to New Orleans from an extended stay abroad and settled into her mother's townhouse. She then went directly to *Belle Fleuve*. Her Irish temper had flared the moment she saw the odious notice nailed to the front door: Auction Due to Failure to Pay Back Taxes.

Kate had ripped down the offending poster and immediately returned to the city. She'd marched into the tax office and used funds from her inheritance to pay the back taxes on *Belle Fleuve*, but with the stipulation that she remain anonymous. On the very day she ripped up the foreclosure notice, she had vowed to see the place restored to its former glory.

The passage of time had only added to the decay. Even more windows were broken. Finely carved woodwork was rotted. Gallery railings were splintered and missing. Inside, shredded wall coverings and crumbling stucco exposed interior walls constructed of Spanish moss and sand—*bousillage entre poteaux*, as the French called them.

Her vision was needed now more than ever.

When the carriage suddenly stopped Kate forgot all about the state of the house. Colin was home. How would he receive her? She'd grown up since they'd seen each other last. In a moment or two she would be looking into his eyes again, hearing his voice. Her gloved hand trembled. Kate tightened it around the plans, then tried to relax.

Myra touched the sleeve of Kate's short-waisted violet cloak as they waited for the driver to open the door.

"You know there's no shame in turnin' back," Myra whispered.

"Everything is going to be fine. You'll see." Kate smiled at her longtime travel companion and friend. There was no room for fear or doubt here. "I'm not one to back down. Don't you worry. Everything will soon be right as rain."

The minute she mentioned the word *rain*, huge drops began to spatter against the roof of the carriage and the air filled with the scent of damp earth. Kate glanced up at the low, angry clouds. The sky was about to open up.

The driver hopped down, pulled his collar up around his ears, and looked put out as he opened the door. He stepped aside so Kate could exit. She pressed the roll of drawings against her bodice, hunched her shoulders around them protectively, and ran for the door of the *garçonnière*.

Halfway there she noticed another vehicle on the drive. A scuffed, covered buggy was parked beneath a tree not far away. A Negro driver with his hat pulled low was perched on the high-sprung seat. He watched Kate's progress in silence.

Hugging the plans, pressing close to the door of the *garçonnière*, Kate reached for the weathered brass knocker. Before she could grab the ring, the door flew open. Kate stared at a tall, redheaded woman who was apparently just as shocked to see Kate standing there as Kate was to see her. The woman stepped out and slammed the door behind her.

Standing toe to toe with the stranger, Kate inhaled an overpowering scent of cheap perfume. The woman's hair was a garish shade of henna, her cheeks dusted with bright-pink rouge, her lips carmine. Dark kohl outlined her small, close-set eyes. A slim, painted brow slowly arched above her left eye as she studied Kate. Then a slow smirk curled her upper lip.

"Good luck with that one, honey." The frowzy redhead indicated the door behind her with a toss of her hennaed head. She looked Kate over from head to toe and barked a harsh laugh. "He'll chew you up and spit you out in no time."

With that, the fancy piece stepped around Kate and ran for the safety of the buggy. The woman scrambled aboard and the vehicle started down the drive. Refusing to let the odious creature shake her confidence, Kate wiped raindrops off the lenses of her spectacles with a gloved finger and raised her hand to knock again. When there was no answer, she twisted the knob and cracked open the door.

"Colin?" Kate held her breath in anticipation. Inside her gloves, her palms were damp.

When there was no answer, she pushed the door open another fraction of an inch.

"I said get out!" The hoarse shout was followed by a deep growl. Something heavy slammed into the door, crashed against the floor, and shattered.

Kate stood tall and quickly thrust the door open. Broken pieces of a ceramic vase crunched beneath her sturdy traveling boots as she stepped inside. Across the room, a tall, lean man, fully clothed but barefooted, was stretched out across a narrow bed. His thick, wavy, black hair reached past his shoulders. The lower half of his face was hidden beneath a heavy beard and moustache.

He bore little resemblance to the young man with the ready

smile and deep laugh, the man who never would have wallowed in such a state of dishevelment. His once-bright eyes were glassy, his full lips hidden behind his shaggy beard. Kate's fantasy was shattered in that very instant. A bittersweet ache filled her soul. The Colin Delany she knew was gone and in his place was this broken, angry remnant of a man.

Paralyzed with shock, Kate stared at him. The task she'd set for herself was too great. No doubt she could save the house, but Colin? Was he beyond redemption?

With one leg stiffly extended, he stretched as far as he could but his hand fell just shy of an oil lamp on the bedside table. No doubt if he reached it, he had every intention of hurling it at her. Not exactly the welcome she had imagined.

"Colin, stop!"

At the sound of his name, he drew back and his head whipped around. He skewed her with a cold, fathomless stare. Dark shadows stained the skin beneath his deep-set black eyes. The slightest movement caused him to wince in pain. His dark eyes bored into hers, and then when he finally realized she was not the woman who had just left, something between a rusty laugh and a snarl escaped him.

"You're not my type either," he rasped. "So get."

Shielding the architectural plans, Kate stepped closer to the bed. Determined to give him a piece of her mind, she was careful to remain out of reach. Her heart faltered when she noticed a cane propped against a bedside table littered with a tray of uneaten food and a half-empty brown bottle of laudanum.

The pieces fell into place. What he must have suffered suddenly came clear.

Her heart ached for him, for the past. This time she barely whispered, "Colin, it's me. Kate. Katie Keene."

Katie Keene.
Colin stared through a laudanum-induced haze at the bespectacled young woman clutching a roll of paper. Was he hallucinating or was she real?

She was a far cry from the wench who had brazenly shown up earlier willing to do anything for a price. This one was no bigger than a minute and modestly turned out in an expensive traveling ensemble.

Her initial shock had faded. Now she appeared to be carefully studying him from behind her spectacles, her features shaded by the brim of a small hat jauntily poised atop thick hair of rich, dark brown.

His gaze swept from the lace around her high collar to the toes of her rain-spattered boots before returning to her face. Behind small wire glasses, her intense blue-eyed gaze never wavered. Something about her silent perusal forced him to search through long-forgotten memories. He knew this young woman but he had no idea how.

Katie Keene. Suddenly he was assailed with painful flashes of recollection, memories of giggles and crinolines, hoop skirts with cascades of ruffles, pleas for his time and attention. He pictured his sister, Amelie, and remembered.

Katie Keene. His little sister's best friend.

His eyes narrowed. Colin tried intimidation with a cold stare. She had nerves of steel, he'd grant her that. She hadn't budged an inch, nor did she appear to be frightened of him. Clutching that long roll of papers, she was dug in; Katie Keene wasn't going anywhere.

Or so *she* thought, but he didn't care who she was.

No, the truth was he cared too much because she had known him before. He wanted no witness to what he had become. She was too painful a reminder of a life that vanished long ago.

He wanted her out. "Leave, Katie Keene, and don't come back." She lifted her stubborn chin.

"It's Kate now, and I'll not go until I've had my say."

"Nothing you have to say interests me."

"Oh, I think it might." She dared to take a step closer.

He made another attempt to grab the lamp until searing hot

pain shot from his ruined ankle to his groin. He turned a groan into a growl, hoping to frighten her away.

"Oh, Colin —" Concern stained her blue eyes. She took another step forward.

He held up his hand. "Stop right there. Don't you dare come any closer."

Thankfully, she halted.

"I want you *out*." He didn't need her help or her pity. He needed her gone.

For a second he thought she was going to comply. Instead she glanced around and walked over to a wooden chair beside a drop-leaf table. She pulled the chair to the center of the room, stopping just out of his reach.

Late summer rain spattered hard against the windowpane behind him. This dismal day was proving to be even more tedious than all the other miserable days he had suffered of late. Kate Keene was apparently determined to make this one the very worst.

As she perched on the edge of the caned chair, she carefully positioned the long, rolled pages of newsprint on her knees. Then, acting as if he hadn't just bellowed at her to leave, she took a deep breath and started talking.

"The minute I heard you were home I came to help."

"I don't need or want help. Yours or anyone else's."

"You may not want my help but it appears you need it. And *Belle Fleuve* needs me. The place is in total ruin, and I can assure you that I'm just the one to manage the restoration. Thanks to your father's inspiration, I've spent years educating myself and am now an architect. I don't pretend to be as talented as he was, but I know Patrick Delany would have wanted someone who truly cares about the house to bring it back to its former glory. I spent part of the war in Boston and afterward I went to Ireland where I studied ..."

In seconds she had worked up a full head of steam, unaware that he was in excruciating pain. He didn't care who or what inspired her any more than he cared about restoring the house to its former glory. The place was in complete shambles, just like the entire South. So was he, for that matter.

What he *did* want was for her to leave him to his misery. Pain weakened his resolve to end his dependence. He was in dire need of a hefty dose of laudanum and her blathering on about living in Ireland and studying architecture on her own only made things worse.

"Miss Keene, I have no intention of restoring this place." *Not even if I had the money. Not even then.*

His words shocked her into silence—but unfortunately only for a moment.

"Of course you are going to restore *Belle Fleuve*. You must."

"Why?" He closed his eyes and took a slow, deep breath.

Taken aback, she blinked her magnified owl eyes.

"Why? Because it's your home. Because it's ... historic and magnificent. I mean, it was magnificent and it can be again. I have designs that will make it so." She shrugged. "I'll admit I've made a few changes and additions, but I assure you they will not ruin the integrity of the original colonial design. The adjustments I've made take into account the needs of not only the home's occupants, but the staff."

Staff? His meager savings was almost gone. He had nothing left to spend on anything but food and payment to the former slave who cooked for him in exchange for lodging for her and her husband.

Kate Keene began to untie the thin black ribbon wound around the drawings.

"Don't bother, Miss Keene." He willed her to listen. "I have no intention of living in that house ever again. I'd be rid of it in a heartbeat if I could find someone to take it off my hands. If I hadn't enlisted in the army after the war and exchanged a gray uniform for Union blue, I'd have lost possession of this land years ago."

She opened her mouth and surprised him by snapping it shut again. Her cheeks were on fire.

He was elated to see her apparently struggling for words, but she didn't struggle long enough.

"You can't be serious about selling."

His unkempt appearance, his surly attitude, his rudeness, even the threat of flying missiles had not stunned Kate Keene as deeply as the declaration that he couldn't care less and wanted to be rid of *Belle Fleuve*.

"This is your home, Colin, your heritage. Your ancestors are buried here."

"I look forward to the day it's no longer mine," he reiterated. "I have no use for this place anymore. It's not worth the paper the deed is written on."

As far as he was concerned, the grand, pillared mansion was nothing but a tomb that housed memories of halcyon days faded to a cloudy dream. His father and mother had passed on years ago, victims of the war.

"What about Amelie? What if she comes back looking for you?"

Would he ever lay eyes on his sister again? He had no notion of her whereabouts or if she was even still alive.

"There's no need for you to live like this." She waved her hand indicating the interior of his small dwelling. "You could move into the house if we make a few basic repairs."

"I have no desire to move back in there." He doubted he could travel the length of the narrow walk that connected the *garçon-nière* to the mansion even if he wanted to face the memories locked inside those walls. His gaze slipped to the laudanum bottle and then back to meet hers.

Kate Keene's sharp eyes became calculating.

"I'm tired, Miss Keene. Please do me a favor and leave."

She formed her words slowly, as if choosing them very carefully.

"Even if I wanted to, Colin, I owe it to Amelie and your parents to not leave you in this state. Obviously, you need far more help than I ever imagined. I feel it's my Christian duty to stay on."

Astounded, he forgot his injury and was forced to clamp his jaw against a shout of pain when he tried to sit up. He closed his eyes and waited for the intense throbbing that snaked from his shattered ankle all the way up his leg to recede. Finally, he managed a shuddering breath.

"Stay on? There is no way in h——"

She cut him off with a quick wave of her gloved hand. "There is no need to be vulgar. I can see that you are in no mood to discuss this today. Perhaps in the morning you'll be more receptive."

"In the *morning*?" He couldn't believe her audacity.

Miss Keene rose very slowly, taking great care in handling her plans. Then she made a show of shaking out her skirt before she returned the chair to its original location. Moving back to the center of the room, she paused, her long-lashed lids fluttering behind her spectacles.

Then Miss Katherine Keene smiled a very slow, extremely irritating smile.

Either he had gone completely mad or she was insane.

"Please try to understand. There's no way I'm leaving you like this, Colin." Her words were laced with Southern syrup and a hint of something more. "I'll send my companion back to town for our things and find some way to make myself comfortable for the night. We'll have the house livable in no time. You'll see. You simply can't stay holed up out here like this." She gazed around at the dingy paint and cracked plaster walls and shook her head. "It's depressing. No wonder you feel so terrible."

Colin shoved the fingers of both hands through his hair, held his head, and gritted his teeth.

He pinned her with a hard, cold stare. "You are not wanted or needed here. Turn yourself around, go back to New Orleans, and *don't come back*."

Kate walked slowly to the door, crunching across the broken vase as if it weren't there. Before she reached for the knob, she carefully turned to face him again. Her tone was laced with soft-ness, but there was no denying her determination.

"Your parents once assured me that I was always welcome at *Belle Fleuve.*"

"My parents are dead."

"Which is a blessing. If they were here, they would be appalled by your appearance and rude behavior. Since you are obviously not yourself, I'm going to forgive you for such odious conduct. I will see you again tomorrow. Perhaps then we'll have time to go over the plans."

"You will leave *now!*" he bellowed.

She smiled her irksome smile again and he noticed a dimple in her left cheek.

"I'm sorry, Colin, but I'm not going anywhere until you are capable of throwing me out yourself."

S tubborn, bullheaded ..."
Kate muttered to herself as she hurried back to the carriage. The sight of Colin had been an appalling shock to say the least. Had she passed him on the street she would have never recognized him given his current state of deterioration. She'd longed to see him for years and he hadn't even recognized her. There was no denying his confusion. She certainly hadn't expected him to hold her in the same regard she held him, but she had expected him to show some enthusiasm simply because of her past connection to his family.

The horrific reunion was a not-so-gentle reminder that she'd never been more than a visitor here.

Certainly some terrible fate had befallen him. His face drained of color every time he moved. His skin was jaundiced, and deep shadows haunted his dark Creole eyes. His curly hair hung past his shoulders. His thick dark beard emphasized the hollows beneath his eyes.

Thankfully, guarding against flying objects had kept her from crying out at the sight of him.

The rain squall that had started before she entered the *garçon-nière* had been short-lived. To the west, the sky already showed a hint of blue, though overhead, gray clouds still threatened. Surely tomorrow would be brighter. Kate anchored a smile on her face. No need to let Myra know they were definitely not welcome.

But if Kate had been one to take no for an answer, she would have never completed her architectural training. Her heart was set on restoring *Belle Fleuve*, not only because the place held so many memories, but as a showcase for her talent. She wasn't going to give up without a fight.

She nodded to the waiting driver. When he opened the door, she saw Myra hadn't budged.

"Well? Is he crazy?"

"No," Kate said. "But he's not well. In fact, he's in such desperate need that I've decided we must stay on."

"Here?"

Kate's mind was racing. "We'll walk to the house while the driver pulls the carriage around to the back door. Once we take inventory, you can return to town for supplies and our things."

"I wouldn't be back until tomorrow night at the very earliest. I can't leave you here all alone."

"You can and you will. I'll be just fine."

"Who was that woman? The redhead who walked out just before you walked in?"

"I have no idea." The strong scent of the woman's perfume had lingered in the air in the *garçonnière*, mingling with the smell of the stale food on Colin's tray.

"A common strumpet, if you ask me." Myra wrinkled her nose.

"She's of no concern." Did she come here often? What was that woman to Colin?

"So he's really not a maniac?" Myra worried the notion like a dog with a bone.

Kate paused for a bit too long. How much should she tell her companion?

Myra's eyes widened. "He *is* insane then?"

"No, he is most certainly not. He's … he's injured and apparently can't or won't walk. There was a tray of half-eaten food but he doesn't appear capable of cooking for himself. Not in the *garçonnière* at least. If someone is preparing his meals, then that someone has to be nearby and can tell us more."

"Was he injured in the war?"

"I don't know. I think more recently."

After Myra stepped out, Kate asked the driver to pull the carriage around to the back door. Myra continued to stare at the *garçonnière* until they started down the path to the main house.

Myra observed, "'Tis a real shame Mrs. Delany's gardens are in ruins. I always loved her roses."

And Colin is in ruins. Can I save him? Kate wondered.

The garden, formally laid out in the French *parterre* style, was overgrown with weeds. The ground was uneven where holes had been dug, seemingly at random, and poorly refilled. Hedgerows were altogether missing in places. The roses Colin's mother once prized were in dire need of pruning, struggling valiantly against the weeds.

Kate focused on the back of the main house. Many of the lacquered window shutters were missing. Bits of peeling paint clung to those that remained. Two of the back steps had rotted away.

As they passed the kitchen, an outbuilding close to the main structure, Kate saw someone through the window. Since her last visit a few months ago, a vegetable garden had been planted behind the kitchen and another near the first dwelling in a row of former slave cabins.

Kate knocked on the kitchen door and, to her delight, a former slave named Eugenie, who had been the Delanys' cook before the war, answered.

"My stars if it ain't little Katie Keene." The tall, slender woman in her early fifties was all smiles.

"I go by Kate now." She indicated her companion. "You remember Myra O'Hara?"

"Your nanny? Why, sure I 'member her. Welcome, Miss Myra." Eugenie ushered them both inside the kitchen and her expression darkened. "You seen Mr. Colin yet?"

Kate nodded. "Just now, unfortunately. I wish I could say he was even half as happy to see me as you are."

Eugenie shook her head. Worry emphasized lines the years had added to her thin face. She crossed her long arms at her waist. "I can't believe you even got past the door. He's not himself anymore, that's for certain."

Myra sniffed.

Kate tried to replace the image of Colin now with the memory she'd carried in her heart for so long. She imagined him in the doorway of the *garçonnière*, smiling down at her, handing her a rose. Surely that Colin was still inside him somewhere.

Eugenie interrupted her thoughts.

"Come have a seat, ladies."

Kate took in the huge hearth and fireplace, the battered and blackened pots and pans hanging from hooks along the mantle. A tea kettle was steaming on the stove in the corner. Eugenie was waving them over to the table and chairs in the center of the room.

"You two sit and I'll fix you up with some hot chicory and biscuits. Sorry I don't have any coffee. We been makin' due with chicory since the war."

As Eugenie puttered, Kate quickly explained that, having seen Colin, she had decided to stay to help him. Taking in the bare kitchen shelves she was glad she'd come.

"You're the answer to my prayers, Miss Kate. Since Mr. Colin got back he seems to be gettin' worse instead of better. There's nobody livin' in the house. No reason you can't stay on for a while," Eugenie said. "The place is in need of a good cleaning. Ain't much in there from the old days, but Simon and I can fix up pallets for you and Miss Myra. Havin' you here might do Mr. Colin a world of good."

After what just happened? Kate doubted it.

"I heard your daddy died and Captain's Landin' got sold a while back. You been living in New Orleans all this time, Miss Kate?"

"Papa sent me away with Myra when the war started. We lived in Boston and then Ireland and didn't come back until just before Father died four years ago. Mother sold the plantation and went off to Europe. Myra and I had been living in her townhouse, but a few weeks ago she sent word she married an Italian count and wanted the townhouse sold. So we've been living in a suite at the St. Charles Hotel."

It was like Nola Keene to simply send a letter and expect things to get done. The woman had had a battery of accountants, lawyers, and slaves to do her bidding most of her life. Kate had never been close enough to Nola to have to dance to her tune very often. That lack of love was something she didn't like to ponder.

"I've come out here a few times over the years and have never seen any signs of life before," Kate said.

"My husband, Simon, and I only been back 'bout three months now. Soon as the war ended we took off. We traveled 'round lookin' for work and tried to find our son, Mica. He disappeared when he drove Miss Marie upriver to her French cousin's place durin' the war."

"You never found him?"

Eugenie's eyes glistened. "Never did. We went up to Cleveland to look for work, but we couldn't find any there either so we came back. We never knew any other life but the one we had here. Figured if no one was around, we'd stay on here until we got thrown out. About a month ago, Mr. Colin come ridin' in. Could barely sit the saddle. He refused to stay in the house so we scrounged up what furniture we could find and set up the *garçonnière* for him. He's been there ever since and I been cookin' for him."

Eugenie served steaming chicory and heavenly biscuits slathered with butter. Kate's mouth watered before she took the first bite. Eugenie hovered over them and finally, at Kate's insistence, sat down.

"How was Colin injured?" Kate ventured to ask. "Did he say where he's been since the war?"

Eugenie shrugged and shook her head. "He's in a bad way. Insists on takin' too much laudanum, if you ask me. He told Simon that by the time the war ended he didn't know anythin' but soldierin'. With both his folks gone and Miss Amelie having run off with that no-account Johnny Reb deserter, Mr. Colin had nothin' to come home to, so he signed up with the Union to fight the Indian wars out in West Texas."

"I had heard that much when I returned. Someone from his old regiment told a friend of a friend of mine he'd enlisted again."

Eugenie went on. "About a year ago, one of them savages shot an arrow clean through his ankle. Tore it near to pieces. It went putrid and he nearly died. It pains him so bad that he wishes they'd have taken his foot and ankle clean off."

Kate stared into the bitter chicory, trying to imagine the wealthy planter's son she'd once known with nowhere to go, no choice but to reenlist and wear Union blue. The old Colin was a far cry from the shattered thirty-two-year-old holed up in the *garçonnière*.

"He's hurtin' too much to walk, but I think he still ought to try 'fore he can't move at all. He ain't left that room. Has me bring his food in and take it out but won't let me tidy up."

Kate finished the tea and stood, thankful that she knew a little more than she had a few moments ago. She reached up and straightened her small hat, then smiled with far more confidence than she felt.

"Who was that woman? The one with the red hair?"

Pursing her lips, Eugenie shook her head in disgust. "That's not the kind of woman you need to know anythin' about, Miss Kate. She came here askin' for Colin this afternoon. I tol' her good luck, be my guest."

"He sent her packing and not too politely, I must say."

"Good." Eugenie sniffed. "We don't need her kind 'round here."

Kate nodded. "Thank you, Eugenie, for the refreshment and the information. I suppose I should tell you that Colin wasn't exactly happy when I told him I wasn't leaving."

Eugenie laughed and shook her head.

"He's always in a wicked mood," she warned. "But you don't have to worry. He won't be comin' over to the house to throw you out anytime soon. That much is certain. For me it's a blessin' you're here. I didn't know what else to do for him."

Kate drew herself up. All of her hopes and dreams rested on a roll of architectural plans, dreams of restoring *Belle Fleuve,* and of seeing Colin again. She'd been given more than a chance to prove herself as an architect. It was up to her to help Colin find himself and be the man he used to be. The man she remembered.

She wasn't a shy, hesitant young girl anymore either. Gone was the cast-off orphan hiding in the shadows. Thanks to her adoptive parents, she was educated, well traveled, and independent. Before she was through here, Colin Delany would definitely have to take notice.

"Helping Colin is the least I can do for Amelie," she told Eugenie. "And for her parents, God rest their souls."

Eugenie smiled through forming tears. "Miss Kate, I know you're gonna have Mr. Colin up and around real soon."

Relieved to have an ally, Kate smiled.

"Thank you, Eugenie. Colin is going to have my help whether he wants it or not."

Gray skies cast Colin's sanctuary into a gloom that matched his mood as he tried to forget the sight of the audacious young woman who had flounced out a few minutes earlier.

The last time he'd seen Katie Keene was on the eve of the war. She had been silent as a shadow, a bookish thirteen-year-old with wren-brown hair and owlish blue eyes trapped behind overly large spectacles.

He had no idea where or how she had weathered the war years, but from the look of her expensive getup and new boots, the Keenes had survived far better than the Delanys and *Belle Fleuve*.

Slowly shifting positions, Colin gritted his teeth and cursed his injury. The incessant pain in his shattered ankle never diminished. The laudanum he'd just downed made it hard to recall Kate Keene's explanation for her appearance. Something about restoring the house.

With what? Was he supposed to pull money out of thin air?

What he'd saved from his army pay was almost gone. On his way back he'd heard talk of federal troops being withdrawn and home rule restored to Louisiana. Once the carpetbaggers were out of office, the reinstated government would demand any current taxes he owed.

Why bring the house back to life just to lose it? It was hard enough living day to day; he was in no condition to worry about the future.

He pictured the smiling, undeterred Miss Keene and her irritating stubbornness. Last time he's seen her he'd been what? Seventeen? Wealthy and confident, he'd known who he was and what he was destined to become. His future as a prominent Louisiana planter was assured.

He'd planned to go on a world tour after the war and had been sure he'd end up marrying someone stunningly beautiful, equally wealthy, and well connected. His Confederate uniform turned many lovely heads.

They were all shocked when the war dragged on and on. Within a handful of years, his family, wealth, and future were gone. Now Kate Keene was back, a living reminder of everything he'd lost.

She and Amelie had been constant companions. Their fathers had been close too; members of the Irish community descended from the first-wave immigrants who helped found New Orleans.

Gil Keene was a wealthy banker who, along with his wife, Nola, preferred spending most of his time at a townhome in New Orleans rather than with Kate at their plantation, Captain's Landing, which neighbored *Belle Fleuve*. They'd left Kate on her own so often she became a fixture here. Though she was always around, she'd been so unobtrusive he remembered little about her. A watchful, quiet child, she was always just *there*, easily overshadowed by his vivacious, lovely little sister.

Colin rubbed his temple, attempting to ease a throbbing headache in his muddled head. When someone knocked at the door he yelled, "Go away, Miss Keene."

"It's me, Mr. Colin. Come with your dinner."

Not Kate Keene, but Eugenie.

"Come in, then."

The woman opened the door, carefully balancing a tray. She halted just inside and stared at the pieces of broken vase littering the floor. Eugenie shook her head and fussed as she set down the tray and then went back outside, returning with a washbowl that she placed on the table near Colin. She struck a match and carefully lit the oil lamp, then pulled a straight razor and scissors out of her apron pocket.

Colin nodded toward the washbowl. "What's all this?"

"Thought since you have company you might like to shave and clean up a bit."

"You thought wrong. I told Miss Keene to leave. She's not wanted here."

"She's not going."

"Tell her I'm flat broke, Eugenie. That ought to do it."

"Miss Kate don't care nothing about your money. She was always welcome here before and she ought to be now. Why, your mamma and daddy would turn over in their graves if they heard you talk like that."

"Fortunately they can't hear a thing."

"How you know they ain't looking down from heaven right now?" She tested the water in the basin with her fingertips. "You want me to put this closer so as you can use it while it's still warm?"

"I want you to take it away."

There was no chance his parents were up in heaven looking down. Fourteen long years of fighting had convinced him there was no such place. Hell, yes. Heaven, no. God had stopped listening a long time ago.

Eugenie sighed and started fussing with the cutlery and bowl on his tray.

"You might change your mind," she mumbled.

"I will not change my mind about eating or shaving any more than I'll change it about Miss Keene."

"Well, she's staying. She sent her nanny back to town for their things."

"The woman still needs a *nanny*?"

"Calls her a travelin' companion now. Seems Katie's daddy sent them up to Boston soon as the war broke out. They lived in Ireland and met a whole passel of Keene cousins. Myra's kin is there too. Miss Katie studied up on how to make them house drawings like your daddy used to do."

"She's an architect." He still couldn't believe it.

"Just like your daddy. She been working on plans for this place for a long time now and promised to show them to me tomorrow. Mr. Colin, she's spent years dreamin' of putting *Belle Fleuve* back together again and—"

"She's got no right."

"But she's got the heart. Never seen anything like the way her eyes light up when she talks of fixin' up the place."

"She can go fix up her own place."

"The Keenes sold Captain's Landing years ago. It never saw half the trials this place has seen; no Union soldiers running through the house tearin' it all up or diggin' up the gardens looking for buried loot." Eugenie paused long enough to shake her head. "Not an ounce of respect for what wasn't theirs." She went to collect the broom and swept up the shards of vase.

"Too bad Gil Keene isn't around to rein in his headstrong daughter," Colin mumbled.

Anyone with an ounce of sensitivity would realize it made him sick to see his home in such a shambles, especially when there was nothing he could do about it.

The Delany wealth had been tied up in slaves and cane, and now both were gone. Even if he had funds, Colin doubted he'd know how to run a sugar plantation on his own. The accounting had been up to his father. Managing the plantation had fallen to their foreman, a man named Bolton.

Now there was no sugar to harvest, no money to hire field hands with. Sooner or later the tax collectors' leniency would reach its limit and this place would be on the auction block.

Eugenie finished sweeping and picked up Colin's luncheon tray. He'd largely ignored his noon meal. Now, oddly enough, the aroma of the steaming stew she'd brought in for dinner was actually tempting. Anger must have piqued his appetite; he was hungry for the first time in a long while.

"You might as well push that dinner tray closer," he bid her. "I think I'll give it a try."

He glanced at the bottle of laudanum that she moved just out of reach. He knew she was less than thrilled about giving it to him. His ankle ached, an echo of pain that conjured memories of the day he was injured. Memories he'd just as soon forget.

The laudanum helped with that too, but it also left him feeling weak and drained and dependent. He wanted some now but he needed a clear head if he was going to deal with Kate Keene. Eugenie was on the woman's side. He had no one to depend on but himself.

"Remind Miss Keene I want her gone by tomorrow noon."

Eugenie mumbled something, but he couldn't make out the words.

"I mean it, Eugenie. I want her out of here."

"Yes, sir. I'll surely tell her." The woman avoided his eyes as she balanced the noon tray, crossed the room, and reached for the door handle.

"Eugenie."

She paused and met his stare. "Yes, Mr. Colin?"

"There's not to be any work done to the house. If Miss Keene balks about leaving, you tell her that."

Eugenie shrugged. "I'll try, but I 'spects you just might have to get up and tell her yourself."

TWO

Mr. Colin still wants you to leave.

An hour after dawn the next day, Kate sat at a small, crudely made table in the corner of what was once the formal dining room on the main floor of *Belle Fleuve*, absently running her fingertip around the chipped edge of a Limoges teacup. The delicate china was one of the few pieces of Marie Delany's extensive china collection to survive the war. How many pieces of the set were gracing Yankee tables up North?

Her gaze traveled around the dining room, cavernous and empty except for a rickety table made of sawhorses and a slab of wood, and her pallet, which was set up in the far corner where she had spent the night. The dining room was in far better condition than any of the other rooms—there were no rat holes in the walls and only a few leaks around the windowsills.

That morning, Eugenie had not only delivered to Kate a breakfast of poached eggs, a mound of grits, and a pot full of thick, black chicory, but she had also said Colin had reissued the demand that she leave.

"But don't you pay him any mind," Eugenie said. "And don't take it personal. That's just the pain and laudanum talking."

"How much does he take?"

"Too much if you ask me."

One more worry. Kate didn't wish Colin pain, and as long as he stayed in a haze he couldn't back up his threats to throw her out, but she didn't want him taking so much laudanum. She wasn't going anywhere until she had him cleaned up and settled in the house again. Surely moving in would lift his spirit.

Rumpled and disheveled, she shook out the skirt of her lavender traveling suit and ran a hand through her hair, determined to walk through the house and make notes. Essential repairs simply had to be done whether or not Colin agreed to an entire reconstruction. Surely he wouldn't fault her for making a few minor repairs to keep the roof and sills from leaking and shore up the gallery stairs to the second story.

Built in French Colonial style, *Belle Fleuve* was constructed with wide wrap-around porches called galleries. There were no interior halls for the six rooms on each floor, three across and two deep. To walk the length of each floor one had to pass through the rooms or along the outside galleries. Downstairs, wide double-pocket doors separated two large sitting rooms. Fireplaces were on both ends of the house open to the second-floor rooms as well.

Countless broken windowpanes nurtured dry rot where rain had seeped in and ruined the wood and glaze. Sections of crown molding patterned in a Greek key style were missing. Smoke stains from a clogged fireplace flue marred what were once stunning pale-blue and gold ceiling murals. Wall coverings Marie Delany had personally chosen for their rose and medallion designs hung in tatters. Priceless draperies and furnishings were long gone.

Kate sighed. It was a near-daunting task—almost as challenging as Colin. She grew more and more heartsick as she carefully negotiated the worn stairs to the second floor. Jalousies, long shutters that closed to block out the sun, hung askew on their hinges. Her footsteps rang hollow as she traversed empty bedrooms where an old daybed, its frame broken, and two small bureaus were the only pieces of furniture left.

Kate entered the master bedroom, imagining the way it looked when Marie and Patrick Delany lived and loved there. Gone were their crimson and gold Aubusson rug, the mahogany tester bed, the handkerchief linen spread. Gone were the portraits of the Baudier ancestors who had claimed this land along the Mississippi. Gone was the sound of laughter that once rang in rooms now silent and cold.

After making a few more notations, Kate went through a door in a bedroom that hid a narrow staircase to a small attic beneath the wide hip roof. Small windows at each end of the roof near the chimneys let in enough light for her to make her way, crouched, beneath the low ceiling.

Once her eyes adjusted to the dimness, she saw a few possessions littered across the floor, items with which the ransacking Yankees hadn't bothered. A domed trunk lay open, tossed on its side, its contents spilling out. As Kate stared at the open trunk and the papers scattered around it, a breeze blew in through one of the cracked windows.

A creak in the floorboards sent a shiver down her spine. She glanced behind her and scoffed at herself when she noticed a worn rocking horse gently moving back and forth. Its leather reins were broken. Most of its felt saddle was torn or missing. All that was left of its horsehair mane and tail was stubble.

She walked across the attic and stilled the rocking horse with a touch of her hand and looked around. A spindled child's bed remained intact but its mattress was filled with holes — a home to mice. Other boxes and trunks were opened and emptied. They'd never know what treasures and family possessions had been taken. Her gaze returned to the contents of the trunk where a collection of daguerreotypes and photographs was scattered among papers.

Ignoring the dust and cobwebs, Kate sank to the floor. Her skirt billowed up around her as she knelt and gathered older carte-de-visite images, tintypes, daguerreotypes, and Delany family memorabilia. She dropped them into her lap, then lifted a certificate of some kind and turned it toward the light. It was the official notice of Patrick Delany's death, with the Confederate seal attached. She rubbed dust off the seal with her fingertip. The piece of dusty yellowed paper seemed so little to show for such a kind and intelligent man's life.

Next she picked up a small formal portrait of Patrick Delany, made when he appeared to be in his thirties. His hair was neatly parted, his light Irish eyes near translucent in the likeness. Like her, he wore spectacles. "It's no sin to be farsighted," Patrick had told her upon overhearing Amelie declare it a shame that Kate had to wear glasses and ruin her looks. He would never know how grateful she'd been for his kindness. Nor could she thank him for taking the time to teach a young girl the rudiments of architecture. His inspiration was the foundation for her dreams, and now that she was here at *Belle Fleuve* surrounded by so many reminders, she missed him even more.

Kate wiped away tears and picked up another photograph. She had one very much like it packed away somewhere in her suite at the St. Charles. In it, all of the Delanys were seated together. Amelie was dressed in a fussy, frilly gown with yards of lace and crinolines. The fabric was lemon yellow, Kate recalled, a vibrant shade that was a lovely contrast to Amelie's near blue-black hair, which was plaited into braids and tied into loops on each side—a style long out of fashion.

Marie Baudier Delany sat proudly between her stunning children. The photographer had captured the youthful features and childlike qualities of the woman who was mother to two nearly grown offspring. Colin stood straight and proud, taller than his father. A touch of conceit was in his smile and, indeed, he was handsome with his jet-black hair and dark eyes. How could he not know it?

She touched Colin's image with her fingertip. His expression was so unlike the bitter man in the *garçonnière*. This Colin smiled with a debonair, carefree air. Now the joy in that smile had been replaced by a scowl. The only similarity was the intensity of his dark eyes.

The flowery scroll on the back of the picture dated it 1861. The Delanys, formally portrayed for the last time, had been completely unaware that their way of life was poised on the brink of disaster.

Kate lowered the photograph to her lap and sat in the middle of the attic, surrounded by dust and shadows. She imagined herself hovering unseen in the background, a witness to their unfolding lives, attuned to their routine and exchanges but not really one of them. Her adoptive parents had distanced themselves from her by their age and interests. As happy as Kate was to visit *Belle Fleuve*, her parents were just as happy to let her.

So it was that she became a fixture here for days and sometimes weeks, pretending she and Amelie were sisters. She had only the vaguest memories of her real sisters. They'd been separated from each other when Kate was only six. Lovie and Megan were the oldest. Sarah, the youngest, had ended up at the orphanage too. An adorable little blonde, Sarah was adopted months before the Keenes finally chose Kate.

So out of loneliness Kate had indeed pretended Amelie was her sister and dreamed of ways to get Colin to notice her. But studying the Delany family portrait now and seeing the four of them together, Kate realized the truth for what it was: she might have been a fixture in their home, but she was not a member of the family. After her exchange with Colin yesterday, the futility of her fantasies made them seem bleak and ridiculous.

Kate felt sure things would be different if Amelie were here. Despite the dire circumstances, their laughter would ring out and she would have an ally.

She sighed and gathered the photographs into a pile and set them aside. She picked up a cobalt cloisonné baby rattle, turned it over in her hand, and gave it a shake. A half dozen carved wooden animals were also on the floor, remnants of a Noah's ark set, all missing their mates. She dusted off the animals and lined them up; one donkey, one lion, one elephant, one giraffe. They looked so lonely she scooped them up and set them back in the trunk, and as she did, she tried to dismiss the urge to go to Colin and see for herself how he was this morning.

Best to keep my wits about me. She couldn't let him deter her from her task or forbid her from helping again.

She closed the trunk and tucked some of the photographs behind her notepaper before she descended the stairs to the second floor. The sun was shining, a gentle breeze coming in off the river as she walked through an open door onto the upper gallery. She tested the floor before she stepped out. It wouldn't do to have come this far and drop through a hole in the rotted wood.

She sat down on the top step and turned to a new sheet of paper. Jotting down all the supplies as well as foodstuffs she wanted, Kate checked the list three times and then remembered to add coffee. When she was finally satisfied with the list, she penned two letters, one to her accountant, Dan Rosen, and another to the owner of the warehouse where her mother's furniture had been stored. Nola had given Kate all of her townhouse castoffs, pieces that could be put to good use here at *Belle Fleuve.*

An hour later, Kate met with Eugenie's husband, Simon. His grandfather had been a carpenter who had helped build the original house. Of solid build with short dark hair shot with gray, Simon had hands that were thick and calloused from a lifetime of labor. He rounded up a half dozen able-bodied men in need of work, some trained in carpentry, others willing to do anything. Kate assured them they would be paid fairly.

When the men walked away, Simon lingered, his expression cloudy.

"What is it?" Kate asked.

He cleared his throat and tapped his straw hat against his baggy pant leg.

"Mr. Colin said he ain't got any money, 'cept for what he saved from his army pay."

Kate hesitated. In his present state she had no wish to humiliate Colin by telling him she had paid the back taxes or that she would happily provide all the building materials and money for the workmen.

"For the time being, I'll pay for them, Simon," she finally said. "There's no need to mention that to Mr. Colin right now. He and I will settle up later, when he's got the place up and running again." Hopefully, being comfortably installed in the house again would inspire him to look toward the future and bring the fields back to life.

"When do you want us to start?" Simon seemed relieved.

She planted her hands on her hips and looked out over the back garden where Myra was on her hands and knees tugging at a stubborn patch of weeds.

"I've sent for furniture. Hopefully, it will arrive in a day or two. Have men here to unload and move it into the house. The lumber and supplies should be here within the week. Until then, there is plenty of preparation work to do."

"Sure will be good to see the old place come to life again," he said. "It's been like livin' with an open sore, starin' at the house, seein' it so dark and forlorn. Eugenie and me are sure glad you showed up, Miss Kate. I know in time Mr. Colin will be too."

"Thank you, Simon. I hope you're right."

When he left she looked toward the *garçonnière*. Thankfully, there had been no sign of Colin all morning. Daring him to throw her out yesterday hadn't been enough to rouse him. Eugenie said he hadn't even mentioned her this morning when his breakfast was delivered. Obviously, he had no idea with whom he was dealing; she would never walk away without a fight.

The only way she could succeed was if she avoided him for the next few days. As long as she didn't raise his ire before the repairs were well underway, there was every chance she just might get him to see things her way.

THREE

For three days Colin refused to let Kate Keene bait him. Remaining locked in self-imposed isolation in the *garçonnière* grew more difficult, however, for with each passing day the sounds of hammering and sawing at the main house intensified.

What irked him almost as much as her presence and obvious disregard for his wishes was that Miss Keene refused to let *Belle Fleuve* fall into further neglect. If the house was to be saved, he should be the one restoring the place, not her. But he hadn't the physical strength or the funds. All he possessed was an abundance of regret.

Not a day passed when he didn't berate himself for leaving his mother and sister alone to face the upheaval of war. As the sole surviving male, he should have put in for a discharge and returned home to run the plantation. Looking back now, he realized he might have done as much or more to fight the Union army right here on River Road. At the very least, he may have been able to keep the Yankees from commandeering the house.

Even if he had been forced to lock her up, he could have somehow stopped Amelie from running off with a no-account deserter. He would never forgive himself for not coming home to save his mother, his sister, and their home, but he had had no notion of how bad things were.

His mother's infrequent letters reached him weeks after they were written, and by then there was little he could have done. He hadn't even learned of Marie's death until a letter from a Baudier cousin reached him months after his mother was already gone.

When someone knocked on the *garçonnière* door at noon Colin knew it was Eugenie. He called out to her to come in. She appeared with a covered tray, but neither the food nor her presence drew him out of his malaise.

"I want that infernal pounding stopped," he ordered.

Eugenie shrugged and avoided eye contact. "A few things need fixed is all."

"Who's doing the work?"

"Simon and some of the others."

"On whose orders? Is that woman still here?"

"You mean Miss Kate?"

"Who else?"

"She's still here."

"Then either you or she is ignoring my demands."

Eugenie's eyes widened. "I told her you wanted her gone."

"She's no doubt responsible for all that pounding. Am I right?"

Where was she sleeping? On what? Colin pictured her fine traveling getup and new boots again. She certainly didn't look as if she wanted for anything. A bookish, spectacle-wearing spinster and the pampered heiress of a wealthy banker, she had probably never heard the word *no* in her life. She wouldn't be comfortable very long in the house, not in the condition it was in the last time he'd seen it.

He hadn't been able to manage the stairs, but he knew enough from hobbling around a few of the empty rooms on the first floor that the place had been stripped of everything of value. A few pieces of furniture, mostly broken, were amid the debris. Leaves had blown in through open doors and shattered windows. Water damage stained the plaster ceilings. He hadn't spent five minutes inside before he walked out and gave the house up as one more loss.

Eugenie nodded toward the tray. "There's pork and rice just the way you like it. I'll come back to collect the tray." When she paused, folded her hands at her waist, and turned to him without smiling, he knew he was in for a lecture.

"You know," she began, "the roof leaks. Lots of glass is broken out of the windows. Rain water was rottin' the sills. Miss Kate's only having the men do what needs to be done most to keep the weather from bringing the place down."

She's doing what I should have done.

"Send her over here, Eugenie."

"Miss Kate?"

"Of course *Miss Kate*. I certainly don't want to chat with her nanny unless that would do more good."

"She's busy right now. Maybe tomorrow she'll — "

"*Now*, Eugenie. Not tomorrow. Not even later today." Colin took a deep breath and closed his eyes for a second. When he opened them again he spoke slowly and distinctly. "I want to see that woman right now."

"Yes, sir."

She was irked, but she held her silence as she walked to the door.

"I mean it, Eugenie."

The door closed behind her but not before Colin heard her mumble, "I hear you."

Colin gritted his teeth, steeled himself against the pain, and managed to pull himself to a sitting position against a bank of pillows. He ran his palm over his beard, then shoved his hair back out of his eyes. A soup stain from last night's dinner was on his shirtfront, but it was too late to ask Eugenie for a fresh shirt now. *What do I care what Miss Keene thinks?*

Fine mess you are, Colin.

He imagined his mother's voice, heard the tinkle of her girlish laughter. In Marie Delany's eyes he could do no wrong. If she were to have seen him like this before the war she would have rolled her eyes and ordered one of the house maids to fill a tub full of lavender-scented water and bring him clean clothes.

As he waited for Kate to appear, lethargy mingled with traces of his last dose of laudanum and lulled him into a doze. He was awakened by a knock and discovered the sun was much lower. Kate Keene had taken her sweet time in answering his summons.

Another quick, impatient knock followed the first before Colin hollered, "Come in."

Kate appeared with a rosy blush on her cheeks. Her hair was wrapped in a loose knot atop her head. She wore a pale-blue gown covered by an overly large apron.

Styles had changed since before the war, so much so that even a man could notice. Back then women wore hooped cages beneath their skirts that belled out to completely hide the female form from the waist down. Seeing Kate's shapely figure affirmed that Colin certainly didn't miss those contraptions.

The pockets of her apron bulged with what appeared to be papers and cards. Before he could utter a word, she went back outside and then came back in toting a bucket, rags, and a mop.

"Why are you in that getup?" he demanded.

"Getup?"

"You look like a servant." He pinned her with his gaze, letting his eyes roam over her from head to toe, and was pleased when she blushed.

"I've been cleaning." Kate set down the bucket. "Eugenie said you wanted to see me."

He glanced at the bucket before he met her gaze again.

"She told me repairs are underway and that they're your doing."

Instead of answering, Kate walked over to the drop-leaf table and ran her finger over it. She stared at the dust on her fingertip, brushed it off, and shrugged.

"It's the least I can do."

"I don't want your help. I thought I made that clear."

"It's not for you, Colin. My childhood would have been a very lonely time if not for Amelie and your parents. I'm doing this as a way of showing my gratitude for their many kindnesses." Her voice was soft and melodic with a hint of an accent atop the slow languid cadence of Louisiana.

"Well, they aren't here and I have no money. Your efforts are wasted."

"The repairs are very limited. You have no need to repay me. The South may be in ruins, but thanks to my father, I am not."

"How nice for you, but I don't need or want your charity." He paused, watching her wipe off the tabletop with a floppy rag. "What are you doing?"

"Dusting."

"Well, stop it."

"This place is a pigsty."

"I have expressly told Eugenie to leave it alone, that's why."

"I'm not faulting her." She reached up and wiped the dusty picture frame around a badly executed watercolor. "Amelie painted this one. Do you recall?"

He didn't recall, though lately he'd spent hours staring across the room at the painting, wondering who had wasted his or her time.

"She was never very good at watercolors," Kate said. "But she tried." Suddenly she turned, the dusting momentarily suspended. "It would do well for you to take some pride in this place, not to mention yourself, Colin. Amelie could return anytime, and I, for one, certainly pray she will. Do you want her to see you like this?"

"Did you suffer some kind of head injury, Kate? A fall maybe?"

"No. Nor am I insane. Why wouldn't Amelie come to visit you? When she does, things should be in order. She would expect that."

She turned away and started dusting a cane chair. After she finished the cane bottom, she tilted the chair and wiped off the legs and rungs beneath the seat. When Colin found himself admiring her backside beneath the fall of ruffles down her skirt, he sighed and forced himself to concentrate on the misshapen cluster of roses in Amelie's watercolor.

"After what she's done, do you think I'm going to welcome her home with open arms?"

"I really don't care. At least this place will be looking better when and if Amelie ever does come home."

He cursed under his breath and saw Kate wince before she started dusting the second chair.

"You've been in the company of soldiers too long," she said.

"What do you know about where I've been?"

She considered him for a moment. "I heard you were out west fighting Indians. Wearing Union blue." She finished the chair and turned to him directly, the dust rag forgotten at her side.

"Colin, there's every chance that with a little faith and time, you'll recover—"

He turned to stare out the window.

"It's been months," he said.

"Locked inside all the time, I assume." She picked up a chair and carried it over to the French doors facing the garden. She opened the doors wide and set the chair just outside on the small stone veranda.

"You need sunlight, fresh air, and a change of view." Suddenly she was beside the bed, touching his arm. "Let me help you up."

"Get your hands off me!" She startled him so much his demand came out far harsher than he intended. Kate ducked her head and quickly stepped back.

Does she think I've sunk that far? To think that I would hit her?

"You are very irritating, Miss Keene, but I would never strike a woman."

"I wasn't expecting you to holler like that." She blinked, her round eyes wide behind her spectacles. "Would you like me to help you outside?" She reached for his cane.

He didn't want her help, and he wasn't about to go sit outside where he'd be seen. The truth was that he couldn't bear to see his mother's garden in ruins, her precious roses choked by weeds. Suddenly he heard Marie's voice again.

Look, Colin. A box from France! My new tea roses have finally arrived. Yellow, I think. Why, it's been so long I can't even recall what I ordered.

He had enough unwanted memories before Kate Keene had showed up. Now she'd awakened even more.

"I thought I made it clear I don't want your help. Stop cleaning. And while you are at it, leave the main house alone too."

"I wish you would go see the progress Simon and the others are making. Did you know Simon's grandfather built the original house? Your mother's relations paid him a fair price for his work too."

"Do Simon and the others know they won't be getting paid?"

She hesitated. Frown lines marred her forehead just above the bridge of her glasses. She turned so she didn't have to face him and batted the dust rag along a chair rail.

"I've paid them." Before he could respond she added, "You can pay me when you are on your feet again."

Kate glanced at his injured ankle. She was close enough to see the angry, ruined skin and deep scars extending below the hem of his pant leg.

"You had no right to butt in here, Miss Keene. None at all."

Their eyes met briefly before she turned away. She picked up the mop and shoved it into the bucket. She sloshed soapy water onto the floor. It dribbled over the toes of her leather shoes.

"I won't be beholden to you or anyone," he added. "I'll give the place away first."

"Who's going to want this tumbled-down mess?"

"You, obviously."

"It's yours and Amelie's. As long as you have *Belle Fleuve*, you have a home and you have land."

"Why don't you have a home of your own? Why aren't you browbeating some hapless husband, drawing up house plans and bestowing your fortune on him instead of me? Would no one have you? Is that it? Too much of an intellect are you, Miss Keene? Did you spend too many hours hunched over plans for *Belle Fleuve* to find yourself a husband and have a proper life?"

Kate was tempted to fling the bucket of soapy water on him, but she put her back into mopping Colin's muddy floor instead. He probably wouldn't believe her if she told him she'd turned down half a dozen proposals.

She dunked the dirty mop into the bucket, yanked it out, and twisted the wet, flopping ends before she slapped it against the floor again.

He knew nothing, *nothing* about the offers she'd refused from fine, decent men who would have made wonderful husbands. Men in Boston and Ireland, some from right here in Louisiana. Men who were polite and good humored—nothing like him. A few she denied because they'd seemed more interested in her inheritance than in what she had to offer as a wife. The rest she'd turned down because none had measured up to her ideal. None of them held a candle to the young man who had captured her heart so long ago.

She sneaked a glance in Colin's direction, then let her gaze linger while he stared out the open French doors. She'd all but given up hope of ever seeing him again until the day Myra returned from the market and told her rumors were rampant about the madman living at the Delany plantation. Kate had ignored the gossip and danced a little jig.

Now surly and unkempt, he was straining her patience. She could barely tolerate the way he was treating her. It was hard to imagine what she'd ever seen in him. Myra had tried to convince Kate that the torch she was carrying for Colin was merely child-hood infatuation. The man she thought she loved was not the brooding man who had locked himself away from the world. There was certainly nothing admirable about Colin's anger or his self-pity.

What did she know of him or what he'd become? Was she taking on too much?

Wielding the mop, Kate vowed right then that once he was on his feet again, and once the house was cleaned and repaired, her work here would be done.

Ignoring him for the time being, she finished mopping the floor, then picked up his untouched luncheon tray. Leaving the front door wide open behind her, she marched the tray back to the house. When she returned not more than three minutes later, he remained silent, but she felt his dark eyes boring into her. She toted the bucket outside, tossed the dirty water, and then went back for her rags and mop. She was about to leave when she remembered the Delany photographs tucked in her right pocket.

When she walked over to Colin's bedside, he looked mad enough to spit nails. She ignored his scowl.

"I don't remember you having any gumption before. I don't think I ever even heard you squeak around here," he growled.

"Maybe you weren't listening. I earned my gumption standing up to people who constantly told me no. People who insisted I couldn't be what I wanted to be or learn what I wanted to learn because I was a woman. I learned to fight for what I wanted."

She prayed he would soon muster enough courage of will to fight his pain, to believe in himself and this place again.

"I found these in the attic." She slipped the images out of her pocket. Though she felt like tossing them on the bed, she set them down gently.

"If you're waiting for me to thank you, you're wasting your time." He didn't even glance at the pictures lying within reach, though he balled his fingers into a fist as if to keep from reaching for them.

It suddenly dawned on her that his anger had a purpose—it kept everyone at bay. He used it not only to isolate himself, but to hide his pain.

Kate softened the moment the realization hit her.

"Would you like me to trim your hair?" The words had come out too soft, almost as if she were coaxing a temperamental child. She desperately needed to find out if there was something, anything, left of the Colin she once knew. Perhaps after a haircut and shave . . .

"What I would like is for you to disappear."

"I'm only trying to help, but I'm beginning to think you don't deserve it." Suddenly it didn't matter why he was so angry and morose. Her Irish temper was already strained to the limit. "You have a dark heart, Colin. You didn't always."

She looked at the empty chair waiting beyond the French doors. She so wanted to see him in the dappled sunlight filtering down through the oaks. She started to walk away.

"What would you know of me or my heart?" His softer tone stopped her. "You were a child when you last saw me. I was too for that matter."

She walked over to the open doors and stared outside. The garden was empty. The intense sunshine had driven Myra inside.

"I'd rather have a dark heart than one like yours," he said.

She turned to him. "What do you mean?"

"You have a heart of glass. That's very dangerous, you know."

"Why do you say that?"

"It is too fragile, too full of a disgusting overabundance of optimism and hope."

"What's wrong with optimism? What's wrong with hope?" His words hurt more than anything else he'd said or done. Rapidly blinking away tears, Kate was bound and determined not to let him see how easily he could wound her.

"When it finally shatters and that light is gone, Kate, you won't be able to survive it."

"I don't believe that for a minute. That hope is what sustains me through good times and bad." She took a step closer to the bed and stopped when his frown deepened. "I'd happily share it to see you through this. If only—"

"Are you always like this? Are you *real?*"

"I hope so."

"I would think all that hope is exhausting."

She took a deep breath, shook her head, and forced a smile. "No more exhausting than all of your self-pity."

FOUR

I hate to see you go, Miss Kate."

Kate crossed the open foyer at the bottom of the stairs in the main house and took hold of Eugenie's hands. The woman's eyes widened at Kate's gesture.

"Given how much Colin wants me gone, I've been lucky to have stayed two weeks, but I dare not defy him any longer."

Kate surveyed the changes: The stairs to the second floor were no longer dangerous. Her mother's unwanted furniture was scattered throughout the formal rooms downstairs. Decent beds and bedding now filled the rooms upstairs, and she had left an ample supply of linens, lamps, and rugs. The walls were bare, but at least they'd been stripped of shredded wall coverings.

Kate nodded, satisfied with what she'd done in a month. Now it was time to return to the city and reestablish herself there. She'd done enough to stave off the inevitable at *Belle Fleuve* for a year or two. All she could do now was pray that Amelie would return before then and convince Colin to come to his senses.

"I've done all I can," she said.

Just then Simon came downstairs toting Myra's trunk and a traveling case.

"Where will you go now, Miss Kate?"

"Back to our suite at the St. Charles. I may even look for a permanent residence." She knew some lovely homes could be had for a song in the Garden District, but none that compared to *Belle Fleuve*. "I couldn't have found a better carpenter anywhere, Simon. Please thank your crew for me, will you?"

"'Course, Miss Kate." He set down the trunk, reached into the pocket of his baggy homespun trousers, pulled out a miniature wooden carving that fit in the palm of his hand, and handed it to her.

"Why, it's *Belle Fleuve*." Kate turned the piece over and over, studying the intricate carving and detail. The columns were all there. So too were the gallery railings. It was a small masterpiece. She smiled at Simon through tears.

"I'm honored, Simon. I'll treasure this always."

"I know how you hold this place in your heart, Miss Kate. Now you can hold it in your hand. I'm hopin' it'll bring you back."

"I sure wish things would have worked out different," Eugenie said, as Myra made her appearance on the stairs.

Once her companion was beside her, Kate handed Myra the carving for safekeeping and thanked the couple again. The carriage she'd hired was due at any moment. Eugenie opened the front door, and as Kate walked out she saw a wagon coming up the long drive. Not exactly the carriage she expected.

"You didn't order more supplies, did you?" Simon stepped up beside her as the four of them watched the approaching vehicle. A driver in overalls and a wide-brimmed straw hat was guiding the team of horses.

"Everything's been delivered," she said.

The wagon, loaded with burlap sacks labeled "Rice," made its way to the circular portion of the drive that fronted the main house. The driver pulled back on the reins and set the brake, then looked over his shoulder into the bed of the wagon.

"We're here." He reached down to give someone a shake. "We're here, ma'am."

Someone in the wagon bed coughed. Before Kate cleared the

front steps, two small heads with coal-black hair appeared over the side of the wagon. Kate found herself staring at two children, a girl and a boy. Then suddenly a woman sat up, grasped the side of the wagon, and broke into a fit of coughing. She was thin and pale, her dark hair limp and matted, but Kate would know her anywhere.

"Amelie!" When Kate rushed to the wagon, it was indeed Amelie who grabbed Kate's hand and held on tightly, wincing as if Kate's hold might break every bone in her hand. Amelie's lips trembled so hard she couldn't speak as tears streamed down her pale cheeks.

At the sight of her friend so forlorn and fragile, Kate started rambling to cover her shock.

"I imagine this is quite a start, all of us lined up on the drive staring at you this way. Have you come a long way?" Kate turned to the children. "Why, don't tell me these are your children, Amelie!" She leaned back and drank in the sight of the youngsters, mirror images of a young Amelie and Colin, except for the worry shadowing their eyes.

Simon lowered the tailgate of the wagon so that Myra and Eugenie could help the children climb down. Amelie watched with a mother's eye until they were safely on the ground.

Amelie had barely moved. Kate enlisted Simon to lift her friend out of the wagon. Amelie's condition was shocking. Her once-plump, rosy cheeks were sallow and sunken. A faded calico dress of fabric unfit for the rag bag hung from her thin shoulders. What terrible things must have happened to reduce her to this state?

"Can you stand?" Kate asked.

"I think so." Amelie's voice was hoarse. "But I'd appreciate the help walking."

As Kate took hold of her arm, Amelie introduced her to the kind farmer who had carried them all the way from Baton Rouge. Kate tried to imagine Amelie's suffering on lumpy bags of rice and riding over pockmarked roads for hours.

"No wonder you look exhausted." But there was more to her

friend's haggard, stooped condition than exhaustion. "We'll have you feeling right as rain in no time at all," Kate promised.

When the girl, older and taller than her brother, moved up beside Amelie, the boy trailed after his sister. He didn't appear in the least shy, openly staring at Eugenie and Simon before taking in Myra and Kate.

"These are my children. Marie is ten and Damian is four." Looking at them, a light shone in Amelie's eyes.

"I'm almost five," Damian added. "My birthday is in January."

"Then we'll have to celebrate," Kate assured him. She turned to Amelie. "At least I hope you have planned a long visit." Amelie hadn't mentioned the man with whom she'd run away during the war, so neither did Kate.

Amelie looked toward the second-floor gallery, her eyes bright with tears.

"Is Mama inside?" Her voice cracked.

Simon cleared his throat and stared at the worn toes of his shoes. Eugenie pressed the back of her hand over her lips. Myra shut her eyes and whispered a prayer.

"Let's get you and the children inside, shall we?" Kate acknowledged the driver hovering beside the lead horse with a quick nod. She turned to Eugenie, afraid the cook was about to burst into tears.

"I left my reticule on the trunk in the foyer," Kate quietly told Eugenie. "Would you mind bringing it out to me?"

Eugenie, looking ready to fall apart, seemed thankful for the excuse to leave. She hurried across the gallery. Kate rested her hand on Damian's shoulder. "Eugenie has some molasses cookies in the kitchen. Why don't you go with Myra and have some while your mama and I chat? There's some fresh milk there too."

Damian reached for the hand Myra offered. His sister looked to her mother for permission first. "You go right ahead, honey." Amelie fell into another fit of coughing. "I've known Myra since Katie and I were your age. She'll take fine care of you."

Marie seemed hesitant to leave her mother, but when Amelie bid her go, she took Myra's hand. They headed through the main house to the kitchen in back.

"Do you have any bags?" Kate asked.

Kate wanted to kick herself when Amelie bit her lips and shook her head no. Eugenie had collected herself by the time she returned with the reticule, and Kate paid the driver. When the man asked if he could water the team, Simon volunteered to show him where.

With Kate and Eugenie flanking Amelie, they walked slowly into the house. They'd barely cleared the front door when Amelie looked around and whispered, "She's gone, isn't she? I can feel it. Mama's not here."

They ushered Amelie into the sitting room. She moved as if in a trance as she looked around the sparsely furnished room. Eugenie left them as soon as Amelie was seated on a satin upholstered settee that had recently belonged to Nola Keene.

"All of Mama's lovely things are gone," Amelie noted. She gazed around again, then met Kate's eyes. "I don't seem to have any tears left," Amelie whispered. "I believe I'm all cried out and didn't even know it."

"She's been gone since '65," Kate said. "There was no way to let you know."

"I broke her heart. I'm sure that's what killed her."

"Your mama went upriver to live with your Baudier cousins not long after you left. She fell ill shortly afterward. You mustn't blame yourself."

"I should have never run away." Amelie's smile was wistful when she looked at Kate. "How lucky you were that your father sent you up to Boston. The war ..." she swallowed, shook her head, and squeezed Kate's hands. "The war changed us all. We had to do things we would have never dreamed of, but the world was upside down, Kate. All upside down."

Kate had no notion what to say. Thanks to her father she had

escaped the upheaval. In Boston there was a constant bombard-
ment of news, but the war still seemed removed. While she'd lived
in Ireland the conflict was easy to put out of her mind as she wandered green hillsides, sat in cozy cottages listening to lilting songs,
or romped with her father's Keene cousins. It was far too easy to
forget all about the horrors in America, if not for days then at least
for hours.

Yesterday Colin accused her of having a heart full of hope. If
she'd suffered all the tribulations of war firsthand, would her spirit
have ended up in tatters too?

Amelie stared around the room. "I don't recognize any of these
things."

"They're from my mother's townhouse. She recently sold it and
remarried while traveling the continent."

"Nola remarried? Oh, Kate, your father's gone?"

"He died four years ago. I returned to New Orleans the minute
I learned he was ill."

"At least you got to tell him good-bye." Amelie pulled up the
hem of her skirt and started to weep into the faded calico. Her
hands were red and worn, her nails ragged. Kate reached out and
stroked her friend's limp hair and rubbed her back as one might
comfort a child.

When Amelie finally collected herself, she wiped her eyes and
turned to Kate again. Apprehension was etched on her features.

"Kate, dare I even hope that Colin is alive?"

Kate had been dreading this moment. What if Colin wanted
to turn out his sister?

"Is he here?" Amelie asked.

"He's here." Kate smiled to hide her worry.

"That's wonderful news." Amelie started to rise and then sat
back down. "Unless, of course, he's angry with me. Is he angry,
Kate? If it weren't for the children, I'd never forgive myself for running off the way I did. But I can't imagine life without Damian
and Marie."

"Where is their father?" Kate was stymied. Where was the man now? What happened to Amelie since she left? "Did you marry?"

"We did marry in Kansas, but I'd rather not speak of Billy Hart right now."

"Of course," Kate said. "We have all the time in the world to talk."

When Amelie didn't respond Kate said, "Colin is living in the *garçonnière*."

"The *garçonnière*? Why?"

"Let's just say he's not himself." She went on to give Amelie the few details she knew of Colin's reenlistment and his injury. "It's left him bitter and angry." Kate sighed. "I tried to help him. I wish I could have done more." Amelie was in no condition to suffer a long explanation that would only give her more worry. "Actually, I'm all packed and was ready to leave."

Amelie frowned. "I never even asked why you were here. It just seems so right to find you here." She paused, considering for a moment before she cried, "You can't go now, Kate! Please stay."

"I've already overstayed my welcome, I'm afraid, but—"

"Please, Kate. Now that I'm here, I'll need you. The children will need you."

Amelie looked around, frantic. Kate saw the room through her friend's eyes, the missing artwork and vases, the missing silver candelabra and pianoforte. Holes were in the plaster where sconces once flanked the fireplace. The mahogany mantel was splintered. None of Kate's efforts had yet eradicated the visible signs of ill-use caused by the Yankees and the neglect that moved in after them.

"Promise me you'll stay." Amelie broke into another fit of coughing, grabbed the hem of her skirt, bent and held it to her lips. When she sat up, Kate saw flecks of blood on the fabric. Her own blood ran cold.

"Of course I'll stay." She would not leave Amelie in this state, not with two children in tow and no husband in sight. Not while there was no telling what Colin might do.

They had all been brought together for a reason, just as Kate had hoped. There was no way she could leave now.

"It seems like a dream," Kate said.

"It does, doesn't it, Kate? We were so spoiled all our lives. We had everything and didn't realize it. Now it's as if our lives before the war never happened. We've nothing left but memories." Amelie rested her head against the back of the settee and closed her eyes.

"You're home now. You can build a new life for yourself and the children," Kate said.

Amelie opened her eyes. "You've been kind not to comment on the way I look, but a blind man could see that I'm ill." She took a shallow breath and a rattle escaped. "The truth is, I'm dying. I haven't much time left and must know my children will be safe. I hoped my brother—"

Shaken, Kate stopped her. "Don't talk like that. I prayed that you'd come home and here you are. Now that you're back, things will be wonderful again. Eugenie, Myra, and I will soon have you well. You'll see."

Amelie shook her head. "I have consumption, Kate. The doctor said I'm not going to get well."

"Who said that? Some backwoods prairie doctor? What does he know?" Kate forced a laugh. The idea was nonsense. She refused to believe it. "You'll be fine. You'll see."

"This isn't something you can wish away, Kate. Not like the old days when we wished upon the evening star. This is something not even you can fix." Amelie stared at her work-worn hands. "Not even you," she whispered.

Undeterred, Kate took hold of Amelie's hand and drew her to her feet. "We'll just see about that. Come on now, let's get you upstairs. Your old room is all ready for you. The children can share Colin's, since he's not using it." She would have Simon bring the child's bed from the attic for Damian.

"You won't leave, will you, Kate? If Colin doesn't want me and the children here, I don't know what to do or where to go." Simply walking from the sitting room to the stairs taxed Amelie.

She grabbed hold of the banister as they started up. Kate clung to her elbow, careful not to hold too tight.

"Never worry for a moment," Kate said. "I'll stay as long as you need me." If Colin had the nerve to throw out his sister, then she would find lodging for them all in the city.

The pallet Kate had used when she first arrived was put to use again that night. Amelie was so worn and fragile, so feverish by the time she had bathed and was tucked between clean sheets, that Kate hated to leave her alone. She bedded down on the floor beside Amelie. After a restless bout of fever and cold sweats, Amelie finally slept. Kate tossed and turned, her mind racing most of the night. She had no idea how Colin would take the news of his sister's arrival, but he would be furious when he heard she was staying on at Amelie's request.

Her mind replayed the events from earlier that evening. After placing a cool compress on Amelie's forehead, Kate had listened to her faint whispers as she told the story of her infatuation with Billy Hart, a Confederate enlisted man who walked away from his regiment.

"I found him hiding behind the smokehouse one foggy winter morning," Amelie said. "I hid him in a crawl hole beneath the barn and sneaked him what precious little food we could spare. He was only two years older than me, handsome and a real smooth talker. I was so starry-eyed, I fell in love with his sunshine-yellow hair and bright-blue eyes. He was bold and so charming that it only took him three days to talk me into running away with him to Kansas.

"I asked Mama for permission but my mind was already made up. Yankees were running all over the house by then. Mama had moved out to the kitchen where Eugenie and Simon were always fussing and pampering her. She was trying to pretend none of it was happening, that the Yankees hadn't really moved in. She would throw fits or burst into tears, and some days she even forgot the war was going on at all. When I told her about Billy and told her it was a way out for me, she still refused to give me her blessing, even when I begged her. She wanted me to stay home, to stay here at *Belle Fleuve*."

"But you went anyway," Kate said.

Amelie whispered, "I did. I should have listened to Mama. I should have stayed for her sake, but I was selfish and scared."

"And in love."

"We sneaked off without telling Mama good-bye. Up until little Marie was born, I regretted nearly every day of my life in Kansas. Most of the time Billy left me home alone with his parents. I was forced to do farm work. They barely eked out a living on their farm." She sighed. It was a ragged sound. "I'm simply too spent to tell you the rest, Kate, but two months ago Billy was killed in a gunfight in Dodge."

Her voice had barely reached Kate in the darkness. Her friend's weakness added to Kate's mounting worry. Kate finally gave up tossing to stare at the ceiling. She tried to equate the life Amelie had lived in Kansas with memories of the two of them running through luxuriously appointed rooms playing hide-and-seek and teasing the smug French dance teacher, who was forced to put up with the antics of the spoiled offspring of wealthy planters. Together they had dreamed of the galas they would attend after the war, the gowns they would wear, and the handsome gentlemen who would line up eager to court them. One of their last times together, they had polkaed around this very room—the night Kate had kissed a pillow and pretended her imaginary suitor was Colin.

Those gilded days were over now, vanished like the thriving cane fields of *Belle Fleuve*; but at least they had survived—she and Amelie and Colin—and though her own strength was being tested, Kate was convinced they would all thrive again.

Up well before dawn, Kate looked in on the children in the room next door as Amelie slept on. Sometime during the night, Damian had left his own bed and crawled in with Marie. The two slept holding hands as Kate smiled down at them.

She hurriedly dressed—all her things still in bags and trunks that had been hauled back upstairs by Simon and deposited in the guest room she would share with Myra. Out in the kitchen she found Eugenie piling hot biscuits on a plate for Colin. The cook added a slice of ham steak and slathered it with gravy.

"I'll take the tray out to him," Kate volunteered.

"Are you sure?" Eugenie paused in the act of pouring a cup of coffee.

Kate nodded. "I must tell him Amelie is back."

"What if he turns her out?"

"This is her home too. I'm just so thankful the place wasn't sold or boarded up when she arrived."

"That poor child." Eugenie's eyes filled with tears. She shook her head. "What's gonna become of those children when she goes?"

Kate's fear flared in the form of anger.

"That kind of talk must stop immediately, Eugenie. Amelie is going to be just fine. We're all going to see to it."

Looking doubtful, the cook finished readying Colin's tray in silence. Eugenie didn't have to say a word; Kate could tell the woman didn't believe it.

"I mean it now." Kate fought to reassure herself as much as Eugenie. "She's going to be just fine. Good as new in no time."

A few minutes later Kate was standing outside Colin's door. She knocked gently, and there was a pause before he called out for her to enter.

"I thought you left yesterday."

"I'm still here."

"Lucky me."

She set down the tray. "You are lucky indeed. The most wonderful thing has happened."

"You've decided to leave today and never return?"

"Actually, no. I may be staying for quite a while now."

"Listen here, Miss Keene—"

"Your sister is home, Colin."

He went completely still. Kate walked over to the table, pulled out a chair, carried it closer to the bed, and sat.

"Just make yourself at home, why don't you?" He shook his head.

"Thank you, I will." She smoothed her skirt over her knees.

"Why didn't she come to see me herself? Is she too ashamed? Or too afraid?"

"Ashamed of what she did? Or afraid of your reaction?"

He crossed his arms and waited for an answer. This man, this hard-hearted Colin, didn't deserve her concern or her care, but Amelie did. Instead of walking away as she was tempted to do, she took a deep breath and met his hard gaze.

"She's worn out, Colin. It was a long, trying journey and her life has been far from easy. In fact, she's admitted that running off was a big mistake."

"So now she's come crawling back."

"She hardly crawled, and she's not alone."

"She didn't dare bring that lily-livered deserter with her —"

"Her husband is dead. She brought her children, Colin."

"Children? As in more than one?"

"That's what the word usually means, yes. A ten-year-old daughter and a four-year-old son. They're beautiful. Wait until you meet them. I'll help you walk over to the house if you —"

"Absolutely not."

"Then I'll ask Simon to help you."

"I'm not going over there. I don't want to see them."

"Fine, then stay here. You know where they are." She didn't look forward to telling Amelie that he refused to see her when what she needed most right now was loving care, not her brother's rejection.

"It's still my house," he reminded her.

"Amelie's too, remember."

"But not yours."

Kate sighed. "No. Not mine."

A s soon as Colin saw Kate Keene swish her shapely bustle out the door, he reached for the photographs on his bedside table. He stared at the images in the family portrait. He didn't need a mirror to tell him how much he'd changed. He doubted Amelie would recognize him.

And what was she like now? A grown woman with two children. He hadn't even asked their names. Ten and four, Kate had said. The girl was a few years shy of Amelie's age the last time he'd seen her. According to the odious Kate Keene, Amelie's life had not been easy and her husband was dead.

Was it possible his sister had changed as much as he had?

He'd been mired in self-pity for so long it was hard to think of life outside the walls of the *garçonnière*, hard to imagine Amelie home and living here with her children. Kate Keene was no doubt feeling smug for predicting as much. Did she expect him to thank her for making the place livable?

She'd be waiting a long time. He hadn't asked for her help nor did he want it now. He had been too broken, and his wounds too raw, to take up the challenge. He should have been here during the war to keep Amelie from ruining her life. Apologizing now wasn't enough. How could he ever admit he had nothing left to give, no way to provide for her and her children?

All he knew how to do was soldier, and thanks to the Comanche, he could no longer wear a uniform. Colin tossed the photo aside and picked up his breakfast tray. Eugenie's biscuits were impossible to ignore and she knew it. Every tray she brought in of late had a generous pile of biscuits on it and this morning they were smothered in gravy. Determined to gain back some strength, he started in on the ham. Glad he'd tapered himself off his laudanum, he glanced at the hateful cane propped within reach. It was high time he try to get on his feet again.

Miss Katherine Keene had been running things at *Belle Fleuve* long enough.

FIVE

Three days later, accompanied by Simon, Kate followed a narrow dirt path to a ramshackle house perched on stilts in the bayou not far from River Road.

She stopped long enough to glance up from the path toward the weathered cypress-wood house ahead and then walked on, studying the ground, taking care not to trip over any exposed roots or stones on the path. None of Eugenie's remedies had helped Amelie. Together they had concocted and doused her with all manner of peppers and honey and teas that Eugenie swore almost always worked. They'd also tried applying steaming plasters to Amelie's chest. And when someone told Eugenie that milk was the best curative for consumption, they began pouring it down Amelie at every turn until the poor woman begged them to stop.

When Simon suggested Kate go to Cezelia Mouton's place and ask the Cajun *traiteur* for one of her potions, she balked.

"I don't hold to any superstitious hoodoo," she told him. She'd heard tell of the *traiteur*, or treaters, as the Cajun practitioners were called, but neither her parents nor the Delanys had ever consulted one.

But after spending several sleepless nights watching Amelie suffer through night sweats and fever, Kate became desperate. The Cajun woman's place was closer than seeking out a physician in

New Orleans, so she slipped away with Simon, leaving Eugenie and Myra to watch over her patient.

As Kate climbed the steep, narrow stairs to the sagging front porch, she took in the surrounding landscape — the silent water so still on the surface but running deep beneath, the spears of sunlight streaming through the tall cypress, the knobby cypress knees poking up out of the muddy water.

A shiver ran down her spine. She knocked on a front door painted bright red.

"'Allo?" A young woman peered around the edge of the door. She was a bit shorter than Kate and around the same age, or so she seemed.

"I wish to speak to Cezelia Mouton," Kate said.

"I am Cezelia."

"Cezelia Mouton? The *traiteur*?"

The young woman's dark eyes swept Kate from head to toe and then she smiled. "You thought perhaps I would be older?"

Kate nodded. "I had heard you were older."

"My grandmother was also Cezelia Mouton. Sadly, she died last year." She shrugged. "She taught me what she knew and now I am the *traiteur* in these parts."

Cezelia stepped outside and closed the door behind her. Two wooden chairs stood together in the far corner of the porch. She indicated Kate should sit. Soon they were seated side by side. Simon waited at the far end of the footpath.

"How can I help you?"

"My friend is very ill. I need something to relieve a cough and fever. A doctor told her she has consumption."

Cezelia stared off into the distance. Kate wondered if she was paying attention until the young woman said, "Tell me her symptoms."

"Night sweats, a constant cough. She's very weak. A higher fever at night with body pain. She has trouble breathing and cannot catch her breath."

"She coughs up blood?"

Kate hesitated. "Specks, that's all."

"Can she walk?"

"Yes..." Kate paused. "Actually, she's been in bed for three days now, but I'm fairly sure she can still walk."

Cezelia shook her head. "I'm not certain I can help."

Irritated, Kate jumped up. "I knew better than to turn to hoodoo."

Cezelia rose and looked down at Kate. "I do not practice hoodoo, Miss Keene. I am a *traiteur*. I believe in the power of prayer and God's intercession."

"As do I."

"Then you know your friend is in His hands."

"Yes, but I need to do something. If you didn't think you could help people you wouldn't have taken up this calling."

"I am but a tool, a woman who dispenses concoctions that may ease pain. Sometimes people are cured, but I am not stupid enough to believe it is all my doing and neither are you."

"I'll go to New Orleans. I'll find the best doctor in the city."

Cezelia sighed. "I'm afraid even the best doctor cannot help your friend at this point, so beware of those who claim they can. Soon her throat will crackle with each breath. Her bones will start to crumble. Her lungs will hemorrhage—"

"Enough!" Kate fisted her hands at her sides. "I won't hear more."

"Wait here."

Cezelia went inside for a moment and was back with a small jar. She handed it to Kate.

"This is a mixture of camphor, eucalyptus, and turpentine. Rub it on the soles of her feet."

If the woman's shuttered expression was any indication, the salve wasn't going to help. Kate blinked back tears of frustration as Cezelia added, "Try boiling an onion for ten minutes. Pour the liquid in a cup and give her the onion juice with a little honey while it's warm. As much as she can drink. At least two or three times a day."

"Will that cure her?"

"Only prayer can save her now."

Prayer and a real doctor, Kate thought, as she thanked the woman and started down the stairs. Prayer was not a problem. Finding the best doctor in New Orleans was.

SIX

Furious, Kate stared out at the *garçonnière* and watched the rain streak down the windowpane in Amelie's room. Colin had ignored his sister and the children for too long. According to Eugenie, he hadn't once even asked after them. Nor had he made any attempt to see them in the four days since their arrival.

When she heard a soft knock at the door, Kate turned away from the window. Amelie was still sound asleep, her hair spread out across her pillow, and her skin sallow against the white linens. Cezelia's salve and the onion potion had eased her cough only slightly, but enough that Kate held a little more hope.

She hurried to the door and, when she saw it was Eugenie, stepped out onto the gallery and gently closed the door behind her.

"How is she today?" Eugenie's dark eyes were shadowed with deep concern.

Kate forced a smile. "She still has a fever, but she's finally getting some much-needed sleep."

"You could use a full night's sleep yourself or you won't be much help to Miss Amelie. That poor child was so weak yesterday. I'm sorely worried, Miss Kate."

"Did you make up some more of Cezelia's onion potion?"

Eugenie looked doubtful but she nodded. "Soon as she wakes up I'll try to get some more down her."

"Where are the children?" The last Kate had seen of Marie and Damian, they'd been playing checkers in the sitting room with Myra.

"In the kitchen. They're bored to tears. I was lettin' them make pralines until they ate nearly all the extra pecans. Little Marie is worried. You could tell time by that girl. She asks after her mama ever' five minutes. I wish for their sakes this rain would let up so Myra can take them outside berry pickin'."

Kate tapped her foot, as impatient with Amelie's lack of response to the curative as she was Colin's avoidance of his sister and the children.

"Will you sit with her a few moments, Eugenie?"

"'Course."

"I'll be right back."

Kate hurried downstairs, cooled by the mist of the rain falling beyond the open gallery. When she reached the kitchen, she found Damian running around the outbuilding with a tin pudding mold on his head. She plucked it off as he ran by.

"Hey!" Looking like Colin, Damian crossed his arms and pouted. "That's my helmet," he said. "I want it back."

Kate held it out of his reach. "It's a pudding mold, not a helmet."

"Aunt Kate, I need it. I wanna be a knight in shining armor."

Marie said, "It's not shining armor. It's a pudding mold. Besides, you shouldn't be running around having fun with Mama so sick." Her eyes filled with tears she swiped away with the back of her hand.

Kate put her arm around Damian's shoulders and walked him over to Marie where she embraced the girl too.

"Damian, run into the sitting room and ask Myra to find our umbrellas," Kate said. "We're going visiting."

The boy's eyes widened. "Really?"

"Really." Kate nodded.

"How's Mama?" Marie's eyes spoke of fear.

"She's sleeping," Kate said.

"I don't want to go anywhere." Marie crossed her arms.

"We aren't going very far at all," Kate tried to reassure her. "In fact, we're only going next door. To the *garçonnière*."

"What's a garden-air?" Damian hadn't gone to fetch the umbrellas yet.

"It's the tall funny building with the pointy roof next door," Kate said.

"Mama thinks it looks like a castle tower," Damian added.

Kate nodded, pleased. "Exactly. It looks like a turret, but it's six sided. It's a building where young men can be away from the rest of the family."

"Young men like me?" Damian wanted to know.

"Older than you," she said. "A bit older anyway."

"Who lives there now?" he asked.

"Our Uncle Colin, remember?" Marie folded her arms across her chest. "I don't want to meet him. I heard you and Mama talking the other night," she told Kate. "She thinks he's angry with her. Is that why he hasn't come to meet us? Is he angry at us?"

"He was a soldier and he got injured. He still has a hard time walking. He—"

"How did he get hurt?" Damian leaned his arm on the kitchen table and propped his chin on his hand. "Daddy used to talk about the war. Was Uncle Colin shot by some Yankee son of a—"

Both Kate and Marie shushed him at the same time.

"I heard he took an Indian arrow in the ankle. You might want to ask him yourself," Kate said. For a moment she wondered if she should be encouraging Damian to speak of Colin's injury, but decided Colin could fend for himself. "Right now, you need to go collect the umbrellas from Myra so we can be on our way."

"Should we take Uncle Colin some of our pralines?" Marie asked as Damian ran out of the room. "Mama always says it's not polite to go calling without a little something to give."

It was something Amelie would say. Kate tried to picture her living on the Kansas prairie so far from family and home. Did

Amelie have neighbors she could call upon in a time of need? From the little her friend had revealed, Kate doubted it.

"I think a few pralines would be a lovely gift. Especially since you made them yourselves." Kate reached for a bread plate and handed it to Marie. "Let's use this for the candies."

The three of them hurried through the rain beneath two bobbing umbrellas. Kate held hers over Marie, who carried the plate of pralines. Damian trailed behind, explaining that they knew all about castles and knights and towers because their mama had told them many fairy tales before they fell asleep. When they neared the *garçonnière*, Damian bolted ahead and pounded on the door.

"Just a minute!" Colin shouted.

Kate was shocked to hear him respond so quickly. Usually he took his sweet time answering.

She smiled to reassure the children. "He's not as bad as he sounds."

"Let's go back," Marie whispered.

Kate knocked again, harder this time. "Colin, it's raining out here, in case you haven't noticed."

Inside, something clattered against the floor. Hopefully he wasn't back to throwing things. She began to doubt the wisdom of the visit when he yelled, "Come in!"

Kate folded her umbrella, took Damian's from him, and then opened the door. She ushered the children in first. They took a few tentative steps into the room and stopped to stare at Colin. Kate closed the door and propped the umbrellas against the wall before she turned around.

"You're gaping like a fish up for air, Kate." His voice was laced with sarcasm.

She closed her mouth and tried to cover her shock. He'd shaved off his beard. The lower half of his face was intensely pale. Without the beard he appeared even more wan, far thinner than before, but still staggeringly handsome. The Colin she'd known had been a mere boy compared to the man lying down across the room.

He was lounging on the bed as usual, but his forehead and upper lip were beaded with sweat. His dark, curly hair was still long, the curls in front clinging to his damp hairline. His hands were shaking. Kate's first instinct was to go to him, but the sight of his cane lying on the floor stopped her.

He'd been walking, or at least making an attempt. Now he was trying to appear nonchalant, trying to hide his efforts though she could see what they cost him.

He looked at the children for a moment and then turned to Kate with a silent get-them-out-of-here stare.

"Colin," she began, "this is your niece, Marie, and your nephew, Damian. They were going stir-crazy in the house and I thought it was high time you met them." To the children she said, "This is your uncle, Colin Delany."

Marie was clutching the plate of pralines so tightly that Kate asked her to set them on the bedside table. When Marie balked, Damian piped up, "I'll do it, 'fraidy cat."

He took the plate from Marie and, holding it before him like an offering to a king, he used great care crossing the room. He set the plate on the table and then backed away. His eyes never left Colin.

"That's pralines. We made 'em. They're mostly sugar and butter with a few pecans. There woulda been more pecans but we ate them. Wanna taste one?"

Kate held her breath. *Please be civil, Colin. Please try.*

He glanced at her with steel in his eyes, turned to the boy, and shrugged.

"Might as well," he said.

Instead of passing the plate over, Damian picked up a praline and slowly carried it on his palm within Colin's reach. They all watched Colin take a bite, waiting.

"Mmm," he nodded. "Good."

Surely he noticed how much Marie favored Amelie and his mother. Could he tell that Damian looked like him?

The children watched him without a word, their fear palpable. Kate walked over to the watercolor on the wall and told them, "Your mama painted these roses when she was just a bit older than you."

"Roses?" Colin's voice cut the silence that followed Kate's statement. "I always thought they were beets."

"I don't like beets," Damian announced.

"As I recall, your uncle doesn't either," Kate said.

A quick knock came at the door and Kate answered. It was Simon.

"You're needed at the house, Miss Kate," Simon announced.

"Children, stay with your uncle. I'll be right back." She carefully avoided eye contact with Colin.

"Kate Keene, don't you dare leave," he warned.

"I'll be right back," she said, before she slipped out the door behind Simon. As they walked back to the house, Simon looked so concerned she reassured him. "Right on time, Simon. Thank you."

"You sure this is a good idea?" He frowned at the door.

"Why, they'll all be just fine." She hoped.

Colin watched the silent pair stare at him with frightened eyes. Kate Keene had just crossed the line. If he could only get his hands on her—

With tears glistening in her eyes, his niece reminded him so much of Amelie that he forgot about the irritating Miss Keene. He'd never been able to withstand his sister's tears, or any woman's tears for that matter. Whatever Amelie had done was not the fault of these innocents.

"I don't bite," he said.

Neither moved.

He tried to smile but he was sorely out of practice.

"Are you really our uncle?" The boy, Damian, had momentarily bent over to rub a spot of mud off the toe of his shoe.

"Yes."

"Should we call you Uncle Colin?" Young Damian was content to chatter while his worried sister merely watched.

Colin hadn't thought about what they should call him. He hadn't thought past these walls in weeks.

"I suppose you can."

"We got some uncles back in Dodge," the boy said.

"Damian." There was a clear warning in the girl's tone.

"You do, eh?" Colin waited. Dodge. So his sister had ended up in Kansas.

"My uncle Pete is a gunfighter like Daddy was. I don't like him much, though. He was mean to Mama before we all took off."

Colin's gut tightened. "Mean how?"

"After Daddy got shot and died, Uncle Pete tried to kiss Mama. She didn't like it. He said he—"

"Damian, *shush*," the girl said.

"Why?" The boy glared at her.

"That's family business," she whispered.

Damian pointed at Colin. "He's our uncle. He's family, ain't he?"

Marie glowered.

"Sorry," Damian mumbled, scuffing the floor with his toe. "I'm not supposed to tell that story."

"So your daddy is dead?"

"Mama said it was only a matter of time 'fore he got kilt anyway. Hired guns don't live that long. I bet now she wished Uncle Pete woulda got kilt too."

Personally, Colin was glad Amelie's no-account husband was gone. But now what? How was he supposed to care for her and these children when he couldn't even take care of himself?

Kate was right but he'd never admit it to her. By now he should have found a way to get on his feet and should have sold the place.

But if he had sold *Belle Fleuve* his sister might never have found him. He grudgingly had to admit that if it hadn't been for Kate Keene's stubbornness, Amelie and her children would be homeless right now.

When Kate knocked on the door earlier he'd been struggling to walk but the attempt had taken everything out of him. He'd seen by Kate's stunned expression she was not only shocked by his appearance, but that she'd noticed his fallen cane. She was smart enough to deduce what he'd been doing but for now he didn't care what she thought.

What Damian had just said continued to haunt him. How many more secrets did Amelie and the children share? It had been much easier to imagine her happily settled in a new life, but apparently the path she'd chosen had brought her much suffering.

The girl, Marie, kept glancing toward the door. The last thing he wanted was to scare these innocents.

"We should go back," she whispered.

"Because Mama's sick," Damian blurted. "Real sick. She's got the 'sumption. That's why we moved here."

Colin's blood ran cold.

"She has consumption?"

Damian nodded, far too solemn for such a young child.

Colin had seen enough cases of consumption during the war to know just how fatal it was. The wounded, crowded together in damp field hospitals in tents and barns, were highly susceptible. They suffered fevers, fits of bloody coughing, death.

Not Amelie. Please, God. Not Amelie.

Shocked, he realized what he'd just done. Only a fool would believe God actually answered prayers.

Colin watched a tear slide down the girl's cheek.

"Aunt Kate and Myra and 'Genie are taking care of Mama. Aunt Kate says she'll be right as rain in no time at all."

"You sure got a lot of books," Damian announced.

"We used to have a library full." Colin pictured "Aunt" Kate nursing Amelie. Did she realize there was no hope?

"In Kansas we only had a Bible. We don't even got that anymore."

Colin tried to imagine where they'd been born, what conditions they'd lived in.

A thought struck him. "Can you read?"

"Not yet." Damian shook his head. "I'm too little."

"I can," Marie nodded.

Colin tried smiling without much success. "Choose a book and bring it over here."

When neither child moved he softened his commanding tone. "Please."

Marie still hesitated.

"I won't bite," he assured them.

Neither looked certain. Damian was the first to move. The low bookcase with three shelves, each a yard wide, held what was left of *Belle Fleuve*'s library. Favorite adventure stories that he'd read as a boy were there along with books on world geography, history, and botany. Damian stared at the gold-embossed spines.

"Perhaps you should help him?" Colin suggested to Marie, who was watching the boy.

She walked over to the bookcase, tipped her head to read the spines, and then glanced back at Colin.

"Pick one," he encouraged. "Anything you like."

She pulled out a book.

"Now bring it here," he said.

Marie didn't move. Damian took the book from her and walked over to the bedside and handed it to Colin.

"*A Pirate's Tale of the West Indies.* One of my favorites. Too bad my eyes have been bothering me. Perhaps you'd like to read to us?" He indicated the space beside him. Before Damian climbed up to join him, he retrieved Colin's cane and examined it closely.

"Aunt Kate said you were shot by Injuns. Is that true?"

"That's true. A Comanche shot an arrow clear through my ankle. Busted it to pieces."

"Did you keep it?"

Colin looked at his ruined joint. "It probably would have been better to let the doc take it off."

"I mean the arrow. Did you keep it? We found a bunch of arrowheads at the farm. Did it have feathers on it? Did the Injuns dip the tip in poison 'fore they shot you?"

"No. I didn't keep it, and no, there was no poison on it."

"Can I really sit by you?"

Colin sighed. "Why not?"

He closed his eyes, steeling himself for a jolt of pain but the bed barely jiggled beneath the little boy's weight. Marie still hadn't budged. Colin imagined Kate Keene badgering him to be kind to these two. He offered the book to the girl.

"Why don't you pull up a chair and sit close to the bed?" he suggested. "Perhaps you can read to us both."

Kate meant to return for the children within minutes but Eugenie was frustrated by Amelie's refusal to swallow any more of Cezelia's potion. After sitting with Amelie for nearly an hour, tasting the brew herself, and finding she could not even pretend to stomach it, Kate finally hurried through the rain to the garçonnière.

She raised her hand to knock, then out of curiosity, pressed her ear against the door first. It sounded ominously quiet inside until she heard a soft voice.

Kate turned the knob, pushed the door open a bit, and heard Marie reading aloud with confidence in her even, lilting tone.

"'We made the scourge walk the plank. He begged for his life like the worm he was before he disappeared into the fathomless turquoise depths of the shark-filled waters.'"

Kate peered around the door. The scene inside melted her heart. Colin was propped against the bed pillows and pressed alongside him lay Damian. The boy's head was cradled in the crook of Colin's shoulder, his eyelids drowsing lazily as Marie read to them from the chair drawn up close to the bed. Kate could tell Colin wasn't paying attention to the story as he gazed into the distance. When Colin absently reached down and brushed Damian's dark curls away from his eyes, Kate's breath caught. Here was the glimmer of hope she'd been waiting for, a sign that there was something more inside Colin than the hardened, bitter man he seemed to have become. She rapped on the partially opened door.

"May I come in?"

When Marie's voice stilled, Kate stepped inside. Damian sat up straight and rubbed his eyes. Colin crossed his arms over his broad chest and frowned, but that didn't change what she'd seen.

"Is Mama all right?"

The girl's fright was evident. Kate tried to reassure her that Amelie was doing fine. "Why don't you go on back and see how she is for yourself? I'll bring Damian," Kate suggested.

Marie collected her umbrella and was out the door in seconds. Kate stared at the little boy, whose head had dropped back onto Colin's shoulder. His eyes were closed again.

"It looks as if you've gotten on well enough," Kate noted.

"Nothing but scamps. Both of them," Colin said.

She walked up close to the bed, reached for Damian, and hefted him up to her shoulder without waking him. Colin's look might have passed for admiration in any other man.

"Where did you learn that?" he wanted to know.

"I've twenty-seven Keene cousins in Ireland, and I was there for four years." She rubbed Damian's back between his shoulders.

When Colin spoke again, his voice was low.

"The boy told me Amelie is ill."

"She'll be fine."

"She has consumption. Why didn't you tell me?"

"You didn't seem to care one way or the other. Besides, I refuse to believe she won't be up and around soon. All she needs is good care. Now that she's home, she'll be fine. You'll see."

"Marie said they came here to live."

"Their father died. Amelie had nowhere else to go. Naturally, she came to you."

"Did you know he was a gunfighter?"

Kate nodded. "Amelie told me."

Colin's expression darkened. "What am I to do?"

"Do what you were born to do. Run *Belle Fleuve*."

"You're relentless, you know."

"A woman must be relentless in this world."

Damian stirred against her shoulder. She rubbed his back and quieted him again. Colin was staring at the boy now. Hopefully, he *was* worried about Amelie and the future. Now perhaps he would take steps to bring *Belle Fleuve* back to life. She turned to leave and suddenly stopped.

"May I take the photographs? For Amelie?"

He shrugged. "Why not?"

As he reached for the pictures scattered over the bedside table, Kate noticed the empty praline plate.

"You liked the pralines?"

"Who wouldn't?"

He held out the photographs and, due to his immobility, Kate was forced to go to him. Their fingers brushed as she took them. A frisson of warmth shot through her, and she dropped her gaze while fighting to ignore her physical reaction to an accidental touch.

So it's like that, Kate thought. *It's still there.*

After all these years, after his rudeness and dismissal, the mere touch of his hand still set her heart soaring. Was this love then? Again and again it all came back to her feelings for Colin and this place. Did she actually love him or was she infatuated with the idea of him and the past?

If she did love him, then he had the power to hurt her.

But at least she'd seen this softer side of him. His care and concern for the children gave Kate the courage not to give up. It might still be possible to bring him around, to open his heart to Amelie, and if so, maybe there was some hope that he would someday see the love she had to offer.

She shifted Damian higher on her shoulder.

"What is it, Kate? You look so thoughtful." He fell silent for a second and then demanded, "Is Amelie worse than you've let on?"

There was no way she could admit to him — or more especially to herself — the amount of uncertainty weighing on her. She had no idea how long it would be before Amelie recovered or whether or not he could find the will and the strength to help.

She was living here on borrowed time. They all were.

"Amelie will be well very soon. You'll see."

SEVEN

The morning air was already close and humid in the room Kate shared with Myra. She stood alone at a cluttered table near the gallery window where, for a good quarter of an hour, she'd been attempting to sort her drafts and art supplies into some semblance of order before undertaking what she hoped would be a fast and productive trip to New Orleans.

She dreaded telling Amelie she was leaving and certainly wasn't going to explain that she was going in search of a physician. Not when Amelie would insist there was nothing to be done. Prayer and potions hadn't helped. Kate was still determined to find a cure.

She moved a box of watercolor supplies beneath the desk. She hadn't even found time to open the box once since she'd arrived. It had been naive to think she'd find a few quiet hours of leisure time at *Belle Fleuve*. She sighed and shook her head at such foolishness.

The hours had flown while she had supervised Simon and his crew, and since Amelie and the children arrived there hadn't been a moment to spare. She hadn't even returned to the *garçonnière* since she had taken the children to meet Colin three days ago.

Not that she cared to see him while she was still confused about her reaction to his accidental touch. Not while that glimpse of what he was and could be again lingered in her mind.

She picked up the photographs of the Delanys, put a smile on her face, and breezed into Amelie's room.

"You're looking better today!" she exclaimed.

"Poor Kate." Amelie's voice was no more than a hoarse whisper. Ravaged from her nightly battle with fever, she lay limp and wasted against a mound of pillows.

"You *do* look better." As Kate opened the window hoping fresh air would dispel the staleness in the room, she heard Amelie's soft sigh.

Kate walked to the bedside and handed her the photographs. "I brought these in from the *garçonnière*. Do you feel like looking through them now or should I set them on the table?"

Amelie held out her hand. Kate couldn't help but notice the tremor that ran through it.

"Where are the children?" Amelie dropped the photographs in her lap.

"They're out exploring with Myra, walking along the levee and watching the boats on the river."

"They don't know how to swim—" Amelie's worry increased the lines around her eyes.

"Myra won't let them anywhere near the edge of the path. Remember how vigilant she was with us?"

"I suppose." Amelie turned her attention to the photographs, pausing now and again to comment.

"Remember this dress?" She turned the photograph so that Kate could see. Amelie's skirt was draped over a wide hoop, the hems of her ruffled pantalets showing beneath it. "I loved that gown. What a silly creature I was."

"You look like a confection. A crème layer cake." Kate fought to keep her tone light, afraid her voice might crack and give her away.

Amelie took her time perusing through the stack twice, then laid the photographs on the bedclothes draped over her thin frame.

"Thank you, Kate. I'll be seeing Mama and Papa again soon enough." Her voice was so weak Kate barely heard her.

Kate was hard-pressed not to grab the photographs and toss them out the door and over the balcony.

"Don't talk like that." She walked back to the window, clasped her hands together, and tried to still her racing heart. She knew she sounded far too harsh but couldn't control her anger. How was Amelie to get well if she didn't believe it herself?

"Your children need you," Kate said.

"I know they do," Amelie said with more strength than she'd shown in days. "But they won't have me much longer and they need a home. I think that you of all people can understand."

Suddenly it was all back. Her birth mother's illness and death, she and her sisters huddled together crying. Lovie tried to comfort them. Megan angry. Sarah too young to know what was happening. The feeling of helplessness, of emptiness, had been terrifying.

Kate swallowed a sob.

"Kate, turn around and come here, please."

She took a deep breath and collected herself before she obliged. She went to sit on the edge of the bed and took Amelie's hand.

"The children still speak of their visit to Colin. Thank you for taking them to meet him."

"It was nothing." At the very least she should take the children back to visit him again before she left for the city tomorrow.

"He hasn't come to see me yet," Amelie said.

"Perhaps in time ..." Kate looked away from the hopelessness in Amelie's eyes.

"I haven't much time, and I have no idea if Colin will ever forgive me or if he'll be willing to care for my children. I need a promise from you, Kate. Please promise you'll raise my children as your own after I'm gone."

To promise would be to admit Amelie was dying.

Kate shook her head. "I can't. I won't ... because you are going to get well."

"There's no reason for you to give up your dream. Hire a nanny or have Myra care for the children while you work. It's enough to know you'll still be there to guide them, to help them."

Kate had told Amelie of her studies, of the influence Patrick Delany had had on her.

"It's not that. Never that." Kate reminded herself not to squeeze Amelie's hand and cause her pain. "I simply refuse to let you go."

Kate stood up again and paced over to the marble-topped washstand. She dipped a washcloth in a basin of water, twisted the water out, and went back to wipe Amelie's brow.

Amelie closed her eyes. "Please don't refuse me this." A smile touched her lips. "I know how hardheaded you are, Kate. My father used to call you a stubborn Irish lass."

"You're half Irish yourself," Kate reminded her. "Use that stubbornness to fight this, Amelie. If not for me, for the children."

"It's only sheer will that has kept me here this long." She coughed again, taking the washcloth from Kate and daubing at her mouth. Rust-colored stains seeped into the fabric. "You were an orphan, Kate. Would you subject little Marie and Damian to that fate?"

The memory of the orphan asylum in New Orleans came back with a fierce swiftness—the sound of children who had lost their mothers crying themselves to sleep at night; her confusion over wondering where her older sisters had been taken. Kate had even begged the plump woman in the ruffled poke bonnet and the older gentleman who had adopted Sarah to take them both.

She could only imagine how she must have looked with her round, frightened eyes misting behind the new spectacles the nuns had given her, pleading with the strangers to take her too. She swore to them she barely ate anything and promised she would give them no trouble if they would just *please* take her with Sarah.

But Sarah went off alone and Kate was there for months until the Keenes adopted her. Gil and Nola were not loving parents, but they made certain she had a roof over her head and everything money could buy. They had kept her safe and saw to her future, and for that she would be forever grateful.

A motherless child was a crime against humanity. Never, ever would she submit Marie and Damian to an orphanage, never would she turn her back on them. But to agree to Amelie's plea was an admission of defeat. She couldn't do it.

Amelie's warm hand closed around Kate's.

"Please, Kate. You're breaking my heart. I need you to promise to do this for me. It's the only thing I need or want. Please."

Amelie started crying such deep, wracking sobs that Kate wrapped her arms around her.

"Hush, now. I'm so sorry." She held her for a moment and then settled her friend against the pillows. "If what you want is a promise that I will care for your children, of course, I give it gladly. But someday we'll both be old women together and the children will be grown with families of their own. You'll see."

Amelie managed a weak smile.

"Thank you," she whispered as she wiped away tears.

Kate, distracted by movement in the doorway, looked up expecting to see Eugenie with another dose of medicine. Instead, she was shocked at the sight of Colin leaning against the door frame.

Seeing him there was exactly what she wanted, but the cost had been dear. His face was drained of color, his brow glistened with perspiration. His pain was mirrored in his dark eyes. White knuckled, he clutched his cane in one hand. In the other, he carried a book. He fought to stand tall, to hide his agony, and he even attempted a slow smile for Amelie.

Kate was tempted to rush to his aid and usher him to a chair, but stayed where she was to avoid causing him any embarrassment.

How much had he heard?

When Amelie saw him, she gasped and clutched Kate's hand. "Colin—"

At the rasp of his sister's voice, he stepped into the room and limped closer to the bed. Kate got to her feet and drew a chair over to the bedside. She held it steady as Colin lowered himself into it. When he handed over the book to her, she glanced at the spine: *A Pirate's Tale of the West Indies*.

Completely silent, she hesitated to break the spell as brother and sister studied one another for the first time in over a decade. Stepping into the background of the Delanys' lives was familiar territory, and yet this time Kate was uncomfortable in her role as silent observer. She started to edge her way around Colin to leave them alone.

Amelie gave a slight shake of her head and whispered, "Please stay, Kate."

Colin barely recognized his sister. How much she must have suffered. It shamed him to think of his own self-pity. Not only was Amelie ravaged by disease, but her hands were cracked and red, her nails uneven and ragged. Signs of time in the sun marred the skin over her thin, pale cheeks. Seeing her this way, he was happy that her husband was already dead.

"Forgive me, Colin." Amelie's hushed whisper dispelled his dark thoughts.

"There's nothing to forgive. I wasn't here to advise you. I wasn't here to defend you and Mama. I could have come back after our father died, but I chose not to. I could have kept you from running off with that—"

"Billy Hart is dead. That life is over," Amelie interrupted.

"So the children said."

He had more than an inkling of exactly how hard her life had been. The plains were wide open, raw and challenging enough without having to eke a living out of the soil. Far hardier souls than Amelie had been broken by the West.

It was hard to imagine her living on the edge of the rough cow town a few miles outside Fort Dodge. Thanks to the railroad, Dodge grew almost overnight into a watering hole for drifters, cowhands, buffalo hunters, and soldiers. A legendary cemetery was already full of gun-toting braggadocios.

He took a deep breath, shifted on the hard seat of the chair. His heart ached at the sight of Amelie so wan, so pale. She was far more ill than Kate had let on. No wonder little Marie had been so concerned. No child should have to see her mother ravaged like this. Colin reached for Amelie's hand. It felt as fragile as a hummingbird's wing.

"I'm glad you're home." The words, straight from the heart, were out before he knew he was going to utter them. *Home.*

From what he knew of Kate Keene now, he was certain she had painted a rosy wash over his circumstances, and for the moment he was relieved. There was no need to make Amelie's burden any greater.

Amelie's breath rattled as she spoke.

"I'm here for the children's sake. I want them to grow up at *Belle Fleuve* … the way we did." After a fit of coughing through which Colin was forced to sit helplessly, Amelie shook her head and her voice faded. "I didn't realize those days are gone."

She looked at a point over his shoulder before she met his eyes again. "But you are here and, by some miracle, so is Kate. With both of you bringing this place back to life, it will be better than before."

So Kate hadn't told Amelie that he had forbidden her from rescuing the house. She hadn't confessed that she'd gone against his wishes. Kate had let his sister believe he had a hand in the repairs of the newly cleaned and partially furnished rooms.

Making his way upstairs a few minutes earlier, he'd been amazed at how much Kate had accomplished in so little time, but the repairs only highlighted how much more needed to be done.

"How were you injured? How long ago?" Amelie's voice brought him back.

He hated talking of that day on the Texas plains, hated remembering what had been done to a band of innocent women and children in the Comanche stronghold. Hated remembering what had happened to him. An arrow had gone through his ankle, clear through the bone and into his horse's belly. The animal had gone down on top of him, compounding his injuries.

"I took a Comanche arrow in the ankle." He shrugged, ashamed of his self-pity in light of what she was suffering through so bravely. "It's taken quite some time to heal."

Amelie looked over his shoulder again and this time said, "Come closer, Kate."

Until now, Colin had almost forgotten Kate was still in the room.

"I should leave, let you get some rest," he said.

"Please, stay," Amelie said. "Help me sit up."

Kate stepped forward and helped Amelie.

Amelie smiled at Colin. "Kate won't admit how ill I am or that she is powerless to save me. I've asked her to raise my children. I want them in your care too, Colin. They are innocent of what I've done, of what Billy did. I'm just grateful they are nothing like their Hart kin."

"I'll do what I can," he promised. Even though he was the children's uncle, Kate was the obvious choice as guardian. He had nothing of real value to give them, no money to see them through, and his spirit was as damaged as his ankle.

"Did you know that Kate has always loved you?" Amelie asked him bluntly.

Kate gasped and cried, "Amelie!"

Surely his sister was delirious.

"You know very well it's true, Kate." Amelie paused as if to gather strength. "I suspect ... that might explain why you never married."

Colin looked at Kate. Behind her spectacles, her eyes were wide with shock. He continued to stare — to really *look* at her for the first time as more than his sister's friend. Beneath Kate's expensive, well-tailored outfit, her figure was trim and shapely; her hair was thick, a rich brown shot through with russet highlights; her skin was flawless, her cheeks stained with embarrassment.

Kate had been here at *Belle Fleuve* for nearly a month and all he really knew about her was what he'd heard from Eugenie. It was obvious she held *Belle Fleuve* and his parents' memories in her heart, but how could anyone possibly love him? Perhaps before the war, but not now.

Kate was studiously avoiding looking at him. Amelie lifted the family photograph from the bed.

"Since our Bible cannot be found, both of you must swear on this photograph of Mama and Papa and on their memories that you will marry and care for my children ... together."

"Amelie, you can't possibly—" Kate began.

Colin glanced up again, saw the stubborn line of her jaw and knew she was going to refuse. He'd seen enough of death to know what it looked like. There was little hope for his sister, but Kate refused to see it.

Amelie was crying as she stared up at him in silent appeal. He had failed her before when he hadn't come home from the war. He wouldn't fail her again, not when she needed him. He would do anything to give her peace of mind.

Without warning, he grabbed Kate's hand. She tried to pull away but he held tight and forced her hand down to cover the photograph. Slowly her fingers uncurled beneath his until her palm was pressed against the image of his family.

Shocked into silence, Kate watched Amelie struggle to take a breath. Dumfounded, Kate started to protest, refusing to take any such vow, but then she met Colin's gaze. Unshed tears welled in his eyes—tears that melted her heart.

He was doing this insane thing for his sister. How could she refuse?

"I promise," she whispered. "I promise to raise Marie and Damian if anything happens to you."

Colin took up where she left off. "I promise on our parents' memories to marry Kate Keene and raise your children as my own."

Kate's hand trembled beneath his. He gave it a slight squeeze. She found him staring into her eyes. A chill seared her and she shivered, afraid that if he could see into her heart he would see the secret she'd kept hidden there all these years. The secret she'd just tried to deny.

"Promise that you won't mourn me. Promise you will keep my children safe and happy," Amelie urged.

"I promise." There was no doubting Colin's sincerity.

Kate hesitated. She wanted Amelie here.

"Kate, please," Amelie urged.

Kate waffled between anger and the terror of such a loss.

"I promise," she whispered.

Colin lifted his hand and Kate was free. She backed away, and a second later, Eugenie was at the door bearing a tray with a glass of milk. Her surprise at the sight of Colin was evident.

"I'll sit with Miss Amelie if you all would like to go on down to the kitchen and have somethin' to eat."

Now that Amelie had extracted their promises, her eyelids were fluttering. Rather than have her fight much-needed sleep, Kate took the photograph from Amelie's limp fingers and placed it on the bedside table. As she stepped back, Colin reached around her and propped the family portrait against a lamp where Amelie could see it.

Once they were on the gallery, Kate halted Colin.

"I need to talk to you." She was determined not to vent her anger until they were downstairs. The last thing she wanted was for Amelie to overhear what she had to say.

"I have to get off my ankle." He made his way to the stairs, leaning heavily on his cane, then stopped and reached for the ban-ister with his free hand. Kate had been too upset to notice his pallor but was quickly reminded of his struggle.

She took hold of his elbow. He tried to shrug her off.

"Are we going to stand here playing tug-of-war with your arm, or are you going to let me help you?"

He stopped tugging and slowly negotiated the stairs, pausing after every step to take his weight off his ankle. When Kate finally let go of his arm, he headed for the front door.

"Oh no you don't." She took hold of him again. He stared at her hand but didn't pull away. "If you think you're running back to the *garçonnière* after what just happened upstairs you are sorely mistaken. Come with me."

She expected an argument. Instead, he followed her through the house and the gallery. As soon as they were inside the kitchen, she pulled a chair out from the table for him.

"Sit."

He sat.

She was too upset to even think of sitting. She paced over to the stove and back to the table.

"Let's get one thing clear. I have *not* always loved you." That much was true. She hadn't *always* loved him. Only since she was twelve or so until she came back to *Belle Fleuve*. Up until she saw him with the children she certainly hadn't been pining over him anymore.

Worried, yes. But still in love? She would never, ever admit it to him. Certainly not now.

"Surely you know that's not true," she added. She watched his hand tighten on his cane. He looked at it for a second before he looked up at her.

"Of course not," he said. "What woman could love me now?"

"Because of your injury? Hogwash."

"What matters is Amelie, not the past and certainly not some schoolgirl crush of yours."

"What were you thinking, making a promise like that? What made you swear to her that we'd marry?"

"I was *thinking* of my sister. No matter what you believe, she is going to die, and I don't want her any more worried about her children than she already is."

"But marriage is impossible."

"I agreed to put Amelie's mind at ease."

"She doesn't need *ease*. What she needs is hope. She needs to want to live. You've made it *easier* for her to die, Colin."

"How dare you, Kate?"

"I'm sorry." Seeing his outrage, she was instantly and truly sorry. "I'm just so upset ..." She fought back tears and turned away.

"I know," he said softly. "We both want what's best for her."

She turned and watched him prop his cane against the table and use both hands to push himself to his feet before he took up the cane again.

"Is that all? May I leave now?" His eyes were full of pain as he stood tall.

"Would you like something to eat before you go?"

"No. Thank you."

Colin took a halting step, then put a bit of pressure on his bad leg and nearly crumpled. Kate rushed to his side, slipped beneath his arm, and wrapped her arm around his waist. She felt him tremble and didn't let go even when he insisted he was fine. With her body pressed along his side, she looked up and found him staring down at her, his face mere inches away from hers.

"You can let go now," he told her again.

She blinked and stepped back, then pushed her glasses up the bridge of her nose.

"Colin, I'm going into New Orleans tomorrow to find a doctor," she blurted out. "There has to be someone who can help Amelie."

"If it makes you feel better, by all means go. But I hope you don't regret leaving her now to go off on a fool's errand."

Rather than argue, she added, "There is an architect I wanted to speak to about work."

It was time to turn her passion for architecture into a way to make a living. She needed to sit down with her accountant and go over her finances, to make certain there was no way Colin would ever find out she'd paid the back taxes on *Belle Fleuve* before he found sufficient funds to repay her.

Colin negotiated the room and had almost reached the door when he turned to her again.

"Work? How can you think about that now? What about the children?" There was a touch of panic in his eyes.

"Myra will be here to care for them. Eugenie will watch over Amelie. I hope you can summon the strength to visit her again."

He sighed. "It's hard."

She didn't know if he meant walking or seeing Amelie so ill.

"She needs you, Colin. The children need you. I doubt they've ever known an honorable man."

"What makes you think I'm honorable?"

Kate adjusted her glasses again. "I don't think it. I know it."

"You are impossible, you know."

"So you've told me."

"When will you be back?"

"Soon. Day after tomorrow." She watched him struggle to take a few more steps. "Would you like me to help you walk back? Do you need a dose of laudanum?"

"No, I dumped it out."

She took it as a sign of hope.

He paused in the doorway and turned to her. "I can get back on my own. And Kate?"

"Yes."

"Thank you."

For a moment she thought she heard wrong.

"For what?"

"For going against my wishes. I'm glad the place was decent enough for Amelie and the children to move into."

"I'm right about finding someone to help her too. She'll recover. You'll see."

Alone on the path to the *garçonnière*, Colin took his time. Whenever he halted to ease his pain, he studied the garden. Someone had done some weeding since he'd seen it last. A few of his mother's roses were free of the weeds that had been holding them hostage.

He took a deep breath, inhaling the familiar smell of the river, the soil, the damp, fertile earth of Louisiana. Was there some hope for this place even if there was none left for him?

The sound of Damian's laughter floated to him on the breeze off the river. He didn't hear Marie's voice; no doubt she was too worried about her mother to laugh. Watching one's mother waste away was far more worry than a ten-year-old should have to bear.

Colin imagined that the world the children had known was a far cry from the childhood he and Amelie and Kate had shared. Sheltered and privileged, the three of them had grown up believing they were entitled to everything.

Though it caused him much anguish to face the truth, he held no hope for his sister. When she was gone, he would need insurmountable courage to raise two children. Could he do it?

He gazed beyond his mother's garden, past the barn, the smokehouse, and other outbuildings, and past the row of cabins that once housed slaves and now stood empty, except the one Eugenie and Simon occupied. He looked over the old cane fields — the former lifeblood of the South and *Belle Fleuve* — but where there used to be acres and acres of sugarcane, there were but a few straggling islands of ratoon cane.

Yesterday Colin couldn't imagine he would be able to walk from the *garçonnière* to the house, let alone drag himself upstairs — yet he'd done it for his sister. One step at a time, he'd done it for Amelie.

Could he possibly resurrect *Belle Fleuve*?

He had no idea where to start, but nothing could be accomplished without money. His only bankable asset was the Delany name. It was a name that meant something in a city where pedigree counted — especially if a man could claim Creole or Irish roots. Fortunately, he possessed both.

EIGHT

Most New Orleanians' favorite pastimes were dining and shopping, and Kate was no exception. In town she feasted on all the rich foods she loved, thankful that the city was coming back from the long, dark years of the war and its aftermath.

She hurried up and down familiar streets, stopping now and then to purchase clothes and shoes for the children, a McGuffey's First Reader for Damian, and some ribbons for Marie's hair. They also needed stockings and undergarments and hairbrushes. And she found a gold locket for Marie.

Calling on a few of her mother's closest friends, Kate asked for physician recommendations. She set up interviews with the top three recommended doctors. After she described Amelie's symptoms to the first doctor, he told her the best thing she could do was return to *Belle Fleuve* and tell her friend good-bye. Kate walked out and slammed the door behind her.

She left the second visit in a pique when the well-known physician with a spotless reputation told her that Amelie was receiving the same care at *Belle Fleuve* that she'd get at a sanatorium — good meals, fresh air, and rest. Nothing was to be done but make her comfortable until the end.

Kate sat in the third doctor's empty office waiting area, afraid she'd be returning to the plantation alone. A portly middle-aged gentleman wearing a finely cut suit and a wide smile walked in. He was only a few inches taller than she.

"Miss Keene? I'm Doctor Jonathon Ward. How can I help you?"

He had a Yankee accent, which explained the lack of patients in his office.

"I'm seeking help for a friend," she began. "She has consumption." Kate described Amelie's symptoms.

The man actually smiled when she finished.

"Why, Miss Keene, no case is ever hopeless. I'd be most happy to help."

Kate burst into tears. Once she'd collected herself and was seated in a comfortable wing chair near a window overlooking Jackson Square, she listened to the doctor as he explained his plan of attack.

"There are many things to do before we give up, my dear. Many things. Phosphorous is one treatment—"

"I spoke to someone earlier who told me that it's dangerous to use phosphorous when the disease is advanced."

Dr. Ward waved his hand as if batting away a pesky fly. "Pooh. I've used it with much success." He leaned forward with his elbows on his knees. His stare was intent. "I have a very powerful curative made of snail syrup."

"Snails?" Kate loved escargot, but the idea of a syrup made from snails made her wince.

"Snails gathered from the garden in the early morning when the dew is still on the leaves. Bagged and doused with honey, they drip a very powerful restorative."

Kate swallowed. "It works?"

He nodded. "Ninety-nine percent of the time."

The man was overconfident, perhaps even a charlatan. She sat back and stared out at the park in the open square.

"What have you got to lose, Miss Keene?"

"My friend." Her voice wavered. "My dearest friend."

The doctor stood up and walked into the adjoining room. She

heard him moving around, and then he came back to the reception room carrying a square box. He sat and set the box on his knees. Taking great care, he lifted a crystal sphere out of a nest of excelsior and held it in both hands.

"If all else fails, *this* should do it."

She leaned closer to the sphere. "What is it?"

"A very powerful healing stone discovered in the ruins of the ancient city of Rome. It holds the secrets of the ages."

Any other time, Kate would have laughed and thought him crazy. But picturing Amelie's shadowed eyes, her pitifully thin, bent frame, her lungs so infected that every cough was excruciating, Kate was ready to gamble on anything that might work.

"I suppose it's worth a try. As crazy as it sounds, I have no other options," she said.

"I should warn you that my services don't come cheap, Miss Keene."

That much was evident from the cut of his clothes and fine leather boots.

"You are not a charlatan, are you, Doctor?"

"It pains me to hear you ask, my dear. Pains me to the quick."

"Believe me, Doctor, you don't know the kind of pain I can inflict if you are lying. I can have you run out of New Orleans in the blink of an eye."

It wasn't an empty threat. One word to some of her father's former business associates and Dr. Jonathon Ward would be on his way back north.

"Miss Keene, nothing is certain when it comes to cures. Don't you know that all medicine is based on faith? Faith in the doctor, faith in the remedy, and faith in God. I am merely a conduit. All we can do is hope that your friend has the courage to believe."

Kate was reminded of her visit to Cezelia and hoped God was listening.

Kate's accountant, Dan Rosen, ushered her into his office with all the fanfare wealthy clients expected, but the elegance of his carpeted offices full of glossy cherry wood furniture was lost on Kate. She'd been poor, and she'd been rich, but she was impressed only by a person's honesty and generosity, not by a show of wealth.

Dan had proven his loyalty and business acumen time and again. Her father had considered him one of the most honest and qualified accountants in New Orleans. Once Kate convinced Rosen she didn't need to be fawned over, she dealt comfortably with the well-known family man.

"I'm glad you finally returned to town, Kate." Dan took a seat beside her rather than behind his expansive desk. "I was afraid I was going to have to go out to *Belle Fleuve* to see you."

"You look worried, Dan. Should I be worried?"

She had asked Dan to oversee ordering the building materials and having them delivered to the plantation. He knew exactly what she'd been up to.

"You have to stop spending, Kate. You've next to nothing left."

"Next to *nothing*?" Her thoughts ricocheted back to Dr. Ward's warning that his services didn't come cheap.

"I warned you back when you paid off the Delanys' taxes that you should take care. When Nola sold the townhouse I advised you against moving into that expensive suite at the St. Charles."

"But I never thought things would get this dire," she said.

"Hopefully you are through with your pet project."

"I didn't get as far as I'd hoped. I must admit I was very naive about making plans without consulting Colin first. He's tried to run me off. He's a very stubborn man."

"But not crazy, as rumor would have it?"

"Definitely not crazy."

"Does he know how invested you are in that place?"

"No, and I don't intend to tell him until he's on his feet and can make some arrangements to repay me."

"I warned your father not to give you *carte blanche*."

"Because I'm a woman?"

"Because you think with your heart and not your head. It's admirable that you want to help out old friends, but I'm worried about your future."

"This morning I heard from one of mother's friends that Roger Jamison is looking for an architect to act as his assistant. He was a friend of Father's. Perhaps he'll hire me."

Dan looked skeptical. "If you can make enough to cover your living expenses I'll invest some of your remaining funds and try to rebuild your account."

"I'll find more affordable lodging for Myra and myself when we leave *Belle Fleuve*. I certainly hope to make enough to pay our expenses." She spoke with all the confidence she could muster. "Are you really quite certain the situation is that dire?"

"Let's just say you are poised on the brink of disaster. There is certainly no more money to spend on *Belle Fleuve*. What would Delany say if he knew you'd spent your inheritance on the place?"

"He would be livid." Livid was putting it mildly. He was a proud man who loathed indebtedness—especially to her, if Kate were to hazard a guess.

"Hasn't he wondered why the taxes haven't come due?"

"He thinks he was given leeway because he enlisted in the army and took an oath of loyalty to the Union."

"And how did he come by that misinformation?" Dan didn't look pleased.

She shrugged. "Four years ago I asked the clerk at the tax assessor's office to tell him as much."

"Oh, Kate."

"The clerk once worked for my father and recognized my name. When I told him I wished to pay the taxes anonymously, we penned a letter for Colin and put it in his file. I know it's bad, but at the time it seemed like a good idea."

"Tell him the truth now, Kate. Find out what kind of man Colin really is."

"He's a broken man. I hate to tell him now when there's finally a glimmer of hope that he's recovering." She pictured Colin painfully making his way upstairs to visit Amelie. "Don't worry, Dan. Everything will work out. You'll see."

"For your sake, I hope so. Take my advice, Kate. Stop spending. I can grow the small amount of principal you have left, if you're careful."

"I'm sure my father would have tripled what he left me by now," she shrugged. "Business was his gift. Unfortunately, I must have taken after my birth parents. They fled the Irish famine and immigrated to New Orleans."

Like so many others, her parents had died of yellow fever, which her father caught while digging the canals of the city.

"Amelie has come home, and now that she's back, Colin will realize he simply has to save *Belle Fleuve* for her and her children," she added.

"If Patrick Delany had lived he would have invested in the Hibernia Bank. Most of his friends were founders. A Hibernia loan isn't out of the question for Colin."

"Do you think so?"

"It would be a long shot," Dan Rosen admitted. "With declining land values, the plantation is almost worthless. Colin could break the land into smaller holdings, sell them, or rent out parcels to tenant farmers. Surely there's still some sugar-refining equipment around the property."

Kate's thoughts were miles away at *Belle Fleuve* with Amelie, Colin, and the children until she realized what he'd just said.

"Did you say something about refining sugar?"

Dan nodded. "Farmers have been forming co-operatives, pooling their crops. If there's an old sugarhouse on the land, Colin could get it running again. Does he have any resources at all?"

"Apparently not."

She pictured the seemingly endless fields stretched out around *Belle Fleuve*. Was there an old sugarhouse somewhere?

"You've given me a lot to think about." Kate got to her feet. "I have to get ready to go back tomorrow morning."

Dan rose as well. "I hope you make it. There's quite a storm brewing." He walked her to the door. "Remember what I said, Kate. No more spending."

"Don't look so worried. I promise to tighten my purse strings." *After I pay Dr. Ward*, she thought. "Everything will be fine. Please give Susan and the boys my best."

"I will. You have a safe journey back to the country."

Kate's last stop was the home of Roger Jamison, an architect who lived in the Garden District. Jamison's work was as well-known as Patrick Delany's, and Kate considered herself lucky that he'd even agreed to see her on such short notice. Of course, having been Gilbert Keene's daughter helped.

The architect was in his late fifties, whipcord lean, and like her, wore spectacles, but his were the thickest lenses she'd ever seen. His jacket was patched at the elbows, but his shoes were new. He ushered her in and asked if she'd like some tea. She accepted and followed him into the kitchen where he brewed it himself.

"I'll admit I agreed to see you out of curiosity. I met your father on a few occasions. Brilliant mind. What brings you here, Miss Keene?"

Kate stood a bit taller. "I'm an architect, Mr. Jamison, and an admirer of your work."

His brow arched. His expression revealed disbelief.

Kate hurried to add, "I've recently been overseeing repairs to *Belle Fleuve*, the Delany plantation on River Road."

She told him of her accomplishments at *Belle Fleuve*. Once the tea was brewed, Jamison served it in his office.

"I'll admit that there is no shortage of work rebuilding the South, Miss Keene. I'm not getting any younger, and I find it harder to keep up with demands. You've come at an opportune time, my dear. I've been looking for someone who can help, some-one with a fresh eye and new ideas."

"That's certainly me, Mr. Jamison." Before her visit to Rosen's office, Kate would have seen this interview as an exciting challenge. Now she struggled not to appear desperate.

"What actual experience have you had other than overseeing repairs?"

"I studied with Patrick Delany." Jamison's gaze was calculating.

"You must have been a child."

She shrugged, tried not to blush but failed. "Well, yes."

"What else, Miss Keene?"

"I was apprenticed by an architect in Ireland. He's written a letter of reference. Since then I've worked on reconstruction plans for *Belle Fleuve*. I've entered a few periodical contests as well."

"Have you completed the reconstruction of *Belle Fleuve*?"

"No. Colin Delany has no funds available at this point."

"It's a shame you didn't bring your plans along with you. I'd be interested in taking a look at them."

"It would be an honor to show you what I've done."

He sat in silence for so long she feared he was going to dismiss her.

"Miss Keene," he said as he leaned forward in his chair, "I'm not as young as I used to be. Nor am I as patient. The idea of taking on any apprentice at this stage is not to my liking, but it appears that it's a necessity. I never thought to take on a woman, certainly not someone as untried as you. But once, long ago, your father found work for me when I was an impoverished architect down on his luck, and I'll always be grateful. It would be an honor to repay him by hiring you, on a trial basis, of course. Hopefully you can help relieve some of my burdens."

Kate's relief and excitement was only tempered by the thought of Amelie's lying ill at *Belle Fleuve*.

"You won't regret it, Mr. Jamison."

"Please, my dear, call me Roger." He pushed himself up out of the chair, crossed the room, and motioned for her to follow him to a wide table covered with plans. "Now, let me show you what I have in mind for your first assignment. I'd like to hear your ideas."

NINE

Colin stepped onto the gallery, leaned heavily on his cane, and paused to rest his ankle before he moved into the main house. He'd made three trips upstairs in three days, each trip a miracle in and of itself. He brushed the rain off his shoulders and ran his hand through his damp hair. Unable to manage both an umbrella and his cane, each day he'd walked through a steady rain that hadn't been letting up.

He opened the closest door, stepped into the dining room, and heard the sound of the children in the sitting room just beyond. The pocket doors were open a few inches and he could clearly hear their young voices. Colin wiped his face with his sleeve as he listened.

"Have you seen the pirate captain? Have you seen the scurvy cabin boy?" Marie's voice was stronger and more forceful than he'd ever heard it. Whenever he was around the girl, she barely spoke, and when she did, she whispered.

Damian shouted back, "Nay! I haven't seen the blackguards, but when I do I'll have them clamped in irons and make them walk the plank. Or maybe I'll keelhaul them for drinking my rum! Yo, ho, ho!"

Colin began doubting the wisdom of gifting them with *A Pirate's Tale*.

"I'm going to be the captain now," Marie said. "I'm tired of being the wench."

"You're a girl. You can't be a pirate captain. Girls can't be pirates *or* sailors."

"Then I won't play anymore."

"Hey, you come back here," Damian ordered.

The sound of running feet preceded a loud scuffle. Colin had his hand on the sliding doors, ready to walk in, when something crashed to the floor. He opened the doors just as Damian came barreling out of the room, plowing straight into him.

Forced to put his weight on his injured ankle to keep his balance, pain shot up Colin's leg with the white heat of lightning. Reeling, he raised his arm to brace himself against the door frame. Damian let out a yelp and cowered.

"I'm sorry," the boy started blubbering. "I'm sorry, Uncle Colin. I didn't mean to break it."

Colin glanced across the room. Marie stood frozen beside a round side table tipped over on its side. The shards of a ceramic figurine lay scattered beside it.

"We're sorry," she whispered. "It was an accident."

Colin couldn't speak until he managed his pain. He took a deep breath. "I know that."

The boy was visibly shaken and well beyond Colin's reach. *Does the child really think I would hit him?*

"Help me to the settee, will you?" Colin waited as the girl crossed the room to stand beside him. Only then did Damian sidle up closer. The two exchanged a glance and then each put an arm around Colin, lightly to be sure, but they made an effort to help.

Once he'd lowered himself to the settee and the children were shoulder to shoulder in front of him, he rested both hands on the handle of his cane and looked at each in turn.

"You have my solemn promise that I will never hit you. Do you understand?"

Neither of them moved.

"Do you?"

Marie nodded.

"You won't?" Damian stared in disbelief.

"I will not. I promise."

"Even if we're *very* bad?"

"What do you mean, very bad?"

Damian shrugged. "Like that." He pointed at the table and broken figurine.

"That was an accident, correct?"

They nodded.

"Then you didn't intentionally break that ... whatever it was."

"A little dog. Aunt Kate said it was one of her favorite things from a long time ago."

"You didn't mean to break it. But you will take more care when you are playing in the house, and you will have to apologize to her when she returns."

"Maybe we can glue the biggest pieces back together." Marie fiddled with the cuff of her sleeve.

The cuff was tattered. He would speak to Eugenie about it.

"When is Aunt Kate coming back?" Damian asked.

"I've been wondering that myself," Colin mumbled. As much as he didn't want to admit it, Kate's absence wasn't sitting well with him. She'd been gone for nearly three days now, and the house was empty without her. He found himself watching the road, listening for the sound of her voice.

With the storm and impassible roads, it didn't seem likely she'd be returning anytime soon. Both children looked disappointed when he told them as much.

"I'd like you to stand the table up, Damian," he instructed. "When you are finished, go out to the kitchen and ask Eugenie for a broom and dustpan, and sweep up. Your sister will help you."

"That's all?" the boy asked. "You really aren't going to whip us?"

"I gave you my word." Before the boy turned to go to the kitchen Colin asked, "Have you ever been whipped?"

Damian nodded. "My daddy took a switch to us a lot. He didn't tolerate any misbehaving."

Colin's hands tightened on his cane. He wished Billy Hart was standing before him instead of the boy. He'd have a thing or two to impress upon a man who whipped his children.

"I won't tolerate misbehavior either," Colin assured Damian. "But there are other ways to punish. Believe me, I've experienced a good many of them myself."

"Like what?" Damian wanted to know.

"I spent more than a few hours with my nosed pressed against the wall. Once when I was six, my father caught me chewing tobacco and made me fill half a glass with spit before I was free to go. It was terrible." Colin stopped talking when he noticed Damian's eyes were wide with trepidation.

When the boy left to collect the broom and dustpan, Marie sighed. Colin patted the settee beside him and she sat down after a long hesitation.

"Have you come to see Mama?" She studied her hands folded in her lap.

"How is she today?"

"Not very good. She sleeps a lot."

He hated seeing Amelie so weak.

"Uncle Colin?" the girl whispered.

"You really need to speak up, you know. I could go deaf straining to hear you."

She nodded and raised her voice a bit. "What will we do if . . . if something happens to Mama?" Huge tears pooled in her eyes and began to slip down her cheeks.

Unable to stand the sight of her tears, Colin reached over and thumbed them away. She reminded him of a young version of his own mother and seemed just as vulnerable.

"What will we do?" Colin paused. He could lie and tell them Amelie would recover. Or he could be honest. Colin took a deep breath. "We'll do what we all have to do and we will survive. You and your brother will be in my care."

"Will we live here?" She wiped her nose on her sleeve.

He couldn't say for sure. He had no idea what was going to happen to *Belle Fleuve*.

"Wherever we go, we'll be together."

"Aunt Kate too. Mama said Aunt Kate promised to take care of us."

It was his turn to sigh. "I'm not sure about that."

The girl's face puckered into a frown.

"Of course Aunt Kate will look out for you too," Colin was quick to add.

The weight of the old house seemed to press down on him from every angle. He hadn't put much thought into everything Damian and Marie would need. Their clothing was worn and almost too small for them. If he were forced to move out now, he'd have to rent a larger flat. There would be schooling to think about, not to mention boots and shoes and a thousand things he'd never thought about before.

His pledge to marry Kate and raise the children had been purely for Amelie's peace of mind. But how could he actually raise two children with his own future so uncertain?

Maybe it would be better to hand them over into Kate's care and not look back. As close as she was to his sister, Kate was the logical choice as guardian. Besides, Kate would never have to worry where their next meal was coming from.

Damian returned with a broom and long-handled dustpan.

"Uncle Colin, can we hunt for the treasure?"

Colin pulled his scattered thoughts together. "I doubt there is any pirate treasure around here."

"No." The boy shook his head. "*Grandmere* Delany's treasure.

Mama told us *Grandmere* buried her treasures so the Yankees wouldn't steal them."

"She did?" Colin couldn't imagine his mother burying anything herself.

"That's what Mama says. So can I dig for treasure in the garden?"

"After Marie helps you clean up the floor." As an afterthought Colin added, "Don't hurt the flowers, though."

He felt Marie tug lightly at his sleeve.

"Uncle Colin, you should go and see how Mama is doing."

"You're right." He wasn't looking forward to standing, let alone negotiating the stairs again.

"I'll help you," she said softly, "if you'd like."

Surprised at her offer, he was just as shocked when he felt something stirring in the empty space where his heart used to be.

"That would be kind of you. I believe I would like some help."

At the top of the stairs he saw the apprehension on Marie's face as she stared at the door to her mother's room. He sent her back down to help Damian sweep up and was about to open the door when Eugenie stepped out of the room. Her face was drawn, her eyes downcast.

"How is she?" Suddenly Colin had no desire to go into Amelie's room.

Eugenie sniffed and wiped her eyes with a hankie that appeared from her apron pocket.

"Not good, Mr. Colin. Not good at all. She's in and out now. I'm not sure she knows where she is anymore."

He leaned heavily against his cane and wished Kate were here.

"What are we going to do?" Eugenie wanted to know.

He told her what he'd told Amelie's children.

"We're going to do what we have to do."

"I sure hope Miss Kate comes back soon. She was bound and determined to find a doctor who could help."

Colin's wish that Kate were here was not because she'd promised to bring help. It was because she loved Amelie as much as the rest of them. Amelie needed her dear friend beside her right now, and Kate should be here to say good-bye.

The war had taken every vestige of whatever softness Colin had once had inside him. Kate's presence filled the empty space he left behind with the love and hope they all needed—things he could never give.

TEN

The storm stranded Kate in New Orleans for six days, and afterward the Mississippi was running too fast for steamboat travel. But Kate ignored the dire warnings not to travel, hired a carriage, and insisted the driver take her back to *Belle Fleuve*.

Lingering squalls made the roads barely passable. With Dr. Jonathon Ward accompanying her, the journey was nearly unbearable. The man droned on the entire way. Kate tried to ignore him, catching only bits and pieces of his ongoing monologue.

" ... or so the ancient Egyptians thought. Antiquities and medicine go hand in hand, as far as I'm concerned. There is so much modern man doesn't know that ..."

After having spent hours in his company, Kate feared he was more than a bit delusional, but what mattered most was Amelie. If Dr. Ward's insane notions brought her friend even a modicum of relief, then the exorbitant fee she'd agreed to pay him would be well worth it. Since her meeting with Dan Rosen, that fee weighed heavily on her mind.

The journey took twice as long as usual. Trees were downed along the route, though there weren't any they couldn't carefully skirt. There were also a few harrowing moments when one of the carriage wheels became mired in mud, but finally they arrived.

The driver pulled up to the house and Kate scrambled out without waiting for him to assist.

She took a deep breath and let her gaze sweep the tall white columns standing sentry across the front gallery. To her *Belle Fleuve* was not as worn as a favorite pair of old shoes, but as grand as it used to be. Warmed by a feeling of homecoming, she reminded herself she was only there for Amelie, only at *Belle Fleuve* for as long as her friend needed her.

She had no regrets. She was satisfied knowing in her heart that *Belle Fleuve* would survive a few years longer, with or without her.

"Oh, my." The doctor took in the condition of the house. "I'm not certain ..."

"Don't worry. You'll be well compensated, Dr. Ward. Come with me."

Anxious to escape the light mist, Kate lifted her gown and made her way across the crushed oyster drive with the portly man close on her heels. He clutched the velvet-lined box containing his healing stone against his brocade vest.

The heels of Kate's ankle-high boots clipped against the brick floor as she crossed the lower gallery. The front door opened before Kate touched the handle.

She smiled when Myra answered the door, but noticed Myra's shoulders were drooped, her steps slow. Kate took a deep breath. Myra's apparent exhaustion was perfectly understandable; she'd been cooped up in the house for several days with two children to entertain and Amelie to worry about.

"I've found a wonderful doctor," Kate said as she breezed into the main room. She began to pull off her gloves. "If you could ask the driver to pile up the boxes and my bag ... oh! And I have some drawings too. I must take Dr. Ward up to see Amelie immediately."

Myra's lips worked but she made no sound. Kate's smile faltered. It was impossible to ignore Myra's swollen, red-rimmed eyes.

"Praise God you're home." Myra grabbed Kate's hand. "We didn't think you would be back in time."

Kate's stomach dropped. She pressed her lips together and fought off a wave of dizziness. She took a deep breath and ignored the warning bells clanging inside her.

Myra cleared her throat. "She's taken a turn for the worse. There is nothing—"

Kate started shaking and couldn't stop.

"It's a blessing you made it back," Myra finished.

"Where's Colin?"

"Upstairs with his sister. The children are there too. They dare not leave her now."

"Excuse me, Miss Keene." Doctor Ward edged closer to Kate. It was a moment before she recalled why he was here.

Kate grabbed his sleeve. "Hurry, Doctor. Bring that crystal of yours." She brushed past Myra.

All the way up the stairs she prodded the doctor to move faster. He huffed and puffed and when they reached the top, Kate raced along the gallery to Amelie's room with Dr. Ward on her heels.

She skidded to a stop at the door to Amelie's room. Colin was seated on a chair beside the bed. Marie was poised on a stool near her mother's pillow, and little Damian was half-draped across the other side of the bed.

"Colin."

"Kate." Sorrow pooled in his eyes. He sounded relieved to see her.

She walked into the room. "I've found a doctor willing to help."

Kate expected Dr. Ward to be right behind her. She turned and saw him framed in the doorway. She followed his horrified gaze, taking in the pile of bloody towels on Amelie's bedside table and the washbowl of water stained bright red. He started backing away.

"I'd like to speak to you in private, Miss Keene." He clutched his silly box.

"Dr. Ward, I expect you to—"

"There's nothing I can do," he mumbled. "Nothing."

Kate wanted to snatch what was left of his hair off his head.

"Kate, please." Colin's voice was low but it carried. "Come back inside now."

She closed her eyes. Colin and the children. Those faces. They knew. They were willing to face what she couldn't. They were braver than she, truer to Amelie than she had been.

Kate took a deep breath. She spoke to Dr. Ward without looking at him.

"Go outside and tell the driver you'll be returning to New Orleans with him." She sounded calm and assured, but the words drifted out of someone else entirely. Inside she had shattered into countless pieces.

The man hesitated. "But what about my—"

Kate whipped around. "I will see that you are fully compensated for your time. You have my word. Now go."

As he hurried down the gallery, his footsteps clattered on the stairs. Kate smoothed the front of her skirt, then reached up and removed her hat. Myra suddenly appeared beside her, and Kate handed over her hat and gloves. The children never took their eyes off Amelie.

Amelie's eyes fluttered opened. She looked at Kate and rasped, "Good. You are ... home."

"Tell me a story, Mama." Damian begged. "Please?"

"Damian, let your mother rest." Myra started toward the boy.

Colin held up his hand. "Let him be. Please."

Amelie's breath was ragged. She smiled up at her boy. "How about ... I rest. You ... tell me a story."

"But you tell them better."

"Now it's your turn."

Marie lowered her head to the bed and buried her face in her arm. Damian climbed up beside his mother. Kate covered her mouth with her hand and swallowed a sob.

Damian touched Amelie's cheek. "Which story would you like? Blackbeard?"

Her eyes fluttered as she fought to open them again and failed. "Cinderella," she whispered.

Damian sighed. "All right." Stretched out beside his mother, he stacked his hands behind his head and crossed his ankles. "Once upon a time in a small village in ..." He paused. "Where is it, Marie?"

"France," she whispered.

"Once upon a time in a village in France ..."

Kate wrapped her arms around her waist. Amelie's eyes remained closed. Her chest rose and fell, each breath a struggle until she was gone. Damian went on unaware.

Colin remained completely still, leaning forward with his forearms propped on his thighs, his fingers laced together. Was he praying? Marie's muffled sobs and Damian's valiant voice were the only sounds in the room.

"And they lived happily ever after." Damian looked at Colin, then Kate, then raised himself up on his elbow. He traced his fingertips along his mother's face.

"Uncle Colin?"

It was a moment before Colin said, "What, Damian?"

"Mama's not asleep, is she?"

Colin turned to Kate with a universe full of questions in his eyes. What Kate wanted was to break down and sob for her own loss, to be alone, to face her own grief head on. But Marie was crying uncontrollably, Damian's hand was pressed to his mother's cheek, and Colin was silently pleading for help.

Somehow she walked to his chair to stand behind him. When she placed her hand on his shoulder, he cleared his throat. The silence in the room stretched taut.

Kate looked at her best friend, at the sister of her heart. For the first time since Amelie arrived she looked at peace. As if she might just be asleep, dreaming a wonderful dream.

Damian was still waiting for an answer.

Colin reached up and grabbed Kate's hand.

She struggled to smile for Damian, struggled and failed.

"No, honey," she said. "She's not asleep. Your mama's gone."

They laid Amelie out in the front sitting room for visitation. Kate changed into a black mourning gown and avoided going downstairs again for as long as she could. Once there she recognized the cloying scent of Eugenie's myrtle berry candles, the sickly sweet perfume of jasmine filling the first floor rooms. The windows in the sitting room were covered. Myra, also wearing a severe black gown, the same one she had worn after Gil Keene's death, was waiting for her on the gallery.

Myra walked over, took Kate's arm, and tried to lead her farther into the room. But as the heavy candle scent wafted over Kate, her feet failed her. She looked around the room.

Eugenie and Simon stood against the back wall. Eugenie held a dishtowel against her mouth to muffle her sobs. The children, stiff and silent, were seated side by side not far from Amelie. She looked like a life-sized doll laid out in the center of the room on long planks covered with various pieces of sheets and tablecloths. Her hands were folded around a bouquet of her mother's precious yellow roses.

Colin was seated near his sister. As soon as he saw Kate in the doorway, he pushed himself slowly to his feet. She knew what the move cost him, but didn't protest. Her knees trembled so hard she hadn't the strength of will to take another step.

Colin's dark eyes were shadowed with pain and grief as he slowly stood and made his way over to her, one measured step at a time. She had thought him broken before, but today they were both shattered. Once Colin was beside her on the gallery, Myra returned to the children.

When Colin touched her arm, Kate felt nothing.

"Come, let me help you," he offered.

"No." She shook her head, refused to go a step farther. Refused to make this nightmare real.

Colin wrapped his arm around her. He leaned so close his warm breath brushed her ear.

"She loved you, Katie Keene," he whispered.

She longed to pull away, to run outside and down the drive, across the damp lawn, along the *allee* of oaks, to the levee, to the river. She wanted to wail and scream. Most of all she wanted to turn back time.

"We promised not to mourn her, remember?"

"Impossible," she whispered.

She heard a soft hiccup followed by a sob. Marie was doubled over on her chair.

"Go in there, Kate. Help them."

"I can't."

"You have to. It's what she wanted."

His words struck a familiar chord in her heart. Who knew better what it meant to be orphaned? To have no one.

Colin kept an arm around her as together they joined the children in the sitting room. Kate knelt down and hugged Marie. The girl pressed her face against Kate's neck and wrapped her arms around her. Kate held her close and let her cry. Damian slipped off his chair and hooked an arm around Kate's shoulders. In their knot of sorrow, they cried together.

When Kate finally looked up, Colin was seated again. He nodded. Together they would find a way to do right by these children.

Kate gently raised Marie's head and wiped away her tears before she turned to Damian, smoothed his dark curls, and wiped the tears off his cheeks as well.

Fighting for composure, holding their hands, she spoke softly.

"Your mama did not want us to be sad. Why don't you go into the kitchen with Myra and have some chocolate to drink? While you are there, I want you to think of some lovely stories about your mama. Things you remember that will make us all smile. Things we don't know about her. You can each tell one of the stories tomorrow at the burial. It's a very grown-up thing, but I'm sure you can do it. Will you try?"

Damian nodded first. Marie appeared uncertain.

"Can you do it, Marie? For your mama?"

She finally whispered, "I will try."

"Good." Kate hugged them both. Damian tugged on her sleeve. "Aunt Kate?" His eyes were watery and huge in his pale face.

"Yes, dear?"

"What will we do without Mama?"

Kate was out of words. Colin rose and, leaning heavily on his cane, walked over to join them.

Damian's face was pinched with worry.

"Will we have to go back to Kansas?" he asked Colin.

Without hesitation, Colin said, "No, you will not." He softened his tone. "Right now you should have some chocolate to drink and some of those cookies Eugenie made earlier. Try not to worry. You aren't going anywhere."

Myra collected her charges and took them to the kitchen. Eugenie slipped out after them.

"Thank you, Colin." Kate tried to smile, but again failed.

"Why don't you go upstairs? You must be exhausted."

His compassion surprised her. He was acting so unlike the man who had railed and demanded that she leave *Belle Fleuve*.

"No more than you."

"Simon and I will stay," Colin clarified.

The household, except for the children, would take turns sitting with Amelie all night.

"I should stay."

"Go," Colin urged. "Try to rest awhile. We'll be fine."

As she left the sitting room and stepped out onto the gallery Kate carefully avoided looking at Amelie. The setting sun turned raindrops on the trees into crystal teardrops as *Belle Fleuve* mourned the loss of its daughter. Despondent, still shaken, Kate escaped to her room, but she could not escape the memory of Damian's sorrowful eyes.

What will we do without Mama?

She couldn't bring herself to tell him the truth he would soon discover on his own.

You will feel abandoned and alone. You will call out for her in the middle of the night. You will cry yourself to sleep.

You will pray. You will survive. You will go on.

She washed her face with tepid water, stretched out on the bed, closed her eyes, and wished things had turned out differently, wished Amelie were alive.

I promise to raise Marie and Damian if anything happens to you.

She recalled the sound of Colin's deep voice and how he had spoken without hesitation. She still felt the remembered warmth of his hand when he forced hers onto the photograph.

I promise on our parents' memories to marry Kate Keene and raise your children as my own.

Surely Colin would not hold her to it.

He had assured Damian that he wasn't going anywhere, but perhaps Colin would consider letting her raise the children on her own in New Orleans. He could concentrate on *Belle Fleuve*, on rebuilding the plantation. Once that was accomplished and the children were older, they could move back.

Sleep eluded her as Kate wrestled with her thoughts. Finally she left the bed, crossed the room and glanced at the mirror above the washstand. For want of something black, Myra had covered it with a worn piece of calico—no doubt a remnant from Eugenie's ragbag. There was no way for Kate to tell if she looked presentable. No way to see if her deep sorrow and uncertainty showed.

Colin heard Simon shuffling behind him in the shadows of the large, sparsely furnished sitting room where every sound echoed against the bare walls and floors. He turned to the man and indicated the door with a nod.

"Why don't you go too, Simon?"

"Are you sure, Mr. Colin?"

"Yes. I'd like to be alone."

He leaned back in the chair and closed his eyes as Simon slipped out.

Once the man was gone Colin whispered. "What now, little sister?"

His mind went over all the possibilities, all the challenges. He'd made Amelie promises he couldn't keep. Marrying Kate Keene was one of those promises.

The moment he had seen Kate standing in the doorway to Amelie's room, relief had swept through him with the force of a summer storm.

He knew immediately that Kate belonged at *Belle Fleuve* even more than he did.

ELEVEN

The sun appeared for Amelie's burial, bright and golden in a cloudless blue sky. The breeze off the river carried the scent of the gulf to the small knot of mourners gathered beneath the oaks beside the Baudier family crypt, a short walk from the house and formal gardens.

The breeze challenged young Marie's voice as she struggled to speak of her mother.

"Mama told me about her first day at Daddy's folks' place in Kansas. It was called a soddie, and it was made of dirt. Dirt walls, dirt floor, and nothing to see for miles around but more dirt and the sky. That was before they moved closer to Dodge. Anyway, Mama was fresh up from Louisiana and when she found out that she'd have chores, she told Granny Hart that she'd never done chores and never washed a dish in her life and she wasn't about to start." Marie paused and looked to Kate, who nodded encouragement.

"That's the only funny thing I know about Mama. I can't imagine anybody not ever having to do chores. In Kansas we all did chores from mornin' to night." She looked at the crypt and shrugged. "I guess that's one good thing about her dying. Maybe Mama won't have to do any more chores in heaven."

As Marie walked back to Kate's side and took her hand several people shuffled and cleared their throats. Despite the heat of the day, Marie's hand felt clammy.

Kate stared at the crypt, heartbroken that Amelie was the only Delany to rest there. Marie Delany had been buried somewhere upriver at her Creole cousins' home. Patrick's body was in a field cemetery near the site of his last battle. Amelie was alone with her Creole ancestors, but at least she was at *Belle Fleuve*.

Kate had been surprised when a trio of buggies had arrived that morning. Two families that had recently bought homes along the river had come to show their respect. Even now they stared at Colin as if expecting him to do something outrageous and prove the rumors true. Kate suspected they had come more out of curiosity than sympathy. At least their children created a diversion for Damian until the brief graveside service had begun. The third couple turned out to be *Belle Fleuve*'s former manager's son, Jason Bolton, and his wife, Cora, who was expecting their first child.

Eugenie and Myra laid out a cold buffet on the gallery where those in attendance gathered after the burial. Kate's appetite had been nonexistent since her return, so she stood alone, off to the side of the group of neighbors who chatted among themselves discussing crops and weather. Now and again Colin would find her with a glance and understanding nod. Was he as eager as she was for the guests to leave them in peace?

Assured that Myra had the children well in hand, Kate was about to slip inside for some much-needed time alone when Cora Bolton joined her.

"My sympathies." The young woman appeared to be in her mid- to late-twenties and had blond hair and wide-set green eyes.

"Thank you," Kate nodded.

Kate had recognized Jason Bolton that morning when he handed his wife down from their carriage. He was near Colin's age, a handsome, fair-haired man with a strong, even jaw and broad shoulders. Like his wife, his clothes were clean but showed wear.

"Jason told me that you and Amelie were very close." Cora took a sip of water and glanced over at her husband, who was speaking to Colin.

"That's right." Kate struggled to be polite, but she didn't feel like making conversation.

"I'm from Tennessee," Cora said. "We married a year ago, and Jason's been talking about moving back ever since. We're living in a small cabin up the road near Plaquemine. Jason's hoping to get reestablished before the baby comes, so he was happy to hear Colin was back too. He's got some fine business propositions." Cora's face flushed. "But I suppose this isn't the time to discuss them. Sometimes I do go on. You'll have to forgive me." Then she added, "We were so sorry to hear about Amelie. Jason said she was always the prettiest girl around."

What did Jason Bolton hope to get out of Colin? Surely the couple could see there was nothing to be had at *Belle Fleuve*.

"I remember Jason," Kate said, "but I don't recall ever really talking to him at length." She did remember sneaking out to the *garçonnière* with Amelie to spy on Colin and his friends. Despite the fact that the others were wealthy, Jason, who was only the manager's son, was often with them.

"Jason's father worked for Patrick Delany for years. He said Mr. Delany gave his father credit for running the place so smoothly that Patrick had time to concentrate on his architecture."

"Where is the elder Mr. Bolton now?" Perhaps the man might inspire Colin to get *Belle Fleuve* back on its feet. Kate's hope dwindled when Cora said that, like Patrick, Jason's father had died for the Confederacy.

The woman chatted on, discussing everything from a new rice pudding recipe to each item of clothing she'd made for the coming baby. Kate pasted a smile on her lips and let her mind go blank until Marie found her.

"Aunt Kate, I'm tired."

"Please excuse us, Cora," Kate said. "I'm going to take Marie up to her room."

"Of course," the young woman smiled.

Marie trudged along as they mounted the gallery stairs together. "I'm sorry I interrupted you, Aunt Kate."

"You've nothing to be sorry for. I'm exhausted myself. Why don't we both lie down for a while in your room?"

Marie nodded. When she slipped her hand into Kate's, unexpected tears filled Kate's eyes. She felt Marie's hand tighten around hers as they passed Amelie's room. A breeze wafted through Marie's room as the two of them made themselves comfortable on the small bed. Side by side they stared at the ceiling.

"Do you think Mama can see us from heaven?" Marie asked.

"I think she can see us perfectly. She'd be very proud of how brave you were today. You and Damian both."

"Damian is out there having fun with those other children." There was disapproval in Marie's tone. "He's forgotten Mama already."

Kate slipped her arm around the girl and smoothed back her hair. "Damian is younger than you are, that's all. He hasn't forgotten."

"I'll never be happy again," Marie sighed. "I certainly don't see how I could."

"Someday you will laugh and play again. Your life will never be the same, but you'll be happy and laugh and play. You'll see."

As Kate stared at the cracks in the plaster ceiling she wished she could believe it.

Neither slept. They were silent until Marie rolled to her side and slipped her arm around Kate's waist.

"I miss my mama," she cried.

Kate's heart contracted. She curled her arm around the girl and held her close.

"I miss her too, honey," Kate sighed. "I miss her too."

The Boltons were the last to leave. Buoyed by a brief conversation with Jason, Colin watched the couple's carriage roll down the drive toward River Road before he sought out Kate. He hadn't seen her for a good hour and a half, not since she'd disappeared with Marie. He was about to look for her when Damian ran to him in tears. Colin braced himself to keep the boy from knocking him down.

"I don't want to wash up and nap, Uncle Colin. Tell her I don't have to." The boy crossed his arms and glared at Myra, who was bearing down on them.

"I'm sorry, sir, but he's sweaty and exhausted and full of sweets. I think he needs to rest a while," she said.

"No. I won't. I don't have to do what you say. You're nobody!" Damian planted his hands on his hips. "Only Uncle Colin can tell me what to do now, right Uncle Colin?"

Colin studied the boy. Damian needed to know who was in charge now.

"Myra did a fine job raising Kate, and while she's here she will look after you and your sister too. You're to do as she asks and you must also obey Kate and Eugenie."

"But—"

"Go with Myra and let her wash that cake off your face. Then take a nap. There's no shame in resting when you are tired."

Irritated, Damian tapped his foot.

"Go." Colin waited, relieved when the boy finally turned his back and plodded off with Myra in his wake.

Eugenie had nearly cleared the makeshift serving table on the gallery. How long would it be, if ever, before they could afford more furniture? Colin scoffed at the thought. A handful of days ago he'd been willing to vacate *Belle Fleuve*. It was premature to think about furnishing the place.

"Where's Kate, Eugenie?"

"She took little Marie upstairs. Would you like me to fetch her?"

"I'll go." He needed to see Kate, to make certain she was all right.

Eugenie glanced at his cane. "You sure?"

"I'm sure," he said.

He climbed the stairs slowly, stopping at the open door to Amelie's room. The curtains lifted on the soft breeze. The bed was freshly made and a vase of fresh flowers had been placed on the dresser, but the room held an aching emptiness.

He took a step. A floorboard creaked beneath his weight.

Two doors down, Kate opened the door to the children's room and held her finger to her lips. She stepped out and closed the door behind her without making a sound.

"Marie is asleep." She came toward him.

He missed her smile. Once she'd realized Amelie was gone, Kate's sparkle, her hope, the light that kept her fighting to make things better for everyone, had been extinguished.

She wore a heavy black gown that dwarfed her trim frame and gave her the appearance of a child playing grown-up. It washed out her complexion. Her spectacles magnified her red-rimmed, swollen eyes.

He watched her glance into Amelie's room and thought for a moment that she was going to wilt, but then she drew herself up. The light in her eyes was gone, but there was a new hardness to her lips.

"I failed her," she said.

"Do you really think you could have kept her alive?"

"At least *I* was willing to try."

"And I wasn't? Is that what you are saying?"

"You resigned yourself to her death."

Standing taxed his strength but there was nowhere to sit on the gallery. Pain gave an edge to his voice.

"My sister knew she was dying and accepted it. I hope I helped her go in peace. Let go, Kate. Regret won't do any good. I spent years wishing I hadn't gone to war, wishing I had protected my mother and sister." He shrugged. "If I hadn't reenlisted, I'd still be able to walk."

"You are walking."

He shook his head. "Barely."

He waited, expecting a word of encouragement. Expecting the old Kate.

Instead she looked at him a moment and shrugged. "I understand you better than ever now, Colin. I know why you locked yourself up the way you did. Why you gave up. This feeling of loss, of helplessness, is unbearable." She clasped her hands and walked to the railing overlooking the front lawn.

"People die, Kate."

He was going about this badly. This was not the way to put the light back into her eyes.

"Walk with me," he urged. "Let's go down and sit in the garden."

"I'm too tired."

On impulse he took her hand. Shock flashed across her face but she didn't pull away. He was glad. She matched her steps to his slow shuffle as he made his way down the stairs again. Her hand was small, dwarfed by his.

"I thought you were crazy for insisting Amelie might return and that I should be ready," he said. "What happened to all of that determination?"

"What good did it do me? Amelie's gone. The house ... this place ..." She sounded hopeless as they stepped out onto the lower gallery and headed for the garden.

"It wasn't until I buried my sister in the Baudier mausoleum today that I understood what you've been trying to tell me. This place, this land, is our birthright. It's been in my family since 1720. Somehow, some way, I have to restore *Belle Fleuve* and build a life for those children. Talking with Bolton has given me a glimmer of hope. We—"

She cut him off.

"I'm so happy you've had that epiphany, Colin." She clasped her hands and turned away, then walked over to the long windows overlooking the garden maze. "That will free me to go back to New Orleans."

"You can't." Suddenly he didn't want her going anywhere. "I'm barely on my feet."

"You're getting stronger every day." She continued to gaze toward the river. "I ... I must go. I've found work with the architect Roger Jamison. It's a wonderful opportunity to finally put my training to work and become a professional. I can no longer afford to work on drawings in my spare time." Her brow creased with worry. "Because I need ... to be useful." She seemed hesitant to say more.

"I think you may have misunderstood when I said that I would care for Amelie's children."

"You're not going to?" Kate asked.

"Yes, of course I am, but I can't do it alone."

He crossed the room, took hold of her hand, and watched the color leave her face. He wasn't saying anything correctly.

"I can't do this alone, Kate. I need you here pushing and prodding. I need someone who won't quit when things get tough."

She turned. "What are you saying?"

"You can't leave. Not yet."

She laughed, but there was no warmth in it. "A month ago you couldn't wait to see the last of me."

"The children need you." He couldn't imagine dealing with them on his own. When he had no idea what to say to them, Kate did. If it hadn't been for her the house would still be a shambles and he'd be wallowing in self-pity.

"I'll see them often. In fact, I've been thinking of ways we could share—"

"I need you *here*, Kate. We all do."

He needed her to keep him from crawling back into the darkness, but to tell her that would make him feel less than a man.

"Please, Kate, for the children. Stay."

They had paused beneath an oak draped with Spanish moss,

a tree that had seen generations of his mother's family grow and prosper. He let go of Kate's hand, cupped her chin, and made her look up at him.

"At least give me time to come up with a plan." He paused a moment and then smiled. "Unless you already have one?"

"My plan is to move back to town and lose myself in work."

"Just give me a few more weeks. A month at most."

Her gaze searched his face, but she was the first to look away.

"Two weeks," she said with a sigh. "I suppose I can stay two more weeks."

He grabbed her hand again, raised it to his lips, and kissed it.

"Thank you, Kate. After the way I treated you, that's more than I deserve."

Stunned, Kate watched him walk away. The sound of Eugenie's voice as she called out to Damian drifted on the still air. Watching Colin negotiate the path back to the *garçonnière*, Kate placed her palm over the back of her hand where he'd kissed it and closed her eyes. Was her skin really hot to the touch or was she imagining it?

She'd waited years for him to notice her, to see her as something more than Amelie's best friend. She'd waited years to step out of the shadows of this house and have him truly *see* her.

I need you, Kate. Stay for the children.

Stay for the children, not for him.

She opened her eyes to the brightness of one of the saddest days of her life. The sun was shining on the river, dancing like diamonds on the water. The recent storm had turned the leaves and grass bright green. Hidden promise in the soil was waiting to be awakened. She walked over and touched her palm to the rough trunk of the ancient oak and wondered if Colin would find a way.

Two weeks.

She would stay because he needed her, and when she left, she'd leave the better part of her heart behind.

Somehow Kate made it through the evening meal with Myra and the children and saw them tucked in for the night. With the walls closing in on her, she put on a wrap, slipped outside, and found herself at the Baudier crypt. A wrought-iron bench had been placed near a huge cement urn that held a fern so overgrown its roots hung over the lip.

Somewhere an owl hooted. Kate wasn't aware of time. She had no idea how long she'd been sitting in the dark alone when she heard a twig snap behind her. Turning, she thought she saw movement near the oaks, but there was nothing but shadows. A chill went down her spine. A few erratic heartbeats later, Kate saw Eugenie walking toward her.

"Miss Kate, you best come inside. No sense in your sittin' out here in the dark by yourself."

"Night or day, it's just as dark." Kate slid over to one side of the bench and patted the space next to her. Eugenie hesitated before she finally sat down.

"The sadness will ease. You'll see," Eugenie said.

"How do you know?" Kate realized how harsh she sounded. "I'm sorry," she added, immediately contrite. Surely Eugenie had suffered a life that was unimaginable. "That sounded as if I have absolutely no feelings. I'm truly sorry."

"No need to apologize. You're just hurtin'."

Kate thought of the children upstairs aching for their mother, knowing Amelie was out here in the dark. Kate detested the raw hopelessness that held her in its grip.

Eugenie's voice cut through the silence. "I didn't think I could go on when my son went missin'," she said.

"Tell me about him." Eugenie needed to talk as much as Kate needed to take her mind off her own sorrow.

"Mica was fifteen, but he was a big, strappin' boy and always willin' to work alongside his daddy and the others. We were so scared the Union soldiers garrisoned here were gonna conscript him into the army that we kept him busy and out of the way. When the day came that Miss Marie decided to move up to her cousins' place, she had us load up a wagon with the furniture from her room, some linens, and a few of her clothes. The soldiers had taken most everything else, the silver, the china, odds and ends. Miss Marie was frantic and looked wild around the eyes, you know?"

"Was she ill by then?"

"She was thin. Didn't eat much. None of us did 'cause there wasn't much to eat. She was sick at heart. We got the things she wanted packed up ready and told Mica to drive her up River Road to her cousins' place."

Eugenie pleated the skirt of her black gown with her fingers and smoothed it out again. "That's the last time we saw him."

"Would he have run off?"

"No. Never."

"Do you think he was conscripted? Or maybe he went off to fight in a colored regiment."

Eugenie shrugged. "Not without tellin' us. A couple of days later Simon went up the trail and found the wagon. Everything in it was gone, so he went on to the Baudiers' and found Miss Marie there, but by then she was too far gone to tell him what happened."

"Too far gone?"

Eugenie was quiet for a long while before Kate heard her whisper, "She finally lost her mind, Miss Kate. Simon said it was one of the worst things he ever seen."

"Did you tell Colin?"

"He don't need to carry that burden too." She cleared her throat. "We searched the road all the way to Baton Rouge, but there was no sign of Mica. Simon's got a sister up in Cleveland. We found her, but there was no work anyplace with so many newly freed folks lookin' for jobs up north. We couldn't stand the cold, so we headed south and lived here and there. Did what we could until we ended up back here at *Belle Fleuve*. I'm sure the Lord led us home, 'cause two months after we came back, Mr. Colin comes ridin' in 'bout ready to collapse, and we were here to look after him."

"That was a blessing," Kate agreed.

"God always sees us through the darkness, Miss Kate. He'll see you through this."

Kate was used to managing everything, pushing and prodding, lifting everyone else's spirit, fighting to make things right. Now the fight in her was gone.

"I hope so."

"I know so." When the owl hooted again, Eugenie got to her feet. "You better come on in with me now. It's gettin' damp out here."

"I'll be in shortly."

"You promise?"

"I promise. Just a few minutes more."

As soon as she was alone Kate walked through the darkness to the crypt. Whitewashed plaster was cracked and peeling off the thick walls that were shaped like a miniature domed church. Beneath the cross at the apex, Kate pressed her forehead against the cold metal door.

She closed her eyes and saw Amelie as a carefree thirteen-year-old, laughing, dancing, smiling.

"Good-bye, my friend," she whispered. "Good-bye, Amelie."

TWELVE

Three days after the burial, Kate still hadn't found the inspiration she needed to begin her assignment for Roger Jamison. With Damian and Marie under Eugenie's watchful eye, Kate made her way to the main house to find Myra so she could tell her about their finances. Walking along the gallery she heard Colin's voice coming from one of the back sitting rooms. She paused outside the open French doors and found him inside with Jason Bolton.

"Kate." He waved her in. "Join us."

Feeling fragile, she had taken great care to avoid him lately.

"I was just looking for Myra," she said before greeting Jason and asking after his wife. She had paused in the open doorway. "I'm sorry for the intrusion."

"I'd like you to stay," Colin said, "if you have a minute."

She was in no hurry to find Myra so she stepped inside.

"I wanted to ask you about the crew you hired for repairs," Colin said. "I've offered Jason the foreman's house where he grew up. It'll take some fixing, but he's willing to refurbish it and live there in lieu of pay until we harvest our first crop."

She looked at each man in turn. Jason looked fine with his fair hair and eyes, but he couldn't hold a candle to Colin's compellingly dark eyes and rugged features. She lost herself in Colin's intense gaze.

"What kind of crop?" Kate struggled to focus.

"Cane. As always," Colin said.

Jason interjected, "Cotton is doing just as well, but this land has always produced fine sugarcane and there's quite a demand since the war. Hopefully it won't take much to get the old sugarhouse shored up."

"So there *is* a sugarhouse here?" she asked. Dan Rosen had mentioned refurbishing it.

Colin nodded. "What were you thinking about it?" He indicated Kate should sit.

She remained standing. "Simon gathered the work crew for me. They did an excellent job."

"He's already assured me he can round up all the field workers we can afford," Colin addressed Kate and Jason both. "At best it will be a skeleton crew."

Jason added, "Since I've been back, I've met with the other cane planters up and down the road. Unlike cotton farmers, most of them aren't sharecropping their land yet. The labor demands with cane are too great and the freedmen know it, so they have some bargaining power. Most of the planters have finally reconciled to paying for labor, but it hasn't come without violence."

"I'll have no violence here. I've lived through enough of it to last a lifetime," Colin insisted.

"How will you pay them?" Wishing she could help, Kate's heart sank.

"We'll negotiate a fair wage and provide housing. Perhaps even open a store where workers can purchase goods using credit tokens. They'll be able to borrow against the crop," Jason explained.

"I banked my soldier's pay for the past three years. It's not much, but it should help get us started. It's fall now. If we can get the crop in, we'll be able to harvest the cane a year from now."

Now, thanks to Jason's arrival, there was more than a hint of the man Colin used to be.

Jason slipped his watch out, opened the lid, and checked the time.

"I told Cora I wouldn't be long," he said, rising. "She's a bit jittery with the baby on the way. I'd better head back."

Colin was slow to his feet but no longer needed help. He grabbed his cane and indicated that Jason and Kate precede him. Kate stepped onto the gallery into a cool breeze that dropped the temperature in the shade.

She walked to the edge of the gallery with Colin and stood with him in a pool of sunlight until Jason mounted up and rode away. Colin turned to her and asked, "What are you up to this morning?"

It was hard to concentrate so close to him. "I was looking for Myra. I think she's in the garden."

"She's out there so often I'm beginning to think she's searching for Mama's buried treasure. Damian does nothing else."

"Myra loves roses."

"And the children?"

"In the kitchen with Eugenie. She's teaching them to make hushpuppies."

"Hopefully, she's not serving them for dinner."

"I'm sure they'll turn out just fine."

"Obviously, you didn't taste the grits they made yesterday."

Kate hid a smile, tempted to ask if he would join them for supper. He still took his meals alone in the *garçonnière* but she hoped that soon he'd share them with the children in the main house.

"How are they getting along?" His concern was written on his face.

"It's only been a few days, Colin."

"I know exactly how long it's been. I just wondered what you've observed."

"Damian spends most of his time in a fantasy world pretending to be a pirate. He nearly gave Myra a heart attack yesterday when he launched himself off the sideboard at her."

Colin chuckled. Kate smiled for an instant.

"Marie isn't doing as well. She's naturally shy and can't express herself, or won't. I'm going to give her a watercolor lesson later this afternoon. Perhaps she'll open up and talk to me."

"Can you help her much in less than two weeks?"

Her self-imposed deadline was quickly approaching. Colin was studying her closely.

"I really need to speak to Myra." Uncomfortable, Kate started to step off the brick gallery floor onto the drive.

"Wait." He caught her arm, forcing her to stop.

When he lifted his hand and reached toward her cheek, Kate's breath caught. She watched in silence as he leaned closer. His fingertips grazed her cheek and then he wrapped the escaped tendrils of her hair around his index finger and gently untangled them from the hinge of her glasses.

"There." He leaned back. "Now you can be on your way."

Kate's heart was still racing as she rounded the corner of the house and spied Myra kneeling in Marie Delany's rose garden. Since the burial Myra had spent every spare moment on her knees attacking weeds and turning the earth around the base of the bushes.

Myra looked up as Kate approached and started to rise. "Are the children finished?"

Kate shook her head no and waved her back down. She sat on the ground near Myra, carefully tucking her skirt and petticoat around her ankles.

"You'll dirty your skirt." Myra leaned back and wiped her brow with her sleeve.

Kate smiled. "Always watching out for me," she noted. "The dirt will shake off. The children are still busy cooking. I'm here because there's something important we need to discuss."

"You sound very serious, Katie Keene."

"I am."

"I've been wantin' to talk to you too."

"Let me start." *Before I lose my nerve.* Kate reached for a weed, twisted it, and gave it a tug, then tossed it onto Myra's pile. "There's no easy way to say this."

"Then out with it."

"I met with Dan Rosen in New Orleans, and he warned me that I've nearly gone through my inheritance."

Myra's blue eyes widened before she dropped her gaze to the weeds again. "I started worryin' back when you paid off the back taxes on this place. What will you do?"

"Fortunately, I found work while I was in the city, and I've given up our suite at the St. Charles. We'll find a modest place to live, but I'm afraid I won't be able to pay you much of a salary, at least not until I'm established."

"It won't be easy for you," Myra warned. "Dabblin' in men's work."

Kate didn't have the energy to argue.

"I don't see it as dabbling. If I'm frugal I'll make enough to support us both."

"You don't need a nanny anymore, Kate."

"Of course I don't, but we've been together forever."

"Aye." Myra set down her trowel and rubbed her hands together to dislodge the dirt. "I was only nineteen when the Keenes hired me. Thought I'd be tending to an infant until I found out they adopted a seven-year-old."

"If you want to find other employment, I'll understand." Kate couldn't imagine life without Myra O'Hara in it.

She waited for Myra to agree, but the woman remained silent and picked up the trowel again.

"I've been thinkin' of the future a lot lately, what with Miss Amelie up and dying so young. I'm near forty now and if I'm ever going to have a life of my own, it's high time I start goin' about it. I've decided to move back to Ireland."

"Ireland?"

"It's my home, you know. I still know plenty of folks there." Myra's blush gave her away.

"Is there someone special waiting for you?" Kate clasped her hands together in her lap. "Is that it?"

Myra studied the basket without looking up. When she finally met Kate's eyes, hers were aglow.

"Aye. There is and I turned him down when we left, but he said he'd wait for as long as it took me to change my mind. When we buried Miss Amelie, I decided it's time to see if he's still waitin'."

"Oh, Myra." Kate blinked away tears.

"Now don't go carrying on, Katie Keene. I'm worried about how you're going to get on alone as it is."

Kate raised the hem of her skirt and slipped it beneath her spectacles to wipe away her tears. She thought of all the years they'd been together, their wartime journeys. Gil Keene had trusted the young Irish woman enough to accompany Kate halfway around the world. To have found and lost Amelie and now to lose Myra—there was no denying it hurt. Kate smiled to hide her pain.

"I'll get on just fine. You can count on that. You must follow your heart." Kate grabbed Myra's hands. "Just remember you'll always have a home with me."

"I hate leavin' you at a time like this."

Kate pulled another weed. "I feel as if I've fallen down a deep, dark well. I felt sad when my father died, but nothing like this."

Myra set her trowel down and brushed off her hands. Then she leaned back against her heels.

"That's because your father lived a long, full life. Amelie was too young to suffer the way she did, and from what those children have said now and again, I know their life in Kansas wasn't easy."

"No, it wasn't. They certainly deserve more than what they've had." Was leaving the children alone with Colin the best thing for them? Surely they were better off here than they were in Kansas.

"I was so lucky to have the life I was given," Kate said, thinking aloud.

"There were times when I wondered, though," Myra said softly. "You had everything money could buy, Katie, but were you happy as a child? Did you resent the way the Keenes left you on your own?"

"I think I was happy. When I remembered what it was like to have parents and sisters and all the laughter and tears that come with family, I felt alone, but those memories faded. I always had you. And I had permission to come to *Belle Fleuve* as often as the Delanys would have me. But many times I wondered why Gil and Nola ever adopted me."

Myra didn't look up but appeared to be concentrating on the pile of weeds.

"Do you know why?" Kate asked.

"Only servants' talk, is all."

"Tell me."

"Nola Keene was a good twenty years younger than your father and proud of the standin' his money gave her in New Orleans society," Myra said.

"I've been fairly certain for years that she married him for his money."

Myra nodded. "What I heard was one day Nola took it in her head to adopt an Irish orphan to set an example for her high society Irish friends. Didn't want a babe, though. Wasn't about t' be puttin' up with any crying or messes. You were a smart, biddable little thing. Sharp as a tack and quiet as a mouse. I always thought that was why she chose you."

"My father always gave in to her."

Myra nodded. "That he did. She wasn't cut out to be a mother, but Gil Keene loved you, no doubt about it. But that man was fifty when they adopted you and he was already set in his ways. Business was his life."

"Which is why they were never around. He was always happier in town."

"And Nola wouldn't ever miss a fancy soiree. At first she used to dress you up and show you off at all the ladies' gatherings, lording it over her friends, tellin' them it was their civic duty to take in one of the many poor Irish children left orphaned by the yellow fever epidemic. It riled me to no end when she got bored and left you on your own."

"I didn't mind. Besides, Amelie and I would never have become such close friends if my father hadn't brought me on a visit to *Belle Fleuve* to meet Patrick Delany's daughter."

"Your father did the best he could. No one thought the war would go on as long as it did or that the South would end up in ashes. Sendin' you away was a blessing." Myra adjusted the wide-brimmed straw hat Eugenie had loaned her to keep the sun off her face.

"How soon will you leave for Ireland?" Kate couldn't bear to think of losing Myra but would never stand in the way of her happiness.

"As soon as you give me leave to go."

"As soon as you can pack then. Life is far too short to waste. I'll send word we need a carriage from town."

"Simon can take me to the river landing down the road. I'd rather buy a steamboat ticket than face the long ride to the city." She studied Kate. "When will you move back to New Orleans?"

"The day of the burial I told Colin I'd only stay two weeks more."

"Eleven days left."

Kate nodded. Eleven days. *So few.*

"You could work here and make trips into town when you need to."

"The longer I'm here the more the children will come to depend on me. Colin is on his feet now. There's no need for me to stay." If she stayed much longer she ran the risk of losing her heart.

"Can't you see what's right in front of your face, Katie?"

"What do you mean?"

"You love this place and those poor children. Colin may be on his feet but he still needs your help. You'll never know what might be if you run away, Katie. What happened to the girl who walked up to the door o' that *garçonnière* willing to face whatever she found inside? Where did she go?"

THIRTEEN

Colin slowly made his way to the house, eager to find Kate. The small successes of each passing day were bittersweet, for as he gained strength in his injured ankle, Kate's time here grew shorter.

He wandered through the first-floor rooms in search of her. She'd set up a work table in one of the dining rooms but he rarely found her there. He paused to look at the plans and paperwork spread over the table.

Sitting atop the plans was a wood carving of *Belle Fleuve* no bigger than his palm and carved with intricate detail. Colin marveled at the craftsmanship. When he turned it over, he saw that Simon had carved his name on the bottom in small, even letters. How little he knew about the couple that had served his family all his life. Colin set down the carving and turned his attention to Kate's plans.

The open drawings were not the ones commissioned by Jamison, but were plans for *Belle Fleuve*. The original section of the house hadn't been touched, but she'd rearranged a few walls, added closets, and moved the kitchen closer to the main structure. Not only that, but there were two additional bedroom wings added to each side of the house and a twin *garçonnière* placed opposite the one he inhabited.

The pages were filled with well-planned, well-balanced additions and renovations. Kate had done nothing that would change the integrity or feel of the house. The thought and love she had put into each and every line was evident, and her talent was more than impressive.

There were notes from Roger Jamison, but Colin saw no evidence that she'd been working on any new plans, and he suddenly felt guilty for relying on her to spend so much time with the children.

As he was arranging the plans the way she'd left them, his hand grazed the stack of Delany family photographs he'd last seen on Amelie's bedside table.

He looked through them again, stared at the images of his family, and whispered, "I lost my way, but I promise that I'll make it up to all of you."

On the opposite side of the house, Kate was waiting for Myra on the lower gallery when she heard her footsteps on the stairs. Kate watched her descend. Her companion was outfitted in a black traveling ensemble and a jaunty black hat with a bobbing peacock feather.

"I can't believe this day has come," Kate said.

Simon had already loaded Myra's bags.

"I'll write you as soon as I get to Ireland," Myra promised. "Where should I send the letter?"

"The St. Charles. I can always collect mail there."

"I've been thinkin' a bit more on your situation," Myra said.

Kate felt her heart drop to her toes as she waited for what Myra had to say.

"Sometimes we don't see what's right in front of our faces. It took Miss Amelie's death to make me realize what I truly wanted. Stubborn determination has gotten you this far, Katie. You've learned your craft despite the odds, and now you have work as an architect. You made certain the house was ready to receive Miss Amelie when she needed it, and you've gotten Colin back on his feet. Don't let your stubbornness stand in your way."

"In the way of what?"

"Don't spend your life alone."

"Oh, Myra, it's not that easy."

Myra nodded. "Just remember, only you can decide where you belong."

Kate had no chance to respond before Eugenie joined them. Colin and the children were soon there to bid Myra farewell too. Kate hugged Myra tightly one last time. Simon helped Myra board the wagon as Kate wiped away tears of joy for Myra mingled with tears of sorrow over another parting.

Settled on the wagon seat, Myra smiled through her own tears and waved good-bye.

Kate and the others watched the wagon roll down the drive toward River Road, and when it all but disappeared, Eugenie announced the noon meal was ready. She collected the children and suddenly Kate was alone with Colin.

"Are you all right, Kate?"

"I'll be fine." *Someday. Somehow.* She took a deep breath, took off her spectacles, and used the ruffle on the edges of her sleeves to wipe them. "Did you have a successful morning?"

Colin let his gaze wander out over the yard.

"Jason and I interviewed the men who showed up at dawn looking for work. All were experienced cane field hands. We hired six with families. They'll have a reason to stay and make a life at *Belle Fleuve.* Each family will have their own cabin. The eight single men we also hired will be divided between the remaining two cabins."

He'd taken on a lot of help and all of them would be banking on a viable crop.

"We believe we've hired a good crew," he went on. "We'll know soon enough. Tomorrow they start moving in and will have time to plant garden plots behind their cabins. There's plenty of fish and game around, and for a time I'll be able to provide a few staples. We need to get the first crop in the ground by the end of October."

"I'm so happy for you."

"I might still be hiding in the *garçonnière* if it weren't for you."

She shook her head. "You'd have roused yourself when Amelie arrived regardless of my being here or not."

He shrugged. "Thanks to you, the house was ready. I hate to admit it, but you and Eugenie may have been right; using my ankle seems to be making it stronger. As long as I don't overdo."

"I'm glad."

"I looked over your plans for *Belle Fleuve* earlier," Colin said as they lingered.

"You did?" Kate turned in surprise, Myra's departure momentarily forgotten. She never imagined he'd take an interest. She never imagined he spent any time thinking about her at all.

"They're wonderful," he said. "How is your work for Jamison coming along?"

"Not well." It wasn't concentration she lacked but inspiration. Her heart wasn't in the project Jamison had turned over to her.

"You were obviously inspired when you drew the plans for *Belle Fleuve*. I could tell they were a labor of love."

"It was something I always wanted to do for all of you."

"Someday I'll be able to pay you for them, unless your work becomes so famous that I cannot afford to. Rest assured I intend to repay you for the repairs to the house."

"They were my gift to Amelie and the children."

"I will repay you regardless." His tone brooked no argument.

Of course he would insist. He still had his pride. Her conscience nagged her to tell him about the back taxes, but this wasn't the time to heap more debt on him. Not after he had spent the morning hiring workers who he hoped to pay from the proceeds of a crop that wasn't even planted yet.

"Shall we go see what Eugenie has for lunch?" he suggested.

"This morning the children learned to make corn pone."

He shrugged. "I survived the grits and hushpuppies. I guess their corn pone won't kill me."

After the noon meal, Kate set up a table for Marie at one end of the second-floor gallery. A slice of sunlight poured across the white sheet of paper on the small table in front of the girl, highlighting her work.

"That's actually very lovely." Kate studied Marie's watercolor. She'd placed a single yellow rose on the table and asked the girl to try to copy it using techniques she'd demonstrated earlier. For a first effort, Marie had done quite well.

"Better than Mama's beets?"

Kate smoothed her hands over the girl's dark curls. "Much better."

"Maybe I'll give one of my paintings to Uncle Colin."

"That's a fine idea. I'm sure he'd like that."

Marie didn't look up as she dipped the tip of her brush in clear water and touched it to the page. "May I give this one to Eugenie?"

"Of course. Your work is yours to do with as you wish."

Marie's smile didn't reach her eyes. "If I had learned before now I could have made something for Myra too."

Ignoring Myra's departure was as impossible for Kate as overcoming her recent sadness. Seated in the warm fall sunshine, she tried to convince herself she was more than ready to be on her own. She had done what she came to do. Colin was on his feet and getting stronger every day. The children were adjusting step by step, though Damian needed a firm hand and Marie still dealt with bouts of tears.

Kate leaned back in her chair and studied Marie. The child's skin was flawless, the tan fading from where she had been exposed to too much relentless prairie sun. Kate would leave a bottle of almond lotion behind and have Eugenie encourage the girl to use it.

"Mama always told us she was your best friend." Marie set her brush down carefully and folded her hands in her lap.

"That's right."

"She said you did everything together when you were girls."

"We did."

"Did you ever get into trouble?"

Kate found herself smiling. "Oh, we were in big trouble one time. We tracked Colin and his friends to the swimming hole. By the time we found them, they were already swimming, so we sneaked up and took their clothes."

Marie's eyes grew wide as flapjacks. "How did they get home with no clothes?"

"We hid the clothes just a little ways upstream and were long gone before they noticed their things were missing. They hid behind palmetto fronds and wandered around till they found their clothes."

"What happened then?"

Kate chuckled. "We'd run home and hidden in the stables. Just before dark, Colin flushed us out, which was a good thing, because we were afraid of spending the night out there."

"Did you get the switch?"

Kate shook her head. "Of course not. It was just a harmless prank. Your grandfather Delany made us apologize and promise not to do it again. The idea of Colin and all his friends parading around naked as Adam except for huge palmetto leaves had Amelie and me laughing so hard that we fell into bed and had to cover our heads with our pillows."

"Did you stay here a lot?"

"All the time."

"What about your parents? Didn't they miss you?"

"Not really. They led very busy lives before they adopted me and afterward as well."

"What happened to your real parents?"

"They died of yellow fever, one right after the other."

"Like my daddy and mama. One right after the other. Were you all by yourself then?"

"I had three sisters. All of them were adopted." At least she hoped so.

Marie's eyes widened. "You were an orphan too."

"Just like you. Except that my uncle didn't keep us. He took me and my little sister to an orphan asylum when he couldn't afford to feed us."

Horror filled Marie's eyes. "He left you at an *orphanage?*"

Too late, Kate realized what she'd just done.

"Yes, but you don't have to worry. Colin is a fine man. He would never do that to you. *Never.*"

Kate hoped she was right, but what if Colin were to fall on dire straits? What if his crop failed and he was forced to abandon *Belle Fleuve?*

"Besides, if anything ever happened to Colin and for some reason he couldn't keep you, then I would."

"You must be very sad without Mama in the world."

Kate didn't try to smile or mask her own hurt. "I miss her very much. I know you're still very sad too."

Marie nodded and reached for Kate's hand. "I miss her something awful. But don't worry, Aunt Kate. We have each other now."

Colin walked up the gallery stairs, his progress slow but steady. When he reached the top he saw Kate and Marie sitting in a wide swatch of sunlight at the far end of the porch. Watercolor supplies were crowded together on a small table, but the two ignored them as they sat side by side, Marie holding Kate's hand tightly. He heard Marie tell Kate, "We have each other now."

Not for long.

He wished there was a way to convince Kate to stay.

He would have been content to watch them a while longer, but his ankle hurt. Kate must have sensed his presence for she turned his way. She rose from her chair and smoothed her black skirt.

"Colin." Kate hurried toward him. "Come see Marie's painting."

She led him over to the chair she had vacated, and he lowered himself into it. He noticed the rose in the center of the table. Marie had done a credible job of copying it.

"That's very good." He nodded toward the painting.

"Do you know what it is?" His niece waited.

"I believe it's a yellow rose."

Marie beamed. "It *is* a rose, Uncle Colin."

"Of course it is."

"I was afraid you'd say it was a beet." Marie laughed.

"Well, it's not the right color."

Kate was standing at his shoulder. Even if he hadn't seen her, he would have felt her presence and welcomed it.

"She's doing very well for her first day, don't you think?" Kate asked.

"She is, indeed."

Marie picked up her brush again and pulled out a clean sheet of paper. She was in the act of rubbing her brush over a slice of green paint when Colin looked back and noted that Kate's smile was far too tepid.

"Will you be all right with Myra gone?"

"Of course. I'm happy for her. She was excited to be going home to Ireland." She shrugged. "Who knows, someday I may even visit her."

"Are you still moving back to New Orleans next week?"

Marie's hand slipped and the brush tore the page. She knocked over the tall water glass in front of her. Water poured over the edge of the table. The child jumped to her feet, oblivious to the glass when it fell off the table and onto the wooden gallery floor. Thankfully it didn't break, though it rolled perilously close to the edge of the porch before it stopped.

"Are you *leaving*?" Marie demanded.

Kate opened her mouth but nothing came out, and she turned to Colin.

"Kate is just moving back to New Orleans. She won't be far."
His explanation fell short of what the child wanted to hear. Marie
looked back and forth between the two of them.

"But you *can't* leave. Tell her Uncle Colin. She can't leave. You
aren't married yet."

"Marie ..." Kate extended a hand toward the girl. "I can
explain."

"You promised Mama. I heard you. I was in the hallway the
day you both promised you'd get married and take care of us."

Colin stared at the girl in shock. She'd heard the promise to
Amelie?

"I will take care of you, darling," Kate said.

"How can you take care of us if you are not even *here*?" Marie's
breath caught on a sob. "Who will keep Uncle Colin from taking
us to the orphanage? How could you lie to Mama like that?"

"What orphanage?" Colin turned to Kate. Her eyes were huge
behind her glasses. What had she told Marie?

As Marie started to rush past them, Kate reached for her arm,
but Marie shook her off and headed down the stairs. The new shoes
Kate bought her beat out a tattoo all the way down. When the girl's
footsteps faded along the lower gallery, Kate turned to question
Colin.

"How could you just blurt that out?"

He shrugged. "No matter who told her or when, it all boils
down to the same thing: You are leaving."

"You should have let me explain in my own way."

As Kate's gaze drifted toward the river, he stood up. The chair
scraped across the floor but she didn't turn to him. Water was still
dripping from the table with soft plops as he crossed the gallery and
walked up behind her.

"We did promise, Kate." Was it so crazy to think they should
marry? They would already be sharing the responsibility for the
children. She was living in his house. Marriages had been built on
far less.

"What are you saying?" As she raised her eyes, he was shocked by an inexplicable urge to kiss her.

"Seeing you sitting here with Marie just now, the two of you with your heads together like that, I'm thinking Amelie might be right."

"Right?"

"We should get married."

"You said you wouldn't hold me to it."

"I won't, but why can't I still try to convince you? What was all that about my taking them to an orphanage?"

"I was hoping to gain her trust, telling her about my childhood. Letting her know that she never has to worry and that she'll never end up in an orphanage the way I did."

"I'd say that backfired. You were in an orphanage?"

"I was six when my uncle handed my little sister Sarah and me over to an orphan asylum in New Orleans after our parents died." She paused. "Surely you knew I was adopted. It was no secret."

He shook his head. "I don't recall. What did I care about your life, Kate? You were a child, and I was a carefree, self-centered young man back then."

Just then they heard footsteps on the stairs again. Marie was dragging Damian by the hand. He had a white rag tied around his head in pirate fashion and dirt stains on his shirtfront. He was carrying a wooden sword but let go the minute he started running headlong at Kate. The sword clattered onto the gallery floor. Damian wrapped his arms around her and hung on tightly.

"You can't go, Aunt Kate!" His shout was muffled by her clothing. "Don't leave us! Please, don't leave us!"

"Do you see, Aunt Kate?" Marie stood away from them, tapping her foot, hands planted on her hips. Her cheeks were flushed and tearstained. "Do you see what you've done? You can't leave us."

"You were 'posed to marry Uncle Colin," Damian cried. "And take care of us forever."

"What now, Kate?" Colin stared at her over Damian's head.

"This is hardly fair."

"Life isn't fair."

She managed to unclamp Damian's arms from around her waist. She held them tightly and knelt down.

"Listen to me, Damian. Please."

He tried to twist away and drew back his foot to kick her. Colin shoved his cane in front of the boy's ankle.

"Gentlemen do not kick," he warned.

Damian wiped his tears on his shirtsleeve.

"Gentlemen should keep their promises!" Marie shouted. She turned on Kate. "Ladies too!"

Damian howled. "Uncle Colin, don't let Kate leave!"

Kate's tone was soft but firm. "Stop it, Damian. Crying isn't going to help. Stop now."

He stopped shrieking and started hiccupping a string of sobs. Marie put her arm around his shoulders and stared defiantly at Kate.

"You *promised* Mama you would stay."

"Marie," Colin said, "I'd like to speak to Kate alone. Please take your brother downstairs."

"Make her stay," Marie pleaded.

"Go," Colin ordered.

Marie grabbed Damian's hand and started toward the stairs to the lower gallery.

"My sword!" He stopped and ran back, grabbed the wooden sword that was nearly as long as he was tall.

"Where did you get that?" Kate's concern for Damian's safety took precedence over their conversation. "It doesn't look safe to me."

"Simon made it for him," Colin said. "Damian and I had a talk earlier. He swore a pirate oath not to use it on anyone."

Marie was still crying, wiping her tears as fast as they fell.

"Go on now," Colin told them.

Their footsteps echoed against Kate's heart as they walked away with their heads down and steps heavy. Damian's sword knocked against every step as it dragged along behind him.

Colin waited until they were out of earshot before speaking. "I'm sorry, Kate. I should have let you tell them."

The sight of their tearstained faces came back to her with a rush of sadness.

"We did promise Amelie," Colin reminded her.

"You forced me."

"Maybe it isn't such a bad idea. You belong here at *Belle Fleuve* as much as any of us." He stepped closer, touching her cheek.

"But ..."

"You love the children. You loved my sister. This place is your heart. Even if you don't love me, perhaps the best thing we could do for them is consider getting married."

She wanted to tell him that she *had* loved him when she was a child. She had longed to see him again through all the years of their separation. Since their reunion that day in the *garçonnière*, her feelings for him may have dimmed due to his attitude toward her, but they had never really faded. Yes, she cared for him. She loved him still, which was why she hesitated to enter into a one-sided marriage.

"Did you know my parents' marriage was arranged?" Colin was intent on arguing his case. "The Baudiers were bankrupt, and my mother married Patrick Delany to save this place."

"But they were so in love." His revelation was shocking. Had Amelie known?

"They grew to love each other very much."

He was so close that if she stood on tiptoe, their lips would meet. *What if?* she wondered briefly.

She came to her senses and stepped away. Walking to the gallery railing, Kate drew her arms around herself and stared down the lane bordered by oaks.

Colin walked up beside her. She heard his voice near her ear, felt his warm breath against her cheek as he leaned closer.

"Will you at least consider it, Kate? I'm sure there are worse things than marrying me."

I'm sure there are worse things than marrying me.

Not exactly the proposal a woman dreams of.

What excuse had Kate made when she left him standing alone on the upper gallery that afternoon? She recalled mumbling something before she ran off.

Marrying Colin Delany had been her lifelong dream. But now?

She was no longer a starry-eyed child. Could she settle for being his wife and hope that love might grow as a by-product of their union? Could she stake her future on the unknown for the sake of Amelie's children?

Kate slipped a wrapper over her nightdress and went down the hall to tuck in the children for the night. They were seated on the floor shoulder to shoulder. *A Pirate's Tale* lay open in Marie's lap. They both looked up when Kate walked in, but neither of them smiled. They were too young to have eyes so full of worry.

"Time for bed." Kate kept her tone cheerful.

Marie closed the book. Unsmiling, she got to her feet and pulled Damian up off the floor. She placed the book on her bed-side table. Kate turned down the covers on Damian's bed and then Marie's. The children knelt on the floor at their bedsides as they did every night. They folded their hands and pressed their foreheads against them.

"God bless Mama and Uncle Colin and Aunt Kate and Myra and Eugenie and Simon," Marie began.

"God bless Mama's kin up in heaven and Great-Granddaddy Hart," Damian added.

"Please don't let Uncle Colin take us to an orphanage," Marie finished.

Kate closed her eyes as the children said amen and climbed into their beds. She tucked the covers around Damian.

"Thank you, Aunt Kate," he whispered. She kissed him on the cheek and then tucked in Marie.

"I hope you both know that your uncle would never take you to an orphanage. Never."

"We're sorry, Aunt Kate." Tears shimmered in Marie's eyes. "I'm sorry I yelled at you today. I'm sorry I acted so terrible."

"Me too," Damian mumbled. "I was scared."

"I'm still scared," Marie whispered.

"I am too," Kate admitted as she lowered herself to the edge of Damian's bed. He slipped his arm out from under the covers and reached for her hand. Her heart melted.

"What are you scared of?" Marie said. "If you're afraid of moving to the city, then don't go."

The notion of staying here and giving in to her desire frightened her more than moving to New Orleans.

"Sometimes grown-ups get scared when they don't know what to do," she said.

"Ask for help when you say your prayers tonight. That's what Mama always did." Damian nodded and smiled encouragement.

Kate turned to Marie. "You forgot to mention your father in your prayers."

"I don't think Daddy's in heaven," Marie said.

"'Cause he was a gunfighter," Damian added.

Marie sighed. "No, but now that Mama's up in heaven, I hope he's not. He wasn't nice, Aunt Kate. I don't want them meeting up again."

"I see." Kate pondered a moment. "But bad things don't happen in heaven."

"I expect not," Marie agreed.

"I hope I get to heaven," Damian said. "At least then I won't have to worry about getting taken to an orphanage."

Kate closed her eyes and sighed. "You will never end up in an orphanage. I promise."

When she opened her eyes, Marie was pinning her with a hard stare. "The way you promised Mama you'd marry Uncle Colin?"

Sleep was out of the question, so Kate returned to her room and closed the window to the cool, dry fall evening. Outside, the river was hidden by the darkness but still flowing toward the gulf, a certainty in an uncertain world. A single light was shining in the *garçonnière*. Was Colin just as restless? Did he regret proposing?

For the hundredth time that night, Kate weighed her options. She might be in financial straits, but she had talent. She needed to prove it to Roger Jamison. Waiting for inspiration wasn't going to pay for her lodgings or put food on the table. Inspired or not, she needed to complete the work Jamison assigned. If she chose to stay on at *Belle Fleuve*, the money she made would help them all.

Colin's revelation about his parents had been a shock. How long had Patrick and Marie been married before they fell in love? How had Marie ever found the courage to marry a stranger, even to save *Belle Fleuve*? At least Kate had grown up around Colin and had always loved him.

How could she ever forget the sight of Damian and Marie in tears begging her to stay? How could she dismiss the feel of Damian's arms wrapped around her in fear and desperation?

Would it be enough, marrying Colin knowing he was doing it only for the children?

If there were some guarantee that they would eventually be half as happy as his parents, it would be worth gambling away the rest of her life.

But there were no guarantees.

She remembered Eugenie's words. *God always sees us through the darkness.*

Except for the light shining from the *garçonnière*, the world beyond her window was dark and silent.

Maybe it was time to trust again.

FOURTEEN

That looks straight to me." Colin directed work on one of the empty cabins from a tall wingback chair that once graced Nola Keene's townhouse.

Simon had insisted on bringing a chair out for him, but the elegant wingback looked decidedly ridiculous in the middle of the former slave cabin. What would Nola Keene say if she could see the elegant brocade piece now?

"You mind holding this board for me? I'll be quick." Simon pulled out a length of cypress wood and carried it over to the wall where he planned to mount it as the base of the top bunk.

Colin pushed himself up out of the chair, determined to walk across the room without his cane.

"I wish I could do more to help." He rolled up his shirtsleeves.

"No need to worry none, Mr. Colin. If I need help, I can ask one of the men. Three families are movin' in right now."

Simon made a scratch on the wall with a nail and surveyed the frame he had nearly completed. The men Colin had hired were desperate for work and for homes to shelter their families. Jason and Cora were putting their faith into the plan. Hopefully they would all be blessed with fine weather and a good crop.

Simon nailed the top rail to the wall. Colin watched but his mind was on Kate. Was she in shock after his spontaneous proposal yesterday? The possibility that she might accept kept him awake all night. By daybreak he was convinced that it wasn't such an outlandish notion after all.

There was no reason for her to keep her suite at the St. Charles when she could live and work at *Belle Fleuve* and have access to the children. Dividing care of the children would free them both to concentrate on their work.

It might prove to be the perfect partnership — if only Kate weren't inside packing to leave at this very moment.

He was thinking along those lines when he heard footfalls on the wooden porch out front, and suddenly Kate was standing in the doorway. Her cheeks were flushed, her hair slipping out of its pins as usual. She squinted into the dim interior of the cabin until her eyes adjusted to the lack of light. When she spotted him her complexion deepened.

After a second or two of hesitation she stepped inside and greeted him, then Simon. If she was surprised to see her mother's chair there she didn't show it.

"I'm having Simon build four bunks against the walls to leave a bit more room for the men to move around." A sudden nervousness surprised him.

"That's a fine idea."

"You are the expert. Do you have any other suggestions?"

"Perhaps you should put another window in. Let in more light."

He nodded. "That's something to consider. Where do you suggest?"

She studied the interior and pointed out places where Simon could open the wall for a window or two. Then she suggested a series of shelves on the back wall.

"If you have any spare materials," she added.

"Simon is a magician," Colin told her. "He's able to make something out of nothing."

Simon chuckled but kept working. "Anything around here that

has some life left in it, I can make it into something else, that's for sure."

Kate clasped her hands and looked everywhere but at Colin. He gestured toward the door.

"Would you like to step outside?"

She nodded. "I'd like to talk to you alone."

His cane was hanging on the back of the chair. He picked it up and fell behind as he followed her out onto the porch. She looked back.

"Your ankle—"

"A little better every day." She looked skeptical, so he added, "Honest."

He was still nervous as they stepped off the low porch and walked to the empty cabin next door. Kate sat down on the edge of the wooden porch. He joined her. They gazed out over the fields rather than at each other.

"I've been thinking about our talk yesterday," he said.

"I had a feeling you'd come to your senses."

"On the contrary. Ours might be the perfect partnership. The woman who stormed the *garçonnière* armed with nothing but a roll of plans and the determination to get me on my feet again is not the sort to cling to any romantic notions of hearts and flowers."

He took her silence as confirmation and went on.

"I like the fact that you are not influenced by such nonsense. A marriage of convenience will stand us both in good stead."

Kate stared at her folded hands, then let her gaze shift to his bare forearms. With his sleeves rolled up and the faded work trousers he was wearing, he seemed different. Who was this man who had spent the last fifteen years soldiering?

Kate had no idea who he was but obviously he saw her as a no-nonsense intellectual, a bluestocking pursuing a career in a man's world. As a woman who cared nothing for romantic love.

The situation would have been laughable if it wasn't so very sad.

"So what do you think?" Colin turned to her and before she could respond, he took her hand. "Should we join forces, Kate? For *Belle Fleuve* and the children?"

She was twenty-nine and had no other marriage prospects. She'd never wanted anyone else. Adding Marie and Damian's fears and concerns for their future along with her promise to Amelie, Colin's proposal made her wonder if perhaps a marriage of convenience might be the best thing for all of them.

Is a one-sided love enough? she wondered. Did she have enough love in her heart for both of them?

Before Amelie died the old Kate would have found the courage to hope that one day she and Colin might fall in love like Marie and Patrick. Sitting beside Colin in the dappled sunlight on the porch of the abandoned cabin, she missed the old Kate — the Kate who refused to take no for an answer, the Kate who believed dreams did come true. That Kate wouldn't have hesitated to try. She wouldn't have had to convince herself that a marriage for the sake of the children to the man she already loved would work. She would have believed.

She would never know unless she tried.

"When?" she asked.

"As soon as possible, I suppose."

"I'm sure there are formalities. A minister. Not until the weekend, for certain."

"Does that mean yes?"

At last she met his eye and managed a smile.

"That means yes."

She had once dreamed of being wed in a beaded gown of ivory silk faille and Valenciennes lace. On the day of her wedding, however, Kate wore a black satin mourning gown with three-quarter sleeves and black satin-covered buttons. There would be no honeymoon trip, no grand reception, no teas held in the coming days so that she might gather a circle of society friends.

The morning of her wedding, she and the children had gathered ferns and flowers and palm fronds and arranged them in large ceramic crocks around the room. Coffee and fruit ambrosia would be served immediately after the simple ceremony, which was performed by a local minister and witnessed by the Boltons. Eugenie and Simon and the children were there to watch Kate and Colin exchange their vows in the larger of the two sitting rooms. The entire ceremony lasted less than eight minutes.

When the minister pronounced them man and wife, Marie and Damian started clapping and jumping up and down. The minister hushed them with a stern eye before he turned to Colin and announced, "You may kiss the bride."

Kate hadn't thought past saying "I do." In fact, the days before the ceremony seemed to pass as if in a dream. Throughout the exchange she tried to focus on the minister but found that nearly impossible. She'd handed her spectacles to Marie at the last minute. The preacher stood before her in a haze.

After an awkward pause, Colin gently touched her elbow and Kate slowly turned to him. She barely made out that he was smiling, but she felt his hesitancy.

She nodded ever so slightly. He reached for her, held both her hands, and tugged her closer. He lowered his head and gave her a quick, chaste kiss. For a moment she thought it was over, but before she knew it he was kissing her again, slower this time and with more feeling. It wasn't her first kiss, but it was the first to make her tingle all the way to her toes.

When Colin finally drew back, his face was a blur. Was he as shocked as she?

"Congratulations, Colin." Jason startled Kate back to reality as he began to pump Colin's hand.

Cora and Eugenie crowded close to congratulate Kate. Marie

pressed Kate's glasses into her hand. Kate slipped them on as Damian wedged his way into the circle to stand beside the men.

The small knot of well-wishers surrounding her was her family now. A lightness of spirit that she hadn't known in weeks came over her. Kate found herself smiling at Colin. He nodded and smiled back. A shiver ran down her spine at their silent exchange.

Belle Fleuve was finally her home. Without Amelie, though, her joy was tempered.

"Everything's ready in the dining room," Eugenie announced. "I'm sure Miz Bolton would like to set down a spell."

Cora patted her extended belly and sighed. "Not much longer, Eugenie. In fact, I think all this excitement might just hurry this child along." She sounded nervous as she added, "I hope I can still count on your help."

"You just send for me and I'll be there," Eugenie said.

The children ran ahead, followed by the minister and then the other adults. Cora and Kate trailed Jason and Colin, who spoke of business as usual. As Kate studied Colin's broad back she nearly pinched herself to be certain she wasn't dreaming.

Eugenie served the coffee and ambrosia. The minister chatted with them long enough to be polite and then excused himself saying he had a list of ailing congregation members to visit that afternoon.

Colin walked him out, and when he rejoined them, Kate could tell he needed to rest his ankle. She ushered him over to an empty chair.

"I suppose I'll have to get used to you bossing me around," he teased. "Now that you are my wife."

"I suppose so."

Cora turned to Jason and announced, "It's time we left these newlyweds to themselves." She then invited Kate over to the foreman's house at a later date. "I can't wait for you to see the progress Jason has made. We're nearly ready to move in."

Eugenie took the children out to the kitchen, and Simon asked if there was anything they needed. When both Kate and Colin said no, he excused himself as well.

Suddenly Kate and Colin were sharing an empty sitting room as large as a hotel lobby.

"I'm sorry I don't have a ring to give you." Colin's voice echoed in the almost empty room.

"It's not necessary. Really."

Colin was watching her intently. Whenever they'd had a chance to talk this past week they'd spoken of nothing but business. She was working on preliminary plans to show Jamison next week. Colin kept her apprised of Bolton's progress at the foreman's house. They had conferred twice over how best to ensure Damian and Marie's schooling.

But not once had they broached how to handle the intimacies of their wedding night. Kate had no idea whether or not Colin expected her to fulfill her wifely duties. Theirs was a partnership, a marriage of convenience and not a love match, but he was a man and she was his wife. Their union had been sealed by a minister and witnessed by friends. He had every right to expect her to fulfill her wifely duties, and she would never deny him — if they had married for love.

Her face flamed at the very notion of what Colin might expect of her tonight. She certainly wasn't expecting any romantic fantasy. Technically, she knew what was supposed to happen in a marriage bed but wasn't sure exactly how to go about it.

The days were growing shorter faster. The sun was already low in the afternoon sky, and the shadows were deepening in the room. Kate shivered and rubbed her shoulders, chilled more by nerves than from the evening air.

"I'll get Simon to light a fire." Colin started to rise.

"That's not necessary." How long would they feel compelled to share the awkward silence? A lifetime?

When Eugenie walked in, Kate was so happy she practically ran across the room to greet her.

"You're invited to the gallery overlookin' the garden," Eugenie made a slight bow. "Whenever you're ready."

Before Kate could say anything, Eugenie walked out.

Colin rose slowly. Kate handed him his cane.

"Do you know what this is all about?" she asked.

"No, but shall we go see?" He offered his arm.

As Kate slipped her hand into the crook of his elbow she was flooded with warmth.

"Are you all right, Kate?"

"Yes, why?" she asked without looking up at him.

"Your cheeks are very flushed. I hope you aren't coming down with a fever."

Perhaps a fever would save her from tonight.

They walked outside, where twilight was gathering in the garden, to find the gallery lit with the stubs of twenty candles protected by glass jars, which were placed here and there on the bricks and column bases. A small table set for two was near the garden edge of the gallery. A mended tablecloth was covered with the best pieces of mismatched china and cutlery Eugenie had been able to rustle up.

Simon had donned a faded but formally cut black jacket and was waiting to serve them. Eugenie was holding one of Kate's wraps. She slipped the wool shawl around Kate's shoulders.

"I made a special wedding supper for you," Eugenie told them. "I thought seein' as how this is a special evenin' you might enjoy a candlelight supper out here like Miz Marie and Mr. Patrick liked to do."

Kate knew the minute she saw all the candles and the table that Eugenie had tried to recreate one of the Delanys' romantic evenings, the kind she once secretly dreamed of sharing with Colin.

The only thing missing tonight was love.

Kate hadn't time to dwell on the truth as Colin thanked Eugenie and slowly escorted Kate to the table. Kate thought of the nights she and Amelie had spied on Marie and Patrick and missed her friend with a bittersweet ache.

Once they were seated, Eugenie watched over Simon as he poured amber liquid into their wine glasses.

"Where did this come from?" Colin asked.

Still mute, Kate tried to quell her nervousness.

"I made it from dandelions," Eugenie told them. "Been hoping we'd have a special occasion to celebrate someday. There's been enough sadness around here to last a lifetime."

Colin tasted his and nodded. "Not bad, Eugenie. Perhaps we can go into the wine business as well as cane."

"Simon will serve crawfish *étouffée* while I keep those children busy to give you some privacy," Eugenie said to Colin.

Butterflies warred in Kate's stomach.

As promised, Simon soon appeared with two steaming dishes of *étouffée* over rice along with warm bread and butter. Kate took a sip of wine but had no appetite. She forced herself to take a few bites of buttered bread and tried to marshal her missing courage.

She set down her fork and looked at Colin.

"Do you remember your parents' candlelight dinners out here?"

He studied the table and surrounding gallery ablaze with candles in jars.

"They always used the tall silver candelabra, crystal, china, and fine linens." He shook his head. "Everything they treasured is scattered to the four winds."

"I like to think they would have been just as happy without those things."

"Is living here like a church mouse a novelty for you, Kate?"

"If you think this is a game to me, you don't know me very well."

He smiled. "Finally."

"Finally what?"

"I've been waiting for a glimpse of that gumption, waiting for some sign that the Kate who stormed the *garçonnière* not long ago is still in there somewhere."

Unnerved to be so captivated by his smile, Kate studied a particularly large crawfish on her plate.

"I wasn't an infant when my birth parents died. I still remember being poor quite well. My parents fled the Irish famine and died in the yellow fever plague." She touched the rim of her plate, too nervous to take another bite.

"What of your sister?" he asked between bites. "The one left at the orphanage with you."

Kate stared into a candle flame trapped inside a jar. "She was adopted shortly after we arrived there. She was younger, only four, and very beautiful. I've no idea what happened to my older sisters."

"Older sisters?" Colin rested his fork on the edge of his dinner plate and studied her carefully.

She blushed and nodded. "Lovie and Megan. My uncle told us they were taken in by a wealthy family and were living like princesses." She shrugged. "I suppose that's why I wasn't in awe of the Keenes' wealth when they adopted me. I expected to be as lucky."

He was finishing off what was left on his plate. If he noticed she hadn't had more than a few bites he didn't comment on it. Kate filled the silence.

"I tried to find them but there's no record of them anywhere. Sometimes I'm surprised they haven't ever looked for me, but then again, the war turned everything upside down." She shrugged. "Who knows where they are or even if they are still alive."

"Maybe you'll find them one day." Colin finished his wine and leaned back.

"Maybe so. No matter what, I'll always remember them."

He frowned and gazed over the land, which was now bathed in darkness. "Do you really think Jason and I can bring in a crop next year?"

"Of course."

"You say that without hesitation." His voice low, he added, "I wish I was as certain."

If only she were as certain about their future together. Uncertainty about what was to come tonight overshadowed everything else in Kate's mind. Colin seemed perfectly at ease as he finished his meal. But, skittish as a frog on a hot griddle, Kate ate very little and declined coffee when Simon offered it.

Simon had just served Colin a cup of coffee and a plate of almond cookies when they heard a shout followed by a loud thud inside. Then they heard Marie scream.

Kate jumped to her feet and dashed across the gallery and into the dining room. Marie was at the far end of the room kneeling beside Damian. The boy lay spread-eagle on his back staring at the ceiling. His shirtsleeves were rolled up, and his hand still clutched the handle of his wooden sword.

"Is he dying? Help him, Aunt Kate!" Marie leapt to her feet.

Frantic, Kate knelt beside Damian, but he didn't move. She heard Colin limp up behind her.

"What happened?" he demanded.

Marie cried, "He was jumping off the sideboard but he slipped off the edge and landed on his back. Is he dead?"

Suddenly, the boy's mouth began to open and close, but he didn't say a word.

"Damian." Colin was calm but firm. "Damian, look at me."

Slowly, Damian rolled his eyes toward Colin.

"Oh, Colin, do you think his neck is broken?" Afraid to touch him, Kate fought the urge to pull the boy into her arms.

"I think he's knocked the wind out of himself," Colin said. "Breathe, Damian. Take a slow, deep breath. You're all right."

Damian focused on Colin. His chest rose and fell. Tears replaced the fright in his eyes.

"Are you all right?" Kate brushed the dark curls back off his forehead.

Finally, Damian nodded. Gasping for breath and crying in earnest, he tried to sit up. Kate took his hands and pulled him up with care. She wrapped her arms around him.

"I think it's time you surrendered your sword," Colin said.

Damian let out a wail. "How will I storm the bulwarks or carouse like a real pirate without a sword?"

"You are not to storm the bulwarks or carouse, especially in the house."

"You could have been killed." Marie was white as parchment, her hands fisted at her sides.

Kate took one of Marie's hands but kept an arm around Damian.

"Damian is just fine. He simply knocked the wind out of himself."

Colin asked the boy, "Is this the first time this has ever happened to you?"

Damian wiped his face and nodded.

"Then let's hope it's your last. Now, do as I say and hand over your sword for safekeeping."

Damian's lip quivered. "Will I get it back?"

When Kate saw the corner of Colin's lips twitch and knew he was holding back a smile her heart did a somersault.

"Only if you can obey the rules of your pirate commander."

"You mean Aunt Kate?"

"I mean me."

"Oh." Damian reached for his sword. He cradled it for a moment. "Simon worked very hard to make this for me."

"I'll take good care of it." Colin took the sword and tucked it under his arm.

"Will it be a long time before I can have it back?"

"That depends on how well you follow the rules around here. Show us you've given up leaping off the furniture, and you'll be a buccaneer again before you know it."

Damian let Kate help him to his feet to dust him off. Marie kept an eye on her brother as if she thought he might keel over again. Damian tugged up his pants and straightened his shirt.

Marie finally separated herself from Kate and took Damian's hand.

"I'll help you upstairs," she said.

Before the unarmed pirate left the room he stopped and looked up at Colin.

"You were nicer before you got married," he said.

"Just remember," Colin said, "it was your idea."

Colin hoped Kate hadn't taken his words as an insult. "You know I didn't marry you simply because the children insisted," he said as soon as the children were out the door.

"I know how complicated this is."

He looked at the sword and shook his head.

"So much for our first crisis. I think we handled it very well, don't you?"

"Do you mean for two people who have no idea what they are doing?"

"Speak for yourself."

"By the way, when were you promoted to commander?"

When Colin saw the sparkle in her eyes he was happy for another glimpse of the old Kate.

"It was a self-appointment," he said.

Her smile faded too quickly.

"When I saw him lying there like that …" She didn't go on, but her silence said more than words.

"It scared me too. But having been a boy once myself, I'm fairly certain this won't be the last time he gets hurt."

"I'm not sure I can take many scares like that."

"I'll be here to help."

"Will you?"

He nodded.

An awkward silence lengthened, much like the moments that had passed between them outside.

"I suppose I should go up and see to their prayers." Kate hesitated, then surprised him. "Would you like to join me? I'm sure they'd be happy to have you tuck them in."

"I don't think I could make it up the stairs tonight. I'd best get back to the *garçonnière*."

Kate's eyes were huge behind her glasses; her face flushed. Was she about to burst into tears?

"What is it, Kate? Damian is all right. There's no need to worry."

She glanced out the door. The light in the *garçonnière* window beckoned.

"Would you ...? Should I ...?"

Suddenly it hit him. Over the past week they discussed the children, her work, the cane crop, and field workers, but never once had they discussed the intimate guidelines of their marriage. Kate wasn't sure what to expect.

He set the sword on the sideboard and took Kate's hands in his. Hers were as cold as ice.

"Thank you, Kate."

"For what?"

He could barely hear her.

"For the sacrifice you've made for the children and for me."

She looked so vulnerable and confused that he couldn't help but kiss her. Unlike during the ceremony, this time Kate kissed him back. Tempted by her response, Colin longed to deepen the kiss, but he had no intention of toying with her. He pulled back. Kate's face was still tipped up, and she blinked at him as if she'd just had the wind knocked out of her too.

He rubbed his thumb against the vulnerable underside of her wrist. Was Kate Keene unwittingly storming his heart the way she had *Belle Fleuve*?

"I can feel your pulse. Your heart is racing," he whispered.

"I ..." She dropped her gaze. Her cheeks flamed.

"Kate, there's no need to be frightened. I will never press you for more than you are willing to give."

"I thought that you might be moving in with ... us."

"I'm comfortable in the *garçonnière*."

Another moment passed before she met his eyes again.

"Thank you," she whispered.

He kissed her hand before saying good-night and walking away.

FIFTEEN

Somehow Kate survived the first week of her marriage without dying of embarrassment. Thankfully, Colin never once mentioned their awkward wedding-night exchange.

They quickly settled into a routine; he spent his time overseeing the work on the cabins and making sure the new hands and their families were settled. Together he and Jason met with other planters on River Road.

Kate spent the time completing the plans Jamison had assigned and tending to Marie and Damian. The day after the wedding, she approached Colin about taking his evening meals with them, stressing that she felt it was important for the children to see them as a united front. He immediately agreed.

The first time he joined them in the dining room of the main house with his shirt open at the neck and his damp, dark hair tied back, she almost wished he would have chosen to continue eating alone in the *garçonnière*. The lamplight in the dining room hid the lines and hollows on his face, making it hard to remember that he was not the Colin she knew in her youth and that theirs was a partnership, not a marriage.

The four of them gathered around the table was a stark reminder that Amelie was gone. Sometimes Damian or Marie would struggle to fill awkward silences. On occasion Colin tried to make conversation, but often seemed distracted. Kate suspected he was either worried about the future or in pain.

To someone peering through the window they might seem an ordinary family, but the reality of the situation was achingly clear; they were trying to cobble together a life and none of them knew how to go about it.

As much as she wanted to concentrate on her duties as the wife of a struggling plantation owner, inexperienced mother of two, and fledgling architect at *Belle Fleuve*, duty demanded that Kate make the trek to New Orleans to meet with Roger Jamison.

Upon arriving in New Orleans Kate walked the Garden District, enjoying perfect fall weather and admiring the architecture. A few homes were made of brick and stucco like in the French Quarter, but most were made of wood and were surrounded by large gardens with enough room for oaks and magnolias. Though she enjoyed New Orleans, with Colin and the children never far from her mind, the city no longer felt like home.

When she finally reached Roger Jamison's stately house, she rang the bell and then admired the decorative ironwork used on the side gallery as she waited for him to answer. He opened the door, pleased to see her.

"Miss Keene, come in. Come in. I'd all but given up on you." He noted the roll of plans in her arms. "I see you've brought the designs along. Good. Good. I've been anxious to see them."

He led the way into his office. Kate followed, hoping that her work would meet his approval. The plans were not very inspired, but she thought she'd produced some good, solid additions.

"I'm sorry this has taken so long," she began.

"I heard that Amelie Delany passed." He cleared space on his design table, his expression one of sympathy. "Are you still at *Belle Fleuve*?"

She nodded and tried to hide a blush. "Actually, yes. Colin Delany and I were married last week."

He peered at her over his spectacles.

"That was rather sudden, I take it?"

"Amelie returned with two children, a boy and a girl. Colin and I promised to look after them together."

"So you married him?"

"It's more of a partnership, actually."

"I suppose this means you won't be able to assist me after all." He hadn't even seen her plans but sounded disappointed.

"On the contrary, I'm hoping the designs meet your approval and you'll keep me on as your assistant—as long as I can work at *Belle Fleuve*. Naturally I'll come and meet with you when needed."

"As long as the clients are happy, I don't see why that should be a problem." He took her plans and spread them out. As he studied them intently, the only sound in the room was the tick of the clock on the mantle and Roger's occasional "Ah."

When he was finished he slipped off his glasses, folded the stems, and set them down. Kate held her breath.

"I must say this is very nice work, Mrs. Delany."

Hearing him address her as Mrs. Delany caught Kate off guard. It was a moment before she responded.

"Thank you, Mr. Jamison."

"Having known Patrick Delany's work, all I can say is that he would be proud to have you carrying on the family name."

She thanked him again, and he rolled up the plans and invited her to sit down over tea to discuss a project he wanted her to start on immediately: the remodeling of a home recently purchased by a steamboat captain from Baton Rouge.

"It's a place with good bone structure. Perhaps you'll have more luck persuading him to change some of the crazy notions he's come up with."

"Crazy notions?" She was intrigued as well as concerned. "Will his ideas ruin the integrity of the house? If so, what should I do?"

"Make him happy, Mrs. Delany, or forfeit the work and I'll find someone who will." He gave her a nearby address.

"I'll walk past it on my way back to the French Quarter," she told him.

"You don't have a carriage waiting?"

She hadn't wanted to spend the money when she was quite capable of walking.

"It's a lovely day for a walk," she said.

"That it is."

They shared a pot of tea, and then he gave her the original plans he'd found in the New Orleans city archives to study.

"Captain Stevens will want to meet with you on his next trip to town."

"Just send word and I can be here whenever you say. I'll go over these drawings and come up with some of my own ideas before we meet. Hopefully he'll be pleased."

"Is there anything else we need to discuss? I have an appointment with my accountant in an hour," she added.

"Just one more thing." He disappeared into his office, returned with a bank draft, and handed it to her.

"Payment for your first assignment," he said.

Kate looked at the check in her hand. A few weeks ago it would have seemed modest. Today she was not only happy to have it and pleased to have become a professional architect at last, but elated that Jamison had said Patrick Delany would be proud.

"I hope this is just the beginning of many successful projects." Jamison opened the front door for her.

"Thank you, sir. I hope so too."

As Kate bid him farewell and walked away smiling, her steps felt a bit lighter and so did her heart.

An hour later she was in Dan Rosen's office in the French Quarter.

"I don't know what to say, Kate."

"You don't have to say anything but congratulations," she said.

"Your father asked me to do what I thought best for you, to counsel you."

"You're not my father, Dan."

"When your mother sent word from Italy that she'd married a count I wasn't surprised. It was exactly something Nola would do, but your marriage to Delany *is* quite a surprise." He shook his head and added, "Then again, maybe I should have seen it coming."

"What do you mean?"

"You didn't think twice about paying off years of back taxes on *Belle Fleuve*. Where that place is concerned, you throw caution to the wind."

"Is that what you think I've done? Married him to get *Belle Fleuve*?"

"When did Colin Delany propose?"

"Shortly after Amelie died."

"So it's not as if you are in love with him."

What would Dan say if he knew she had always been in love with Colin?

"We've entered a kind of partnership," she admitted.

"A partnership." He studied her carefully. "Does he know your inheritance is almost gone?"

"I don't think he knew I had an inheritance to begin with."

"Really, Kate?"

"Yes, Dan. We married to raise Amelie's children together."

"If you run out of money, how do you plan on feeding them? Does Colin have any resources at all?"

"He saved some of his army wages."

"I believe soldiers are paid less than two hundred per year."

Kate sighed. "I have my first paycheck in my reticule, and you are going to rebuild my account."

"You're as stubborn as ever."

"You don't know how happy I am to hear you say that. I haven't felt much of anything lately, let alone trying to muster the strength to argue with anyone."

"You say this is a partnership, Kate. Am I to assume it's platonic?"

"I can't believe you're asking me that."

"I'm concerned for your welfare. If the marriage isn't consummated, you can always engage a good lawyer and have it annulled."

"I don't want it annulled."

His brows shot up. "So that's how it is. You *are* in love with him."

"You have no idea how *it* is." She straightened her hat and stood up. "Now that I've delivered my news, I'll be leaving."

"Kate, don't take this the wrong way. I'm merely concerned. As I said, your father bade me to watch out for you. Now I'm afraid I haven't done a very good job."

"I'm twenty-nine and perfectly capable of looking out for myself."

"I don't doubt it." Dan pushed off the corner of his desk where he'd been sitting and walked her to the door. "If you need my help with anything, don't hesitate to let me know."

Kate had the rest of her belongings moved out of the suite at the St. Charles, and by late the following day she was back at *Belle Fleuve*. Though her trip to the city was brief, it seemed she'd been gone forever, and she was happy to be back.

No one was there to greet her carriage when she arrived so she had the driver unload her things before she went in search of the children. When she didn't find them upstairs, she went out in the gardens to look for them.

There was no sign of anyone there either, so Kate continued out to the yard and walked over to the row of cabins. Simon and Eugenie's place was empty, but a very young woman with a toddler was standing on the porch of the cabin next door. Kate introduced herself.

"I'm Portia," said the girl. "This is Betsy." She bounced the baby on her hip.

"Have you seen Eugenie or Simon?" Kate asked. "Or Mr. Delany and the children?"

"Eugenie went to the foreman's house to help birth the Bolton baby. Mr. Delany took a few of the men over to another place to load up some cane cuttings, but they came back a few minutes ago. He's still over at the barn."

Eager to see him again, Kate hurried across the stable yard. She soon heard his voice coming from the dim interior of the barn. His low, mellow tone sounded confident again. She took a deep breath and paused long enough to tuck a strand of hair back beneath the front brim of her small hat. She gave the hem of her short jacket a tug and tried to ignore the flush of excitement she felt.

Kate smiled as she stepped into the barn. Colin and Simon were covering a wagon bed with canvas.

Colin felt her presence before he saw her. Thinking only of Kate, he turned around and stepped off the wagon bed onto his bad leg. The pain made him stagger. Kate was beside him in an instant, slipping her arm around his waist, supporting him as he fought back a wave of dizziness.

"Are you all right?" Concern for him shadowed her expression.

"I am now." He almost kissed her but Simon intruded.

"Here's your cane, Mr. Colin." Simon handed it over.

"Thank you, Simon. I'll leave you to finish here." He turned to Kate, hating for her to move away. It felt natural to have her tucked beneath his arm. "We just picked up a load of cuttings. Got them for a good price. We'll start planting soon."

"I hear Eugenie's at the Boltons'."

He nodded. "Jason came to get her. It's Cora's time."

"Where are the children? Not with Eugenie, I hope."

Did she seem loathe to let him go? She took her time moving away.

"They were with us." He looked around and shrugged. "They were right here a minute ago."

She walked the interior of the barn and came back looking piqued.

"They aren't here. Did you see them leave, Simon?" She placed her hands on her hips.

"No, ma'am."

"There are snakes everywhere and alligators that come up from the marsh and a thousand other ways Damian could get hurt."

"Kate, they were just here. I'm sure they're fine."

"You have to watch children every minute." She marched to the barn door and surveyed the property. "We have to find them."

"I'd come with you," Colin offered, "but I'd only slow you down."

She turned to Simon. "Saddle Colin's horse in case they wandered away from the house."

"Can you ride?" Colin tried to picture her tearing across the fields like a madwoman.

"I'm not the best rider in the world but I can manage."

"You could also break your foolish neck. Simon will go look for them."

"They're our responsibility, not Simon's and not Eugenie's." Her alarm was contagious.

"Fine, but I'm telling you they can't be far. Maybe they're back in the house by now."

Colin admired the flash of her ankle when she hiked up her skirt and ran back to the house before he turned to Simon.

"You have any idea why she's in such a lather? Those two can't have gone very far."

"Eugenie would snatch us bald if she knew those children had slipped away someplace when we weren't watching."

Colin lifted his hat and wiped his brow with his shirtsleeve.

"I'll go saddle up your horse."

"Hold off, will you? I'll take care of this." The last thing he needed was for Kate to break her neck.

Colin heard her voice echoing through the house calling for Damian and Marie. He was halfway across the stable yard when he noticed a stem of wild geraniums lying in the dirt. Marie had gathered an armful of the flowers that had been growing beside the road. Seeing the flowers on the ground, he knew where the girl was headed. Hopefully, Damian was with her.

Colin was sweating by the time he reached the house. He called out to Kate and she came running. She had shed her hat and gloves and her hair had slipped loose around her shoulders.

"Did you find them?"

"I think I know where they are. Come with me."

He walked around the house, sensing Kate's impatience at his slow pace. When they rounded the overgrown hedge, the Baudier crypt came into view. Marie was seated on the bench in front of the monument where she'd placed the wildflowers.

Relieved, Colin turned to Kate.

"You see? No need to panic."

"But where's Damian?"

Just then Damian called, "Aunt Kate, Uncle Colin! Look at me!"

"I still don't see him." Kate shaded her eyes and stared across the lawn.

Colin spotted Damian in the limbs of the nearest oak.

"He's right there."

"That's a good twelve feet off the ground!" she cried.

"No snakes, no alligators."

"What if he falls?"

"We'll be here to pick him up."

They started across the lawn together, Kate adjusting her pace to his.

"Can we do this, Colin? I'm not sure my heart can take it."

"If anyone can do this, Kate Keene, it's you."

"Mr. Jamison called me Mrs. Delany yesterday. It felt odd."

"How was the meeting?"

"I'll tell you once Damian is out of that tree. Do stop him before he goes any higher."

Marie ran toward them.

"Aunt Kate, you're back!" She greeted Kate as if she had been gone for weeks instead of two days. With one eye on the oak tree, Kate hugged the girl tight.

"I see you brought your mother some lovely flowers," Kate said.

"Come see, Aunt Kate. There are so many pretty ones. Uncle Colin had Simon stop the wagon so I could pick them."

Kate turned to him, fear clouding her blue eyes.

"I'll get Damian down." Colin continued across the wide lawn toward the oak wondering what would it be like to have Kate greet him with open arms?

Talking Damian down from the tree took a while. By the time the two of them joined Marie and Kate, Colin's ankle was on fire.

As always, Kate sensed that he needed to sit. She helped him lower himself to the bench near the crypt.

"There's a butterfly!" Damian yelled. "Can we catch it?"

"You can try," Colin said.

"Stay beside the hedge where we can see you," Kate warned.

The children ran off, and Colin leaned back.

"Are you all right?" she asked.

"I will be. Tell me about your meeting."

"Mr. Rogers liked my work," she said. "He gave me another assignment and my first pay. I cashed the draft while I was in town."

"You've already invested enough in this place." He noticed that she blushed and quickly looked away. "Kate?"

"What?" She continued to avoid meeting his eyes.

It shamed him to think he might have to ask her for money sooner than later. The cane cuttings he just purchased cost more than he had planned on spending, but he'd come home with enough to plant a sizable crop.

"I don't want your money," he told her.

Finally she turned and looked deep into his eyes, her irritation more than evident. "If we need it for the children, you will most *definitely* use it, Colin Delany."

"Fine." He couldn't help chuckling.

"Why are you laughing?"

"I'm just happy to see signs of the old Kate again."

The foreman's residence at *Belle Fleuve* was quite modest, but with a fresh coat of whitewash inside and out, crisp cotton muslin curtains, and Cora's loving touch, the wood frame house was warm and welcoming.

"It's wonderful," Kate said as Jason ushered them across the wide enclosed porch into the main room. "I can imagine it must have needed a lot of work after sitting empty for so long."

She glanced back to see if Colin and the children were following, but they had stopped to pet a hound that came running to greet them. Each time she had tried to initiate conversation on the drive, Colin had answered in short syllables or grunts, his eyes focused on the road.

As Kate walked through the door, Jason pointed out where he had carved his initials into the wood as a child.

"My family was very happy here. I can only hope my children find as much happiness. It's exciting knowing my son will grow up alongside Marie and Damian the way I did Colin and Amelie."

Proudly cradling their newborn, Cora greeted Kate. She rocked the babe in a chair Jason claimed his great-grandfather had made.

"This chair has rocked a whole passel of Boltons." He smiled as he ran his hand over the top of the headrest.

Cora pulled back the blanket and Kate smiled down at the little boy named Jake. She marveled at his round chubby cheeks and plump hands.

"He certainly looks healthy," Kate said.

"Would you like to hold him?" Cora offered.

Kate hesitated. "He looks so content. Perhaps later."

She glanced over her shoulder as the children and Colin came through the door. Marie carried the gift they had brought for the baby and handed it to Jason, who remained beside the rocking chair smiling down on his new son.

"Open it," Damian encouraged.

Jason held the small bundle in his hands. Marie had helped Kate wrap it in a piece of ticking from Eugenie's scrap basket.

"I'm painting you something for your wall," Marie said. Cora thanked her and claimed she couldn't wait to see the finished product.

Colin had little to say. As a career soldier, he probably cared nothing about visits to see newborns. Or perhaps his dark mood was due to pain. Kate made sure he was comfortably seated before she returned her attention to the baby.

Jason opened the gift and held up the cobalt cloisonné rattle for Cora.

"It's so beautiful." Cora carefully shifted the baby and held out her hand.

"Kate found it in the attic," Damian informed them.

"It was in an old trunk of things the Yankees decided they didn't want," Kate said.

Cora shook the rattle. It made a ringing sound.

"This is surely a family treasure," Cora looked to Colin. "We're thrilled to have it, but you really should keep it for your own children."

Kate flushed. Colin stretched his injured leg out in front of him. He shrugged and deferred to Kate.

"We wanted you to have it for Jake," Kate assured her.

Cora handed the rattle back to Jason. "We're honored. We'll treasure it and make a gift of it when you have your first."

Thankfully, Damian drew their attention to a rocking horse near the window.

"This is too big for a baby." He touched the dappled gray horse's wooden head, inspected the oiled leather reins and the bright blue and yellow felt saddle. "Too bad nobody's riding it."

"Would you like to? I'm sure Jake won't mind," Cora encouraged.

"Slowly," Kate advised when Damian jumped on the rocking horse and lunged forward. When she noticed Colin staring at the toy she said, "There is one almost like it in the attic."

"I thought it was familiar. I'll have to tell Simon to find it and see if he can bring it back to life," Colin said.

Before long he asked Jason if they could speak outside, and soon after their conversation ended Jason returned and announced that Colin was in the wagon and ready to leave. Kate shepherded the children out. They scrambled into the back. Kate sat next to Colin and blushed every time their shoulders touched. Still preoccupied, Colin didn't seem to notice.

"Is everything all right?" she finally asked.

He drummed his thumb impatiently against his knee. "I can't stop thinking of the large portion of my savings I used to buy cuttings that may or may not yield a crop next year. I have cabins full of families dependent upon me to help see them through until harvest. All it would take is one hurricane or drought and we'd be finished. You want to know if everything is all right? Who knows, Kate? Who knows?"

Before Amelie's death, Kate would have given him endless encouragement. She would have assured him that everything would work out. But now she wasn't sure of their future, or of anything else for that matter.

Even though he was right beside her, Kate didn't feel as if she could talk to Colin about how she felt and add to his burdens. She was still thinking of the blissful look on Cora's face as she nestled Jake and of Jason's loving expression whenever he looked at his wife. Watching the two of them together, Kate was sorely reminded that she was twenty-nine years old with no children of her own and little hope of having any if her situation remained the same.

Kate still believed she'd done the right thing for Marie and Damian, but in doing so, she might very well have sacrificed any chance she had for her own happiness.

They rode along isolated in thought as the children chattered in the back of the wagon. When they neared the house, Kate's gaze wandered toward the garden. She imagined Myra kneeling there in Eugenie's floppy straw hat and hoped that soon she would receive the promised letter from Ireland.

"Do you know who that is?" Colin's question broke her reverie. "Where?"

Colin pointed and Kate looked toward the back of the main house. Eugenie waited on the gallery beside a man in a double-breasted, navy-blue coat and cream-colored trousers. He reached up and rubbed the muzzle of what was obviously a very expensive piece of horse flesh tied to the hitching post.

"I have no idea." She scooted to the edge of the wagon seat, curious to see who had come to call, thankful it wasn't Dan Rosen. Though she trusted him to be discrete, she wasn't ready to have Colin meet him while the issue of the taxes was still a secret.

As Simon pulled up close to the back of the house, the gentleman waiting for them shoved his hat back off his forehead and stepped toward the wagon. He reached up to help Kate down.

"Mrs. Delany?" He had an infectious smile beneath a thick, golden moustache.

"Yes, I'm Katherine Delany." She smiled in return.

He helped her climb down and held her hand a moment longer than acceptable. Kate shook the dust off her skirt and wished she'd worn a hat. She smoothed her hair into place.

"I'm Captain Ezekiel Stevens. Roger Jamison told me you'd be working on my house designs."

"It's nice to meet you, Captain Stevens. I told Mr. Jamison I'd be happy to discuss things with you at his office."

"That's exactly what he said, but I didn't want you to have to make the journey."

Stevens studied Colin as he slowly made his way over to them. Both children were on his heels, staring at Captain Stevens with wide-eyed curiosity. Eugenie excused herself and went back to the kitchen while Simon drove the wagon back to the stable area.

The captain wore an expensive saffron brocade vest, and a thick gold watch chain and fob dangled from his vest pocket. He was tanned by the sun and stood with his feet anchored wide.

Colin stepped closer, but before she could introduce him to

Stevens the man said, "I heard congratulations are in order. Jamison told me you were just married."

"That's right." She paused a moment and wished Colin would smile. "This is my husband, Colin Delany."

"I'll admit when Mr. Jamison told me a woman would be designing my plans I pictured someone older. More matronly." He shrugged and flashed her another smile. "How wrong I was."

"She's older than she looks." There was no warmth in Colin's tone.

Pain might explain his lack of manners but his dark scowl was an embarrassment. Kate gave him a look that she hoped communicated her displeasure.

"Let's all go inside," she said. "I'll have Eugenie serve tea."

"That's a fine-looking animal," Colin complimented Stevens, perhaps trying to negate his cool welcome.

"Thanks. Brutus comes from one of the greatest Arabians ever imported to these shores." Stevens turned to Kate again. "When I admire fine things I don't let anything stand in the way of my acquiring them."

"We should go inside." Kate stepped back and took Colin's elbow.

As they started into the house, Damian began tugging on Colin's coat.

"Uncle Colin, can Simon get the rocking horse now? Please?"

Colin nodded. "You and Marie run and get Simon. Tell him it's up in the attic." He turned to Kate, "You did say the attic?"

"I did."

As the children ran off, Stevens watched them. "They look just like you, Delany," the captain noted.

"They're my niece and nephew."

Colin sounded barely civil, but Stevens' smile didn't dim a notch.

"Perhaps you could tell Eugenie we'd like some tea," Kate said. The tension in the room was impossible to ignore. Kate hoped the sooner she separated the two men the better, but Colin's expression darkened at her suggestion.

He looked from her to Ezekiel Stevens and finally gave her a cool nod.

"Enjoy your discussion," he said before he walked out.

Kate turned to Stevens, trying to hide her embarrassment. Colin had been testy all morning but now his mood was completely sour. She would have plenty of time later to find out what had come over Colin. She led the captain into the dining room where her work was set up.

"It's a shame this place is in ruins," he commented as they crossed the floor.

"You should have seen it a few weeks ago." Kate tried to forgive his bluntness. To insult *Belle Fleuve* in any state was to insult her. "Someday we'll remodel. It's important to save these old homes and preserve the integrity of the River Road plantation designs for the sake of history."

"I'm of a mind history should be left in the past where it belongs. I'm a forward thinker."

Please the client.

She touched the plans on the table. "These are the original plans for your home that Mr. Jamison obtained from the city archives."

Stevens barely glanced at them until Kate leaned over to point out the features of the house she thought worthy of keeping.

Eugenie came in and left a pot of tea and two cups. Kate served. The captain ignored his tea, but Kate took a few sips. Awkward beneath the man's silent stare, she took up pencil and paper and offered him a nearby chair.

"I'll just stand here." He leaned casually on the edge of the table. "You'll need to be comfortable to write."

When Kate sat down, he slid closer. It was hard to ignore him. He leaned over her as she wrote his name at the top of the page.

"Now, tell me a bit about what you're planning," she began.

"I want you to make my house look like a riverboat."

Kate was speechless.

"That's right, Mrs. Delany. A riverboat. With a capital R." Big, bold, dramatic, he punched his fist in the air. "There won't be anything else like it New Orleans, and we'll both be famous."

"A riverboat?"

"I've never seen anyone's eyes get that big before," he laughed. "You really should see your expression."

"I'm trying to imagine—"

He began to pace the room, waving his arms like an opera singer as he spoke. He was bold and dramatic and nothing like Colin. He never stopped smiling.

"I'm picturing white railings, a ship's wheel, three stories graduated in size right up to a room that mimics the wheelhouse. Oh!" He snapped his fingers. "Round windows like portholes. Maybe we should use real portholes."

"All of the windows?"

"Not all, but some."

Kate envisioned the flat roofs with their potential for leaks.

"Lots of spindles and chandeliers," he added.

"How about a paddle wheel?" she joked.

Stevens turned on his heel and hurried back to the table.

"Why, that's a fabulous idea, Mrs. Delany. I knew we'd get along the minute I laid eyes on you."

"I wasn't serious, sir."

He sobered, but only for a second. He leaned far too close and, in a conspiratorial tone, said, "You can do it, can't you?"

Please the client.

Kate sighed. "Of course I can."

"So you say, but I sense some hesitation on your part, Mrs. Delany."

Of course she sounded hesitant. He wanted her to turn a perfectly fine home into a steamboat on land. She risked becoming the laughing stock of New Orleans. Not only that, but Roger Jamison's reputation was at stake as well. She couldn't wait to hear what he would say when she discussed Stevens' insane notion with him.

She was so appalled she didn't notice that Ezekiel had moved until she looked up and found him looming over her. He was uncomfortably close, so close she was forced to lean back.

"I'm somewhat of a purist when it comes to remodeling historic homes, Mr. Stevens."

"Mine isn't that old."

"Another reason not to change it."

"Jamison assured me there would be no problem."

She looked down at her notes wishing she could feign enthusiasm.

"Maybe I'll have to use my charm to convince you." He leaned even closer. She drew back.

Was he flirting? His overtures came as a shock not only because she was married, but she suspected she was a year or two older than he. That fact didn't seem to matter to him in the least.

"We found it, Aunt Kate!" Damian yelled as he ran into the room, and Kate glanced over her shoulder. Colin was in the doorway holding the rocking horse, his gaze pinned on Stevens as the man lingered on the edge of the desk, effectively trapping Kate in her chair. Finally, Stevens rose and sauntered a few steps away.

"Aunt Kate, we have the rocking horse." Damian ran over to her and took her hand.

"That's wonderful." She watched Colin set the wooden horse down before he continued into the room.

His eyes never left hers. "I thought you would give us some suggestions as to how to go about restoring this thing." When Kate failed to respond, Colin added, "Unless you two need to be alone?"

She didn't care for the cynical arch of his brow nor the suspicion in his cold perusal. She'd done nothing wrong and yet she felt as if she should apologize.

Just then Stevens spoke up.

"I believe we're done here, aren't we, Mrs. Delany?" He was smiling at Kate as if they shared a secret. "You have your notes, so I'll leave the rest to your fertile imagination. I'm excited to see what you can do."

I'll just bet you are, Captain." Colin left Damian chatting to himself and inspecting the woefully worn and faded wooden creature from nose to tail as the adults paid him no mind.

Was Kate aware that he had seen the way the captain had her pinned in her chair? Stevens had been far too close for proprieties' sake, yet Kate hadn't said a thing to put him in his place. What was she thinking, letting a stranger that close? Or any man for that matter?

The bounder had the kind of polished looks women probably found attractive. Had Kate been so dazzled by Stevens' charm that she was powerless to tell him to keep his distance?

Colin was grateful for Damian's presence. The boy kept him from entertaining a physical altercation with the captain but not from crossing the room to stand behind Kate. Colin wrapped his hand over the back of her chair.

It was hard to forget what he'd seen. If Stevens had leaned over another inch or two, he would have been close enough to kiss Kate.

Would she have let him?

Kate glanced up at Colin as she stood. The captain started the horse rocking with the toe of his boot. "I believe this thing is beyond repair."

When the captain looked over at Kate again, Colin had an urge to slip his arm around her shoulder.

"That horse is only as old as I am, Captain," Colin informed him. "It might not look like much, but with some care it will be as good as new."

Stevens eyed him carefully. "For the boy's sake, I hope so." The man turned to Kate. "I'll be in touch with you soon."

"When I finish the preliminary sketches, I'll have them

delivered to Mr. Jamison. We should all meet together at that point to see if you approve. No need for you to come back out here."

Colin was relieved to hear she planned to be with Jamison when she presented the plans.

"Stopping by is no problem. I'm constantly up and down the river. The plantation just south of here has a landing. I used it today."

"But you rode your horse," Damian piped up to remind him.

The captain smiled. "I did, but from just down the road. Brutus is as at home aboard the steamboat as I."

"Can we please, please go for a boat ride?" Damian begged.

"Damian," Kate corrected, "the captain is a very busy man."

"I'd be happy to take all of you for a ride anytime," Stevens said.

"That's very kind of you, but ..."

When Kate protested, Colin found himself smiling triumphantly at Stevens. The captain pointedly ignored him.

"Perhaps when we meet in New Orleans we can set a date. Until next time, Mrs. Delany." He had the nerve to reach for Kate's hand and carry it to his lips.

Kate's work meant so much to her that Colin held his silence. He could best Ezekiel Stevens in a duel, but how could he explain calling a man out and shooting him at forty paces to Damian and Marie? Or to Kate for that matter?

Once Stevens was mounted up and headed down the drive, Colin heard Kate sigh.

"I hope that was a sigh of relief," he said.

Kate walked back into the house. Colin followed her with Damian close on his heels.

"He wants me to turn a perfectly good house into a riverboat on land." Kate paused beside her desk, frowned at the original house plans.

Damian was still waiting.

"Run outside and find Simon," Colin told him.

"But ..."

"Go. I need to talk to your Aunt Kate alone." As soon as Damian was gone Colin sat down near the table. "What would Jamison say if you told him you thought taking this commission would be bad for business?"

"He made it clear I'm to please the clients."

Colin studied her profile as she read over the notes on her desk. Her skin was smooth as porcelain. He longed to slip her spectacles off her pert little nose and watch her eyes grow wide with surprise.

"How far would you go to please Stevens, Kate?"

"What are you suggesting?"

"I saw the way he looked at you, how close he was sitting."

"Surely you don't think that I ..."

"You have no ring to remind him you're married."

"Jamison told him we had recently wed. I introduced you as my husband—"

"Only after some hesitation."

"What's wrong with you?" She stepped back and crossed her arms. After contemplating him for a second, she slowly shook her head. "Why, Colin, if I didn't know better I'd say you were jealous."

"Jealous? Of course not." To admit to jealousy would mean he cared more deeply for Kate than he even realized. "I just don't like him, that's all."

"I don't like him much either, to be honest. I found him far too loud and brash, and I certainly don't like his ideas."

"The style might catch on."

"You don't really think so, do you?"

"Who knows? But if you don't like him, then tell Jamison to find someone else to work with him. We'll get by."

"I can't turn down my first real assignment no matter how odious Stevens is. I need this chance." She picked up the miniature carving of *Belle Fleuve*, turning it over and over in her hands.

"When did Simon give that to you?" he asked.

"The day Amelie arrived. He made it as my going-away gift." She set it on top of her notes and gave Colin her full attention.

"I'm glad you stayed, Kate."

Having her here felt right. Comfortable. Without Kate to care for and encourage them all to be better, their odd little patchwork family wouldn't feel whole.

"It's your time to shine, Kate. Design the first-ever steamboat house. I know you'll do everything you can to make it wonderful no matter how you feel about it."

"Or the captain."

"Or the captain," he agreed. She looked so serious, so determined, that Colin was tempted to kiss her just to see how she would react.

They heard Damian and Simon approaching.

"Do you really think I can do this, Colin? Do you think I can design something as ridiculous as a house that looks like a steamboat?" Her expression was still troubled.

"If you gave up easily, Kate, I wouldn't be standing here right now."

SIXTEEN

Kate sat at her desk putting the final touches on her work. Then she leaned back, slipped off her glasses, and rubbed her tired eyes.

Inspired by Colin's faith in her, she had worked on the preliminary plans for Ezekiel Stevens' riverboat house for the better part of a month. Once they were the best they could be, she created an alternate set of plans to give Stevens. Hopefully, he would understand how he could improve on the existing house without going to extremes.

Marie was on the other side of the room with her watercolor papers spread out over the floor. Kate had assigned her the task of writing and illustrating a story. Marie had quickly become absorbed and set to work quietly. Kate found she enjoyed the girl's company.

"Are you almost finished, Aunt Kate?"

"I'm not sure I'll ever be really finished, but I'm going to make myself stop," Kate said.

Marie walked across the room and draped her arm around Kate's shoulders. Kate smiled a little smile knowing Amelie would be pleased.

"Those drawings just look like a bunch of lines to me," Marie sighed.

Kate pointed out the various rooms and doors and windows in the Garden District home.

"Pretend you're up above the house looking down into the inside. Like looking into a dollhouse if you took off the roof."

"I've never seen a dollhouse."

Kate put her glasses back on. She wished she had kept the dollhouse the Keenes had given her on her first Christmas with them. Of museum quality, she had gifted it to the orphanage before she left for Boston.

"Well, someday perhaps you'll have one."

"I'm too old for dolls." Marie drew herself up to her full height.

"No woman is ever too old to collect dolls."

Marie looked skeptical. "You don't have any dolls, do you?"

"Actually, I have one somewhere in those boxes and trunks stored in the barn. I'll have to look for her once I send these plans to New Orleans."

She still hadn't found time to unpack the things that arrived from the St. Charles. Somewhere in her boxes was a lovely doll that her father had presented to her. The two of them had shared dinner at Antoine's on one of their rare occasions out without Nola. Kate had thought she was too old for dolls by then, but Gil Keene was so pleased with the gift that Kate treasured it as a reminder of that special evening.

She was jotting a note to remember to look for the doll when Colin and Damian walked in.

Not as shy with Colin as she used to be, Marie left Kate's side to show him her paintings. Damian ran over to Kate's desk and climbed up onto her lap. Unlike Marie, he had warmed to her quickly. Kate wrapped her arms around him. It was hard to remember what her life was like before the children were part of it.

"Are you finished yet?" Damian asked.

"Almost."

"You've been saying that for weeks. Me and Uncle Colin have a surprise for you and Marie."

"What have you been up to?"

"You have to come see."

"First you'll have to get off my lap."

He laughed and hopped off, dragging Kate over to join Colin and Marie.

"Are you really almost finished?" Colin looked doubtful.

Kate didn't blame him. The task had taken far longer than she hoped.

"I just need to make a few small notes and adjustments. It shouldn't take long. How about you? I thought you were going for a ride through the fields." Less than a week ago he'd managed to mount his horse. Happy to be back in the saddle, he rode a while longer every day.

"Damian convinced me that all work and no play makes me a dull uncle."

"If that's true then I'm in good company. I'll be glad to see the last of Captain Stevens' riverboat house."

"Next you'll be designing steamboats."

"Can we have a steamboat?" Marie asked.

"I doubt we could get your uncle off the plantation long enough to use it."

Kate smiled, secretly happy that Colin was so busy. If he wasn't out surveying the fields and the newly planted cuttings, then he was meeting with neighboring planters to discuss the cooperative they were forming.

Damian took Kate's hand and led her over to the middle of the room. Colin accompanied Marie.

"Now close your eyes, Marie," Damian said.

"You too, Kate." Colin moved to her side and put his hand over her eyes. "No peeking."

Damian called out, "Come in, Simon!"

She heard the boy run across the floor. Colin dropped his hand away from her eyes and a second later Damian cried, "Open!"

Kate opened her eyes. Colin, Damian, and Simon stood behind the beautifully restored rocking horse. Marie clapped her hands and ran over to join them. Kate went to inspect their handiwork and knelt down beside the horse as Simon excused himself and left.

"He's wonderful." Kate lifted the new leather reins and then smoothed her hand over the red flannel seat. "I'll bet he's even better than he was when he was new." She looked up at Colin and found him watching her with a thoughtful expression.

"Not as good as new," he said, "but at least he's no longer useless."

Kate ran her hand over the newly sanded and refinished wooden horse. The rich, warm wood tones shone beneath the varnish.

"What's his name?" she asked Damian.

"Uncle Colin can't remember. I wanted to call him Brutus."

"I told him your Captain Stevens already used that name."

Kate glanced up at Colin again. "He's not *my* Captain Stevens."

He shrugged in response. Obviously, the captain was still a sore point with him.

"So I named him Blackbeard," Damian told her.

"A fine name for a pirate's horse," Kate said.

"Pirates don't ride horses," Marie sniffed.

Damian's face puckered. "They do, don't they, Uncle Colin?"

"Whenever they're on land. How do you think Jean Laffite got around when he was on land?" Colin folded his arms and nodded, his brow beetled into a frown. "I'm sure they had a fine stable of horses."

"Stolen horses!" Damian shouted.

"Nicely done, Colin," Kate said softly.

"Jean Lafitte didn't have to steal horses. He had plenty of money to spend on them," Colin clarified.

"Stolen treasure!" Damian yelled.

"I'm not certain that you can get out of this." Kate gave the horse a nudge and set it rocking then got to her feet. "But I'll love hearing you try."

Colin took Damian's hand and led him over to the chair at Kate's table and sat down. He rested his hands on Damian's small shoulders.

"Stealing is a sin, Damian."

"I know." The boy shrugged and tried to pull away but Colin held firm.

"It's an offense against the laws of God and man."

"I know. Thou shall not steal. Mama told us the commandments all the time."

"Good. I'm glad you know that." Colin looked over at Kate. She smiled back.

The boy was still talking. "Thou shall not kill either, but my daddy was a gunfighter. Somebody kilt him. And you were in the army. Did you kill anybody?"

The sound of Colin's sigh traveled across the room.

"There's a difference between being in the army and being a gunfighter."

"What is it?"

Again Colin's silence was a cry for help. Kate walked over and ruffled Damian's curls.

"That's something your uncle will explain when you're a bit older."

"I've been really, really good lately, haven't I?" Damian looked to them both for an answer.

"I think so," Kate said.

"As far as I know," Colin said.

"Then may I have my sword back?"

"I'm drowning here," Colin told Kate.

"I'm not much help, I'm afraid. You promised you'd give it back if he was good."

"I *have* been good," Damian insisted. "Now that I have my horse, I *need* my sword. Please?"

"I'm not sure I want you careening around like a pirate," Kate told him.

"What if I turn into a soldier? Didn't you carry a saber when you fought the Injuns, Uncle Colin?"

This time Kate sighed.

"It appears," Colin said, "that we have our work cut out for us."

It was dark by the time Colin returned to the makeshift office looking for Kate. He paused in the doorway and watched her in the glow of the lamplight as she tied a string around her plans. She'd removed her glasses, and her expression was soft and vulnerable. The halo of light showed off her perfect complexion. Her brow crinkled in thought, and when she pursed her lips, he remembered the taste of her kiss.

What was she thinking as she stared intently at the thick roll of plans?

He knew how much she wanted Roger Jamison's approval, but what of Ezekiel Stevens'? Was she just as concerned about pleasing the overbearing riverboat captain? It had been weeks since the man's visit and yet the memory of Stevens casually sitting on the edge of Kate's desk leering at her still set Colin's teeth on edge.

"Kate." He said her name softly, afraid to startle her as he stepped into the room.

She looked around, squinting toward the shadows. The rustle of palmetto fronds on the night breeze drifted in from the open gallery doors.

"Why, it's already dark." She was astounded. "I must have lost track of time."

"Are you hungry?" he asked. "You said that you'd join us for dinner."

"I'm so sorry. Surely you've already eaten, I hope. I don't know what I was thinking."

"I had Eugenie feed the children earlier. They're already upstairs and tucked in for the night." He nodded toward the desk as he moved closer and touched the ribbon around the plans. "It looks like they're finally finished."

Her smile revealed her relief. "All wrapped up and ready to send to Jamison. Tomorrow I'll have Simon drive me to post them. What about you? Have you eaten?"

He shook his head. "Not yet. I was going over some accounts and thinking about how best to keep the men occupied once the cane is in the ground. I've been trying to find out what each of them does best; some are better at hunting than fishing; one is an expert net maker. There's crab and crawfish for the taking in the river. Alligator meat is good if you don't lose a hand taking one. I thought of assigning the tasks they like to do so they can keep each other fed. Simon claims one of them is even a boat builder."

He warmed to her smile. She was listening intently.

"You should be proud of what you're doing, Colin. I know your father would be pleased."

"You're the one who would amaze him. He loved architecture above all things."

She shook her head. "Not more than he loved *Belle Fleuve* or his family."

"I couldn't have done this without you, Kate." Colin meant every word. Her cheeks flamed at the compliment.

"Come with me. I have a surprise," he urged.

He waited as she turned down the lamp and followed him through the house. On impulse he took her hand and drew her along. Lit only by the milky wash of moonlight pouring in through the windows, the huge, silent house enfolded them as they moved toward the gallery.

He had asked Eugenie to set a simple table under the moonlight —nothing so extravagant as their wedding night supper, but the setting was still intimate and everything was ready when they stepped outside.

"Oh, Colin," Kate turned to him with such delight that his heart tripped over itself.

"I remembered how much you enjoyed our dinner outdoors. I'm happy the weather has cooperated."

He pulled her chair out for her, a simple feat, but one he hadn't been able to manage the last time. Tonight there were no candles, no light other than the hurricane lamp in the middle of the table, but there were biscuits and jambalaya with sausage and rice, raisin pie, and even some of Eugenie's dandelion wine.

Once he was seated he raised his glass. "Here's to the completion of your plans." They each took a sip. Hungrier than he'd thought, Colin ate heartily. "What will you do next?"

"I'll have to see what Mr. Jamison has in mind. It will all depend on how well these plans are received." She reached for a biscuit, broke it in half and slathered it with a generous hunk of butter. "I have collected a few periodicals that feature house design competitions. I'm going to enter."

"Architectural competitions in women's periodicals?"

"Who knows what a woman requires in a house better than another woman? Some winners are awarded prizes. Some have their plans printed in the publication."

"Have you entered before?"

"Twice, but without any luck."

"I'll bet no one ever entered a set of plans for a steamboat house."

"Nor will I."

She laughed and he was glad he could make her happy.

They ate in silence for a few minutes until curiosity got the best of him.

"Will you have to see Stevens again? Or will Jamison handle him now?"

He tried to sound as if it didn't matter and was shocked that it did — far more than he cared to admit.

Kate paused, appearing thoughtful. She took a sip of wine.

"I will probably have to see to him," she said. "Mr. Jamison assigned me to the project. I have to see it through."

When she slowly licked a bit of butter off the corner of her mouth, Colin pictured setting down his fork, getting up, and walking around the table. What would she do if he picked her up, carried her to the *garçonnière*, and locked her inside like a princess in one of the French fairy tales his mother used to read?

It would take a miracle for him to be able to carry her anywhere.

"Colin?"

It was a moment before he realized she had spoken.

He swallowed. "Pardon me. What did you just say?"

"I asked if you would care."

"Care about what?"

"When I have to meet with Captain Stevens, will you care?"

How much should he reveal? No matter what their living arrangements, she was his wife. There was no shame in having proprietary feelings about her. Nothing wrong with being possessive, either. But he had never worn his heart on his sleeve or had such strong feelings for a woman.

"Let's just say I wouldn't be very happy about it," he admitted.

She put down her fork, folded her hands at the edge of the table. "Why?"

"Because, as I told you the day I met him, I don't like the man. I don't trust him."

"Trust him?"

"To keep his hands off you."

She surprised him by laughing again.

"I doubt a man like Captain Stevens would find someone like me desirable," she said.

"Any man would find you desirable, Kate."

She went completely still and clenched her hands together so tightly her knuckles whitened. Silent seconds ticked by. When she finally spoke, he barely heard her.

"Do *you* find me desirable?"

He had no idea how they had started down this road but it was too late to backtrack. Her eyes were wide and blue behind her round spectacles. In the glow of the lamp's flame, her hair was not only rich brown, but highlighted with copper and gold. The light shimmered on her moist lips. Her glasses magnified her thick lashes. She was trim, her slim figure emphasized by the expert cut of her black gown. Even the evening breeze off the river seemed to have stopped, waiting for his answer.

"Of course I do."

The truth came easily. What would she do if he kissed her? *Really* kissed her? There was only one way to find out.

He waited until dinner was over. When they were finished he walked around to her side of the table.

"Are you tired?" he asked. When she stood and turned to him he was tempted to take the pins out of her hair and watch it fall around her shoulders.

"My eyes are tired." She seemed in no hurry to leave. He reached down and turned out the flame on the lamp.

The moon was high, the gallery and land beyond bathed in silver light. The oaks were black, hulking shapes beneath the moonlight. Kate hadn't moved. He reached for her glasses, slipped them off, and set them carefully on the table.

"Better?" he said.

She rubbed her eyes. "I can see well enough." She didn't sound so sure.

"You already know what I look like—tall, dark, and limping."

"Oh, Colin. Don't make fun of your injury. It was valiantly won."

"Was it? How do you know?"

"I know you."

"I'm luckier than many. They say over six hundred thousand Americans died in the war. That's what happens when a country turns upon itself." He paused and stared out at the silhouettes of the oaks, bent and twisted, raw and beautiful at the same time.

"I'm sorry to spoil the evening with such melancholy talk," he said. "Thank you for putting up with my dark moods."

"You seem happy tonight."

"Pain stays as long as it's nourished. What of you, Kate?"

"I'm a little better every day. Eugenie reminded me that God shows us the way out of our darkness."

"Do you believe it?"

"Maybe He's slowly lighting the way for us."

Colin drew her into an embrace, prepared to release her if she balked. To his surprise she slipped her arms around him as if she did it all the time.

"Are you happy here, Kate?"

"I'd be lying if I said I am as happy as before Amelie died. The world looks different to me now. I've learned we can't force things to go our way. We hurt, we lose those we love, but we have to go on and learn to survive, to become someone new, someone hopefully stronger and wiser."

"You don't regret marrying me?"

"I'm glad we did the right thing."

"So am I, and not just for the children. We're good together, Kate. We're partners. I like to think we've become more than friends." He was surprised at how easily the words poured out of him.

"More than friends," she whispered.

"I'll admit seeing you with Stevens made me jealous."

"You don't have to be jealous of anyone, Colin."

"Lately I've thought a lot about how much you willingly gave up for the children and me. You walked into this knowing you might never have a real marriage or children of your own and for that I owe you more than I can ever repay."

She was staring into his eyes, her lips so close, so tempting that he found himself lusting after his own wife. He didn't question when or how it happened, but he had fallen in love for the first time in his life.

"I married you willingly, Colin," she whispered. "I . . ." She fell silent without completing her thought.

He pressed her lips with his, kissed her long and deep and held her close as their hearts beat as one. Kate didn't protest. She returned his kiss with so much fire and spirit that he was afraid to let it go any further lest he lose control.

He lifted his head and gazed for a moment longer into her eyes. What was she thinking?

It didn't matter. He'd said what he wanted to say and now he had to leave before he broke his promise not to press her. She would come to him when she was ready.

"Thank you, Kate." He hated to let her go. "For tonight. For the sacrifices you've made for my family. For your trust and faith in me. I thank you."

He picked up his cane and followed the moonlit trail to the *garçonnière*, stunned to realize he'd fallen in love with his own wife.

Kate somehow managed to walk back to the table and sit down. Her hand shook as she reached for her glasses. She had trouble slipping them on, and when she looked back down the path to the *garçonnière*, it looked empty. A moment later, lamplight bloomed in the window.

Her lips were still warm with the taste of his mouth and wine and moonlight. His kiss was so much more than she'd ever imagined. So much more.

More than friends.

Was it a sin to long to sleep with a man she'd vowed to love and cherish for the rest of her life?

She spread her hands wide, palms down against the table, and tried to keep them from shaking. Her breath was ragged. Colin had left her wanting more. Trembling, Kate took a deep breath and tried to think of something else. Anything else.

For a second she considered clearing the table but was afraid she'd drop every dish, every glass, every last thing she touched.

Smoothing her hair back, Kate straightened her glasses and then traced her lips with her fingertips. She stared at the lamplight escaping the *garçonnière* window.

She left the gallery and went upstairs. Stopping to look in on the children, she found them sound asleep. She smoothed the covers over each of them and kissed them.

Kate undressed by moonlight and slipped on her nightgown. Seated on the edge of the bed, she pulled the pins from her hair and brushed it out before she carefully removed her glasses and set them on the bedside table.

As she turned down the bed, she caught sight of her reflection in the mirror. Silhouetted by the moon she appeared as elusive as a shadow and nothing at all like a woman made of flesh and blood.

SEVENTEEN

Colin sat on his bed, an open book forgotten in his lap. He wanted to blame the full moon for his inability to sleep. The truth? Thoughts of Kate kept him awake and restless.

It was bound to happen sooner or later, he supposed. They were a man and a woman living in close quarters, sharing meals and plans and children.

Was this how his father and mother came to fall in love?

A knock at the door interrupted his musing.

"Simon? Come in." Was there an emergency? It was the first thing that came to mind with all the new people here. One small disaster would be a setback.

The door opened slowly. It wasn't Simon. It was Kate. She was wearing a long white nightgown that swept the ground. Prim and full, it covered her from the lace at her throat to the cuffs of her long sleeves to her toes. She clutched an emerald shawl around her shoulders. Her hair was down, her glasses gone. There were spots of color on her cheeks, otherwise her skin was as pale as her gown.

"Is everything all right?" He struggled to his feet and crossed the room. "Damian? Marie? Are they all right?"

Kate nodded. She shivered and her hands tightened on her shawl. What catastrophe had sent her running to him barely clothed?

"Kate?" He touched her shoulder. "Please, tell me what's happened."

She blinked and looked around as if she had no idea where she was.

"I will be all right. I'm sure I will be all right." She spoke so softly, he had to lean closer. "Right now I'm just frightened."

"Of what? Did someone break into the house?" He thought of all the men he hired. He didn't know them. Not really.

"No. It's nothing like that."

His erratic heartbeat slowed. Maybe she was upset about her work. What else mattered so much after the children?

"Are you apprehensive about sending your plans to Jamison tomorrow?"

"No. Of course not."

"What then? What has you trembling this way?"

"The unknown."

"Kate, why don't you sit down?"

"I don't want to sit down."

She'd come unhinged. Why else would she be standing here in her nightclothes, barefoot, her hair hanging loose around her shoulders, her big blue eyes wide and frightened?

"I'm sorry. I shouldn't have come," she turned.

He stopped her. "Whatever the matter is, we can work it out, Kate."

"Yes. For you are my partner. My friend. More than a friend, you said."

He took her hand and led her over to a chair. She refused to sit.

"What did you mean by that, Colin? When you said that we are more than friends, what did you mean?"

"I meant . . . well, I meant that what we have here is something special. We made an agreement, we . . ."

"We spoke our vows before a man of God."

"Yes. We did."

"We are more than friends. I am your wife. And you are my husband."

"That's right." Heat began to creep up his neck.

"The way you kissed me tonight ... it was not the way friends kiss."

"I'm so sorry, Kate. I owe you an apology. I don't know what came over me."

She pressed her palm against his shirtfront, took a step closer, and stared into his eyes.

"It came over me too, or didn't you notice?"

"Oh, I noticed, Kate. It must have been the setting, the moonlight."

"Perhaps," she said. "Or perhaps I am the sort of woman who clings to silly female notions of hearts and flowers and romance after all."

"You don't sound very certain."

"I'm not certain of anything right now. I'm not even sure I should be here."

The hand she placed over his heart trembled. Colin closed his eyes. She was too close. He fought the urge to run his fingers through her hair, to cup her head, pull her close, and kiss her.

"Why are you here?" He was afraid to hear the answer. Had he gone too far earlier?

"On our wedding night you told me that you would never press me for more than I am willing to give."

"And I never will. I promise."

"Nor I you," she whispered. "But I am here now, if you want me."

"Oh, Kate."

She tried to pull away. "I'm sorry if I misunderstood."

"Don't go." He drew her back into his arms. "You understood very well. You understood more than I. You felt what I've been trying to deny for weeks. I want you, Kate. I want more than a business arrangement. I want ours to be a real marriage. I want to be your husband in every way."

"As I want to be your wife, Colin, but …"

"What is it, my darling?"

She dropped her gaze. He tightened his arms around her.

"I don't like to fail, Colin, which is why Amelie's death shook me to the core. I try to rise to every challenge, but tonight, I …" Her words faded into a whisper. "I have no idea what to do."

He cupped her chin, forced her to meet his gaze, and smiled. Then he lowered his head and whispered against her lips.

"Trust me, Kate. By tomorrow morning you will be an expert wife."

A shaft of sunlight streamed through the window and woke Kate. It took her a moment to realize that she was not in her own bed, but in Colin's. She slid her hand across the sheet. He wasn't there. She sat up and called his name. There was no answer. There was nowhere in the small six-sided room for him to hide.

She glanced over at the cuckoo clock that ticked on despite the sad wooden bird dangling by a wire from its broken perch. She was too far away to read the time so she got out of bed and crossed the room.

Nearly nine. She shoved her tangled hair back off her face and tried not to panic. The children were early to bed and early to rise. By now they would have been up for a good three hours, no doubt asking after her.

She pressed her hands to her burning cheeks and stared down at her bare feet. How was she going to sneak back to the house without anyone seeing her?

Maybe Colin was with the children already. Had he told them where she was? What about Eugenie?

She pressed her palms to her cheeks. She had planned to return to the house long before dawn, before anyone knew she had spent the night in the *garçonnière*.

She found her wool shawl hanging over the back of a chair and then tried to finger comb her hair into some semblance of order.

Looking around for her glasses, she remembered leaving them in her room and groaned.

Padding over to the window, she didn't see a sign of anyone about. She opened the door and slipped outside.

She darted across the lawn toward the hedge and followed it around until she was at the front of the house. Thankfully, there was still no one in sight. She hiked up her nightgown and started running across the sun-warmed grass.

The gallery was empty so she hurried upstairs and locked herself in her room.

Eugenie always brought hot water upstairs just after dawn. It was tepid now. Kate washed up, changed into clean clothes, and pinned up her hair. She grabbed her glasses and walked to the mirror to survey the damage.

She looked tired. Her eyes were puffy from lack of sleep. She leaned close to the mirror and stared at her lips. They were tender to the touch and a bit swollen.

No sense hiding all day, as if anyone would allow it. Sooner or later Colin or the children or all of them together would come looking for her. Better to face the world head on, suffer the embarrassment, and be done with it. They were married. They'd done nothing wrong. She took a deep breath.

Yesterday she was a well-educated, twenty-nine-year-old spinster who thought she knew all she needed to know about life and love. How very wrong she'd been.

But last night had been worth a little embarrassment.

The smell of coffee drew her out to the kitchen. As soon as she entered the small building Eugenie turned and smiled a knowing smile.

"Good mornin', Miz Delany." It was the first time Eugenie had ever addressed her by her married name. "I kept the coffee warm for you, but it'll be a might strong by now."

Kate thanked her and quickly glanced at the table, which was already cleared.

"Where are Colin and the children?"

"Mr. Colin told them to let you sleep in this morning and turned them over to Simon. They're corralled in back of the barn pitching horseshoes."

"Colin left?"

Eugenie handed her a mug of coffee and then shooed her over to the table.

"I got a plate of grits and eggs for you in the warmin' oven." She walked over to the stove. "Mr. Colin went into N'awlins with Mr. Bolton. Said to say he took your plans in for you and that he'll drop 'em by the architect's office. Said today was a special day for him too."

Embarrassed, Kate dropped her gaze.

"Special seein' as how you are done with your plans and he and Mr. Bolton were going to see about gettin' a loan."

Kate glanced up so quickly she sloshed the hot coffee on her hand and winced. She carefully set the mug down and went after a dishrag.

"Colin went to New Orleans for a loan?"

Eugenie nodded. "He left a letter on your desk."

"I'll be right back." Kate eyed the plate of food. She was ravenous but wanted to read Colin's note. She hurried into the dining room to her desk.

The letter was centered beneath the carving of *Belle Fleuve*.

Dear Kate,

Thank you for last night. The last thing I wanted was to leave you today but Jason and I planned this trip before I knew that we would . . .

Well, before last night.

Leaving you this morning was one of the hardest things I've ever done. I cannot wait to see you again. We've gone to apply for a loan and should return in two days. I have your

plans and will personally deliver them to Roger Jamison before
I do anything else.

> *Until I return, love,*
> *Colin*

Kate stared at the page in her hand.

Until I return, love.

Kate folded the letter and tucked it into her bodice, then picked up the miniature of *Belle Fleuve*. She thought of Marie and Patrick and smiled. At long last she was a Delany.

EIGHTEEN

There was no other city in America like New Orleans.

The *Vieux Carre*, situated on a bend of the Mississippi, spoke of old-world charm transplanted from Spain and France. That charm thrived behind walled courtyards and balconies hanging over narrow streets. A languid pace masked the constant hum of life on the crowded streets of the French Quarter, the ongoing commerce at the wharf, the constant ebb and flow of the gulf tides. The mighty river carried money and people from all over the globe into New Orleans.

Colin and Jason arrived in town in the late afternoon. Jason introduced Colin to the Edisons, a young couple who had offered them accommodations. Jason had served with Derek Edison during the war until Derek had been wounded and captured, spending months in a Yankee prison camp. Since then he had not been able to cope with everyday life or hold a job, so his wife took in laundry and sewing. They had no children as Derek refused to bring a child into what he believed was a world of darkness.

The man's depression and lack of interest in the simplest tasks reminded Colin of himself. He'd existed in the same void, the same darkness. If only it hadn't taken Amelie's death to inspire him. What would he have done without Kate?

Colin soon left Jason alone with his friends and ventured out to deliver Kate's plans. He found Roger Jamison's quietly elegant home situated on a shady street in the Garden District. The man was obviously surprised to see him so late in the day but ushered him in with a warm welcome nonetheless. He offered tea, which Colin declined.

"What brings you to the city?" Jamison asked.

"I'm here on business. I wanted to meet you and drop off Kate's plans for Captain Stevens' house." Colin handed the architect Kate's drawings.

"She's well, I hope."

"She's very well indeed."

"I knew your father. Fine man. Great architect." Jamison carried the plans to a long table and looked eager to see what Kate had done. "I see the rumors of your insanity are greatly exaggerated."

"Insanity?"

"It was all over town that you returned from the war a madman. When people heard Katherine Keene had gone to your rescue, there were those who feared for her life. All gossip fed by unfounded rumors, I see. You can imagine how surprised I was to hear that the two of you were married."

"No more surprised than I." So everyone was certain Kate had rescued him from the brink of madness.

Roger continued to study Colin. "I'm happy for both of you. Patrick would be so pleased to have an architect in the family again. Congratulations, by the way."

"Thank you, sir." Colin tapped his hat against his thigh and felt heat rise to his face. He couldn't stop thinking of Kate in his arms last night. She'd done so much for him. What exactly had he contributed to their marriage?

He wished he'd been there when she awoke this morning. Wished he'd been there to say good-bye.

Jamison smiled as if he could read Colin's thoughts. "Kate is a very charming and intelligent woman."

"She has great plans for *Belle Fleuve*."

"I agree. I've seen them myself."

"With any luck we'll have the money for restoration someday." Colin's mind wandered. What was Kate doing now? Was she with the children? Or working at her desk? Perhaps she and Marie were in the garden painting watercolors, or maybe Damian was on her lap learning his letters—

"She could have built her own mansion to her taste, from what I hear."

Built her own mansion? Exactly how rich was she? Colin didn't know what to say.

"I'm eager to see what she's designed for Captain Stevens," Jamison said again. Taking note of Colin's reaction, he added, "I can tell by the look on your face there's a problem."

"Ezekiel Stevens showed up at *Belle Fleuve* to speak to Kate personally."

"You don't like him."

"I don't mean to interfere with Kate's opportunity, but you should know he was very forward with her. At least I thought so."

"I'll make certain he doesn't bother her at home again." Roger peered at Colin over his spectacles. "In fact, she needn't be present at our meetings. I can certainly confer with them separately."

Colin could just imagine how Kate would take that news.

"That won't be necessary. My wife has put much time and effort into the plans even though she wasn't in agreement with his suggestions. I'd not jeopardize the project or Kate's presence at the necessary meetings simply because I ... well, because I may be over-reacting to what might have been completely innocent overtures."

"I understand. You just wanted me to be aware."

Colin nodded. "That's right. Thank you for understanding." He extended his hand. "It was a pleasure meeting you. Now I must be off to my business meeting."

"Best of luck to you, Delany." Jamison walked him to the door.

"Thank you, sir," Colin said. "I'll need it."

Colin found New Orleans much the same and yet things were

different. The city's most talented chef, Antoine, had moved his restaurant to St. Louis Street and then gone back to Marseille to die, leaving his wife to run the place.

Colin stopped on the street outside the restaurant to gaze through the windows at rooms aglow with golden light from the chandeliers. Silver and crystal sparkled on a sea of starched white linen tablecloths. He pictured Kate seated at one of the tables, her bright blue eyes shining. This was the lifestyle she was used to, the kind of life the Keenes had given her. Gilbert Keene had left her well off: Kate's clothing was of the finest fabric and latest styles and her suite at the St. Charles hadn't come cheap—but her money was her own.

He wasn't about to take charity from his wife.

His wife. It still seemed impossible—incredible even—that Kate was his. And now she was his in more than name only. Colin stared at his own reflection in the restaurant window. Dark, worried eyes stared back. His tall form listed to one side as he leaned heavily on his cane. He was thin but not as gaunt as before. The lines etched on his face belonged on someone much older. He was in need of new clothes. The black suit he was wearing, which he'd owned before the war, showed its age. If he wasn't so thin it wouldn't fit at all. As it was, the jacket was snug across his shoulders.

He didn't have much to show for a life of thirty-two years. How had Kate ever agreed to his proposal? Colin had definitely gotten the best of the bargain.

He headed for Tujague's on the corner of Madison and Decatur. As he drew closer, his mouth watered for the restaurant's special shrimp *remoulade*. Dinner at the eatery would cost more than he wanted to spend, but one splurge in ten years could be forgiven.

Nearly there, Colin hitched his horse to an iron post and was about to cross the street when someone approached from behind.

"Why, if it isn't Colin Delany." The woman's throaty voice sounded familiar.

Unable to place it, Colin was careful not to trip on the

cobblestones as he turned and found himself face to face with Tillie Cutter, the red-headed prostitute he had met on the train from Texas. She'd chatted on for hours though he hadn't been in the mood to talk. He had told her his name and little else, but somehow she managed to track him down at *Belle Fleuve*. Had Tillie showed up at the *garçonnière* on the very day Kate had arrived? He'd been too drugged at the time to be able to recall exactly.

Without warning or invitation, Tillie slipped her hand into the crook of his free arm. She was so heavily doused with cheap perfume that the air quickly became thick with the scent.

"You look a sight better than the last time I saw you," she told him.

"Thank you. That's because my wife has been taking good care of me."

Tillie hid her surprise well. She tossed her head, which set the ostrich feather bobbing atop her frilly hat.

"Your wife?"

"Yes."

Tillie shrugged. "Most men don't let that spoil the fun when they're in town."

Colin took in her long, black, velvet gown that was threadbare at the elbows and had unraveled white lace cuffs. Her shoes were scuffed, the leather cracked across the toes. Even though her eyes were rimmed with kohl and her cheeks rouged, a layer of face paint couldn't hide the lines around her eyes and mouth. A man with a woman like Kate at home would have to be insane to turn to Tillie.

"I'll help you across the street." She tugged his arm. Together they started across St. Louis Street.

"Where are you staying?" Tillie wanted to know. "I'd be happy to take you back to my place. You can stay as long as you like, and I'll only charge you for an hour."

He knew there were high-class brothels on Basin Street — three-story mansions decorated better than some of New Orleans' finest homes. Mahogany floors and walnut woodwork, the finest carpets from the Orient, and sterling and china all added to the ambiance. But Tillie had been a camp follower in Texas, trailing after army regiments, sometimes miles into Mexico. She'd never seen the inside of a truly fine gentleman's establishment, nor would she ever.

As soon as they were across the street, he extricated his arm.

"I'm going to have to turn down your generous offer, Tillie."

Her smile quickly disappeared. "You think you're too good for me?"

"I'm very partial to my wife." He was more than partial. He was in love.

"That'll change. Mark my words."

Colin hoped not.

"You take care of yourself, Tillie."

They were on the corner in front of Tujague's when Ezekiel Stevens came walking out of the restaurant with a tall, expensive-looking blonde on his arm and a Cuban cigar in his mouth. The minute he recognized Colin, the captain's smile grew even wider. He looked Tillie up and down before he had the nerve to laugh out loud.

"Imagine seeing you here, Delany." He looked pointedly at Tillie again. "Where's the lovely Mrs. Delany this evening?"

Hitting the captain in the mouth might be worth a night in jail, especially if it erased the man's smug smile. For Kate's sake he refrained.

"Kate is at home. I'm here on business."

Stevens looked at Tillie again. "I see."

"I'm afraid you don't," Colin said. "Miss Cutter and I met on the train from Texas a few months ago. She was inquiring after my health. Not that it's any of your business."

"Something tells me she's very attentive to your health." Stevens drew on the cigar and blew a blue smoke ring. "From what I've heard it would be more lucrative for you to stay home and cater to Mrs. Delany."

Colin took a step toward Stevens and the echo of his injury sent a spear of heat up his leg. Forced to back down, Colin turned to Stevens' companion.

"I haven't had the pleasure, ma'am," Colin introduced himself.

Stevens smiled around his cigar. "I doubt you would ever be able to afford the pleasure of Miss Alicia Rhodes' company, Delany. Not unless your wife extends you a loan."

"You're insulting me, Captain. Why is that?"

"I heard about how you fell on hard times and your lovely wife came to your rescue. Quite a love story."

"Rumors of my insanity were greatly exaggerated too." Colin turned to Tillie. "Thank you for your concern, Miss Cutter. No need for you to tarry any longer."

Tillie bestowed a smile on the captain.

"I hope we meet again, Captain." She ignored Colin as she walked away.

"Speaking of the lovely Katherine," Stevens said, "how are my plans coming along?"

Colin unclenched his jaw. After last night there was no reason to be jealous. He refused to let his pride stand in the way of Kate's career.

"I delivered the plans to Roger Jamison this afternoon. He said he'll look them over and meet with you to discuss the project."

The captain's smile flared again.

"That's the best news I've had in a long while," he said. "You tell Kate I'm looking forward to seeing her again soon."

It was all Colin could do to hold his temper in check. Captain Stevens turned to the woman on his arm. "Ready, my dear?"

"Always ready as rain and you know it." The comely young woman looked no older than twenty.

Stevens winked at Colin as the two of them said good-night and walked away.

His run-in with Stevens soured Colin's appetite even more than having had to deal with Tillie again. He looked through the door of Tujague's, thought about what a meal there would cost, and decided to head to Café Du Monde in the French Market. Coffee and pastry would be enough for tonight.

T his is a perfect day for treasure hunting, isn't it, Aunt Kate?" Damian trailed alongside Kate and Marie as they crossed the far end of the front lawn between the oak *allee*.

"It surely is." Toting the shovel Simon loaned them, Kate agreed. The clear sky was a fine backdrop to the warm fall day.

"Where do we go next?" Damian moved closer to his sister, trying to grab the map she was carrying. "Let me hold it."

Marie held the page out of reach. "You might tear it."

"Let's stop, shall we? We'll all study it together," Kate suggested.

Yesterday after Colin left, the three of them had worked on the map together. Kate thought it a fitting activity for stepping off yards and inches, drawing the layout of the front lawn and garden, and adding the lane lined with oaks and the border of River Road.

Marie had used her watercolors to decorate the map once the details were drawn. Damian was using the map to learn how to read the words for tree, lane, oak, rock, road, and other landmarks. Kate was happy with their progress and at the same time concerned that sooner rather than later they would need to hire a real teacher.

The three of them bent over the map for a moment and decided to count the paces to the central oak in the lane.

"Mama was certain *Grandmere* Delany's treasures are buried here somewhere." Marie scanned the yard before she rolled up the map, put her head down, and started counting off paces.

"She told us lots of stories at bedtime. My favorites were about the buried treasure. Why did *Grandmere* Delany bury it anyway? What was it?" Damian questioned.

"The Yankee soldiers came during the war and took things that didn't belong to them. They saw the planters around here as their enemies," Kate said. There was no simpler explanation for spoils of war or the sadness that still pervaded the South. "As for what your grandmother buried, I have no idea. In fact, I'm not convinced she actually buried anything."

"But Mama said she always talked about it. Too bad Mama never found out if it was true. She could have told us where to dig," Marie added.

"The Yankees believed the planters and landowners buried silver and gold and other valuables, but I have a feeling those are mostly tall tales," Kate said.

"But *Grandmere* Delany really did." Damian was not going to be swayed. "We just gotta find it and we'll all be rich."

They finally stopped at the central oak.

"One hundred and sixty-three steps." Marie walked around the tree trunk trailing her fingers over the rough bark as Damian set down his sword and reached for the shovel.

"Be careful," Kate said as she handed it over.

Damian took a deep breath and buried the tip of the shovel in the soil. When it failed to break the dirt, he jumped on it. His weight didn't budge the shovel. Marie sighed.

"You should let me dig. I'm sure *Grandmere* would have buried it deeper than a few inches," she said.

"I think he's doing just fine." Kate was glad Damian wasn't stronger or Simon would be filling much deeper holes.

Marie sat down on grass warmed by the sun and spread her skirt out around her. Kate joined her, content to let Damian work his way around the base of the oak.

"Are you happy you married Uncle Colin?" Marie asked, smoothing her skirt over her knees. "Or are you sorry we made you keep your promise?"

Kate's cheeks grew warm but not from the sun. She closed her eyes and lifted her face to the sunlight.

"I'm very happy."

"He's nicer than I first thought," Marie said.

"He has changed a lot since you two arrived."

"How?"

How much should she tell the girl? "He was in a lot of pain, not only from his ankle wound, but from what had happened during the war. He'd moved himself into the *garçonnière* and didn't want to let anyone in."

"Not even you?"

"Especially not me." Kate smiled remembering. "I came here to help him repair the house, then found out he was the one in need of repair. He didn't see it that way. I refused to leave."

"Did that make him mad?"

"Oh yes," she nodded. "Very."

"But you stayed."

"I stayed. I tried to help. But it wasn't until you two and your mama arrived that he had to put aside his sadness."

"How did he do it?"

"By thinking of someone other than himself, something other than his own pain."

You can hold on to pain as long as you need to. She was thankful that they were both finally letting go—not forgetting Amelie, never that, but letting go of the pain. She hoped the children were too. She slipped her arm around Marie and the girl laid her head on Kate's shoulder.

"Do you think Mama's watching us?" the girl asked.

Kate scanned the sky. "I know she is. I can feel her spirit here."

"I can too," Marie said.

Just then Damian raced past trying to hang onto both his sword and the shovel.

"Come on!" he shouted. "Let's move to the next tree. There's nothing here."

"Nothing here but his little piles of dirt," Marie shook her head. "But at least he's busy."

NINETEEN

When the hired hack stopped at the office of Tom Gilmore on Camp Street, home of the Hibernia Bank, Colin stepped out carefully and waited for Jason to join him, then paid the driver. Before Colin took a step toward the front door, Jason stopped him.

"Let's hope our luck holds today." Jason centered his tall black hat and gave the top a tap.

"Luck?" Luck hadn't been a staple in Colin's life lately.

"The drills are dug, the cane ready to plant. We seem to have hired a good crew of field hands. If our luck holds, we'll get this loan to tide us over."

"Sometimes all the luck in the world counts for nothing."

"Then let's pray God's on our side."

Colin nodded, but God hadn't been on his side in a long time.

"We missed you at dinner last night," Jason said.

"I didn't want to burden your friends." Colin kept the details of his stroll through the French Quarter to himself.

"Derek filled me in on the men who started Hibernia Bank. Twelve wealthy Irishmen." He gestured toward the building in front of them. "They started right here in these law offices five years ago. When I mentioned your wife was Gilbert Keene's daughter, even Derek had heard of him. That should bode well for us."

Colin tugged on the cuffs of his suit and wished he looked

more presentable. Then again, he did look as if he needed a loan. Despite what Jason had said, the last thing Colin wanted to do was capitalize on Kate's name. Especially since the whole town was convinced he was already living off her charity. He wanted the loan on his own merit.

They walked in, were ushered into a waiting room, and were told that bank president Patrick Irwin was out of town but acting vice president Brandon Hovard would be happy to meet with them.

For *Belle Fleuve* to survive, Colin would do whatever he had to. He took a deep breath and studied the well-appointed waiting room. The bank seal displayed on the far wall featured a harp, the national symbol of Ireland.

"Wonder who Hibernia is." Jason, obviously in awe, spoke so softly Colin barely heard him.

"Hibernia was the Roman name for Ireland."

Just then the connecting door opened, and when Hovard walked in, Colin and Jason stood. Looking dapper in a double-breasted waistcoat beneath a dark brown jacket, knotted tie, and high collar, the man was far younger than Colin expected, but he had a welcoming smile and a way about him that put Colin at ease almost immediately.

"I'm sorry Mr. Irwin is out of town. If you'd prefer to wait until—"

"Not at all," Colin said. "We're happy to meet with you in his stead."

"Then please join me in the office, gentlemen." Hovard ushered them into the next room and waited until they were both seated before he sat down behind an expansive cherry desk.

"Since I'm originally from Baton Rouge, I took the liberty of finding out about you both."

Had Hovard heard the talk of Kate footing all the bills? Were they all wondering why the loan?

Hovard started with Jason. "Mr. Bolton, your father was the manager at *Belle Fleuve*. Is that right?"

"Correct, sir."

"And do you feel you've acquired his skill?"

"I hope so, sir."

Jason opened up, chatting easily with Hovard about his upbringing, his years in the Confederate army, and his recent marriage and move back to the plantation.

Hovard made a few notes before he turned to Colin.

"Your father was not only a plantation owner but also an architect, right?"

"Mostly an architect. When he married my mother, the former Marie Baudier, he became a gentleman planter. Bolton's father was responsible for the success of the cane production."

"Then you and Mr. Bolton should make successful partners as well."

"We hope so," Colin said.

"You recently lost a sister." Hovard stopped reading his notes and looked up.

"Yes. Amelie. She left her children in my care."

"Your wife is the former Katherine Keene."

Colin nodded. Waited.

"Gilbert Keene was one of our investors. He wasn't one of the original twelve, but he came in shortly after the founders. You shouldn't have any problem securing a loan."

Colin made a move to rise, ready to walk out. Jason touched his sleeve and Colin relaxed. He needed this loan, if for no other reason than to salvage his tattered pride.

"No liens on the place?" Hovard sifted through some papers and then looked up. "Just a formality. I have to ask."

"My parents owned the plantation outright."

"The taxes are current, I assume? So many planters fell behind after the war."

"Property taxes on *Belle Fleuve* were waived because of my recent service in the Indian wars out west."

Hovard frowned over his notes. "That's odd. I've never heard of such a thing."

"I was given a letter when I returned. It's dated three or four years back." He'd remembered to bring it along and showed it to Hovard.

"You received this from the tax office?"

"I went directly there after I left the army and returned to Louisiana. The letter was in their records."

"When was that?"

"Not long ago. A few months." So much had happened he wasn't certain.

He had been in terrible pain and in a laudanum-induced haze when he returned. He tried to piece the story together.

"Upon arriving back in the city I ran into a neighbor who told me about all the foreclosures and auctions. He advised me to visit the tax office before I went on to *Belle Fleuve*." Colin hadn't kept up with any tax payments and was certain he would find himself homeless.

Hovard remained silent. What was he thinking? Beside Colin, Jason shifted.

"If I do owe any back taxes, could you add the amount to the loan? Of course, I prefer to keep the amount as close to what I've requested in my application as possible."

Finally Hovard leaned back in his chair. He steeped his hands and tapped his fingertips together.

"There shouldn't be a problem. We'll need proof that your property tax payments are current. It would be more expedient if you went to the tax office and asked for documentation yourself while I put the paperwork in order. If you wouldn't mind," he added.

"Not at all." What he wanted was to go home. What he needed was the loan granted with all haste. "We will make time."

Jason nodded in agreement.

"Fine." Hovard got to his feet. "Then I'll meet with you here this afternoon and we'll finalize the loan. You'll be on your way home by tomorrow morning."

On the third day of Colin's absence, while Eugenie and the children continued their treasure hunt, Kate concentrated on the prairie house and barn designs she planned to submit to the periodical contest. She started with a plain country house and stretched her imagination. The first floor included all of the usual rooms and an indoor kitchen. Then she added two wide verandas front and back. She included fireplaces in all of the first-floor rooms and many of the second. The upstairs mirrored the first floor with a spacious hall separating the bedrooms. She chose economical woods of pine and ash and stipulated no paint or graining.

After drawing in a staircase at the end of the central hall, she included a circular stained-glass window at the first landing to lighten the stairwell and give the stairs a warm glow in the daytime.

She closed her eyes and envisioned the house standing tall and inviting on the prairie, a home full of life and laughter and hope. As Kate penciled in the round window above the staircase, she fancifully filled the circle with the outline of a shamrock.

Just as she finished the detail, Marie and Damian ran in. Kate greeted them with a smile.

Damian leaned against Kate's chair while Marie studied the plans.

"Eugenie said we plum tuckered her out," Damian told Kate.

"I imagine you did," she laughed.

"Are you finished?" Marie wanted to know.

"Almost. Any luck with the treasure hunt, Damian?"

He shook his head. "No, but I'm not giving up."

"What's that?" Marie was pointing to the window with the shamrock. "If it's a four-leaf clover you forgot one of the leaves."

"It's a shamrock. Shamrocks are a symbol associated with

Ireland, the country where I was born. Your great-great Delany grandparents were born there too."

"Shamrock," Damian repeated.

"It's pronounced *seamrog* in Irish." Kate traced the design with her finger. "My mother only had one piece of jewelry, a round, brass pendant with a shamrock in the center. She never took it off."

"Your mother who died?" Marie looked thoughtful. "Or the one who adopted you?"

Kate nodded. "The one who died."

"Did she get buried with it on?" Damian started kicking the leg of the table.

"Please stop," Kate said before she answered. "I'm not sure what happened to it. Perhaps one of my sisters has it."

"The one who went to the orphanage with you. Maybe she has it," Marie suggested.

Kate shook her head. "No, she didn't. Perhaps one of my two older sisters though."

"Where are they now?"

"I don't know. I've tried to find them, but I haven't had much luck." Now that money and time were both dear, it would be a while before she could continue the search.

"Maybe they never got out of the orphanage." Marie's eyes took on a panicked look. "Maybe they are still there."

Kate shook her head. "They're all grown women now."

Damian lost interest, picked up one of Kate's pencils, and started drawing on a blank page.

"Would you like to see them again?" Marie asked.

"Of course," Kate said. "I still hope to find them all someday."

She tucked a strand of Marie's hair behind her ear. "Will you help Damian wash up for supper?"

They left the room hand in hand, reminding Kate of when she and her sisters used to make a chain of linked hands and drag Sarah, the youngest, along behind them.

For all she knew one of them might be living right down the road. Would she know them if they met by chance? Would they recognize her?

It was still sunny but the afternoon held a chill, so Kate donned the sweater she had draped over the back of her chair. She made a few more touches to the drawings, and when she was finished she walked over to the window to gaze out into the late afternoon light. The oaks were lit with a golden glow; the gray moss hanging from the trees appeared as silver. The lane leading to River Road was deserted.

It wasn't the first time she'd come to the window to watch for Colin. She had expected him to return sometime today and was disappointed. She missed him more than she thought possible. She looked forward to seeing him riding across the fields and watching him talk with the crew.

When she'd last seen him he'd had a genuine smile on his face—a smile for which she was responsible.

Kate pressed her palms against her cheeks and tried to think of something else but it was nigh impossible. Their night together still seemed like a dream, one that filled her with longings she'd never imagined.

Had Amelie ever known such happiness with Billy Hart? Perhaps in the beginning. Kate hoped so. Thanks to Amelie the children had thrived despite their situation in Kansas. Damian was rambunctious, but that was to be expected. It was impossible to know what life had in store for them. Hopefully, they would never lose each other the way she'd lost her sisters.

Pulling the edges of her sweater close she looked at the encircled shamrock on her drawing of the prairie house for the periodical contest and instead saw the rolling green hills, high cliffs, and rough seas of Ireland. She could almost smell a Yule log burning on the hearth and wasn't sure if she was confusing memories of her earliest years in Ireland with her time there as an adult.

Thinking of Ireland, she decided it would be fun to have an

Irish Christmas at *Belle Fleuve*. Surely there was enough to spare in her account for a simple Christmas.

Once she finished for the day, she went to find Eugenie, who told her Damian was upstairs complaining of a scratchy throat and Marie was reading to him.

Kate fixed a pot of hot chocolate and a tray with three mugs. As Kate entered the children's room with the chocolate, she found that Marie was indeed reading to her brother. The girl put down the book when Kate entered. Her lovely Baudier eyes reflected her concern.

"He doesn't have a fever," Marie quickly informed Kate. "His forehead is very cool."

Kate took Marie's hand. "Don't worry yourself. Little boys get colds all the time. So do little girls for that matter. He'll be right as rain tomorrow. You'll see."

"I hope so." Marie looked doubtful.

Kate made certain Damian was comfortable amid a mound of pillows before she poured them each a cup of chocolate. She sat down and told them she'd been thinking of how she'd spent Christmas as a child in Ireland and thought it might be fun to celebrate some of the old customs with them this year. Then she asked Marie to continue reading.

The girl really did have a talent. When Kate had money to spare she'd find an art tutor for Marie. A quiet hour passed and then Eugenie brought in a dinner tray for the children. Once they were settled, Kate stepped outside with Eugenie.

"Miss Kate—" Eugenie began.

Kate was eager to convey her thoughts. "You were right, Eugenie. I'll always grieve for Amelie, but life does seem to be getting brighter. We have so much to be thankful for."

"Amen to that," Eugenie said.

"The day I came to *Belle Fleuve* and barged into Colin's life, I never dreamed that we would be married with two children to raise." She clasped her hands at her waist and smiled. "Perhaps I should eat with the children. I've no idea when Colin will be back, but since it's already twilight, I assume it won't be until tomorrow. I surely hope he won't be gone much longer."

"Why, he is home, Miss Kate. I was 'bout to tell you. Turns out he's been here 'bout an hour or so. Simon just came in and told me 'fore I brought the tray up."

"Colin's home?" Kate's hand flew to her hair. Did she have time to change into something fresh. "Where is he?"

"In the *garçonnière*, I expect."

"Then please set the table in the dining room. I'll eat with Colin." She couldn't wait to see him, couldn't wait to hear if the trip was successful. "I'll just take a moment to freshen up and comb my hair." Kate started toward her room.

"Mr. Colin told Simon he didn't want dinner," Eugenie said.

Had the meeting gone badly? Kate hid her concern.

"Why don't you set the table for dinner anyway? He should have a bite of something. I'll go after him in a moment."

Eugenie left and Kate hurried to her room. She took five minutes to wash her face and let her hair down because Colin had whispered to her that he liked it falling around her shoulders. She decided to leave her glasses on; it was better to see his expression than give in to vanity.

Twilight dusted the sky with deep violet as Kate made her way along the path to the *garçonnière*. Halfway there an owl swooped across her path. Startled, she paused to watch it dip and disappear into the branches of a nearby tree. Her shoes crunched against the crushed-shell path. Before she reached the door she saw Colin lurch away from the lamp in the window as if he'd lost his balance. She picked up her pace, anxious to make sure he was all right.

"Colin," she called out as she rapped twice on the door. "It's me." She couldn't stop smiling. With a hand over her racing heart, she pictured him flinging open the door and sweeping her into his embrace. But the door didn't open. Her smile faltered. With her heart in her throat, she leaned close to the door and tapped again.

"Colin? Are you all right?"

She heard him shuffle across the room and breathed a sigh of relief. The door slowly opened and there he was, towering over her, weaving a bit on his feet. The odor of whiskey permeated the air around him. Even through the dark days of Amelie's illness and death he had never once drank to excess.

His expression was dark, his mouth set in a grim line.

"Oh, Colin." She wished he would step back and let her in. "Whatever happened, we can face it together. If you didn't get the loan ..."

He leaned against the doorjamb and stretched out his arm, effectively blocking her way.

"Colin."

"Ah, my lovely wife." There was a sneer in his tone that chilled her to the core. "Ready to solve all my problems again."

"What's the matter? What happened?"

"Exactly what *I've* been wondering. What *really* happened here, Kate? What else have you lied about, I wonder."

"I've lied about nothing." She glanced over her shoulder, thankful no one was around to overhear. She pulled her sweater closer. "Please let me in so we can speak privately."

He shrugged but didn't budge. "Everyone already knows our business anyway." Colin shifted but continued to block her way. "Is there really such a thing as a twenty-nine-year-old virgin?"

Her anger instantly flared. "You *know* better than that."

"Yes, unfortunately I do. Now, thanks to our one night together, it will be much harder to get out of this."

"Get out of what?"

"Ah, Kate. You gave me your innocence but not the truth."

Her mind raced in circles. What could have made him this incredibly angry?

"Did you run into Ezekiel Stevens in New Orleans? Is that it? Surely you don't think that I—"

"I don't know what to think about you anymore. Jamison sings your praises but he's of the same opinion as the Hibernia bankers. Everyone tells me I made a very fortuitous marriage to Gilbert Keene's daughter. They all believe that I was insane and down on my luck and you paid my way out."

"Don't be ridiculous."

"That's exactly what I am. Ridiculous. A laughingstock. But then again, how was I to know all of it? You could have told me so many times, Kate. So many times. But you didn't. Not even the night I held you in my arms. Not even then."

He closed his eyes and his mouth tightened as it did whenever he was in pain. He'd been standing too long. Colin stepped away from the door, making his way into the room. Kate followed him inside.

When he stumbled she rushed over and grabbed his arm. He shook her off, nearly throwing them both off balance. He managed to get to the table where he yanked out a chair and lowered himself onto it. Leaning on his elbow he stared at her, his eyes black with fury.

"Too bad I had to hear it from everyone else, eh?"

"Hear *what*?"

"Imagine my surprise when I walked into the tax assessor's office and found out the back taxes on this place had not been waived because I had reenlisted in the army. There is no such waiver, Kate. No other soldiers were as privileged as I. None of the other struggling planters had a generous anonymous donor pay off years of back taxes for them. At least none that I know of. Is *Belle Fleuve* the only recipient of your largesse, Kate?"

"Oh."

"Yes. Oh."

"That was four years ago."

"How could you *forget* you paid out such an exorbitant amount?"

"I didn't forget. I was waiting until the time was right to tell you."

"We're married, Kate. I would think that sometime before the wedding would have been appropriate? Maybe the day you agreed to my proposal? Something like, 'Oh, Colin, by the way, I spent a fortune on your taxes four years ago.'"

"I was waiting to tell you until you turned a profit and were in a position to pay me back. I knew you'd be angry. Obviously, I was right."

Suddenly he was up off the chair and headed for her. Kate stood her ground. He grabbed her arm.

"What else have you lied about?"

"Nothing!" She tried to twist out of his hold. "Let me go!"

The minute she said it he let go and shoved his fingers through his hair.

"Colin, believe me. I only wanted to help, to save this place for you and Amelie. I did this for you both years ago. Please don't be angry. I had no idea things would evolve this way. Everything has happened so quickly."

"You could have told me countless times. You knew I didn't want your charity."

"I don't consider it charity. I wanted to repay all the kindnesses your parents showed me. I did not do it to insult you."

"Leave me alone."

"But we need to talk."

"About what? About how it appears you bought yourself a husband? After all, if Amelie was right, this is what you've always wanted. I'm sorry you had to pay such a high price for me."

"I bought *time*. Time for you to save *Belle Fleuve*."

"Why not just buy the place for yourself?"

"I didn't want it for myself. I wanted it for *you*." She clasped and unclasped her hands. "You've been drinking. Obviously, you're not thinking clearly."

"Oh, I'm thinking clearly enough. We can't undo this sham of a marriage now but I can still throw you out."

The last time they'd been together in this room he'd held her close and whispered gentle words of love.

"You don't mean that. You can't." Her knees were shaking. She warned herself not to crumble in front of him and mustered her courage to withstand his glare.

"You don't belong here, Kate. You never did. You just wished you belonged. You wished you were a Delany so much that you bought your way into this family through deceit."

"I never deceived you."

"You finagled the tax office into hiding the truth from me. Did you bribe someone?"

"Of course not."

"How, Kate?"

She dropped her gaze, unable to meet his. "One of the clerks once worked for my father."

"So I heard. The long arm of the great and powerful Gilbert Keene. How convenient for you. It must be grand to be an heiress of such stature. If it weren't for sticking your nose into the business of the poor Delany clan you wouldn't have a care in the world."

His words did more than wound; they stoked her Irish temper. She wasn't about to let him ruin what they'd worked so hard to salvage. Not when the last time they'd been together they'd shared such a deep physical and emotional connection.

"Colin, stop it. I'm sorry I took matters into my own hands. I did what I thought was right at the time. Can we please move on from here?"

"I was humiliated yesterday. I needed proof that the taxes were current for the vice president of Hibernia Bank and ended up in the tax office where everyone in the place heard the story of how you concocted a plan to explain why the fees were waived. All around me were men without hope, men who will lose their homes and their livelihoods. They all heard what happened. They all know I was stupid enough to fall for that letter."

"And what if I hadn't paid the taxes, Colin? Where would you and the children be now?" With all the anger and turmoil, Kate had almost forgotten why he'd gone to New Orleans in the first place. Remembering, she calmed herself and attempted to redirect the conversation. "Did you get the loan?"

"We got the loan. I first refused to go back to the bank after the scene at the tax office, but Jason finally convinced me not to let my pride harm more than just me. Our workers are depending on me and that money to ensure our success. Jason reminded me I could deal with you once I was home."

Jason had witnessed his humiliation, but Colin had secured the loan. Now he could pay the hands and buy supplies before the harvest. All they had to do was sit out the next few months and pray for good weather, and the crop would be successful. He would calm down. Things would work out.

"Everything will be all right, Colin. You'll see. We'll put this behind us and when you get ahead, you can pay me back." Kate managed a shaky smile.

"Things will work out. You're right." He shifted on the hard chair, turned away from her, and stared at the wall. "But we won't be working them out together."

He was angry. Humiliated. He'd get over it. She'd make certain of it. She went to him, tried to put her arms around him.

"Oh, Colin, don't say that."

He pushed her away.

"I mean it, Kate. It's over. I want you out. I can't bear the sight of you."

"But you can't mean that."

"I can and I do. This time do me a favor and listen to me. Leave."

Blinded by tears, Kate ran back to the house. Avoiding the kitchen, she hiked up her skirt and ran up the gallery stairs to her room. The French door banged against the wall as she tore it open. She heard the distinct sound of one of the glass panes cracking but didn't bother to turn around.

Anger replaced her tears and Kate began to pace the room.

"You thought you'd rid yourself of me before, Colin Delany. Well, think again. I'm not going anywhere." Her words echoed in the sparsely furnished room.

She crossed to the gallery. Clutching the railing, she stared at the *garçonnière*. Colin's light was still on. Did he regret his harsh words? By morning he would apologize.

Or was she dreaming again?

She walked along the gallery to the children's room where they were sound asleep. Damian had kicked off his covers so she drew them up to protect him from the night's chill. Marie slept on her stomach, her cheek pressed against the pillow, her fist clenched. Her brow was marred by a frown, her worry a constant even while she slept.

Kate smoothed her hand over Marie's blanket, then slipped out of the room. She saw that Colin's lamp had been extinguished. Was he any closer to reason? Was he sleeping off all the whiskey he'd consumed?

She hoped not, for she doubted *she* would get any sleep tonight.

But the fingers of dawn's light found her asleep in one of her mother's wingback chairs. Unfortunately, that's where Colin found her too.

"Wake up, Kate."

His voice came to her through the haze of sleep. She smiled before she remembered. Her eyes flew open. He was standing over her. His hair was windblown as if he'd already been out riding.

"I'm sorry," she said, as she tried to rouse herself, rubbing her neck where it was stiff. Her right arm was asleep from leaning on it. She shook her hand, felt pins and needles. "What time is it?"

"Nearly eight." He walked to the open gallery doors.

She thought he was going to leave without another word, but he turned in the open doorway, a tall, imposing silhouette against the morning sunlight.

"I've taken the children to the Boltons' so they won't be here to see you leave. Simon has the wagon hitched and he's already loaded up most of the things you left in the barn." Colin half turned, presenting his profile. His strong jaw, broad shoulders, and proud stance did not give away his feelings.

Panicked, Kate started toward him with one hand extended.

"Stop right there," he said.

"But Colin, surely we can discuss this civilly."

"There's nothing to discuss."

"You're throwing me out?"

"I'm hoping it won't come to that. I'm merely asking you to leave."

"But you're not giving me any choice ..."

"This won't work, Kate. I was a fool to propose in the first place."

"But what will the children think?"

"They'll get over it. They're far more resilient than I thought."

Tears threatened, but Kate was determined to hide them.

"This isn't what Amelie would want."

"No, but it's what I want. Simon is waiting." His tone was devoid of emotion, which Kate found incomprehensible.

"I understand that my actions embarrassed you—"

"Humiliated is more like it."

"That's what this is about, isn't it? Your humiliation? Your pride? Colin, I have apologized. I will again: I'm sorry. I didn't think beyond saving *Belle Fleuve* for you."

"You didn't think, Kate. You forgot that New Orleans is a city that lives on gossip. You forgot that there are circles within circles there. The Irish, the Creoles, the Americans. There wasn't one person I spoke with who didn't make some offhanded comment about us. Everyone believes I married you for your inheritance."

"My *inheritance*?" She nearly blurted out that she had nothing left. It would be folly to let him know she'd exhausted her funds on *Belle Fleuve*. He would never, ever forgive her.

"Since when do you care what anyone thinks, Colin? You didn't seem to mind when rumor had it that you were insane. You didn't care what anyone would think when you were willing to lose this place."

"Let's just say I've come to my senses."

She watched his shoulders rise and fall as he took a long, slow breath and turned her way. Her heartbeat quickened.

"Have you, Colin?" she asked softly. "Have you come to your senses? Then please tell me you see how crazy this is. Please."

Had she reached him? When she saw his hands fisted at his sides, she knew she had lost.

He looked away. "Don't make this any harder than it has to be, Kate."

Harder? Had he just admitted throwing her out was difficult?

Perhaps it was best that she give him time alone. Leaving him with the children and his responsibilities might work in her favor. If she meant anything to him, in a week or two he would come to his senses, forgive her, and take her back.

"Fine," she was barely able to whisper. "If that's what you want, I'll go." She turned away so that he couldn't see the anguish on her face. "If you'll send Eugenie up to me, the packing will go faster. Tell Simon I'll be down before eleven."

Colin's anger propelled him out of Kate's room and down the stairs. Once he found himself alone, he paused to lean against one of the massive gallery pillars. He had expected her to put up more of a fight but he had had no idea what he would do if she outright refused to leave.

He stared out across the recently tilled fields. If all went well the cane would go into the ground soon. When it grew to well over six feet and bloomed, the tassels would whisper a chorus of hush-hush sounds on the breeze. It would be a welcome sound he hadn't heard in years.

His head was banging in time to the rhythm of his heartbeat. So much for trying to drown his troubles in cheap whiskey. He should have known better; getting drunk had never worked before.

Before he'd awakened Kate she'd looked so vulnerable and inviting. Her head resting on her arm; her loose hair falling around her shoulders. But that vulnerability hadn't moved him enough. He still couldn't forgive her.

If he let her stay and was forced to see her hour after hour, day after day, he'd forever be reminded of his shock and humiliation, the embarrassment he'd suffered not only in the tax office but in Hovard's office when he confessed that his new wife had paid off his back taxes. He sat there simmering. He'd been bought and paid for. How long would Kate have kept her secret?

If he let her stay, sooner or later he would give in to her charm and wind up in bed with her again. Sooner or later he'd forgive her.

He wasn't about to play the fool twice.

Kate had removed a pile of gowns from her closet by the time Eugenie came in. The woman was in tears, continually wiping her face on the hem of her apron.

"You shouldn't go, Miss Kate." Eugenie shook her head when she saw Kate's things all over the bed. "You got just as much right to be here now as he does. More even. Why if it wasn't for you, we'd all be without a home."

Kate paused in front of the marble-topped washstand with her back to the room and closed her eyes.

"What makes you say that?" Kate turned to Eugenie.

"Portia came home from helpin' over at the Boltons'. When Mr. Bolton got back last night Portia heard him tell his missus that he was with Mr. Colin when they found out you paid the taxes on this place a long time ago and Mr. Colin had a fit."

Jason had witnessed his embarrassment and knew what she'd

done. If Eugenie saw her as *Belle Fleuve*'s savior, then so did the others. Keeping the secret had done exactly what she never intended—cut Colin down and emasculated him.

Kate surveyed all of her things as Eugenie began making order out of the piles.

"If I was you, I'd stay and fight," Eugenie sniffed.

"Any other time I would," Kate said. "But Colin is furious. Maybe if I leave for a while he'll have time to calm down and reconsider. If I stay he'll constantly be reminded of what I did."

"You didn't do anythin' wrong."

"Not telling him was wrong. I had ample opportunity."

"Where will you go?"

Kate paused. She could no longer afford a fancy hotel suite, but she could certainly stay at the St. Charles for a night or two.

"I'll go back to the St. Charles, of course. If you need me, contact me there."

Eugenie pressed her lips together, pulled a handkerchief out of her apron pocket, and blew her nose.

"Please don't fret." Kate patted the woman's shoulder. "I have my work with Mr. Jamison to keep me busy. Hopefully Colin will come to his senses soon and I'll be back before you know it. Until then I'll miss you all terribly."

"What if he doesn't? What if he just puts you out of his mind?"

She was willing to bet that Colin could no more put her out of his mind than she could him. Not even for a heartbeat.

"I'll have to take that chance," she said.

"What about Marie and Damian? Won't you stay long enough to tell them good-bye?" Eugenie gave up folding clothes and sank to the edge of the bed with her hands clasped in her lap.

"I don't want to upset them. It would make Colin even more furious if I caused a scene. I won't use them to plead my case." Kate walked to her armoire and pulled out a valise. "I'll write them a letter. Hopefully, Colin will let me visit them soon."

"Visit? You're married to him, Miss Kate. How can he keep you from seeing the children?"

"They're his kin, remember. Not mine."

An annulment was impossible now, but even the notion of living apart from him was breaking her heart.

"Colin will come to his senses, Eugenie. You'll see. I just need to give him a little time."

TWENTY

What started as a light mist soon turned to rain as Colin rode across the land. Surveying the rich, alluvial soil, he was afraid to hope, afraid to believe that the crop might thrive. Around him field hands dropped two-foot cane stalks into shallow troughs four to five feet apart.

Time and again over the past three weeks he'd found himself thinking of things he wanted to tell Kate before he remembered that she wasn't here, that he'd sent her away.

He'd moved into the house the day she left, and the walls whispered her name. He had put his few personal possessions into the master bedroom, though it still didn't feel right to sleep in his parents' old room despite it being furnished with Nola Keene's castoffs.

He was mad enough he'd thought about sending all the Keene furniture back to Kate. Every piece he looked at only reminded him of how indebted he was already. But common sense prevailed; the children needed something to sit on, somewhere to eat.

For two days after Kate's departure Colin avoided telling them that she wouldn't be coming back. At first he explained that she was in New Orleans working for Mr. Jamison.

"Is she working on Captain Stevens' house?" Damian wanted to know. "Why can't we go see it?"

Remembering his run-in with Stevens only fueled Colin's ire.

Eugenie demanded that he give the children Kate's letter. "I don't care if you fire me. Send me away too, but those children deserve to hear Miss Kate's letter."

Colin could hire more help and get along without Eugenie and Simon, but he'd be hard-pressed to find help as devoted to *Belle Fleuve* or as trustworthy, so eventually he gave in to Eugenie's demand.

He handed the letter to Marie without opening it. Grabbing her brother's hand, she took Damian upstairs and closeted them in their room. An hour later they sought him out.

"How long is Kate going to have to stay in New Orleans? If it's for a long time, then when are you going to take us to visit her?" Marie wanted to know.

"She's missing us too much," Damian added.

Their guileless faces had the effect of a bucketful of water tossed on his head. With his temper gone, he had to remind himself that Kate was the source of his public humiliation. The one person in the world he should trust had deceived him.

As the weeks had passed Colin found himself missing Kate more than he ever imagined possible. For someone who had been part of his life for no more than a handful of weeks, she had wormed her way into his heart and mind. But despite how much he yearned for her, his pride wouldn't let him apologize until they were on equal footing. Not until he had a way to repay her and had something to offer.

Had she taken up her old life in New Orleans? Kate was as resilient as a cat. By now she'd surely recovered from the shock of his rejection. No doubt she was surviving. She had her work and enough money to live the grand life she was accustomed to, but did she miss him at all?

The sky opened up as he rode back to the house. Lightning cracked overhead. He dismounted just inside the horse barn and handed the reins to a boy — probably a year or two older than

Marie—that Simon had put to work in the stables. Colin studied the boy's round face and dark eyes.

"What's your name, son?" Colin's mind had been elsewhere when Simon told him before.

"Edward, sir."

"Thank you, Edward. Be sure to rub him down," he added.

"Yes, sir."

As the boy started to walk the horse toward its stall, Eugenie came running out of the kitchen and into the barn, holding her apron over her head. Worry furrowed her brow like the billows of a Cajun's concertina.

"Mr. Colin, we've got trouble," she shouted over the pounding rain of a cloudburst.

"What is it?" He steeled himself against bad news. If anything had happened to Kate—

"I can't find the children anywhere. They're gone."

Eugenie had endured slavery, war, and heartache. She didn't scare easily, but she was clearly frightened now. Colin tamped down rising panic and looked out the stable doors through a curtain of rain.

"They have to be around somewhere. Have you looked through the house? Checked all the rooms and cupboards?"

"All of them."

"They're probably out treasure hunting."

"They usually don't go any farther than the garden, and especially not in a rainstorm."

"They might be hiding from us."

"They aren't here. Damian can't stay still or quiet all that long, and I've been looking for them for a good half hour."

Colin nodded toward the back of the barn. "Ask Edward to leave my horse saddled and bring it round to the door. Have Simon come help me search the house."

He knew he was the last person the children wanted to see.

They had made that abundantly clear ever since he had come up with excuse after excuse for not taking them to visit Kate.

Upstairs he found their hobbies spread out over a low work-table Simon had made for them. Marie's watercolors covered most of the surface along with her paints and glasses of mud-colored water. Damian's treasure map lay forgotten on the floor near his alphabet blocks. The map had been folded and unfolded along the same crease lines so many times that it was worn through. The boy rarely left it anywhere. Colin picked it up and fingered the page as he looked around.

On the table, along with Marie's watercolor supplies, were a McGuffey Reader and an atlas of Louisiana and its counties that Kate had retrieved from the *garçonnière*.

Kate had been teaching them to read maps in the atlas and to understand distance and miles and hours and measurement. They'd been learning about the river and its tributaries, the marshes and bayous as well as the roads.

Colin picked up the atlas and found a scrap of paper marking the page that showed a map of River Road and routes to New Orleans. The children had become distant and secretive since he'd given them Kate's letter and had declined his invitations to take them to visit the Boltons or other planters nearby. He had figured the moping would eventually end.

As he began to suspect where they'd gone, he moved as quickly as his ankle allowed.

Making his way downstairs, he found Edward at the back of the house waiting with his horse. Eugenie was there along with two of the men. They all looked more worried than before.

"They're not there. I'm going to look for them on the road," he announced.

The rain had stopped, though gray clouds still threatened. The stable boy was staring at him until Colin met his gaze, and then he looked at the ground.

"You know something, son? Tell me." Colin glanced at the men watching him in silence. "Do you, Edward?" He kept his tone even, but he was anything but calm.

Edward cleared his throat before he could speak. "Yesterday afternoon they asked me do I know how far it is to N'awlins. I said not for sure, but I heard it was purty far."

"Did you see them this morning?"

"No, sir. If they left the house they must have gone out the front. I got a clear vision of the back door from the stables and I ain't seen 'em all mornin'."

Colin led his horse to the wooden mounting block Simon had built for him. Once he was in the saddle, he turned to Eugenie. She still hadn't forgiven him for making Kate leave.

"I'll find them," he promised.

She gave a silent nod but looked less than hopeful.

He headed out, skirting around the house, and rode between the lines of live oaks standing sentry along the *allee*, as they had for over one hundred years. Planted by his French ancestors, the oaks had survived two wars, four flags, life, death, and every drama in between. Colin hoped to find the children on the property, perhaps sheltered beneath the wide limbs and branches of one of the oaks, but he reached River Road without any sign of them.

How far could two children get on foot? He pictured Damian urging on the more cautious Marie. They were babes with no experience of the world at large. They knew nothing of the dangers of the marshes and swampland beyond the fields or of strangers with false smiles. He prayed no one had picked them up.

Colin stayed on the road. Whatever tracks the children might have left had been erased by the last cloudburst. Rain was falling again with annoying steadiness. He glanced up at the low-hanging gray clouds. Down the road, he saw something black bobbing along. His top hat kept little rain out of his eyes, so he had to wipe his face with the back of his coat sleeve and look again.

Whatever he thought he had seen had disappeared. He rode on and found himself at the end of a lane that led to Langetree, a plantation recently purchased by a Northerner. He debated inquiring at the house until his gaze was drawn to a magnolia in a stand of trees near the drive. Two umbrellas formed a shelter near the base of the tree. The toes of two small pairs of shoes showed beneath the edge of the umbrellas.

Relieved beyond words, Colin nudged his horse into motion and walked the animal closer to the umbrellas. He didn't move or say a word. His horse tossed its head.

"You may as well show yourselves." He had to raise his voice to be heard over the rain drumming on the fabric of their umbrellas.

After a bit of frantic whispering, the children pulled in the toes of their shoes and lowered the umbrellas even farther. Colin sighed, dismounting with care.

Once he was on the ground he realized he'd made a tactical error. He had no way to mount up again. It would be a long, painful walk back—but at least he wouldn't return empty-handed.

"You gave Eugenie quite a scare, you know." He tapped his riding crop against his thigh. *Not to mention me.*

"Are you going to whip us?" It was Damian's greatest fear. Colin slipped his riding crop back into a loop on his saddle.

"Of course not, but I am upset with you. You scared everyone. We had no idea where you went."

They raised the umbrellas. Marie stared across the road and refused to look at him.

"We're going to New Orleans to live with Aunt Kate," Damian said. His sister shoved her elbow into his rib. He cried out, "Ow! We wanna see her," he continued. "We miss her."

The ache in the boy's voice irritated Colin. He'd done everything he could for them and still they wanted Kate. For that matter, so did he.

"Will you please take us to see her, Uncle Colin?" Damian begged.

"Not in this rain. I'll be lucky if we don't all catch our death of cold."

Marie turned to him with terror in her eyes.

"That's just a figure of speech. No one's going to die of a cold." Not if he got them back quickly and into hot baths. Most likely Eugenie already had water boiling.

"Will you take us soon?" Damian asked.

"This isn't the time to discuss it." Colin noticed the rain had stopped again. "Get up and let's get going before it starts pouring again." Rain still dripped from the trees and plopped on the carpet of dry leaves around them.

Marie got to her feet and pulled Damian up beside her.

"Kate said in her letter that she hoped we could visit."

"It's very, very far, isn't it?" Damian sounded discouraged by the hike.

"Too far to walk." Colin turned toward the road. "We'd better get going."

Marie stalled. "We won't go until you promise you'll take us to visit Aunt Kate."

Colin wasn't ready to see Kate for fear he'd beg her to forgive him, beg her to come back home. He had nothing to offer yet and his pride wouldn't let him forget. He couldn't go after her until they were on equal footing.

Marie tapped her foot against the soggy grass. She wasn't giving in.

"Perhaps Eugenie will take you. Cora can go along too, and you can all spend the day together in New Orleans. When the weather is better, that is. Now let's go home."

Damian turned to Marie. She shrugged.

"All right," Damian told Colin. "We'll go."

They folded up their umbrellas and picked up the damp bundles that probably contained no more than their nightclothes. Not even the precious treasure map. They'd been willing to leave everything behind to see her.

Together the three of them slowly trudged up the road toward *Belle Fleuve* in silence. Colin led his horse. It was slow going and his ankle was aching after five minutes of struggling on the muddy road. He was about to call a halt to their forlorn little parade when he spotted Simon driving the wagon up the road.

Simon climbed down off the seat and helped Colin onto his horse. Once Colin was back in the saddle, Simon loaded the silent, bedraggled children into the wagon.

"Eugenie made you some hot cocoa," Simon told them. "Bet that'll taste good right about now. But first she's gonna dunk you in a hot bath. Chase the cold out of you."

"Can we have some biscuits and honey?" Damian wanted to know.

Simon started the rig moving. "I 'spect so."

Nudging his horse into a trot, Colin led the way. With the children safe, all was right with the world.

Almost.

Once they were home Eugenie reprimanded the children for giving her such a scare and clucked over them, promising hot chocolate once they were free of wet clothes and muddy shoes and socks. Colin took their bundles out of the wagon and carried them upstairs. As he set down the larger of the two, a folded piece of paper fell out. Kate's letter.

He glanced over his shoulder before he unfolded the page and ignored the way his hand trembled as he read her words.

My dears,

You know all about my work for Mister Jamison in New Orleans and how I told you I would be going to meet with him sometimes. There is much to do right now and so I must stay in the city for a while. I am so sorry that I had to leave without telling you good-bye, but just know that I can imagine the hugs we will share when I see you again.

While I am away, please continue your studies. Marie, it is up to you to help Damian with his letters and numbers and keep up your own reading. I'm sure your uncle will help you choose suitable books from his library in the garçonnière.

I know you will both be very, very good. Do what Eugenie
asks and take care of each other and Uncle Colin. Remember
to make your mama proud. She is always watching over you
from heaven.

I miss you, and I hope to see you very, very soon.

Many hugs and kisses.

Love, Aunt Kate

Were the tearstains on the page Kate's or Marie's? Or was
it rain?

Colin reread the letter and carried it onto the gallery into the
brisk air. He had expected recriminations. At the very least he
thought Kate would accuse him of sending her to the city, but
she'd laid none of the blame at his doorstep.

Her consideration was more than he deserved. He folded the
letter and slipped it into the poorly tied bundle. The children were
safe. So why was his heart heavier than before?

A lone in New Orleans, Kate buried herself in work, which
brought some light into otherwise long and empty days.

Roger Jamison was a wonderful mentor who entrusted her with
more work—so much work that she was becoming known around
town as more than Gilbert Keene's daughter; hopefully she would
soon make a name as a talented architect in her own right.

When she asked Dan Rosen what rumors, if any, were circulat-
ing about her leaving her new husband to take up residence in the
city, he said no one was giving it much attention. Nola had always
been more than content to live apart from Gilbert; folks assumed
that Kate took after her mother.

Let them talk, Kate decided. Speculation was far better than
the truth.

After two weeks in the city without any word from *Belle Fleuve*,
she was certain she had made a big mistake by leaving. After three
weeks she was heartbroken. She should have stayed to plead her

case. How else could she convince Colin the last thing she ever wanted was to hurt and embarrass him?

Just as she made up her mind that it was high time she returned to the plantation to reason with him, she stopped by the reception desk at the St. Charles. A letter from Cora Bolton awaited her. Cora and Eugenie were making the trek to New Orleans with the children. They were all looking forward to visiting her for the day. She read the brief missive over and over. There was no mention of Colin.

Her heart sank. If he was sending the children to visit, there was little hope of reconciliation anytime soon.

Kate shook off her disappointment and tried to see the bright side; soon she would be with Damian and Marie again, and perhaps Cora or Eugenie could shed some light on Colin's mood.

"I won't be in tomorrow," she reminded Roger, as she handed him her latest drawing.

He smiled as he peered over his spectacles. "I may be in my fifties but I've still got my wits about me, young lady. That's the third time you told me today."

"I'm sorry. I'm just excited. The children are coming to visit."

He sat down on the arm of a chair and studied her.

"You know, Kate, there's nothing good to be had by living apart from Colin. I know a man in love when I see one, and he was certainly in love with you when I met him. Why don't you go home?"

She sighed a small sigh and shrugged. "It's not that easy."

"This has nothing to do with Ezekiel Stevens does it?"

"Not at all." Kate wished things were that simple. "I assured Colin he had no reason to be jealous of the captain. I'm certain he believed me."

Roger was a true gentleman, and Kate had come to consider him not only a mentor and employer, but also a friend. Still, she could tell him no more.

"I had a client in here last week, a man named Sparks. He and his wife saw your plans for *Belle Fleuve* and wondered if you'd be willing to copy them. They're preparing to build on some land they recently purchased on the river."

A replica of *Belle Fleuve*?

"I'm afraid *Belle Fleuve* is far too precious to me. Besides, the original plans belong to the Delanys. They belonged to the Baudiers before them."

"He'll be very disappointed."

"I'd be more than happy to come up with something equally lovely for them. Something with the same colonial feel."

"Good. I'll let them know." He put the new set of drawings on the table.

"Any word yet on your periodical contest entries?"

Kate shook her head. "Not yet."

"Don't be discouraged. I'm sure you're going to become so sought after that I'm afraid I'll lose you." Roger was headed around his desk.

"I'm not going anywhere."

He gave her a thoughtful appraisal. "You'll be going home soon, Kate."

Her heart contracted with a familiar ache of longing. She hoped he was right. Weeks ago nothing could have kept her from *Belle Fleuve*, not even Colin's temper. Now she wasn't certain of anything.

The day of the visit dawned on the chilly side, but it was warm in the sunshine. Still wearing mourning colors out of respect for Amelie, Kate chose one of her finest day outfits, a long jacket of striped gray silk with plain sleeves. She donned a small felt hat with short feathers. Kid gloves the color of her narrow-cut boots and matching silk bag completed the ensemble.

She might not have much left in her account, but she had never scrimped when she had money, so her wardrobe wasn't lacking. She could always have her things altered to keep up with trends. She set her hat at a jauntier tilt and then adjusted her glasses before she looped the silk drawstrings of her reticule over her wrist. Finally, she was ready to await the children in the grand vestibule of the St. Charles Hotel.

The place was already bustling with businessmen and government officials. As it had been for decades, the hotel's famous Parlor P was still the center of Southern politics, and during Reconstruction the hotel had been the site of at least six different congressional committee investigations.

Kate waited for the children beneath the grand rotunda. The hotel housed six hundred guests, and it was here that many of the formerly wealthy planters displaced by the war had sought asylum for as long as they could afford it. Who knew she would be experiencing their plight firsthand?

The rotunda amplified even the most hushed sounds rising from the floor beneath it. The many footsteps and conversations exchanged by harried businessmen and politicians combined with the higher-pitched voices of women preparing to venture out created quite a din. Even with all the noise, it was hard to miss Damian's shout as he came running across the room.

"Aunt Kate! Aunt Kate, we're here!"

When she spotted him making a beeline for her, Kate knelt and opened her arms wide. He barreled into her and hugged her tightly.

"Oh, Aunt Kate. We've missed you. When are you coming home?"

She looked over his head and saw Cora hurrying toward them. Marie was clinging to the woman's hand. Kate extricated herself from Damian's hold but kept his hand in hers as she waited for Cora and Marie.

As soon as they were reunited, Marie wrapped her arms around Kate's waist and hugged her without a word. Kate drew back and smoothed her hand over Marie's damp cheeks.

"There now, don't cry on such a wonderful day. I'm so happy you're finally here."

"Can we see your room?"

After a moment's pause Kate said, "I'm afraid it's a terrible mess right now. I couldn't decide what to wear today and my things are flung about as if a hurricane stirred them up."

She reached for Marie's hand and held tightly to both children. She told Cora, "I've planned a picnic for later. We'll all be more comfortable in the park than here at the hotel."

She could tell Cora was both overwhelmed by the grandeur of the place and relieved to hear Kate say this. In her plain serge gown and wide-brimmed bonnet the woman looked neat and clean but hopelessly unsophisticated, and Kate found herself wishing she had dressed down a bit.

"That sounds wonderful," Cora agreed readily.

"Have you been to New Orleans before?" Kate asked.

"Only once, but Jason hadn't time for sightseeing."

"Well, today we'll take our time. The children have never been to a city before. Have you, Marie?"

Marie shook her head no.

"We've never been anywhere 'cept Kansas." Damian was enjoying the echo in the din.

They exited onto the portico and started down the wide marble steps to the street where Eugenie waited with fussy baby Jake. Cora was relieved when they found her safely tucked in the shade away from the steady stream of passersby. Cora reached for Jake as Kate greeted Eugenie. Dressed in somber black, the woman's eyes filled with tears the minute she saw Kate.

"I wasn't goin' to do that," Eugenie said as she wiped her eyes.

"Please don't cry or I'm afraid I will too. I missed you, Eugenie. I've missed you all. How is Simon?"

"He's fine. Everybody's fine. Don't you worry 'bout us."

Kate blinked back tears. "Today is going to be a fine day," she said, leading the way.

They headed for the French Quarter. Damian was thrilled when they paused outside of an old building once thought to be Jean Lafitte's blacksmith shop.

They walked as far as they could, and when Cora tired of carrying Jake and the children were dragging, Kate hired an open carriage and they all piled in. The children's heads swiveled right and left as they took in the sights and sounds. Damian asked why there were so many soldiers on the streets but Kate soon gave up trying to explain the military law established to quell the frequent riots between opposing sides vying for control over the city government.

"Why isn't Uncle Colin soldiering here?" Damian wanted to know.

"Because of his ankle, silly," Marie told him. "He's not a soldier anymore."

At the mention of Colin's name, Kate noticed that Cora busied herself adjusting the baby's blanket. Eugenie had been mostly silent. They visited a toy shop where each child was allowed to choose a small memento. Marie chose a souvenir plate with a paddle wheeler in the center and magnolia blossoms painted around the rim. Damian chose a cup-and-ball game.

They finally went on to the French Market, where Kate kept a wary eye out for pickpockets. She handed Damian and Marie a few coins so they could choose their own items for the picnic in Jackson Square.

"Pralines!" Damian dashed for a cart with a grand display of sugary treats.

"Fruit and cheeses, please," Kate advised when she caught up. "I'll get some bread. Perhaps we'll all have a praline later and definitely some ginger cake." She nodded to Eugenie, who shadowed Damian as he made his purchases. Kate helped Marie choose items for all of them to share.

They walked three blocks back to Jackson Square and found a bench on the river side of the park near the equestrian statue of Andrew Jackson astride his rearing mount. After they spread out their food and sat down, Kate pointed out St. Louis Cathedral facing the square, the *Presbytere*, the *Cabildo*, and the Pontalba buildings.

Once he gave up on getting the ball in the cup, Damian ran around the lanes circling the park. Marie, ever concerned, hurried after him.

All day Cora and Eugenie had avoided any mention of Colin. Kate could take their silence no longer.

"How is Colin?" she asked neither in particular.

"I'd best go keep an eye on the children." Eugenie stood and shook out the breadcrumbs that had fallen on her lap.

Frustrated, Kate watched her go.

"She's very angry at him," Cora volunteered. "I'm surprised he hasn't fired her."

Kate was aghast. "He wouldn't."

Cora shrugged. "Not unless he's lost his mind. She does such a fine job with the children."

"That's good." Kate's gaze found the familiar trio across the park.

"But it's not the same as having you there." Cora paused, considering. "They ran away last week."

Kate dropped the leftovers she was wrapping. "The children ran away?"

Cora shifted the baby to her other shoulder and patted his bottom. "They didn't get far. Eugenie came to the house looking for them. Colin searched the road. I was frantic until Jason came home and told me Colin had found them not far away. They were running away to live with you. That's why Colin agreed to this visit."

What if he hadn't found them so quickly? What if they'd lost them for good?

"I can't thank you enough for bringing them to town." Kate smiled at the babe nestled in Cora's arms. "I'm sorry you had to make the journey with the baby."

Cora looked up and smiled. "It's not bad by steamboat. Colin had the men restore the old river landing so now *Belle Fleuve* has its own dock again."

"Things are going well then?"

"As well as can be expected. Jason and Colin are constantly inspecting every acre. The cane is finally in the ground but they'll be nervous as mother hens until it's grown. Colin seems particularly driven."

Kate waved at Damian, who was across the park calling her name. He started running again.

"You should come home, Kate. Christmas is in a few short weeks and you should be there with your family."

Kate turned to face the river. Christmas at *Belle Fleuve*. How often had she dreamed of it? Christmas was the one time of year her parents insisted on acting their part and kept her with them in New Orleans for the festivities. Once she had asked why she couldn't spend Christmas with the Delanys and was told holidays were for families and she couldn't intrude.

For the first time she had a family of her own—a hodge-podge, cobbled-together family of sorts—but a family nonetheless. She had every right to be celebrating with them at *Belle Fleuve*. But she would not be with them this year unless Colin showed up at the door and asked her to come home.

She had more hope of a flock of pigs flying over Jackson Square.

Full of ginger cakes and pralines and toting souvenirs, the little party trudged to the wharf where they would board another steamboat back upriver. The children had become more withdrawn with every step and both of them balked when it was finally time to bid Kate farewell.

Determined not to cry, Kate knelt down and held them close.

"We'll have none of this." She spoke as cheerfully as she could. "If you go home all red-faced and sorrowful your uncle might not let you visit again."

"But ... you'll be home soon, won't you, Aunt Kate?" Marie had taken a step back but Damian had a tight grip on Kate's skirt.

"Sooner than anything."

"Why don't you come with us now? Please?"

Kate drew a shaky breath but held onto her smile.

266   JILL MARIE LANDIS

"I've still too much to do here. Besides I must pack my things before I return." Her heart was breaking.

"You said we'd have Irish Christmas this year," Damian reminded her.

"So we shall, another time." She closed the subject. "I'll write you a letter as soon as I get back to my room. That way it will chase you home."

Kate was close to falling apart and looked to Eugenie and Cora for help. Eugenie stepped forward.

"You'll see your aunt for Christmas. I'll make sure of that myself." Eugenie gently pried Damian loose from Kate's skirt. "I will see to it," she whispered to Kate. "That man's not gonna keep you from these children on Christmas."

Just then, as if Kate hadn't enough to deal with, Captain Ezekiel Stevens stepped out of the crowd at the wharf and joined them. Kate introduced him to Cora. He gave a nod to Eugenie.

"You remember Damian and Marie," she added.

"The niece and nephew. Of course." Tall and broad shouldered, the captain's red-gold hair was thick and wavy beneath his white hat. He gave the children little more than a glance.

"I heard you were in town." Stevens ignored everyone but Kate.

"On business." She took Damian's free hand and began walking toward the boat ramp. "If you'll excuse me, the children are heading home."

Undeterred, the captain fell into step beside her. Once they reached the end of the gangplank, Kate gave Damian a kiss and a hug and then bestowed the same on Marie. The girl turned away without a word and went aboard. Kate called out to her but Marie kept going.

"I'll see to her," Cora said. "Thank you for a lovely day, Kate. I'm sure the children will remember this for a long time. So will I." Snuggling Jake close, she hurried after Marie.

Eugenie urged Damian along but the boy stopped in his tracks.

"We got to ride on a boat after all," he told Stevens. "A steamboat like yours."

"Almost like mine," Stevens said, eyeing the packet. "Not as big or as fancy."

"I'll still ride on yours sometime if you wanna take me," Damian volunteered. "We got a dock built at the plantation now."

"Anytime."

Two shrill whistles warned the passengers milling on the dock to hurry aboard.

"Give your uncle my regards," Ezekiel Stevens told Damian. "You be sure to tell him I said hello."

Eugenie told Kate good-bye and led the boy up the gangplank.

Despite Stevens standing there, Kate couldn't leave, though she wanted to get away from him. Not with Damian and Marie and the women waving good-bye from the ship's rail. She waited as the steam packet got underway, then waved until her arm grew tired and the steamboat finally disappeared around a bend in the river.

"I'll walk you home," the captain said, offering his arm.

"No, thank you." Her nerves were frayed. She started walking.

He fell in beside her. "What will your husband say when he finds out we met here?"

She turned on him. "What do you mean?"

"I saw your face when I told the boy to say hello. I know Mr. Delany doesn't hold me in high regard."

"Mr. Delany doesn't care for men who are so forward with me." She almost told him that she didn't either — but she was still working with him on the reconstruction of his silly steamboat house.

"Then Mr. Delany should be keeping a better eye on you. If you were mine I'd never let you out of my sight."

"Colin trusts me."

"Does he?"

Not anymore, she remembered.

"Of course." She started walking again.

"Do you trust him?"

"Yes."

"Your trust may be misplaced then. I saw him a few weeks ago here in town with a redhead on his arm."

A redhead. The redhead she'd run into at the *garçonnière?* Stevens gave her no time to react.

"Why aren't you living at *Belle Fleuve?*"

"Who says I'm not?"

"It's pretty much common knowledge."

"I hardly think so in a city this size," she said.

"Ah. It may be a large pond but the puddles around it are very small."

She fell silent, hoping that he'd get the hint and leave her alone. He had done enough damage for one day. Instead he shortened his long strides to match her pace.

"Mrs. Delany. Kate. You've had a trying day. I can see it on your face. How about I take you to dinner at Antoine's?"

"No, thank you."

"Coffee then?"

"No, thank you, Captain."

"Some other time then?"

Kate extended her hand.

"Thank you for the kind offer and your concern, but I prefer to be alone. Good afternoon."

She forgot he was one for kissing hands until he bowed and raised her hand to his lips. His moustache grazed her skin.

When he raised his head his eyes twinkled above his smile.

"You find me funny, Captain?"

"I find you challenging, Mrs. Delany, and I'm a man who loves a good challenge."

It had been a long, emotional day and Kate was beginning to wilt. As if he knew he'd pushed her far enough, Stevens suddenly bid her good-bye and walked off.

Kate watched him go with a heavy heart and sense of

foreboding. There was no denying he was handsome, if one liked his type, but he wasn't Colin.

Colin. He'd been seen with a redhead when he was in town. Had he sought out the woman the minute he arrived? Or had he turned to her to help him forget his humiliation?

TWENTY -ONE

Colin and Jason were going over accounts in the sitting room as Eugenie entered. She wore an irritable expression of passivity that set Colin's nerves on edge. Not only had her anger dissolved into pity, but he caught her looking at him as if he were a lost cause.

"It's almost time to tuck the children into bed, Mr. Colin."

"Thank you." He watched her as she left, but she didn't say another word.

"Where has the time gone?" Jason looked at his watch. "It's high time I headed home."

Colin escorted him to the gallery. "Thank you for taking the time to meet with me. I know you'd rather be with Cora and your boy."

"You're driving yourself too hard, Colin. There's nothing more we can do before harvest."

"I have to succeed at this."

"Times may never be as good as they were before the war," Jason reminded him.

"I'm aware of that." Colin's need to succeed wasn't just about putting food on the table. Until he and Kate were on equal footing there was no way his pride would let him ask her to come back.

"Cora said Kate misses you."

"Did Kate say so herself?" Colin tried to imagine Kate speaking so openly about him.

"Cora said she could tell." Jason paused a moment as if debating his next words. "You know, there's stubborn and then there's stupid stubborn. You deserve to be happy, Colin. There was a time before we went to New Orleans I thought that might be possible, before you let what happened at the tax office ruin everything."

They'd never spoken of that, not once.

Colin regretted taking Jason with him to the tax office that day weeks ago. As he thought about Jason's comment, he recalled what happened.

They were forced to stand in a long line of landowners waiting to plead their cases. When they reached the head of the line Colin presented his letter.

"I was given this, which tells me my taxes were waived. Now I've applied for a loan and need proof the property is free and clear."

They waited while the *Belle Fleuve* file was located. The clerk took his sweet time reading over page after page of documentation and receipts, many dating back to the establishment of the plantation. He paused to peer over his glasses at Colin.

"Is there a problem?" Colin asked.

"Just a moment, please." The man walked toward the back of the room to confer with someone else.

Would he come back and say Colin owed thousands of dollars?

The man returned with another clerk who looked over the letter, then shuffled through the file.

"Ah, yes. Here it is."

Colin tried to read the receipt in the man's hands. The second clerk spoke up again.

"I remember now. A Miss Keene, Gilbert Keene's daughter, paid off the back taxes four years ago. Quite a substantial amount as you can see." He handed the receipt to Colin. The amount was staggering.

"She made quite an impression as I recall. Came in with a fore-closure notice she'd ripped off the door of the property and torn to pieces. She had heard somewhere about you enlisting in the army to fight on the frontier after the war, so she wanted the payment to be anonymous. The head of the department knew her father, and together he and the clerk who filed the receipt of payment came up with the idea of this letter. Highly irregular. The clerk is no longer here, by the way."

A third clerk with ink-stained fingers and sleeve protectors walked over to join them.

"I remember you," he said to Colin. "I was here when you first came in a few months ago. I found that letter in the file and gave it to you myself."

Colin didn't recognize the man, but he wouldn't have recognized himself when he returned to New Orleans. The crowd in the office had doubled in size. Beside him Jason stared at the receipt of payment. The amount he owed Kate was more than he could hope to pay back for years.

"You look like someone could knock you down with a feather right now. You didn't know?" Jason asked.

"I didn't know," Colin mumbled. *She didn't tell me.*

Shock blocked out everything. Even the pain in his ankle.

"I'll write up a letter for you. Proof that you're all paid up." When the clerk handed Colin the letter and carried the file away, Colin couldn't face Jason. Letter in hand, he turned to leave and was forced to walk past the long line of men — men with hats in hand, men with no one to bail them out. Men wearing tailored suits with frayed cuffs and hems. Men who were about to lose everything.

They stared at him in silence as he walked out.

Even if Colin forgave Kate, would he ever forget?

"Think about what I've said, will you?" Jason's voice brought Colin back to the present. "Throwing away happiness would be worse than any humiliation life hands you. It's not a shame to accept help, Colin. Not when it's freely given."

Not if the giver is honest about it.

"Tell Cora that I'm sorry for keeping you so late. Daylight has slipped away."

"Solstice is almost here. The days will soon grow longer again."

Every day was too long without Kate.

Colin watched his old friend ride away.

Mention of solstice was a reminder that Christmas would be on them in a few days. Even with two children under his roof Colin had no plans for a celebration other than a midday meal with the Boltons on Christmas Day. His mother had loved the season and had celebrated as her ancestors had done by holding a grand feast, *le réveillon*, on Christmas Eve. Eugenie had directed as the kitchen slaves prepared roast goose and oyster gumbo. There were rich egg dishes and delicate pastries. As a child Colin's favorite had been a cake in the shape of a log, the *bûche de Noël*, like the birch log traditionally burned in the fireplace on Christmas Eve.

He couldn't imagine trying to replicate the festivities on his own, especially so soon after Amelie's death. Certainly not without Kate.

Colin pictured Kate hurrying from room to room, making certain the house was festively decorated, instigating the baking of sweets and treats, hanging mistletoe for luck over the front door.

But Kate wasn't here, and whatever Colin attempted without her would fall short of pleasing the children.

Damian and Marie had returned so buoyant after their visit that he was glad he had let them go. Showing off their keepsakes, they took turns relating stories of the open carriage ride and picnic in Jackson Square. Colin had never seen Marie so animated. Damian went on and on about the St. Charles rotunda, the pirate Jean Lafitte's blacksmith shop, and their ride on the steamboat packet. It wasn't until the boy had mentioned Captain Stevens at the dock that Colin's mood soured again.

That dark mood had settled in and stayed. Captain Ezekiel Stevens had sent Colin his regards, but apparently Kate had not. Was she seeing Stevens now? Was she making a new life for herself?

If so, he had no one but himself to blame.

Colin went directly upstairs to the children. Pausing outside their room he heard Damian ask Marie, "Do you think we'll see Aunt Kate for Christmas? It's almost here."

Marie's voice was so soft Colin had to hold his breath to hear her response.

"I'm not sure. He hasn't said anything."

"Do you think she'll like my presents?"

"Of course. She likes everything."

"Do you think she'll have gifts for us?"

"Of course."

Gifts. Colin hadn't thought of gifts. His obsessions were sugarcane and Kate. Simon had just this morning asked if they could butcher two of the hogs for a Christmas barbeque for the field hands and their families. At least there would be festivities in the cabins.

But if Colin denied the children another visit with Kate, their Christmas would be bleak indeed.

They fell silent as he walked into the room.

"Eugenie tells me you are ready for bed." In their nightclothes, they were already perched on their beds. It wasn't his nature to be as lighthearted or nurturing as Kate. No matter how deep her sorrow, she had always tried to keep her spirit up when around them.

He sat at the end of Damian's bed. Both children scrambled out from beneath the covers and knelt to say their prayers. Colin knew what was coming. He'd endured the nightly ritual alone for nearly two months now.

Marie folded her hands and went first. "God bless Mama and watch over her. Bless Granny and Grandpa Hart and don't let them miss us too much. Bless Eugenie and Simon and the Boltons and baby Jake. Bless Uncle Colin and keep him safe, and please bless

Aunt Kate. Keep her from missing us too much. Please, please bring her home for Christmas."

Damian pressed his forehead against his folded hands. He glanced up at Colin before he closed his eyes.

"Dear God, bless Granny and Grandpa Hart. Bless Eugenie and please let her make pralines soon. Bless Simon and keep him strong and healthy so he can make more toys. Bless baby Jake and Jason and Cora. Please make the sugarcane grow so Uncle Colin won't be so worried all the time, and make his ankle all better."

Apparently everyone was aware of Colin's worries.

Damian wasn't finished. "And God, please guide me to the buried treasure. I really, really need to find it so I can buy a steamboat and go see Aunt Kate whenever I want."

"And please bring us all together to celebrate Jesus' birthday," Marie whispered.

As their amens faded, the children climbed back into bed. Still awkward with his duty, Colin smoothed their blankets over them and kissed them on their foreheads.

"The way Mama used to," they had instructed the first time. "The way Aunt Kate does."

As he walked across the room to snuff the lamp, a piece of paper crunched beneath his boot. He picked it up, expecting it to be one of Marie's projects.

It was a letter from Kate, written in her bold, even script.

"That's mine," Marie said.

The letter burned in Colin's hand.

"When did this come?"

"Right after we saw her. Eugenie gave it to me."

Without mentioning it.

"Have you gotten many letters from Kate?"

Marie shook her head. "Just the one."

"She isn't lying," Damian added.

"I didn't think she was." Colin started to place the letter on their low worktable, but hesitated. "May I ... read it?"

Marie hesitated. "Yes."

He quickly scanned the short missive written the day of their visit.

> *Dear ones,*
>
> *I was so happy to see you today. Please thank your uncle for letting you come to visit. I so hope I will see you again soon. It's my fondest wish that we'll be together again at Christmastime.*
>
> *Your loving Aunt Kate*

Marie hadn't passed on Kate's thank-you.

Colin carefully folded the page and set it on the table, said good-night again, and snuffed out the lamp. Alone on the upper gallery, he began to pace.

It's my fondest wish that we'll be together again at Christmastime.

All of us, Kate? Or just you and the children? Was the letter an appeal for him to let her spend Christmas at *Belle Fleuve*?

After Marie and Damian's visit, Kate made it a point to sort through the boxes she had not unpacked in ages. It was time to get rid of things. Many she decided to sell on consignment at a nearby secondhand shop, and clearing out gave her an opportunity to find the lovely doll her father had given her.

Complete with blonde human hair, eyes that opened and closed, a beautifully painted bisque head, and an exquisite gown with layers and layers of lace and ruffles, the doll would make a perfect gift for Marie.

Kate had no idea what to buy for Damian, and as it turned out, she was thankful she left it until the last minute. On the eighteenth of December a letter from the *Prairie Home* magazine arrived for her at Roger Jamison's office announcing that her plans for a country home had won first prize.

Along with a year's subscription to the periodical, she received a draft for one hundred dollars and the news that her drawings would be displayed at county fairs all over the western states.

A day later, a letter from Colin was waiting for her at the St. Charles. She broke the seal before her courage failed her and held her breath as she read the brief note he'd written himself.

Dear Kate,

    I will be sending the children to celebrate an early Christmas with you. Eugenie and Simon will accompany them on the twenty-second of December. They will meet you as before around 11:00 a.m. in the vestibule of the St. Charles.

    They are looking forward to spending a few hours with you. They speak of nothing else. I hope this missive finds you well.

Colin

Had he cast her out of his heart as well as his home? Had he moved the redhead in?

Kate read the letter over and over, wishing he'd said something personal, wanting there to be more than *I hope this missive finds you well.*

Finally she tucked the letter away. There was no time to waste on maudlin thoughts. She had less than three days to prepare.

Apparently he didn't want her at *Belle Fleuve* so she would have to make the best of what she'd been given. Her prize money would help give the children a grand afternoon. She purchased a set of lead soldiers made by Mignot from Paris for Damian. As she wrapped the large wooden box, she pictured the boy and Colin lining up the figures together, hoping Colin would make time to play.

By eleven-twenty, as Kate waited beneath the rotunda with the children's gifts, she feared they were not coming. Since receiving Colin's letter she'd been plagued with worry. It was one thing for Eugenie to travel with the children with Cora along, but on her own or even with Simon it could prove dangerous. Freedom had been hard won, but things were far from peaceable under the Reconstruction government and martial law. The thought of the

pair escorting two white children to New Orleans had had Kate
tossing and turning all night.

"Aunt Kate!" It was Damian's shout.

She spotted the children running to greet her and quickly set
the gifts on the floor. When they barreled into her she hugged them
close. Expecting to see Eugenie and Simon, she realized they were
most likely waiting outside.

After many hugs Damian cried, "Are those presents?"

Kate picked up the gifts and when she straightened, juggling
the packages, she found herself looking up into Colin's eyes.

For a moment neither of them spoke. Colin—who was also
holding wrapped parcels—nodded. Kate struggled to find her
tongue.

"Kate. Merry Christmas," he said.

"Merry Christmas, Colin." She finally remembered to smile.
He was far more collected than she. His appraisal was cool and
distant.

"Eugenie couldn't come. She's ill," he said.

"Nothing serious, I hope."

"I have a feeling she began to recover as soon as we left."

Both children immediately demanded her attention, so Kate
could not ask what he meant. There were so many questions to
answer: yes, they could open their gifts soon; no, they were not
going back to the park; yes, she was certain she would love the gifts
they brought.

Was Colin really here? Kate ached at the image of him with
the hard-eyed redhead on his arm, but this wasn't the time or the
place to mention it.

"I hope you don't mind. I made a reservation for dinner here at
the hotel," she said.

"If you'd rather be alone with the children ..."

"Uncle Colin, don't go." Marie's smile had vanished. "We
should all be together."

"Please, Colin," Kate barely whispered. "We don't have very long, not if you still plan to leave later this afternoon."

"Yes, I do still plan on that. We must get back."

"I understand," Kate said.

"The hotel dining room will be fine."

She could tell her plan was anything but fine.

Colin followed Kate and the children into the main dining room at the St. Charles, where Kate was immediately relieved of her packages.

"I'll just carry these for you, Mrs. Delany, if I may." The maître d' greeted Kate with familiarity and nodded at Colin. "If you will all follow me, we've arranged for you to have your favorite table."

They were promptly seated at a table covered in damask and set with cut-crystal goblets with gold-embossed rims, sterling silver polished to a high sheen, and a centerpiece of holiday greenery.

Surrounded by opulence, Colin thought Kate was still the crown jewel. Not once did her smile falter as she gave both children her attention.

Awed by their surroundings, Marie leaned close to Kate and whispered, "May we open our presents before we eat?"

"Of course. I can't wait either." Kate excused the waiter hovering at her elbow.

Colin had yet to open his menu. He doubted he had brought enough money to cover dinner for the children, let alone for all of them. Once more he found himself in an embarrassing situation.

Kate handed Marie a large box. The smaller one was for Damian. Colin watched Damian appraise the difference in sizes. Before he could stress manners, Kate touched Damian's hand.

"Your box is a bit smaller but I promise it has lots inside," she said.

Damian smiled. "Can I go first?"

Kate turned to Marie. "Is that all right with you?"

Marie nodded. "I think he might burst if he has to wait."

Damian ripped the tissue off the package and then took great care lifting the lid of the polished wooden box to reveal a legion of lead soldiers complete to the last detail. He fingered each of them, touched the point of their sabers, and then began to take them out.

"Best you leave them in the box," Colin advised, "until you get home."

"Will you play with me?"

Colin glanced at Kate. She had given the boy something she thought they could enjoy together.

"Certainly," he said.

Damian was all smiles. He got out of his chair so that he could hug Kate and then took his seat again. "Now you," he said to Marie.

She took her time, carefully unwrapping the doll. Colin watched Kate. Behind her spectacles, her eyes sparkled with joy. Her cheeks were flushed.

"She's beautiful, isn't she, Uncle Colin?"

"Yes. She's beautiful." It was a second before Colin realized Marie was speaking about her doll.

Marie stood the doll on her lap, careful not to knock anything off the table. "Thank you, Aunt Kate."

Kate straightened the lace on the doll's bodice.

"I'm glad you like her."

"Does she have a name?" Marie asked.

"You can name her anything you like but I used to call her Lovie. I named her after my oldest sister. She had blonde curls too."

"Then I'll call her Lovie." Marie smoothed her hand over the doll's curls. "It's the perfect name for her. Thank you so much."

Kate hugged the girl and helped her rewrap the doll.

Colin stared at Kate. Was she really as calm and collected as she seemed? Or were her insides as unsettled as his? Hopefully he could string more than two words together when they were forced to converse again. Hearing her voice and looking into her eyes had left him in a daze.

"Uncle Colin!"

Damian demanded his attention. "Yes?"

"I *said*, would you please give Aunt Kate my presents?"

Colin reached for two small parcels wrapped in plain brown paper and handed them across the table to Kate.

"Those are from me," Damian said proudly.

Kate opened the first, turning it round and round in her hands.

"I'm sure you recognize it," Colin said, trying to jog her memory.

"Is it the Staffordshire dog that was in the sitting room?"

"You guessed! I glued it back together for you." Damian was thrilled with his success.

"I see that," Kate glanced over at Colin.

"It had a run-in with a pirate," he said.

"That was an accident," Damian shrugged. "Accidents happen. That's what Uncle Colin says."

Marie studied the piece in Kate's hand.

"His head is glued on backwards," she noted.

"That's all right," Colin said.

"It's just fine," Kate said at the same time.

They both fell silent.

"Because he's looking backwards now," Damian explained.

Colin caught Kate fighting a smile.

"Now he can see if any pirates are sneaking up on him." Kate rewrapped the figurine carefully.

"Will you keep it in your room and think of me?" Damian wanted to know.

"Of course." Kate reached for the second package. "But I always think of you without any reminders."

Colin wanted to look away but couldn't.

"I think of all of you all the time," she added.

He had to take a deep breath to restart his heart.

Kate opened the second gift from Damian and held up a

necklace of peanuts in the shell strung on a piece of twine. Each peanut was painted a different color.

"How lovely!" She carefully drew the peanut necklace over her hat and head until it rested on her shoulders.

"I made it," Damian announced. "Eugenie helped me string 'em and Marie let me use her watercolors."

Diamond earrings dangled above the peanuts, but Kate wore the necklace just as regally. Colin was lost.

Next she opened a set of paintings from Marie, scenes from the gardens at *Belle Fleuve*.

"Thank you, Marie," Kate said. "You've gotten quite good. I'll treasure these always." Her eyes glistened suspiciously bright as she studied the paintings.

There was one more gift to open from Marie. Colin wasn't certain what his niece had created that was in this rolled, wrapped, and ribbon-tied package. Kate carefully untied the ribbon and then unrolled the long page to reveal a detailed map.

"Me and Marie worked on it together," Damian explained.

"I let him paint in the larger portions," Marie added.

"It's ... it's quite wonderful." Kate seemed to be having trouble getting the words out.

"It's a map of *Belle Fleuve* and River Road."

"I see," Kate said.

Marie leaned over and slipped her arm around Kate's neck.

"We didn't want you to forget the way home," she whispered.

I'll never forget the way home.
Could Colin see her tears? Kate caught him staring at her more than once that evening, but for the most part he was withdrawn. She prayed the woman Captain Stevens saw him with wasn't the reason. She made slow work of rolling up the map and retying the bow until she composed herself. Then she suggested they study the menu. Kate helped the children order and the waiter headed for the kitchen.

Marie said, "I wish we were going to have Irish Christmas at *Belle Fleuve*."

"I'm sure that you'll be happy not to have to clean the house, for that's a big part of Irish Christmas."

"Clean the house?"

She nodded, careful to avoid looking at Colin.

"From top to bottom. Every piece of glass, every mirror and windowpane must sparkle. The yard must be swept clean and the stables mucked out. A candle is placed in the front window."

"Why?" Damian asked.

"To welcome Mary and Joseph."

"Who are out in the cold night seeking shelter," Marie reminded him.

"But not really." Damian sounded uncertain.

"It's to remind us of their story. When it's time to blow out the candle, it's customary for someone named Mary to do it." Kate smiled on Marie. "Did you know that Marie is another pronunciation of Mary?"

Marie beamed.

"For dinner there are lots of traditional dishes, including spiced beef and soda bread," Kate added.

"How will we celebrate, Uncle Colin?" Marie asked.

"I don't want to clean the house." Damian shook his head.

Kate was slow to look up and when she did she found Colin frowning at his plate.

"We're going to the Boltons' on Christmas Day."

"But what will we do at *Belle Fleuve*?" Marie pushed.

"Simon's going to butcher a couple of hogs. I imagine we'll also have some of Eugenie's sweet potato pie." Colin reached for his water goblet and took his time drinking water.

"Did Saint Nick come to *Belle Fleuve* when you were a boy?" Damian wanted to know.

"No, he didn't."

Colin was clearly uncomfortable, looking at Kate as if to say *this is all your fault.*

Damian shrugged. "Well, he didn't come to Kansas either. My Grandma and Grandpa Hart said there wasn't any such person as Saint Nick."

Kate ached for all the wonder and magic they had missed. Before she could comment Colin carefully lined up his fork and knife on his empty plate and sat back.

"In Louisiana we call him *Pere Noel.* On Christmas Eve we used to line our shoes up by the fire, and he would come and fill them with treats. We burned a birch log on the fire and my mother would make certain the grand dinner was complete with all of our favorite dishes."

"Do you think *Pere Noel* will come this year? Will he know there are children in the house again?" Damian's eyes were full of anticipation.

Kate held her breath, willed Colin to say yes.

Colin shrugged and met Kate's gaze. "I don't know. Perhaps."

She fought the urge to take him aside later and promise him that she would go to the French Market in the morning and send him a box of the finest fruits—a pineapple and oranges—along with pecans and candies. Colin would only see such a gesture as another intrusion that would leave him further indebted to her.

The meal proceeded far faster than Kate wanted. For dessert, they ordered an old Creole favorite, *pain perdu,* a bread pudding topped with candied pecans. She had made arrangements for the fare to be paid later but Colin asked for the bill.

"That's been taken care of already, sir," the waiter informed him.

"As usual," Colin said as the man walked away.

Kate shifted in her chair and then sat tall. She refused to let him ruin her day.

"I invited you all to dine with me, Colin. It's entirely proper that as hostess I take care of the charges."

"As you like, Kate."

His cool silence assured her this would be his last visit.

As they left the dining room and headed through the lobby to the entrance, the children walked ahead chattering about their presents. Kate found herself beside Colin. If he intended to say anything of a personal nature, this was the opportune time.

She looked his way and caught him staring at her. The intensity of his gaze spoke volumes.

The warm appraisal in his eyes told her he hadn't forgotten their night together any more than she had. If only they had more time. If only she could speak to him privately.

The children stopped at the entrance.

"Will you come to the dock with us, Aunt Kate?" Damian clutched his box of soldiers to his chest.

"Not this time."

Marie's eyes filled with tears. Kate thumbed them away.

"We'll have none of that, Marie. Just think of the next few days. Cora will make certain you'll have a wonderful Christmas Day." Kate wished she could say the same of Colin.

Unwilling to suffer another long good-bye, she suggested, "Let's say good-bye here. You'd best be on your way if you're going to make the boat."

She hugged them both twice, made certain Damian's jacket was properly buttoned, and forced herself to smile as they walked down the steps.

Beside her, Colin remained cool and silent. There was a second when she thought he would take her hand, but he didn't.

"Good-bye, Kate. Thank you." He made a stiff bow.

She wanted to tell him she hoped to see him again soon, to assure him that she still loved him and wanted to come home, but the words stuck in her throat. He was the one who'd sent her away. He would have to ask her to come back. A silent nod was the best she could do, and then they were gone.

On the morning of Christmas Eve the mouthwatering aroma of roasting pork filled the air at *Belle Fleuve* as Simon and the other men tended the barbecue near the cabins. In her day, Marie Delany had presented new clothes to all the slaves—dresses, kerchiefs, and aprons for the women and girls; new shirts and pants for the men. All Colin had to give he'd already given—a place to live, essential provisions, and the promise of better days to come.

Eugenie found him that morning. The aches and pains that had been her excuse for not going to New Orleans were gone by the time Colin and the children had returned. She'd been bustling about all day.

"I made some sugar cookies and a batch of candy for all the children. I'll leave Miss Marie and Damian's up in the top cupboard for you to put out tonight after they've gone to bed. Simon was able to trade some crayfish for oranges and we got some pecans put by. I'll leave you some of them too."

"I don't deserve you, you know?"

"I know that, Mr. Colin. I surely do."

She hadn't mentioned his visit to Kate, nor had he volunteered any information. Most likely she'd heard all the details from the children anyway.

"Simon got plenty of wood gathered up to haul to the levee for tonight," she said.

"Wood?"

"For the bonfire."

Colin had forgotten all about the bonfires that would be lit along the levee. It was a Christmas Eve tradition he'd taken part in every year until he left home. More and more he was reminded of how much of his past had been stolen by the war. Seeing the flames from all of the pyramids as they burned for miles along the edge of the levee was a spectacle to behold.

"Those children should see it," Eugenie said.

He knew she was right.

"Thank Simon for me," he said. "Tell him to round up a couple of men. I'll meet him in front of your cabin at noon to drive down and build the pyramid."

That night Eugenie left them a light dinner in the kitchen and Marie helped Colin dish up. They ate quickly and then Colin told them to bundle up because they were going somewhere special. Simon had all of the children from the cabins loaded in the back of the wagon already, and when he pulled up to the back door, Colin, Damian, and Marie climbed up onto the high-sprung seat.

"What's so special, Uncle Colin?" Damian asked.

"What's the surprise?" Marie wanted to know.

"Please tell us where we're going."

Colin only nodded and said, "You'll see."

They arrived at the levee where some of the men waited by a low fire burning near a tall pyramid made of dried ratoon cane, willow branches, and logs. A riverboat aglow with lights drifted slowly on the current.

"That looks like a haystack." Damian pointed at the pyramid. "What is it?"

"Just wait and watch." Colin caught their excitement.

"Should be near seven by now," Simon noted.

"Just about." Colin took out his watch and turned it toward the low firelight. Promptly at seven the steamboat whistle blew.

"Light 'er up!" he called.

Simon lit a long torch and instructed the other men to do the same. They tossed them into the center of the pyramid. The dry tinder caught almost immediately, sending flames and sparks high into the sky.

"They're everywhere!" Marie pointed out other pyramids to Damian. "Bonfires are up and down the levee on both sides of the river!"

"Ours is the biggest!" Damian clapped and jumped up and down.

Colin doubted it was the biggest. In fact, most of the stacks looked to be exactly the same height. But as a child he had been just as excited watching the fires burn. The flames were reflected in the water, and sparks vied for attention with all the stars that dusted the cool December night sky.

Seeing Marie's upturned face gilded by the bonfire's glow, it was as if Amelie were beside him again.

"Bonfires are an old tradition the Cajuns brought to Louisiana."

"Who are the Cajuns?"

"People who were forced to leave their homeland and move here. They were afraid the Christ child wouldn't know where they were, so they lit the string of fires to show Him the way."

Colin felt Marie slip her hand into his. "It's so beautiful," she said. "I wish Aunt Kate could see this."

"Me too," Damian added.

"So do I." Colin's words slipped out without warning.

"I can just imagine the Christ child following the light," Marie said. "He is the light of the world."

And Kate is the light of my life.

The touch of Marie's hand and her innocent clarity moved Colin in a way nothing else had and melted his heart. He'd nourished the darkness of all the war years, all of his exile. He'd locked that darkness inside until Kate walked into his life and pushed and prodded and demanded he save him from himself. She'd rescued *Belle Fleuve* for him, for the children. And he'd been too wounded in body and soul to accept the sacrifices she had made out of generosity and love. She had not avoided the truth to shame him, but to spare his feelings.

The sadness behind her smile at the St. Charles and the way her eyes misted with tears she had tried to hide were impossible to forget. She'd accepted the children's gifts with grace and worn Damian's peanut necklace as if it were precious as gold.

Colin had fallen in love with his wife and sent her away when everything she'd done she had done for him. Because she loved him.

That he'd lashed out and put his wounded pride before his love for her was his greatest shame of all.

Up and down the river, the bonfires sparked and raged like towers of light. Overhead the stars became part of the festival of light. Colin stared up into the heavens.

Forgive me my pride. Forgive my anger. Bless me with Your strength and love. Walk with me as I beg Kate's forgiveness and let me bring her home again.

His prayer was inspired by the night and the words of a child. Once he had spoken, a peace he hadn't known in years settled over him.

Damian, worn out from running and jumping around the bonfire, walked over and tugged on the hem of Colin's jacket.

"Do you think *Pere Noel* will find us?" the boy asked.

Colin waited as if considering.

"Maybe."

"Maybe we should put our shoes out by the fireplace just in case," Damian decided.

"I'll light a candle in the window," Marie added.

Damian clapped his hands. "Good idea, Marie. If Aunt Kate follows our map tonight, the candle will show her the way."

TWENTY -TWO

On Christmas Day, Kate donned a coat and decided to go for a long walk. The streets were nearly empty. Strolling past a church on the corner of Canal and Dauphine she stopped to admire the Gothic architecture, complete with buttresses and a central tower. Its architecture never failed to amaze her. Would she ever leave a mark on New Orleans other than Captain Stevens' steamboat house?

The doors of the church opened and members of the congregation poured out. They were families mostly, but there were also a few single individuals like her. She was weaving through the crowd when she recognized the jaunty white cap and thatch of gold hair of Ezekiel Stevens. Before she could disappear into the throng he saw her.

"Kate!" He jostled his way through the crowd until he reached her side. "Merry Christmas!"

"I'm surprised to see you here."

His grin widened. "Don't you believe I'm a God-fearing man?"

"Actually, I have suspected you aren't."

"Because I've flirted with you unmercifully? What are you doing here, Kate? Were you inside?" He stepped aside to allow a woman with an overly large bustle pass between them.

"I was walking and got caught up in the crowd."

"A bit brisk out for my taste." He caught her off guard when his smile faded. "You should be with your family, Mrs. Delany."

Loneliness swept over her and he noticed.

"Oh, Kate, I'm sorry." He took her arm. "Let me make it up to you."

She forced a brighter smile. "I'm fine. Really."

"Have an early dinner with me. It's nearly two."

"Really, I can't."

"Why not? It will just be between friends. Or between client and architect, if you like."

"I'm sorry, Captain."

"I owe you an apology. Let me make it up to you."

"An apology?"

"The day I appeared on your doorstep at *Belle Fleuve* I teased you unmercifully and I baited your husband. But only because you are tempting. If you were only free ..."

"But I am not."

"It's obvious you love your husband, though I can't imagine why."

"Captain—"

He held up a hand. "I'm sorry. Really. I'll settle for your friendship because I enjoy your company, and I refuse to let you spend Christmas Day alone. We can at least share a meal and talk about how the house is coming along. Which is very well, I might add. You are making my vision come to life even though I know you actually abhor it."

Kate couldn't deny it.

"Thank you, Captain. I'm glad you like the way it's turning out."

He offered his arm again. "So, come with me. We'll have dinner and a nice, long chat, and you'll be on your way. I'll be on my best behavior. I promise."

If it hadn't been Christmas Day, if he hadn't just walked out of the church and shown her another side of himself, she would have turned him down outright. What would it hurt to share a meal with a business associate?

He added, "If I wanted to make more of it I would invite you for a tour of the steamboat and dinner in my cabin. But I won't. This is completely an innocent gesture."

Kate sighed. The alternative was a lukewarm soup in her room.

"I'd be happy to join you," she said.

"Is Antoine's all right with you?"

"Antoine's on Christmas? Do you have a reservation?"

"Oh, we'll get in, I assure you."

As usual, Ezekiel's confidence brimmed over. That they would get in she had no doubt.

Colin walked into the St. Charles surprised to find the lobby somewhat empty. Then again, most New Orleanians had been out on the streets until the wee hours of the morning celebrating after midnight mass.

He headed straight for the registration desk where a young clerk who appeared to be no older than twenty was sneaking bites off a plate half-hidden below the counter. When he noticed Colin waiting for service he set down his fork, dabbed his mouth on a napkin, and rose to his feet.

"May I help you?"

"I am here to see Mrs. Katherine Delany."

The young man ran his finger along one page of names and then another.

"We have no Mrs. Delany listed as a guest of the hotel. I'm sorry." His gaze wandered to his dinner.

"Perhaps she's registered as Katherine Keene." Colin recalled that he'd heard the maître d' call Kate by her married name.

"She's not registered by that name either. Perhaps you have the wrong hotel."

"No, she is in residence here."

"No, sir. I'm sorry."

"This is where she's lived for ... well, I have no idea how long. I'd like to speak to your supervisor."

"Sir, I've checked all the lists ..."

"Now." Colin assumed a tone of command he'd abandoned the day he left the army. The clerk headed for a door behind the desk and disappeared. He was back in an instant, a slim, balding man in his wake.

"May I help you, sir?"

"I'm Colin Delany. I wish to see Katherine Keene Delany, my wife, and I've been told she doesn't live here."

The assistant manager stared at him in silence for a moment.

"That's correct. Miss Keene, excuse me, I mean Mrs. Delany, is no longer in residence here, sir."

"But I have met her here twice. We were told this is where we can reach her."

The assistant manager glanced at the young clerk who was listening to the exchange and then motioned to Colin to follow him to the far end of the counter. He lowered his voice and leaned across the marble surface.

"Mrs. Delany has not been here for quite some time, sir."

"But we had dinner here the day before yesterday."

"That may be, but she's no longer in residence. She moved out quite a while ago."

Colin searched the man's expression. He appeared to want to be helpful.

"Do you know her? She lived here for a time with her companion, a woman named O'Hara."

"I know Mrs. Delany, sir." The man sighed and then glanced around the lobby. "She receives mail here—letters and parcels— but I can assure you, she does not live here anymore."

O utside the massive hotel Colin stared up and down the street with no idea where to start looking for Kate, until he remembered Roger Jamison. Surely her employer knew where she was staying.

He hired a hack and rode to the architect's home. He asked the driver to wait and walked up to Jamison's front door. The sound of laughter and conversation drifted out onto the portico.

Relief tempered his anxiety as Colin lifted the door knocker. Surely Kate was inside.

A maid answered the door.

"May I see Roger Jamison?" Colin asked.

"He's having dinner with guests."

"I'm here on a matter of import. If you wouldn't mind disturbing him I'd appreciate it."

The maid left and in a moment Jamison appeared carrying a linen napkin. He smiled when he recognized Colin.

"Merry Christmas, Delany. This is quite a surprise."

"Hello, sir." Colin removed his hat. "I'd like to see Kate. Is she here?"

"Why, no, she's not. She was invited but decided to spend the day at home."

Colin felt his collar tighten. "Where is home? I thought she was staying at the St. Charles."

Roger Jamison waved Colin inside and closed the door behind him. The aroma of a holiday feast, along with raucous laughter, filled the house.

"Why I also assumed she was in residence at the St. Charles," Jamison said.

Colin's heart sank. "They *claim* she isn't."

"I doubt Kate would have them lie to you."

"They didn't appear to be lying. Do you have any idea where she might be staying? Are you sure she never mentioned it?"

"I'm sorry, Delany. You can bet I'll ask her when she comes in after the holidays."

"If you find out before I do, please let me know."

"Is everything all right at *Belle Fleuve*?"

There was no denying the man's sincerity. "Everything's fine."

"You're welcome to join us."

"Thank you for the invitation, but I'd best be on my way."

Though he was hungry, joining a group of merry revelers was the last thing on Colin's mind as he walked back to the carriage.

"Where to, sir?" The driver looked as if he'd rather be at home enjoying his own dinner.

"Give me a minute."

How was he ever going to find Kate in a city this size with no idea where to start? He looked down the street. Holiday greenery decorated the front doors of the well-appointed houses. Here and there couples and families with packages in hand rang doorbells and joined others in celebration.

Colin had left Damian and Marie to celebrate with the Boltons so that he could see Kate. He could return to the St. Charles, leave Kate a note, and let her know that he had been here, but it would be hours before he was home again. He needed to eat before he began his journey back.

The driver opened the door for him and Colin instructed, "Take me to Antoine's."

Ezekiel Stevens held the door for Kate as she stepped out of the restaurant. Pausing on the sidewalk, she made certain her hat was tipped just right, pleased that the captain had kept his promise. He hadn't flirted once, nor had he encouraged her to confide in him about her marital problems.

They had discussed his steamboat house project and then shared some other outlandish ideas he had for future projects. By the end of the meal Kate found her mood lightened. She wished she knew a suitable young woman who might be interested in Stevens, someone as strong and charismatic as the captain. But seeing as how he had ogled every woman in the room, she doubted he was looking for a lasting relationship.

The street was even more deserted than before, the sun sinking low in the afternoon sky. Two- and three-story buildings cast the street in shadows that grew chillier by the moment.

"Thank you for a delicious meal and for sparing me a lonely afternoon," she said.

Ezekiel gave the corner of his hat a tug.

"Thank you, Kate. The pleasure was all mine. Let me just say your husband is a fool."

"He's stubborn, that's all."

"And so are you."

She smiled. "You're right."

Too stubborn by half. It was time she went home and forced Colin to listen to reason.

"I'll walk you back to the hotel," he said.

"No, thank you. It's not far and I need some time alone. Besides, you're so close to the wharf that it would be out of your way. I'll be all right."

"Promise me you won't dawdle. I don't like the idea of you out alone after dark, Kate."

She shook her head and gave him a smile. "No need to worry on my account. I'll go straight home."

The hack pulled up at the corner across from Antoine's and Colin was about to step out when he spotted Kate walking out of the restaurant with Captain Stevens. He'd taken punches to the gut that hurt less. His wife adjusted her jaunty feathered hat. The captain smiled as if he'd just won a round of faro. The couple was in no hurry. They lingered in front of the restaurant laughing and talking.

Had Kate ever looked at him in the carefree, buoyant way she was smiling up at Stevens?

When have I ever given her reason to smile?

Had he lost her?

Colin stayed inside the dark interior of the hack and watched them the way a starving man stares at a loaf of bread. Had Stevens given Kate back her joy? Were the haunted shadows in her eyes gone?

When the captain offered Kate his arm, Colin held his breath. To his amazement Kate shook her head. The two chatted a moment longer before she started up the street alone. Stevens walked off in the opposite direction, whistling as if he hadn't a care in the world.

Colin drew back as Stevens passed by on the other side of the street.

The driver leaned down. "Change your mind, sir?"

Colin lowered his voice. "Follow the woman in the black dress, but keep your distance."

A minute or two passed. The driver waited for Kate to walk farther down the street before the carriage started rolling. The horse's hooves clattered with a slow, steady beat on the cobblestones. The driver hung back far enough not to draw suspicion.

Colin leaned back against the leather seat, tapping his fingers against his knees with impatience. They followed her up St. Louis Street for a number of blocks until the carriage turned in the opposite direction of the St. Charles and eventually stopped at an alleyway between two buildings. The driver climbed down off the box and stood in the window.

"She's gone down this alleyway, sir," he whispered. "You'll have to go on foot from here."

Colin climbed out. He could follow only so far before his ankle gave out. Afraid he would lose her, haste made him clumsy and he fumbled with his coins as he paid the driver.

The sound of the departing carriage wheels echoed between the buildings as Colin started down the narrow lane in a rundown section of the French Quarter. Kate was a good block ahead of him. Colin tried to ignore his pain as he hobbled along.

Ahead, Kate suddenly stopped and disappeared inside a building.

He waited in an alcove, but when it appeared she was not coming out, Colin continued on until he reached a small shop front. The window was lettered with the name of a cobbler. Like the others on the street, the exterior was coated with cracked and peeling stucco. The interior of the shop was dark. A small sign on the door read: Closed until the New Year.

Colin cupped his hands and pressed them against the window to look inside. There was no sign of anyone and certainly not Kate. There was another door beside the shop window, this one painted the color of rust. A cracked windowpane was centered in the door above the handle. Colin peered inside this window and saw a dark, narrow stairway leading to the second floor.

He tried the knob, found it unlocked, and went in.

The stairs were old and worn and Colin figured the building had been standing since the French flag had flown over New Orleans. He used the handrail, grateful for its presence, and slowly made his way to the landing.

On the second floor, a dingy hall was lined with four doors, all closed. Stale odors mingled with the smell of onions. Kate was behind one of these doors.

He knocked on the first and no one answered. The second door opened and an elderly man in shirtsleeves and a stained waistcoat blinked at Colin like a mole unused to sunlight.

"Help ya?" He had but two upper teeth.

"I'm looking for Katherine Keene Delany."

"What you want with her?"

It had been a long day, Colin's ankle hurt, and he wasn't in the mood to be polite.

"I'm her husband. Now where is she?"

The man thumbed toward the door at the end of the hall. "I don't want no trouble here, mister."

Colin was already limping down the hall.

A lone in her small room above the cobbler's shop, Kate slipped the hat pin from her hat, rethreaded it, and set her hat on an overcrowded dressing table. She barely had room to move between the bed and the armoire crowded against one wall. A washstand and a chair completed the furnishings. Kate liked to deny that a life of privilege had spoiled her, but with no one there to hang up her clothes, there were pieces of clothing strewn all over the bed.

Kate had found the small room by chance two days after leaving *Belle Fleuve*. She'd been walking the streets and alleyways, studying balconies and ironwork on older buildings for design inspiration when she saw a small sign in the window of the shoe repair shop on the ground floor.

The flat was passable, highly affordable, and the landlord did not insist upon a lease. Dan Rosen had congratulated her on her thriftiness. Kate was certain he'd be appalled and worried about her safety if he ever actually saw the place.

Kate had expected to be there a week or two at the most. Now, two months later, she was still dealing with the cramped room.

She picked up a small tin of matches to light the candle she'd placed on the windowsill last night. The flame danced, reflected in the glass as it bloomed. Outside, evening shadows expanded around the buildings.

There are far worse things than being alone on Christmas. *Far worse things.*

Kate jumped when a firm knock sounded on the door. Not once had anyone sought her here.

As she threaded her way around the bed, she smoothed her hand over her hair.

"Who is it?"

"It's me, Kate. Open the door."

She immediately recognized Colin's voice and the thread of impatience in it and closed her eyes. How on earth had he found her?

Fear for the children set her heart racing. Her fingers fumbled on the lock before she opened the door. He was tall and imposing, a formidable force in the narrow, dingy hallway.

"Come in." She stepped back to give him room. It must have cost him dearly to climb the stairs. There was nowhere for him to sit so she tossed a pile of clothes off a chair and onto the bed. She folded her hands together to keep them from shaking.

"Please, sit down." She saw the room through his eyes: Damian's peanut necklace hanging around a lamp shade; the repaired Staffordshire dog sitting beside her miniature of *Belle Fleuve*; Marie's paintings tacked up to the wall over her bed. The pages of Myra's long-awaited letter were scattered across the pillows. Kate's clothing was everywhere, and various pairs of boots and shoes littered the floor.

"I'm sorry things are in such upheaval." Kate knitted her fingers together. "Are the children all right? Is there an emergency?"

She longed to smooth the deep creases from his brow. Instead she waited, felt the anger roiling off him even from across the room. Had he come to ask for a divorce? Would he go that far?

"The children are fine. They are at the Boltons'. There is no emergency, Kate, but had there been, how would I have found you?"

She dropped her gaze to her hands, but he gave her no time to respond.

"I went to the St. Charles earlier and asked for you at the front desk. Apparently you haven't been in residence there for quite a while."

"No ..."

"And yet you led everyone to believe you were—not only your employer, but Cora, Eugenie, the children. Me."

"I'm sorry. I didn't want ..."

"Does Ezekiel Stevens know you live here?"

She met his dark gaze and saw hurt and jealousy there.

"Of course not. Why?"

"I saw you leave Antoine's with him."

"You were at the restaurant? Why didn't you say something? Is that how you found me? By spying on me? Following me?"

"I wasn't spying. When I didn't find you at the St. Charles, I went to Jamison's. He had no idea where you were, so I decided to have dinner before I left town. That's when I saw you and the captain coming out of the restaurant—"

"I ran into him coming out of church. He asked me to dine with him." She met Colin's unwavering stare with one of her own. "That's all it was. As you are well aware, I returned alone."

She expected a comment. He fell silent. The tension in the air was as thick as gumbo.

"My dinner with the captain was completely innocent. Can you say the same for your association with the redheaded woman Stevens saw on your arm when you came to town seeking your loan?" It was impossible for Kate to imagine him going to another woman after what they had shared the night before.

His brow knit in obvious puzzlement. "Redhead?"

Kate held her breath.

"You don't mean Tillie Cutter?"

"I don't know. Do I?"

"She's a prostitute, Kate."

She pressed her hand to her heart, aghast.

"She means nothing to me," he insisted.

"You slept with her?" she whispered.

"Of course not. I originally met her on the train from Texas, and I ran into her when I came to town with Jason. She helped me cross the street, that's all. That's when Stevens saw us. I'll bet he couldn't wait to tell you."

Kate wanted to believe him.

"Oh, Kate, come on. Ask yourself why he would want to make more of it than it really was."

Stevens' behavior had been above reproach today, but it wasn't beyond the captain to try to stir up trouble between them.

"I sent Tillie away when she came to *Belle Fleuve*, and I sent her on her way that night too, Kate. Please, say you believe me."

She met his gaze and saw the truth. There were far more threats to their marriage than Tillie Cutter. Awkward silence stretched between them in the confined space.

His gaze traveled to Marie's paintings on the wall above the bed, to the map showing the way to *Belle Fleuve* above her desk. Then the heat of his stare returned to her.

"Oh, Kate, why are you here" — he indicated the room with a wave — "living like this?"

Like the candle in the window, a flicker of hope ignited inside her.

"Why are *you* here, Colin? What do you want?"

Colin wished she'd move closer. How could he even begin to tell her what was in his heart when he was so worried about what she was doing in a place like this?

Suddenly he surged to his feet and crossed the room. Kate's eyes widened as he took hold of her shoulders. She had to tip back her head to stare into his eyes.

"Tell me you did not spend your entire inheritance on *Belle Fleuve*." He could see her mind racing and could feel her shoulders rise and fall on a sigh.

"I have not spent everything on *Belle Fleuve*, not that it would matter to me if I had. My accountant warned me my funds are running low, but he is making investments for me." She smiled at Colin as if she hadn't a care in the world. "I'm sure that soon I'll have no worries. *We'll* have no worries. I'm staying here to save money. That's all." She shrugged. "I don't need more than this."

He glanced at the mountain of clothing on the bed. "You might not need more room but you could certainly use some help."

"I've told you what you wanted to know," she said. "Now tell me why you are here."

He swallowed and smoothed his palms along the black silk across her shoulders.

"I came to apologize." He felt lighter already. "I came to take you home."

Tears filled her eyes. He hated himself for causing them.

"If you can forgive me," he added. "If it's not too late."

She reached up, traced her fingertips across his brow.

"I had no idea my actions would cause you such embarrassment and pain. I had no right ..."

"You saved *Belle Fleuve*. You saved *me*, Kate."

Colin slipped his arms around her, pulled her close, and kissed her, hoping that his kiss would convey everything his words lacked, everything that was in his awakened heart. When Kate kissed him back, when she melted against him, his heart soared.

He lifted his head and cupped her face in his hands.

"You weren't gone long before I regretted what I'd done, but I'd backed myself into a corner. I thought I couldn't ask you to come home until I was solvent and successful and had some hope of repaying you, but I was a fool for not factoring in the time it will take for that to happen. I never knew how much I would miss talking to you, hearing the rustle of your skirt. I miss having you there in the evening presiding over our table. I miss touching you. I even miss seeing you make certain your hats are on just so and your glasses are on straight. I've been haunted by the memory of our last night together, the beauty and promise of what we shared."

"Oh, Colin." She drew his head down until their lips met again. When their kiss ended her smile took his breath away.

"Last night I took the children to watch the bonfires along the river and saw the celebration through their eyes. They believe in the magic and joy of the season as I used to, the hope of the season, the promise of a new beginning for the world. I prayed Kate. I prayed for a new beginning for us too. I can't live without your love. I can't live without the light you bring into my life."

"Oh, Colin." She started to say something, but he gently pressed his finger to her lips.

"You saved *Belle Fleuve* for me, Kate. You saved me with your love. I can't go down on one knee, but I beg you, come home where you belong."

"Of course," she whispered. "Of course I will. I love you, Colin. I wish we could leave right now. But I should see to my things, and I have to tell Roger I'll be working from the plantation again."

"I was going to leave on the last boat upriver. I'm afraid I may have missed it." He paused, looking around the room.

"Stay with me tonight," Kate whispered.

He turned, cupped her cheek. "Are you sure?"

"We can leave together tomorrow."

"I told Eugenie not to worry if I was delayed. She and Simon will collect the children from the Boltons."

Kate pictured Damian and Marie. "Did *Pere Noel* find them?"

"Thanks to Eugenie, he left treats in their shoes last night." He glanced at the bed piled high with clothes.

Kate blushed. "Perhaps we should get a room at the St. Charles …"

Colin grabbed up an armful of gowns and tossed them aside.

"Anywhere is fine as long as we're together."

EPILOGUE

OCTOBER 1877

B*elle Fleuve.*
The pungent smell of the boiling cane was cloying, but it was a reminder of a successful harvest, of security, of prayers, hopes, and dreams coming to fruition.

Belle Fleuve's first harvest in sixteen years had been underway for two weeks. Since the old sugarhouse was one of the few still standing, Colin had opened it to his neighbors. Despite the hectic pace, the constant coming and going of wagons, the cutting and harvesting in the fields, and the round-the-clock boiling, Kate had never been happier. God had seen her through the darkness.

A true Delany at last, she belonged at *Belle Fleuve*.

Outside the huge boiling shed she watched Colin supervise the men as they unloaded yet another wagon filled with cane. Blessed with love, a home, and a family, Kate's only remaining wish was to find her sisters.

Colin spoke to Jason Bolton before he made his way across the yard to join her in the shade of a willow. His countenance had changed. With every day that the weather cooperated and the sugarcane thrived he relaxed a little more and smiled more. He even laughed. Once the sugar was processed they would be solvent if not wealthy.

"Are you feeling all right?" He lifted his hat and wiped his brow with his shirtsleeve.

Kate placed her hand protectively over the slight mound of her belly and smiled.

"We're both feeling fine. Do you need to sit down?"

He shook his head. "Not yet."

"We're bringing in a fine crop, Kate. More than a novice should expect. Here come the children." He nodded toward the road from the main house.

Marie was driving a bright blue-and-yellow pony cart Dan Rosen's children had outgrown. Damian began to climb down before the old pony even stopped trudging along. With a crimson scarf tied around his head and one of Colin's cravats as a sash, he tossed out his sword and then his favorite shovel.

"Ahoy!" He waved the shovel around. "It's a fine day for treasure hunting, mateys!"

Marie set the brake. "Be careful, Damian." She shook her head as her brother ran over to Kate.

"Where should I start today?" Damian asked Colin.

Colin pointed to a spot far away from the men and the hubbub but close enough to be able to keep an eye on him.

"Don't go any farther than that hickory tree."

"I won't. I promise." Damian jogged away with his sword in one hand and the shovel in the other.

Kate laughed and Colin chuckled. Marie held up a sack.

"Eugenie helped us string some more pecans for *chapelets de pacanes*. May I have someone dip them for me, Uncle Colin?"

"Very good French, Marie," Colin complimented.

As far as he was concerned they were the brightest, most fascinating children in all of Louisiana.

"I'll wave you over when someone is free," he promised.

Kate remembered the excitement of stringing pecans on a

thread and having them dipped into an open kettle of boiling sugar. The sugared nuts were a special treat for all.

"Did you bring your sketchbook?" she asked the girl.

"It's in the cart."

As they waited for Colin's signal, Marie touched Kate's elbow. "Have you chosen a name for the baby? You said you would decide by today."

"For a boy, not yet. If it's a girl, we'll name her Amelie."

Marie's smile bloomed. "Mama would like that."

"I think so too." Kate slipped her arm around Marie's shoulder and hugged her to her side.

Another vehicle was coming up the road. Simon accompanied it on horseback. The carriage was driven by a man in a brown suit and bowler hat, and two women were in back. As the carriage bounced in a deep pothole in the lane, one of the women grabbed her broad-brimmed hat.

"Who is that?" Marie wanted to know.

"I'm not sure," Kate said.

Guests and visitors from nearby plantations had been coming and going since the harvest started. Though the work was back-breaking and the schedule demanding, there was a festive air during harvest season. Planters and their families called on one another to ask about progress and volunteer help if needed.

Hopefully, there was enough lemonade and an assortment of tea breads left for Kate to serve to these new guests. Eugenie was busy with the other women overseeing the field hands' meals. All day long they dished up mouthwatering deep-pit barbequed pork and beef accompanied by pots of rice and skillets of corn bread cooked over open fires.

Kate headed toward the newcomers as the phaeton came to a stop. Simon dismounted and waited alongside to help the women down. The dark-haired gentleman driving the carriage doffed his bowler hat and smiled at Kate. She smiled back watching the women descend. They appeared to have no interest in what was going on at the sugarhouse but were focused on her. She lifted her hand to wave and then gasped.

"What is it, Aunt Kate? Are you all right?"

Speechless, she grabbed Marie's hand.

"Aunt Kate, what is it?"

Kate's knees were trembling so hard she could barely stand.

The women wore expressions of yearning and uncertainty. One was smartly outfitted and wore a wide-brimmed hat with a bobbing ostrich feather. A full-figured blonde, her hair was thick and curly, her eyes sky blue. There were dimples in both her cheeks.

The other was a few inches taller and far slimmer. Her hair was dark brown and her skin was fair with a smattering of freckles across her nose. Her eyes were green, and she wore a navy ensemble that was understated but stylish with its white trim and bustle.

Kate stared at them through a wash of tears.

"Lovie? Megan? Don't you know me?" She opened her arms.

The women rushed to her, hugging Kate between them. They laughed and cried and swayed together in a tight knot until the blonde's hat tumbled to the ground. Kate's glasses were shoved askew.

When they finally had their fill of hugs and exclamations, they released her. Kate wiped her eyes on her lace cuffs.

"Aunt Kate?" Marie whispered. "What's happening? Who are they?"

"Marie, these are my sisters." Her joy overflowed as she indicated the blonde. "This is Lovie." Then Kate turned to the brunette. "And this is Megan."

The man in the brown suit handed Lovie her hat. Without dusting it off, she anchored it in place.

"Why, hello, Marie," Lovie said. "I'm very pleased to meet you. My name is Laura now. Mrs. Laura McCormick. I have a daughter at home who is almost your age." She studied Marie a moment longer. "You are a very lovely child."

"Marie was the daughter of my dearest friend," Kate said. "She's my daughter now."

The younger of the two older sisters was once more composed, even thoughtful. Her expression was as serious as Marie's.

"I go by Maddie now," Megan told Kate. "Maddie Abbott." She reached for the gentleman in the bowler hat and he took her hand. "This is my husband, Tom. He's a Pinkerton agent."

The gent smiled and bowed to Kate and Marie. "Pleased to meet you ladies."

"What's a Pinkerton?" Marie wanted to know.

"A detective." Kate turned to Tom. "Was it you who found me?"

"I wish I could take all the credit, but it was Laura's husband, Brand, who discovered the clue that finally led us to you."

Laura nodded. "Brand took the children to the county fair in August. When he stopped to view an exhibit for the winning home designs shown by the *Prairie Home* periodical he saw the name Katherine Keene Delany on one of them."

"But there are countless Katherines in the world," Kate said. "How did you know it was me?"

Maddie responded, "Brand didn't know at first, but the name and the shamrock gave him the idea."

"The one in the window," Laura said. "The circular stained glass window with the shamrock inside."

"Mama's necklace," Kate whispered. The signature she placed in every set of her original designs.

"When Brand saw the shamrock in the round window it reminded him of our silver pattern. I had the same design reproduced on the handles of our silverware. When he saw that your name was Katherine, he was quite sure he was on to something. He purchased a copy of the periodical, and we sent the information to Tom and Maddie."

"I finally had a name to go on," Tom said. "We've been searching for you and for Sarah, but so many records were lost."

"I tried to find you too," Kate told them.

Abbott said, "I did some digging into the architect Katherine Keene Delany's background and found she had been adopted by the Keenes shortly after you had been taken to the orphan asylum with Sarah."

Maddie said, "I've known that you were working for an architect in New Orleans since September. It's been torture waiting to find out if you were our Katie."

"Why didn't you contact me sooner?"

"That's my fault," Laura said. "When Tom was certain we had found you, I made them promise to wait until I could get here from Texas."

Kate turned to Maddie again. "Do you live here in Louisiana?"

"We live right in New Orleans, and we have a small house on the bayou. I grew up in the city, but that's a story for another time."

"My parents had a townhouse in the city," Kate said. "To think that we were so close ..."

"I doubt we ever crossed paths." Maddie sounded quite certain.

Kate turned to Laura again. "You've come all the way from Texas?"

"Mine is quite a story too." Laura smiled. "And a long one, but we have lots of time to get to know each other again. Lots and lots of time."

Colin had seen the black phaeton drive in, but Jason had drawn him back into conversation about one of the mules turning the wheel of a cane crusher. He heard the squeals of excitement and hurried to join the group surrounding his wife.

"Visitors?" He nodded in greeting.

Seeing the tears in Kate's eyes he asked, "Are you all right?"

"There's no need to frown so, Colin. These are my sisters!" She introduced Laura and Maddie and Tom Abbott and explained how they'd found her. His concern for Kate was foremost as he greeted them all. They had lost a babe a few months back, and even though

Eugenie had predicted this one would be carried to term, Colin still worried.

"Let's go up to the house and get out of the heat," he suggested.

"It appears you've quite a production here," Tom commented as they headed for the phaeton. "I'd be interested in a tour when you have time."

"I'd love to show you around," Colin agreed.

Marie said, "Should I get Damian?"

Kate pointed him out to her sisters. "That's Marie's brother, Damian."

"Is he planting something?" Maddie wondered.

"What happened to him? Why is his head bandaged?" Laura squinted toward the tree where Damian was standing on the shovel.

"That's not a bandage. It's a pirate scarf. He's digging for treasure. That's about all he ever does." Marie sighed.

"My sister told him that our mother buried valuables to keep them out of the hands of Yankees," Colin explained. "He believes it wholeheartedly."

"He's dug holes all over the garden." Marie sighed again.

Colin whistled and waved. Digging faster than before, Damian ignored him.

"Why don't you all go up to the house and have some refreshments? Simon can drive you up in the carriage, and Tom can ride back with me. We'll bring Damian." Colin wanted Kate out of the heat.

"We didn't mean to invade," Laura began.

"Yes, we did," Maddie laughed.

"Nonsense." Colin shook his head. "You're all welcome here for as long as you like. We have a guest room for Tom and Maddie, and Laura can stay in the *garçonnière*."

"Yes," Kate insisted. "You must stay. I can't let you go so soon."

As the women started toward the phaeton, Colin pulled Kate close and whispered in her ear, "You are beaming, wife. I'm not certain I can keep my hands off you."

"I'm afraid you'll have to now that you've filled our home with guests."

While Eugenie was preparing tea and refreshments, Kate and Marie prepared to take the sisters on a tour of the house.

"Before we start, we have something to tell you," Laura began.

"We may have found Sarah," Maddie finished.

Kate clasped her hands.

"How wonderful! I saw the people who adopted her—an older couple—I even begged them to adopt me too. I never heard their names or had any idea where they lived."

"Tom has traced them from Louisiana to Arkansas, and then they moved to Texas," Maddie said.

"My stepson Jesse has gone to see if he can locate them," Laura added. "We should be hearing from him soon."

"I can hardly believe we might all be together again." Kate was interrupted by a shout from the gallery.

"I found it, Aunt Kate! I *told* everybody I would find it!" Damian raced in filthy but triumphant and ran straight to Kate. "I was digging too close to the house before. *Grandmere* buried the chest out near the sugarhouse. But I found it! We're rich! We're rich!" He jumped up and down and ran back outside.

Tom led the way as Colin carried in a small wooden chest no more than two feet wide and a foot deep. It had a domed lid and was stained with dirt. The hinges and lock showed signs of rust. Damian ran around the two men.

"I can't believe it," Laura said with awe. "Buried treasure."

"If I had any idea we'd be in for so much entertainment I would have broken our promise to Laura and come sooner," Tom laughed.

Colin headed for the library table covered with Kate's latest drawings. He was forced to step around a dollhouse surrounded by a brigade of metal soldiers on the floor. Kate moved the drawings aside and Colin set down the chest.

"Do you really think your mother buried this?" Kate asked him. Everyone crowded around.

"This is exciting no matter what's inside." Maddie stood beside Tom.

Marie nudged her way into the circle gathered around the table. "If it's not *Grandmere*'s, then it was probably buried here years and years ago by a handsome pirate. Jean Laffite used to visit *Belle Fleuve*, you know."

"I had no idea there were *handsome* pirates." Laura laughed.

"Oh, yes. Quite handsome," Marie assured her.

"Marie's writing a romance about a pirate and drawing all the illustrations." Kate smiled with pride.

"Romance. Yuck." Damian tugged a chair over to the table and scrambled up between the adults. "Open it, please, Uncle Colin."

"I'll have to be careful." Colin glanced at Kate. "No telling what's inside." He picked up Kate's letter opener. Aided by time and humidity, he barely touched the rusted lock before it crumbled.

Everyone held their breath. The lid creaked as Colin raised it.

"What is it?"

"Is it gold?"

"Silver?"

"Priceless jewels?"

Colin lifted out a large book covered in hand-tooled leather and embossed with a gold family crest.

"How lovely," Laura said.

Colin ran his hand over the cover. "It's the Baudier French Bible. It's been in my family for well over a century."

He handed the Bible to Kate, reached into the trunk, and pulled out a large card. He studied it a moment and then showed it all around; it was a photograph of his family taken on the same day as the one they'd found in the attic.

"Is that all?" Damian's shoulders sagged in disappointment. "An old book nobody can read and a picture?"

Colin reached inside again and pulled out a small silk pouch.

He opened it and a gold ring set with a sapphire surrounded by diamonds tumbled into his palm.

"My great-grandmother's wedding ring." He stared in awe. "My mother wore it as well."

"Gold and jewels!" Damian jumped down and headed for the door. "Maybe there's more out there. I'll be back!"

Colin turned to Kate. "A Bible, a photograph, and a ring. So many things to choose from, so many things of value, and my mother buried these," he said.

Kate slipped her arm around his waist, leaned into him, and looked at her sisters. She heard Damian out in the garden. She turned to Marie, reminded of Amelie. Then she looked up and saw the love in Colin's eyes. In that moment Kate understood Marie Baudier Delany's choices perfectly; they were symbols of her marriage, her faith, and her family. Marie Delany had buried the treasures of her heart.

The house was quiet. Kate was tucked in bed in her nightgown and on her lap was the heavy French Bible with the Baudier and Delany family history recorded inside. Though she struggled with the French, she could read the names back to the sixteen hundreds. She traced them with her fingertip and tried to picture the men and women who had come before them, especially those who first settled this land.

She heard Colin's slow footfall on the gallery and smiled as he walked through the door.

"You're still dressed," she said.

"I have to return to the sugarhouse to visit the men working the night shift."

"I forgot it was your turn. You look tired, Colin. Handsome but tired."

"I am tired, but also invigorated. It's been quite a day."

"I'm exhausted but I don't know if I'll be able to sleep. I hate to miss a minute with my sisters."

He sat down on the side of the bed next to her hip.

"You might be too tired to sleep, but the babe needs rest. You'll see your sisters again in the morning."

She reached up and traced his cheek with her thumb. "Thank you for welcoming them."

"They are part of our family too." He gave her a long, slow kiss and then reached into his vest pocket. "I finally have something I've wanted to give you for a year now."

"You've already given me everything my heart has desired and more."

He took her hand in his and slipped his great-grandmother's ring on her finger. "At last you have a wedding ring."

She gazed at the sparkling sapphire and diamonds.

"It's beautiful, but you know I was perfectly happy without it."

"You shine brighter than any diamond, Kate. You're my light and my love."

"And you are mine." Kate admired the ring again and smiled. "It fits perfectly."

"Of course," Colin said as he shrugged. "It's been waiting for you."

Heart of Stone

A Novel

Jill Marie Landis
New York Times *Bestselling Author*

She had the darkest of pasts. And he had everything to lose by loving her.

Laura Foster, free from the bondage of an unspeakable childhood, has struggled to make a new life for herself. Now the owner of an elegant boardinghouse in Glory, Texas, she is known as a wealthy, respectable widow. But Laura never forgets that she is always just one step ahead of her past.

When Reverend Brand McCormick comes calling, Laura does all she can to discourage him as a suitor. She knows that if her past were discovered, Brand's reputation would be ruined. But it's not only Laura's past that threatens to bring Brand down — it's also his own.

When a stranger in town threatens to reveal too many secrets, Laura is faced with a heartbreaking choice: Should she leave Glory forever and save Brand's future? Or is it worth risking his name — and her heart — by telling him the truth?

Available in stores and online!

Heart of Lies

A Novel

Jill Marie Landis,
New York Times *Bestselling Author*

Raised in a tribe of street urchins, Maddie Grande was taught to be a thief and beggar on the streets of New Orleans. But Maddie doesn't know her real name or where she came from.

Raised by Dexter Grande, Maddie and her twin "brothers" have recently left New Orleans and moved to the bayou. The twins are rarely there, but Maddie has come to love the swamp. She has learned to fish and trap and sell pelts at the local mercantile.

Maddie longs to change her life but knows that her brothers will never give up their lawless ways. When they kidnap the daughter of a wealthy carpetbagger, the twins force Maddie to hide the precocious eight-year-old while they return to New Orleans to wait for notice of a reward.

Pinkerton agent Tom Abbott is assigned to the kidnapping case, in which Maddie has become an accomplice. In a journey that takes them to Baton Rouge, a mutual attraction becomes evident, but Tom and Maddie cannot trust each other.

Will Maddie ever discover who she is? Will her real family ever find her? Will Maddie and Tom listen to their hearts? Or will they choose honor over love?

Available in stores and online!